Sam walked over to the window and rested her head against the glass.

'You are dead,' she said out loud. 'You died in nineteen seventy-four, when I was four years old. You fought in Oman. You were killed in Oman. You were buried with full military honours in the SAS cemetery at St Martin's, Hereford. I visit your grave every year. I've carried your dog tags in my pocket since you died. Every day I've rubbed them between my fingers like a rosary. I summoned your ghost to help me when I fought. I miss you. I mourn you. Your absence has made me.'

This was the story Sam had built her life on.

She had been a champion fighter.

She was now a private investigator, specializing in missing persons. When she was working for her clients, she knew there was really only one person that she was ever looking for: the man whose ghost had cast a bloodless shadow across her entire life, her father. Sam knew in every cell of her body that her father was dead. She *knew* it. But as she looked out of the window at the weary faces of the passengers on the top deck of a number 22 bus, which had stopped exactly level with her window, she knew that now, where she had been certain, she doubted. A headache began to pound out a familiar tattoo on the inside of her skull. She peered at the postmark on the envelope.

Oxford.

A city where dead men wrote letters, a city that was calling her home.

Victoria Blake was born in Oxford and brought up in Queen's College. She read history at Lady Margaret Hall and then qualified as a solicitor in London. Deciding law was not for her and at a loose end, she began dogsbodying for the publisher, Gerald Duckworth, and stayed four years. Since leaving Duckworth, she has divided her time between writing and bookselling. Having carried books and packed them, invoiced and shelved them, sold and returned them, she is delighted to have finally written one. She lives in west London with her partner and the ubiquitous cat, percipiently named Dashiell Hammett.

BLOODLESS SHADOW

VICTORIA BLAKE

ORION

An Orion paperback

First published in Great Britain in 2003
by Orion
This paperback edition published in 2004
by Orion Books Ltd,
Orion House, 5 Upper St Martin's Lane,
London WC2H 9EA

A CIP catalogue record for this book is available
from the British Library.

ISBN 0 75286 396 7

Typeset by Deltatype Ltd, Birkenhead
Printed and bound in Great Britain by Clays Ltd, St Ives plc.

For Maureen, *sine qua non*

My special thanks to:

Sahera Chohan, Nigel Watts, Alison Fell and Robert Drake, all inspiring teachers; Richard Collier, Rose Lamb, Keir Lusby and Faith Noonan of the Whitton Writing Group for five years of constructive criticism; Francesca Howard for her wisdom and compassion; Maggie Gilson and Gerry Platt for being there right at the beginning; Nicky Badman, Rose Collis, Hilary Goodman, Jennifer Jaeger, Jennifer Leslie, Katy Richards, Susan Sciama and Phil Welton for being part of the journey; Michael Ellison for Frank Cooper; Henry Hart for *Bloodless Shadow*; my sisters, Deborah and Letitia Blake, and my parents Patricia and Robert Blake for their love and support; Kitty Dobson, my great-aunt, for her generosity; Kate Mills and Nicky Jeanes at Orion and finally Teresa Chris for her boundless enthusiasm and good advice.

PROLOGUE

Park Town, North Oxford
October 2002

It was five o'clock in the morning. The woman stood in the kitchen sipping her tea. It was quiet upstairs; his children were still sleeping. She was dressed in standard city attire: blue court shoes, an open-necked shirt and a hip-hugging blue skirt. A silk scarf of gold and burnt orange was tied around her neck; the gold the same colour as her hair, which dropped in an even bob to her shoulders, the orange the same colour as the leaves tumbling across the soggy, windswept lawn.

She put her cup of tea on the table and pulled a maroon Filofax from her thin leather briefcase. She flicked it open and looked at that day's date. Perhaps she was looking at her appointments, perhaps she was searching for something else. Her finger flicked through the pages, tracing back through the previous month and her lips moved, as if counting. Then she nodded decisively and walked through to the front of the house. You would think she were on her way to work.

John O'Connor padded softly down the stairs. Brown hair, going grey over his ears, stood up in tufts on his head and round glasses perched halfway down his nose gave him an owlish look. As he stepped into the hall, she grabbed hold of the collar of his thick, red, towelling dressing gown and pulled him towards her in a fierce kiss. He smelled of the sex they had just had. She breathed it in.

I

'I can smell me on you.'

He smiled and stroked her face.

'I want to do it all over again, now. Here in the hall.'

He laughed nervously, assuming that she was joking. He was anxious for her to be gone. She had rung late last night, remembering that Meg, his wife, was away and suggested she might come round later, after the boys were in bed. At first he had resisted.

'Absolutely not,' he'd said. 'Not here.' The risk of discovery was too great. No way.

'But they'll be in bed,' she'd said.

He had laughed at that. 'You don't know much about children, do you? They don't necessarily stay there, you know. Not when they're seven and four.'

'Such a pity. I'll be away for a few weeks and I so much wanted to see you before I go.'

Then she had fallen silent, waiting for him. She hadn't had to wait long. He hadn't seen her for weeks; weeks in which he'd been consumed by thoughts of her. Weight of work, she'd said, each time he suggested they meet. So there was just this night.

'Take it or leave it. After this I won't be able to see you for a while.'

And of course he had taken it, despite the risks, despite the worry that the boys might wake, despite everything. He was desperate to see her – at any cost. They'd been lucky; the boys hadn't woken up. But now he wanted her out of here.

At any rate, that was what he thought before she touched him.

'I mean it, darling,' she said, her voice hoarse. 'Now, come on. Please, there's time.'

Afterwards, as he leaned forward to untie her, his face brushed against hers and she bit him on the cheek, hard enough to make him wince. 'To mark you as mine, darling,' she said. She smiled at him and he was shocked to see blood on her teeth, before he realized that it was just lipstick. She pulled up her tights, picked up the scrap of torn black silk and rubbed it against the side of his face then across his lips. 'That's another pair you owe me.' She pulled down her skirt. 'I must run,' she said, suddenly business-like.

He rubbed his cheek where she had bitten him. 'Yes,' he said. 'The boys will be up soon. You really must...'

But she wasn't listening. She stood in front of the hall mirror, reapplying her lipstick, unhurriedly. She placed a red nail on his mouth. 'Wasn't that fun?'

'Yes, yes, but—' he began.

She kissed him lightly on the lips. 'I must run.'

And now they could hear small feet on the floorboards above their heads.

He hustled her towards the front door.

'My briefcase,' she said.

He was frantic. 'Where?'

'The kitchen.'

He ran into the kitchen, grabbed the case and then bundled her outside. She kissed him on the doorstep, not giving a damn about his urgency. He held the door to, behind him. She turned and waved. He waved back.

'Flasher,' she mouthed, and he looked down and pulled his dressing gown together. Behind him he felt the door being tugged. He waited until she was out of sight before letting go of the handle.

His son, Bill, stood there, rubbing his eyes. 'What you doing, Daddy?'

John's heart was pounding. He looked down at his son. Exactly, he thought. What the hell *am* I doing? How could I be so bloody stupid? I must be completely and utterly insane to take these risks, to risk Bill and Ian, to risk my marriage. 'Just getting the milk,' he said, ruffling his son's hair.

Bill looked at his empty hands. 'Where is it?'

3

'I thought I heard the milkman. I must have been mistaken. It's not here yet.'

They walked back into the house and headed for the kitchen.

'What's this doing here?' Bill said, swinging on the red dressing gown belt, which was still attached to the banisters.

'Don't do that,' John said. 'You'll break it.'

'When's Mummy back from London?'

'She's picking you up from school today.'

As he walked into the kitchen to start breakfast, he saw the maroon Filofax lying open on the kitchen table. God, he couldn't leave that about the place. He glanced at it. This day and the couple of days before it were marked with a red star. He flicked backwards through the diary and found the same markings in the previous month. He frowned, put it in his bag and made a mental note to remember to give it back to her. But as he opened an overhead cupboard and took out two large cartons of cereal, he remembered the expression in her eyes, while they had been making love, disconnected and mildly amused.

CHAPTER ONE

Putney
Two weeks later

'So, she didn't turn up to pick the children up from school?' Sam Falconer asked.

John O'Connor shifted in his chair. 'No.'

'And she didn't let anyone know that she wasn't going to do that?'

'No. The first thing I knew about it was when the school phoned to tell me Bill and Ian were still there.'

'I presume that's why the police were concerned. Usually they won't investigate if adults go missing. It's no crime to disappear. But they do get worried if the missing person is a child or someone obviously vulnerable. A mother not picking up her children, they would view as suspicious.'

He nodded.

'And there was no response to your televised press conference?'

'No.'

'I have to tell you these sorts of cases are never easy.' She tucked a strand of curly blonde hair carefully behind her right ear. Staring into the air above his head, she continued. 'It can be very expensive and not produce the results one expects. I tell all my clients this because at the end of the day, if you'll pardon the cliché, there is the bill to pay . . . irrespective . . .' She paused and placed her hands flat on the desk.

John O'Connor frowned. 'Sorry, I wasn't ... my mind was somewhere else.'

She looked up. 'Irrespective of the result. I mean, if you hand over money for a sofa, you know that you will have a sofa to sit on. And it will be the same sofa you paid for. If you hand over money to me expecting a certain result you may be sorely disappointed.'

He rubbed a bruise on his cheek. 'You mean I may end up with a three-legged stool?'

'You may end up with nothing.' Her gaze slid across the surface of his face, and settled on his left ear lobe. 'Sometimes people go missing and no one ever knows why. Sometimes people simply walk or are taken out of their lives and never located.'

He tried to look her in the eye. Located. A neutral word to cover dead or alive. 'So, I may not even end up with a stool?'

'No. Two hundred thousand people go missing every year. Most turn up within a couple of days. But ten thousand go missing and stay missing, and of those, three thousand are never seen again.'

He sighed. 'Your brother says you have a very good success rate.'

'Mark's biased. I'm relatively new to the investigative business.'

'More yellow belt than black belt?'

She stared at him. 'If you like. I've been lucky so far.'

'You mean you've found the people who've gone missing?'

'Yes.'

'All of them?'

'So far.'

'Alive?'

She blinked once and looked away from him. Her fingers ran carefully along all four sides of the leather folder on her desk.

'I'm afraid I can't discuss my cases. You're a therapist, I'm sure you understand about client confidentiality.'

'Of course. I'm sorry. I think I read about one of your cases in the paper recently.'

'Perhaps.'

'It must have been very upsetting.' She didn't say anything so he continued. 'Do you think that a duty of confidentiality extends beyond death?'

She looked up. 'Oh, absolutely. Because the dead are incapable of giving their permission.'

'Mark's been a very good friend to me through all this. He got in contact as soon as he heard about Meg. He mentioned the judo thing. He was always very proud of you.'

'Ditto.'

'So, I suppose I was expecting someone . . .' He waved his hand in the air, struggling for the right words.

She sat back in her chair, allowing him to flounder. 'He presumably omitted to tell you that my fighting weight was under forty-eight kilos.'

John stared blankly at her.

'To the metrically challenged, that's seven and a half stone.'

He laughed. 'He's tall and dark, so I was expecting someone similar. But he did say you were useful at school for warding off bullies.'

'Mark was always a peacemaker. He doesn't have a violent bone in his body. All the fighting genes in the family seem to have skipped him and landed in me.'

'From your father to you?'

She looked startled. 'You know about that?'

'Yes, Mark told me. I'm sorry, I didn't mean to upset . . .'

She stood up abruptly and walked round the desk. Her hand was in her jacket pocket and John heard the noise of metal sliding against metal. It didn't sound like loose change.

'Are you sure you wouldn't prefer an investigator based in Oxford, Mr O'Connor? I could suggest—'

John swivelled in his chair, trying to keep her in view. 'No, no, I want someone who has been recommended. I . . . I'm very fond of your brother. I trust him. So his recommendation means a lot. I know this is the first time we've met but I don't want a total stranger digging around in my life. Our life. Do you see? There are the children to consider. You understand the territory.'

'Oxford?'

'I meant the emotional territory.'

'Oh,' she said, '*that.*'

'I mean, if you feel that it's inappropriate for you to take on a case in Oxford, I suppose—'

'No, no.'

'It's not as if it's a city you're unfamiliar with.'

Her face was impassive. 'Oh no, I'm all too familiar with it. Inside and out.'

She walked back to her desk and took a piece of paper out of the leather folder and handed it to him. 'This outlines our charges and the services we can provide. I'll leave you to read that in peace.'

She walked behind him and he heard the door open and the babble of noise from the other offices in the building waft into the room momentarily before the door closed, muffling the sound again.

John glanced cursorily at the piece of paper he had been handed. Across the top ran the name of the company, Gentle Way Investigations, an odd name for a firm of private investigators. The room was remarkable for its absence of any distinguishing features; an interview room, not her office. There was nothing in here to identify the room was in use – no filing cabinets and no telephone. He stood up, dropped the piece of paper on the desk and walked over to the window. From here he could see the Thames, glittering in the sunlight, snaking under

Putney Bridge. The tide was out and a heron stood motionless in the shallows, being mobbed by a flock of gulls. On the opposite side of the river, three red tower cranes moved elegantly back and forth over a half-built building, like surgeons over a body.

He turned back into the room. He wished it were her office. He wanted to pull open the drawers and rifle inside. After all, wasn't that exactly what he was giving *her* permission to do? Go rifling through his life, their life, in order to find out the truth? He wanted to get some sort of a handle on this woman. She had had some high-profile successes. She had found that murdered child, Jenny Hughes, and been splashed all over the papers, but could he trust her? She seemed reluctant to take him on and also edgy as hell. But more to the point, could he stand to find out the answer to the question he was posing her, why Meg had disappeared? He flipped open the leather folder and looked at the neat writing, which had carefully noted what he had said to her. The walls and ceiling were closing in on him. Was she watching him now through a hidden camera? He shivered and squatted down next to a weeping fig, hunched in the corner of the room. The door opened behind him and he jumped up.

'You should dust this plant, otherwise it'll suffocate.' He showed her the ends of his fingers, which were covered in dirt.

She looked at the open folder and then at the plant, as if seeing it for the first time. 'I'm not very good with plants. To be honest, I thought that one was plastic.'

'If you are not looking after your plants, then you are not looking after yourself,' he said, and then blushed.

She looked at him as if he had spoken to her in Mongolian. 'Have you decided?'

John waved the unread piece of paper. 'Yes, I'm sure that'll be fine.'

A wave of exhaustion crashed over him. He covered his eyes with his hand and grabbed the back of a chair.

'Just do what you can. I'll wait to hear.'

'Do you need to sit down?' She had moved swiftly across the room and was standing next to him. 'Can I get you some water?'

'No, no, I'm fine. I just need some fresh air. The last few weeks . . .' He began to walk slowly towards the door. 'I keep forgetting to eat.'

'Mr O'Connor?'

He stopped and turned. 'John,' he said. 'Please call me John.'

She nodded but when she spoke did not use his first name. 'I'm so sorry about what has happened.' For the first time she looked at him directly and he saw how very blue her eyes were, also how red the lids and dark the marks underneath. 'I know how difficult it is to be in a situation that is so unresolved. It's very hard to get on with one's life.'

'Yes, it is.' He pulled nervously at the cuffs of his shirt. 'Bill and Ian help. They still have to go to school, to be fed. You know, their lives go on.'

'Yes. Their lives go on.' She paused. 'In a manner of speaking.'

'Of course, you know about that from experience.'

She nodded.

'How old were you?'

'Four.'

'The same age as my Ian.'

She didn't say anything.

He filled the silence. 'So, I'll wait to hear from you, then?'

'Yes. I'll contact the police and read the file. And then I'll probably need to talk to you again. Who is the officer in charge of the investigation?'

'Phil someone. Phil . . .'

A long breath escaped through Sam's teeth. 'Howard?'

John frowned. 'Yes, that's right. DS Phil Howard.'

'Perfect,' Sam muttered.

'Sorry?'

'No, nothing.' She held out her hand and he took it, feeling his knuckles crunch together in her grip. 'Send my love to Mark.'

'I will.' He closed the door behind him and stood flexing his right hand. 'Christ.'

A tall man with short black hair, several earrings in one ear and wearing a tight white T-shirt stretched over a muscular, tanned frame was holding a plastic cup under the tap of a water cooler. He grimaced in sympathy.

'I keep telling her to go easy on the handshakes, but it makes no difference. I just thank God I work with her and don't have to shake hands. On high days and holidays, I pin her arms firmly to her side and kiss her on both cheeks. If there's ever a suggestion of anything more formal, I scream and run out of the room.'

John laughed. 'Well, I suppose you don't get to be a World Judo Champion without having a firm grip. But, my God, that's like having your hand crushed in a steel vice. And she's so petite you don't expect it.'

'When she gets a hold of you on a judo mat, I tell you, you haven't got a chance in hell. It was one of the things that made her such a formidable fighter – she'd never let go.'

'You've fought her?'

'No, not strictly speaking. She holds self-defence classes for GMDL.'

'Sorry?'

'Gay Men's Defence League. There was some rather nasty queer-bashing going on a couple of years back and we decided to get organized. She was recommended to us. You should have seen the expressions on the faces of the Muscle Marys when they copped a load of tiny Sam. Their humiliation when she started throwing them about was something to behold. After the first session one of the Spanish boys nicknamed her El Niño.'

John laughed. 'The wind that brings hurricanes?'

'In Spanish it means The Kid, because she's so small. But the hurricane thing applies just as well.'

The door to the office opened and John stepped away from it.

'Oh, sorry,' Sam said. 'I just wanted to have a word with Alan. I didn't realize you were still here.'

Alan folded his arms and cocked his head on one side. 'What have I been telling you about that handshake?'

Sam hit her forehead lightly with the open palm of her right hand. She turned towards John. 'I'm so sorry, I forgot. I don't do it, you know, to prove ... it's just that I ...' She blushed. 'The truth is, it's just my natural grip.'

'Don't worry,' John said, smiling.

'I'll have to practise a bit more with Alan.'

'No, I've had enough,' Alan retorted. 'They're still bruised from the last encounter.' He turned towards John and whispered. 'I couldn't type for a week.'

Sam laughed. 'The thing is, I don't seem to be able to find the happy medium between a limp fish and a knuckle-breaker and sometimes people get very upset...' She flexed her right hand. 'They think I'm throwing down some sort of gauntlet.'

'Maiming clients isn't good for business,' Alan said. 'And anyway, it's completely at odds with our name.'

'I meant to ask you about that,' John said. 'Strange name.'

She smiled. 'In Japanese, *joo* means "gentle" and *doh* means "way". Gentle in the way a willow tree gives and bends to the force of a strong wind. The wind will then go through the tree rather than blowing it over. It's all a question of balance and how you direct your opponents' force against them.'

'I see.' But he wondered who the opponent was in this case. How did that work when someone went missing?

She seemed much more relaxed out here with Alan than in the office, John thought. Perhaps she was human after all.

CHAPTER TWO

Sam Falconer felt all too human as she fumbled in her bag for her keys and tensed against the biting wind that was cutting down the New King's Road and blowing into her right ear. She looked up at the outside of the Victorian mansion block she lived in, and brought down all the curses she could muster on the head of her landlord, Donald Crozier. Scaffolding, not there in the morning, and not warned of in any letter, surrounded it. Wooden walkways now ran around the outside of the building exactly level with her windows. She pushed open the front door of the block and climbed the six steps to her flat. Rent review must be coming round. Every two years or so, Crozier threw a mass of scaffolding round the place and then claimed exorbitant rent and service charge increases. Most of the flats in the block were privately owned and rented out to young men and women with too much money and not enough sense. There were only three sitting tenants left in the block: Edie, Spence and Sam. Thorns in the side of Crozier, who could only charge a protected rent – £400 per month – and could not get his hands on properties worth close to £250,000 each and rising.

As she put the key in her lock, the front door of the flat to her left creaked open.

'Shocking, isn't it?' hissed a voice through the two-inch gap in the door. The smell of mothballs, overridden with steak and kidney pie, tickled Sam's nostrils.

Sam turned. 'Evening, Edie.'

The door opened a bit more and Edie Redlands's pink cheeks

and large glasses poked out. A long piece of fine brown hair, which had dared to escape from under her black curly wig, was quickly wound round Edie's finger and whisked away behind her ear.

'They've been crashing and banging all day. And there's no security. Down the road they did it properly, put up all that green netting and alarms. This is a burglar's charter. *And* I'm a woman alone. And the mouths on them is something disgusting.'

Sam nodded in agreement but couldn't help smiling. There was nothing vulnerable about Edie even though she did like to play up the poor little old lady routine – especially when she wanted something.

'I don't feel safe in my own home and it could be there for months.'

'Rent review must be coming round.'

'I've a mind to complain,' Edie said. 'Tell him what for. Maybe you could write a letter on your word processing thing. It's more official in black and white, and my hand—'

'I'll see, Edie.' Sam turned the key in her lock.

'All right, dear. You watching the match tonight?'

'I'm not sure. I'm tired. Maybe an early night.'

Occasionally, when the football was on, Sam had Edie in for supper but recently she hadn't been feeling up to it. Edie always insisted on bringing in her own music and singing along to it, and Sam wasn't in the mood for that tonight.

'All right for baccy?'

'Fine. You know I only smoke a couple a day, it takes me months to get through them all.'

'I can't always supply them, babes. You know, winter's setting in and it gets rough out there. The cold gets to my knees. I can't always promise to have it. I'm taking Christmas orders.'

'I'll let you know in good time if I need any more.'

Edie sniffed and slammed the door, sending out a final gust of meat and mothballs. Sam sneezed. She wasn't much of a smoker.

Sometimes she thought the only reason she kept smoking her two or three a day was to give Edie a bit of business. Ever since her husband died four years ago, Edie had been living on the state pension, boosted by a little tobacco smuggling. As Sam opened her front door, a fat and shaggy orange cat burst on to the landing, sniffed at Edie's door and began howling.

'Come on, Frank,' Sam said, turning on the light in her hall. 'You want to be fed, don't you? It's not going to happen out there.'

And her cat, Frank Cooper, after scratching his claws on the blue carpet, trotted back into the flat and, defying the laws of physics that say a fat cat can't possibly run as fast as a greyhound, hurtled towards the kitchen.

Sam had lived in this flat in Fulham for the last three years. It had been her gran's and now it was hers. She knew it was supposed to be a desirable area. Rich parents bought flats for their children here. Estate agents drooled over the place and, not knowing she was a tenant, stuffed leaflets through her door, asking if she was thinking of selling or letting. The trouble was Fulham just wasn't her. There was nothing wrong with it per se. The streets were kept clean, certainly cleaner than any other part of London she had lived in, and it was all very nice with a capital 'N'. If you put your newspapers outside your front door on Friday evening, they were removed for recycling the following morning. There was Putney and the river in one direction and the King's Road in the other. But Sam was suspicious of anything that looked too nice. In her experience nice was not to be trusted and estate agents never mentioned that Jill Dando was shot just round the corner and Suzy Lamplugh had disappeared from Fulham into thin air all those years ago.

Sam had been brought up in Oxford, so she knew all about living in places that looked good. She knew that external beauty could aggravate internal misery in a most unpredictable way, that dreaming spires could hold unexpected nightmares tucked away in their complicated stonework. Dreaming spires often carried gargoyles. She thanked God for Edie and for Spence. Neither of them was nice. No, that certainly wasn't a word you'd use to describe them. It wasn't a word Sam would use to describe herself. Nice was not to be trusted; it was an insult. Cheap rent was the only thing that kept Sam in Fulham. In London, cheap rent was everything and if you had that you stayed put. You'd be mad not to.

She looked down on to the head of Frank Cooper, hoovering food into himself like there was no tomorrow. Frank wasn't nice either. He was Edie's fault. Edie was involved in the Cats' Protection League. She always had kittens to hand and Sam had allowed herself to be persuaded. Well, he'd been sweet when he was little. She just hadn't realized that Frank would turn out to be such a thug. He was huge and hairy, a great big orang-utan of a cat. When he'd stopped growing lengthways he'd started growing sideways. He had a gargantuan appetite and had obviously never read the part of the book that says cats will regulate their own intake of food. No, Frank had sneezed when he came to that page. Edie said it was because he was a feral kitten and had never known where his next meal was coming from, but then Edie believed in fat cats. Occasionally, when she thought Frank was getting too thin, she'd kidnap him for twenty-four hours or so and Sam would then find him sitting outside her door, looking dazed and as if a small football had been inserted in his stomach.

Sam sighed and turned on the kettle. As it roared into life, she heard a knock on her door.

Edie handed her a letter. 'Those bloody foreigners have been taking the post up to the landing and leaving it there.' According to Sam's gran, Edie's first husband had been a 'bloody foreigner', a Turkish chef, but Sam had never heard Edie herself refer to it.

'Thanks.' Sam took the letter and closed the door. Edie checked out everyone's post. She'd probably held this up to the light, or waved it around in the steam of a kettle. Sometimes the letters arrived in such a mangled state it was hard to believe it was just the Post Office's fault. Edie was wasted in twenty-first-century London. She'd have thrived in Cold War Russia, sitting at the end of a hotel corridor in Moscow, watching the comings and goings of tourists and handing out bath plugs in exchange for a tidy sum of dollars or perhaps a nice pair of Levi's.

Sam heard the click of the kettle and walked back into the kitchen. The envelope wasn't wet, but it was wrinkled. As if it had got wet and then been dried on the radiator. Sam didn't really mind, any confidential stuff got sent to the office. She made herself a cup of tea and took it into the living room and turned on the Channel 4 News. She'd started watching this more and more recently. She would have liked to have believed it was because she had a growing interest in current affairs, but she knew in her heart of hearts it had more to do with enjoying looking at Jon Snow and Krishnan Guru Murthy. She sipped her tea, the letter lying unopened on her lap, and admired Jon Snow's tie.

Later that evening, Sam lay under a layer of bubbles and turned on the hot water tap with her big toe. Baths to Sam had never meant anything to do with washing. They had to do with relaxation, with thinking, with reading. If you lay long enough in a bath, the dirt soaked off, didn't it? And there was no need to do anything. Showers were horrible things. Often she got into a bath simply to think, in this instance about John O'Connor.

She had seen him at the press conference crying over his missing wife. God, how that man had cried. Sam shuddered. She couldn't bear it when men cried and she couldn't bear therapists. They fucked with your head and picked at your scars; they made you vulnerable. And all for what? To take your money? To encourage your dependence on them? To screw you up even more, so you would keep coming back and back. Sam knew that if a therapist had got a hold of her, she would never have become the fighter she was. She had managed fine all by herself.

At the age of seven, after she had first set foot on a *tatami*, she had come home and stuck a picture of the twelve-year-old Muhammad Ali on her wall. That was the age Ali was when he had come home after his first session in the ring and told his parents that he would be World Champion. Ten years later he was. On another wall, Sam stuck a picture of Ali after he had beaten Sonny Liston and become champion for the first time. He was leaning over the ropes, shouting at the journalists sitting ringside. None of them had thought he would win. Underneath ran the caption, 'Eat your words.'

That was the sort of psychology Sam could get her head around. By the time a sports psychologist came along, there wasn't much that she could be advised to do that she hadn't been doing for years. If you wanted to be the best you studied 'The Greatest'. Mind you, O'Connor had looked a mess, tugging at the cuffs of his shirt while blinking at her through those circular, rimless glasses, and telling her to dust her plants. He was the one who looked in need of therapy. Yes, Sam thought, with a degree of satisfaction, he looked a real mess.

But then you would, wouldn't you, if you were in his situation? His wife, Meg, had gone up to London on the afternoon of 2 October by bus. That evening she attended a private press view of a new exhibition that was opening in Tate Modern. She dined there with a fellow critic, Zandra Dodds, and travelled home by tube to her flat in Fulham. In the morning she phoned John and spoke to the children before they went to school. She then wrote her review of the exhibition and e-mailed it to her editor, Ian Bruce. They spoke on the phone at eleven o'clock about some changes and that was the last contact that anyone had with her. When she failed to pick up her sons from school, O'Connor reported her missing. Sam had a bad feeling about this case. When a mother failed to pick up her children from school and made no effort to let anyone know she couldn't do it, all bets were off as to that person turning up alive.

Sam dipped her chin into the bubbles. Her brother Mark's involvement wasn't the only reason she'd agreed to take on the case. It was true she adored him and would do anything for him. That's the way it had always been between them. But there was also the fact that since the discovery of the body of the murdered child, Jenny Hughes, Sam needed to work. She needed something to distract her from the nightmares and the waking flashbacks and the headaches that were piling up, closer and closer, and starting to resist the best efforts of the strongest painkillers. The dead child seemed intent on telling Sam something, which Sam knew she didn't want to hear, and she was frightened.

Someone based in Oxford should really have taken on O'Connor; that would have made more sense. But Meg had a flat in Fulham only a few streets away from where Sam lived and Sam had been brought up in Oxford, so there was just about enough of a connection for the thing to stick. The only trouble was that Sam would have to go back to Oxford . . . She allowed her head to drop beneath the water and stayed there as long as her lungs could stand it. No, it didn't look any better from under here. Any way she looked at it, it seemed like shit. But the truth was that somewhere between Oxford and London, Meg O'Connor had gone missing. Sam knew the feeling well.

She broke the surface and wiped the water out of her eyes. How long was it that she had avoided going there? Three years? More like three and a half. She blew on the bubbles disconsolately. Well, maybe it was time to lay a few demons to rest and this was the opportunity. But at this particular moment the demons were far from rested. They fluttered up and down Sam's stomach like butterflies trapped in a jar of meths, and each one bore a different face: her ex-boyfriend, Detective Sergeant Phil Howard, her mother, Jean, her step-father, Peter, her brother,

Mark, and now John and Meg O'Connor. And no amount of bubble bath or hot water could scrub those faces off.

Sam levered herself reluctantly out of the bath, dried herself, shrugged on a dressing gown and walked back into the front room to turn out the lights. The letter that Edie had handed her lay unopened on the floor, where it had fallen from her lap. She picked it up and tore it open. *Dear Samantha*, it began. Strange, because not many people called her Samantha. Her eyes skipped down the letter, not recognizing the handwriting and turned the page. *With love from Dad*. Sam's whole body jumped and the letter floated to the ground. She stood staring at it, as if it might explode and then taking a deep breath, picked it up and began to read.

> *Dear Samantha,*
>
> *I know you think I am dead, that I died in 1974. This is what they wanted everyone to think, my mates, my family, the SAS. But I didn't die. I went missing. Things were going on. Things I don't want to write of in this letter. I had to go. I had to go at once.*
>
> *I know how well you've done. I've watched your fights. I was there in Paris in 1990 when you first became World Champion. I was so proud. I wanted to tell you but I couldn't. I wanted to run out of the audience and grab hold of you. Hold you up and say 'This is my daughter, a champion.' You are a fighter like me, small but so strong. I know what it takes to become a champion. I know about fighting. I know about winning. I want to explain.*
>
> *Please give me the chance. I know you may be angry with me. You may not believe me. But please do. Know that I am your father and I'll be in touch soon. I'll explain everything. Please keep this secret. It could be a matter of my life, my death.*
>
> *With love from Dad.*

Sam walked over to the window and rested her head against the glass.

'You are dead,' she said out loud. 'You died in nineteen seventy-four, when I was four years old. You fought in Oman. You were killed in Oman. You were buried with full military honours in the SAS cemetery at St Martin's, Hereford. I visit your grave every year. I've carried your dog tags in my pocket since you died. Every day I've rubbed them between my fingers like a rosary. I summoned your ghost to help me when I fought. I miss you. I mourn you. Your absence has made me.'

This was the story Sam had built her life on.

She had been a champion fighter.

She was now a private investigator, specializing in missing persons. When she was working for her clients, she knew there was really only one person that she was ever looking for: the man whose ghost had cast a bloodless shadow across her entire life, her father. Sam knew in every cell of her body that her father was dead. She *knew* it. But as she looked out of the window at the weary faces of the passengers on the top deck of a number 22 bus, which had stopped exactly level with her window, she knew that now, where she had been certain, she doubted. A headache began to pound out a familiar tattoo on the inside of her skull. She peered at the postmark on the envelope.

Oxford.

A city where dead men wrote letters, a city that was calling her home.

CHAPTER THREE

Sam jolted awake as the coach slowed on reaching the Heading-ton roundabout. She stretched and moved her head from side to side, trying to relieve the stiffness in her neck and shoulders. She felt sad; the sadness that comes with a longing for a home that you know no longer exists. She looked up New High Street, which ran left off the main road, and saw the large tail of a shark buried in the roof of one of the houses; that always cheered her up. It was so surreal, rather like her experience of coming back here. The coach picked up speed as it went down Headington Hill towards St Clement's. As a child, Sam had sat on the top floor of the number 2A, watching the bus chase the cyclists down the hill and ducking as the branches slammed on the roof above her head.

She got off the bus outside Queen's, hitched her rucksack on to her back and set off towards Radcliffe Square. The High was seething with buses, cyclists and cars, the pavements with students and tourists. Radcliffe Square wasn't much emptier. A memorial service had just ended in St Mary's, the university church, and large numbers of dons stood outside chatting, their gowns and different-coloured hoods billowing in the strong wind, which was sending white clouds racing across the sky behind the church's tall spire. A group of Japanese tourists took photos of the dons and each other. The Radcliffe Camera sat, squat and golden, in the autumn sunshine. However malignant Sam felt towards Oxford, she could never view the Camera with anything other than wonder and affection. She turned left in front of St Mary's, walked over the cobblestones in front of Brasenose and cut down the alley that ran down the side of the college. Memories crowded in upon her. Every step she took brought forth another and another. Overwhelming and insistent, they poured into her until she felt she would burst. She shook her head and moved her rucksack from one shoulder to the other. But the memories could not be shifted so easily. Like a crowd waving placards, they announced themselves one by one: Look at me! No, me! But I'm so much more important! They pushed and elbowed and the sickness in the pit of Sam's stomach grew.

She reached St Barnabas's College and tapped on the glass of the porter's lodge. A balding, red-faced man, stuffed into a white shirt that was too small for him, took his time raising his eyes from the racing pages of the *Oxford Mail*.

'Well, good grief, where the hell have you been all these years?'

Sam smiled. 'Hello, Jack. How are you?'

He tapped the paper. 'Still losing money on the nags. How long is it? I haven't seen you in—'

'It's about three years.'

'That long? Time flies when you're losing money.'

Sam laughed. 'OK to go up to Mark's?'

'I need to sign you in, love. It's not like it used to be when we let anyone come and go. We've had too many thefts going on. Security's had to tighten up.'

'Modern life impinging even here? I don't believe it.'

He smiled. 'It gets everywhere, you know, that bloody modern life. Nice to see you, love. Don't be a stranger.'

He wrote her name down and nodded her through. Shivering, Sam walked along the side of the quadrangle, which was in deep shade, trudged slowly up Mark's staircase and banged on his door. It was flung open and her brother stood there staring at her.

'God, you look depressed,' he said, and seized her in a ferocious bear hug, which lifted her feet from the ground.

Sam sat back in a deep leather armchair and grinned at her brother. Strictly speaking, he was the kind of man she should have despised. He was too tweedy and too posh for her, with an unruly mop of black hair he kept long to cover the white mesh of scars on his forehead – the result of a childhood accident. He still looked like an overgrown schoolboy, mainly because his feet were so huge. Even though he was six foot four he had never really grown into them.

But because he was her brother she adored him and forgave him, she always had. He lay stretched out on the sofa, tugging at the dog collar round his neck. Outside, Oxford traffic stop-started up and down The High. So, here she was, back again.

'No one's ever managed to make a comfortable one of these,' he complained.

'Maybe it's the hair-shirt principle,' Sam said. 'You know, suffering for your beliefs.'

'Bugger that,' Mark replied. 'Thank God I only have to wear it for a few hours on stage. Even then it's rubbing my neck raw. I don't know how the chaplain can stand it. No wonder he always looks so bloody miserable.' He pulled it off and threw it on the ground next to him.

'I thought you were playing a friar?'

'Correct, Friar Lawrence. But it's being done in modern dress so I get to wear a dog collar instead of a cowl, for reasons best known to the director.'

'So, how's the play going?' Sam asked.

'The director's prone to bursts of paranoid hostility. You know, the whole cast is against me. That sort of thing.'

'The usual then?'

Mark laughed. 'Yes, I suppose so. We're horribly behind in

24

rehearsals and Romeo and Juliet have started shagging like bunnies.'

'Sex and violence, the lot of the amateur actor,' Sam said. 'It's a while since you've done it.'

'The man who should have been playing the role went down with rather a nasty case of mumps.'

'Ouch.'

'Exactly. It's got every male in the cast checking his gonads on a minute-by-minute basis.'

'That must be interesting for the female members of cast.'

'Well, they keep checking their breasts.'

'So everyone is fondling themselves?'

'Absolutely, it's like "Eurotrash".'

'And why are you doing it, exactly?'

'I knew the director, James, from college, and he knew I'd done the same part back then so he called me up, asked if I'd give it a whirl. The trouble is Friar Lawrence has very long speeches and he was worried about someone learning it all in time.'

'But you did that years ago. Can you remember it?'

'I will be brief, for my short date of breath is not so long as is a tedious tale. Romeo, there dead—'

'OK, OK, I'm bored already,' Sam said.

Mark laughed. 'Mind you, the one thing Friar Lawrence isn't is brief.'

'Do you like the cast?'

'Well, they've gone through that whole bonding thing. You know, from weeks of rehearsal.'

'Especially Romeo and Juliet?'

'Yes, so they're not exactly welcoming me with open arms. But it makes a change from trying to din English Literature into the brains of undergraduates. None of mine this year are very exciting. Hard-working seconds at most, no one to really get my teeth into. It's great to see you, sis. It's a long time since I've been able to tempt you down.'

'Well, you know how I feel about this place,' Sam replied.

'So, what brings you here?' Mark placed his elbows on his knees and his head in his hands. Outside the chapel bell started chiming the fourth quarter before striking the hour. Sam got up and walked to the window. Front quad was flooded with early afternoon sunlight.

'The stone really does look golden, doesn't it?'

He walked over and stood beside her. 'Christ, Sam, I know you haven't come down here to admire the bloody architecture. Spit it out.'

She put her hand inside the pocket of her jacket and handed him the letter. He unfolded it and began to read. She walked away from the window and leaned against the fireplace, waiting for him. When he turned away from the window his face was so white the scars on his forehead were barely visible.

'Who on earth would dream of doing something so cruel?'

'You haven't received anything?'

'No.'

'Mum?'

'She'd have said, wouldn't she?'

She looked at him. 'There's no chance, you think, that . . .' She ground to a halt.

'No, Sam, I don't. I mean we buried him. We must have done, mustn't we? They couldn't have got it *that* wrong.'

'I guess not.'

As if it wasn't bad enough having lost him in the first place. As if she and Mark weren't both defined by his absence.

'Do you recognize the writing?' she asked.

Mark walked over to a filing cabinet in the corner of the room and pulled open the top drawer. He took out a file and handed it to Sam. 'Every piece of correspondence I ever had from him. Every birthday card, every . . .' He stopped and threw himself down on the sofa. 'Pathetic, isn't it?'

She sat down next to him. 'I've got these.' She reached in her pocket and pulled out the dog tags. Mark frowned. He put out his hand and she dropped them into his open palm. His was the only hand she would have let them rest in.

'God, you still carry them around with you?' He ran his thumb over their surface.

'Pathetic, isn't it?' Sam said.

Mark smiled. 'No,' he said.

'Exactly,' she said.

Sam opened the file and took out some cards, comparing the writing to that in the letter. She frowned. 'It's difficult. He'd be a lot older, wouldn't he? Doesn't that change your writing?' She pointed to the word 'Dad' in the card and the letter. 'These are nothing like each other. The writing in the letter is almost childish, like someone has had to learn how to write from scratch.'

'Or like someone who hasn't written for a long time.'

'Yes, they've really had to concentrate on how they form the lines. It wobbles all over the place.'

'It's got to be a hoax, hasn't it?'

'He doesn't say what he's going to do next.'

'No, he doesn't.'

'So, all we can do is wait for him to make contact again.'

'Yes.'

'Did you see the postmark?'

Mark turned over the envelope. 'Oh,' he said. 'So, that's what's brought you here?'

He looked hurt and Sam immediately felt remorseful. 'You never come to London, Mark.'

'I hate it, all that traffic and barging about. London is becoming angrier and angrier.'

Sam pointed towards the window that overlooked The High. 'What's that out there?'

'You know what I mean.'

She smiled.

Mark scratched the back of his neck. 'I hate London and you hate Oxford.'

'I didn't say hate. It's just all the memories. None of them are happy. I get ambushed by them. It's like having a swarm of angry bees buzzing round my head.'

'You were happy fighting.'

'Yes, but I couldn't fight all the time.'

Mark laughed. 'I don't know. You tried pretty hard. Are you going to tell Mum?'

Sam shrugged. 'What do you think?'

Mark shook his head. 'It'd only upset her.'

Sam nodded.

'You going to see her?'

Sam sighed.

'She knows you're in town.'

'You didn't tell her, did you?'

''Fraid so.'

'Oh God, Mark – then I suppose I'll have to.'

'Well, that was the general idea. You know the longer you leave it the worse it gets.'

'I may not have time. I've got work to do on O'Connor.'

'That's hardly an excuse given that he lives practically opposite them.'

Sam didn't say anything.

'He told me he'd contacted you.'

'Yes, and I'd be grateful for a little background. I'll see the police file tomorrow but it's not the same as hearing about him from a friend.'

'We didn't start off as friends.'

'What would you call him, then?'

Mark patted his pockets until he found a packet of cigarettes, took one out and lit it.

'I can get Edie to get you some of those if you want.'

'My God, is that old witch still alive?'

'And smuggling.'

He squinted at Sam through the smoke. 'I'm trying to cut down.'

'You were saying about John.'

'What?'

'You were saying that you didn't start out as friends.'

'Ah, that's right. No, probably the politest and most accurate description of our association would be a one-night stand. Well, it was slightly more than one but you get the general idea.'

'Oh, I see.'

Mark puffed out his cheeks. 'Well, I'm glad someone does, darling, because I didn't and I'm not sure I do, even now. Come on, let's go for a walk.'

Bundled up against a nasty easterly wind, Mark and Sam walked over the bridge that led to the boathouses in Christ Church meadow.

'So,' Sam said. 'He was a good shag, then?'

'Delicately put,' Mark replied. They waited on the sandy path while a shell was carried out of a boathouse on the shoulders of eight burly young men, swung into the air and dropped into the choppy, sparkling water. Then they walked on in silence.

'Do you miss the rowing?' Sam asked eventually.

'Do you miss the fighting?' Mark replied.

'Silly question, right?'

Sam grabbed a bit of Mark's scarf that had unravelled and given her a woolly backhander and tucked it back in his jacket. At least it wasn't one of those terrible college scarves.

'John came up on some kind of military scholarship. You know the sort of thing, he'd passed officer selection and they were paying to put him through college, provided he went into the army afterwards.'

'But he's a therapist, isn't he? From the army to therapy's a bit of a leap.'

'Well, it was obvious to anyone that knew him he wouldn't be heading for the army. I mean he was much too sensitive for that kind of thing, and too anti-establishment. He was a pacifist! I mean, John in the army giving orders, taking them. The whole idea was laughable. Writing essays on Shelley was more his line. He was too much of a free spirit. He always said he'd done the military thing to get the old man off his back and that at the end of the three years he'd do what he bloody well liked. He just had no idea what that was. You know who his father is?'

'No.'

'Who's the most famous O'Connor you know?'

'Well, there was that idiot who was in the Cabinet.'

'The very one.'

Sam whistled. 'My God, that's some family legacy.'

Mark nodded. 'And he was up in the eighties. His dad was in the Cabinet then. So, you can imagine he was always very secretive about his background. Never talked about it much. I didn't find out until I visited him in hospital and his father was there.'

'What was he doing in hospital?'

'He cracked up in his final year.'

'Exams?'

'I don't think so, really. He was very bright, could always do the work, no trouble. Much more easily than me. I think he just couldn't face his dad. It was easier to go mad. And he didn't do it by halves. He tried to kill himself, slit his wrists and ended up in the Warneford. I found him in one of the bath cubicles in college quite by accident. He'd cut the veins lengthways and deep. You know, it was the real thing, not a cry for help. I went to see him in the hospital and was in reception when Sir William O'Connor himself stalks out. It was only then that I put two and two together. When I went in to see him, he was in a terrible state, doped up to the eyeballs, but gibbering on about how his father would never let him do what he wanted, that there was no way out. He wished he'd made the cuts deeper, he wished they'd let him die. Said he never wanted to see me again. That he couldn't forgive me for saving him. Poor John. He said some horrible stuff but he was off his head.'

'So that was the summer of your third year?'

'Yes. Next time I saw him was a couple of years later. I bumped into him at a mutual friend's wedding. I didn't know many people there, so I was glad to see him. It was then he told me that he was training as a therapist. He was always a sympathetic listener. Said it had really worked for him. That he really thought he could help people. And I was pleased. He sounded like he'd found the thing he wanted to do.'

They'd reached the final boathouse and stood looking across at the University Boat Club.

'Were you surprised that he got married?'

Mark shrugged. 'Well, not particularly. You know how it is, and he'd always been adamant about wanting children. And that's not usual in young blokes. Sex, drugs and getting pissed certainly, but not children. But he *really* wanted them. He always said it was a way of starting out fresh. His childhood had been horrible. His father, well, you know his father's reputation.'

'Womanizer?'

'Yes, and then there was all that publicity about the affair with his secretary and her having his child, do you remember? And first he denied it and then refused to have anything to do with it. I think John was ashamed of the way his father behaved. He always said the only way to wipe the slate clean was to do better himself. So, I just figured it was easier for him to do the whole marriage thing. He'd always swung both ways. Maybe it was the children that weighted it one way and not the other.'

'Did you know Meg?'

'No. He met her on an art therapy course. She's a journalist and art critic, and she'd been sent along to write an article on the course he was taking. Her father was a diplomat and she'd been brought up abroad, largely in America, I think. The first time I met her was at their wedding. I liked her. She seemed to have her feet on the ground and be into the same things as John. They seemed well matched. But the main thing about him getting married was that he wasn't marrying Alice Knight; that was a huge relief to all his friends.'

'Who's Alice Knight?'

'Well, she was a contemporary of ours and they'd always had a very intense relationship. It was obvious he was besotted with her but none of his friends could stand her. I don't think they got it together at college, although maybe he wouldn't have told me if they had because he knew how I felt about her. He was always going on about what a brilliant mind she had, but to me she just seemed like a really nasty piece of work. She was the kind of woman who flicks her hair over her shoulder in a crowded tube and doesn't care whose eye she's taken out in the process.'

Sam laughed. 'Plenty of those on the District Line between Earl's Court and Putney Bridge.'

'Mind you, she never did have a hair out of place.' Mark swiped his own unruly mop back across his forehead. 'Always looked as if her nails had just been manicured. And you can't say that about many students. She was very ambitious and we all assumed she was after him because of who his father was. But then there was a rumour that she was having an affair with her tutor, Tony Ballinger. Don't know if it was true or not. But Tony ended up having to resign. John tried to kill himself and she walked away with a First. She was a really chilly woman, but then John always had enough warmth for two. Yes, he was very warm.'

Sam slipped her arm into Mark's and they started to walk back the way they had come. 'Why didn't it work out between you and John?'

Mark shrugged. 'Neither of us wanted to be committed. And

we got together in our third year. And then there was all the suicide stuff. Finding someone in a pool of blood . . . you know, it was a bit much for both of us. And for a while he refused to see me because I'd saved him. It was a mess. Anyway, it didn't work out. Some things don't.'

'No,' Sam said. 'Some things don't.' She squeezed her brother's arm affectionately and wondered if he was lonely. 'Anyone on the horizon at the moment?'

Mark laughed. 'Well, I've got the hots for Maggie Sawyer, the woman playing the nurse. She's a very sexy sixty-year-old.'

Sam laughed. 'Nothing's ever simple with you, is it?'

'With either of us.' They walked on in silence for a few minutes. 'By the way, she's back in town.'

'Sorry?'

'Alice bloody Knight. She became a partner in a City firm of solicitors and then moved back here to set up a new office. There's lots of legal work generated by the colleges. She's going to be doing some teaching.'

'Where?'

'St Barnabas's, actually. You'll probably meet her tonight at high table.'

'Does O'Connor know she's around?'

'Not from me. That woman's trouble. I just hope she keeps away. I haven't told either of them about the other.'

'Oxford's a small place.'

Mark nodded in agreement. 'It would be unusual if he didn't know.'

They stopped and leaned over a bridge close to Christ Church. Mark tucked his hand into the crook of Sam's arm. 'Do you remember, Mum always said this was where the White Rabbit in *Alice* disappeared down the tunnel?'

Sam wrinkled her nose. The water smelled stagnant and was full of algae. What she remembered was the disappointment of looking for a white rabbit that was never going to appear.

'So,' Mark said eventually, when they were walking up St Aldate's towards Carfax. 'You going to see him?'

'Who?'

'Come *on*, Sam.'

Sam sighed. 'It turns out he's in charge of the investigation.'

Mark laughed. 'And?'

'And what?' Sam snapped.

'Well, I don't know. It's all dig, dig, dig when it comes to me and then I ask you a few innocent questions and you clam up good and proper.'

'It's called being a hypocrite,' Sam said. 'So there. And anyway, I'm the private investigator, so I get to ask the questions.'

'I always liked him.'

'Funnily enough, so did I. That's why I stayed with him all those years.'

'I never really knew why you two split up.'

They had turned right into The High and were passing a large building with Old Bank Hotel on the outside. Sam stopped. 'You know that used to be my bloody bank and now they've turned it into a hotel. I mean what's the matter with this town? That's where I first opened an account. Now its address is some stupid PO Box. I want bricks and mortar.'

'Well, if you don't want to tell me, why don't you just come out and say so?'

Sam laughed. 'Let's just say it involved a judo mat and a bruised male ego.'

Mark raised his eyebrows. 'Ouch.'

'He was the secretary of the National Police Judo Association and also their Open Champion. He invited me to come to their annual competition for a demonstration. I didn't really want to do it but he was my boyfriend, so I did it as a favour. But then he set me up. Says we'll have a fight in front of all his mates. *Randori*. No holds barred. He hadn't warned me. He had to see if he could beat me. That's what lay at the heart of it. He couldn't leave well alone.'

'And so you threw him?'

'Not exactly, no. Well, at first.'

'And then what?'

'*Shime-waza.*'

'Excuse me?'

Sam threw her hands in the air in exasperation. 'Well, I was really pissed off with him because he sprung it on me. I was doing him a favour and he wasn't showing me any respect. I strangled him.'

Mark laughed. 'God, sis. You don't do things by halves, do you?'

Sam pulled him to a standstill and faced him. Behind them the Radcliffe Camera sat like a large egg in the dusk. She ran her finger lightly down the side of his neck. 'This is the sternocleido-mastoid muscle. It protects the carotid artery, which supplies blood and oxygen to the brain. If I move the muscle aside and apply pressure to the artery, here, you'll be unconscious in five seconds.'

Mark took her hand away from his neck and held it. 'I feel safer with your hand here, thank you very much. You know it's weird, the last person who told me about that was John after he came back from one of his army weekends all those years ago.'

Sam continued. 'Phil refused to submit so I strangled him until he passed out.'

Mark let go of her hand. 'God! Did you have to do *that*?'

'The trouble was I'd been practising strangles all week. Women don't tend to use them as much as men. But they're very effective in competition. So Tyler had me practising and practising. He'd been goading me. How much do you want it? Will you go for the kill? Go for the jugular. I got into a competitive situation and saw the opportunity to put my training into action. Worked a treat. Phil didn't submit, so I kept the pressure on. When he came round, he said I'd humiliated him on purpose in front of all his mates. He conveniently forgot that the whole thing had been his idea from the start. I'd never really wanted to do it. I'd certainly not wanted to fight him. He set the whole thing up and then complained when it didn't go how he'd planned.'

'The male ego is a fragile thing,' Mark said. 'Look at King Lear.'

'I mean, what did he think was going to happen? I'd just won the European Championships. I was World Champion. I was at my peak. He'd seen me fight. Did he think I'd let him beat me, as if he were a small child? I treated him as a proper opponent. I gave him that respect. He should have submitted but got macho about it and then couldn't take the consequences.'

'Men can be very stupid,' Mark said agreeably.

'The trouble was that because he'd passed out he wasn't allowed to compete, so he lost his Open Champion title by default. We went downhill from then on. Accusation, counter-accusation. You know, the usual thing. The trust went.'

'Well, I always thought he was good for you,' Mark said.

'I liked him until I strangled him. But then he behaved like a complete arsehole.'

'Funny that,' Mark said, gently rubbing the side of his neck.

CHAPTER FOUR

It was all too horribly familiar. Sam sat at high table in St Barnabas's hall, looking wistfully at the tables filled with babbling undergraduates and wishing she were amongst them; down there the conversation seemed to be much more animated. She looked up at the grim portraits of podgy-fingered prelates hanging high above them, portraits from the days when you had to be male and ordained to be an Oxford don. At least there was a smattering of women at this high table. This sort of formality had never suited Sam; she'd had much too much of it as a child. She had tried a bit of desultory conversation with the man on her left. But he, like many dons, seemed to have a constitutional inability to engage in small talk and she soon gave up. In the past she would have tried longer and harder, but she had learned from bitter experience that to jabber away in order to fill the silence rarely made the other person talk more and just made her feel stupid and resentful. If he couldn't be bothered, neither could she.

The year after Sam's father died, her mother moved the family from Hereford to Oxford and started working at the John Radcliffe Hospital as a nurse. Sam loved the large ramshackle house her mother bought in Marston Street, which ran between Cowley and Iffley Road. She loved the students her mother had rented rooms to and she loved the garden and especially the trees: the cherry tree and the big horse chestnut. Good trees for climbing. But all this had changed when her mother had met Peter Goodman, a patient recovering from a car accident and also

37

head of St Cuthbert's College. That meeting had marked an abrupt end to the life that Sam loved. Her mother had remarried and they had moved into the Lodgings. It was certainly bigger and more beautiful than Marston Street, but the garden didn't have a single tree worth climbing, only a huge copper beech, which had no low branches. And when she and Mark began playing football on the large square lawn, the college librarian complained that they were disturbing the undergraduates who studied in the Queen Anne library at the end of the garden. There was nowhere to hide, not even from the tourists who peered through the black metal gate and took photos of the house. Suddenly, the whole family was on show and you never knew who might be there at the breakfast table, and who you might be expected to make polite conversation with. They no longer had neighbours as such, and there were no students filling their kitchen. It's true there was St Cuthbert's – a whole college of students and dons, but over there, beyond the metal gate and that wasn't the same. It wasn't the same at all. There was also her stepfather, Peter, to get to grips with – or not, as it turned out.

'Pass the salt,' she said, and the man grunted and pushed a silver salt cellar across the highly polished table towards her.

She nudged Mark's arm. 'No sense, no feeling,' she muttered.

He smiled. 'Talk of the devil,' and nodded up the table.

Sam looked to where a woman sat to the right of the Provost. 'Alice Knight.'

Sam took in a woman with bobbed blonde hair. She was leaning conspiratorially towards a neat, dapper man who looked more City than Oxford. The woman's hand rested lightly on his pinstriped arm. Her nails looked as if they had been dipped in blood.

Sam reached for her wine glass. 'She looks like she's got him well charmed.'

'Oh, she's charming all right.'

The woman tossed her hair back off her face and patted it into position, then looked up and smiled directly at Sam. Oh yes, Sam thought, this one could charm the birds right out of the trees. Even this old buzzard sitting next to me would probably drop off his perch for her. The Provost threw back his head and roared with laughter. Alice Knight speared a small piece of meat and popped it into a perfectly bow-shaped mouth. She then carefully dabbed at the corner of her mouth with a thick white napkin.

'She's here for a term,' Mark said.

'Should be interesting. I'm surprised after everything you said happened.'

'It was a long time ago. People forget.'

'I wouldn't let her near an undergraduate, would you?'

Mark shrugged. 'She's here now, we just have to get on with it. Some sort of deal was done. She gave advice to the bursar on investments and in return she gets a term here. Her academic credentials can't be faulted.'

'Are you sure the deal wasn't of the flesh as opposed to the markets?'

Mark smiled and picked up his wine glass. 'Knowing the bursar's predilections, I doubt it. Apparently the advice was exceptionally good.'

'It must have been.' Sam nodded at the Provost. 'He looks perfectly capable of giving sound financial advice all of his own.'

'Oh, he is. He was the chief executive of one of the high street banks.'

'Well, there you are, then.'

Afterwards they went for coffee in the Senior Common Room. Sam picked up a white china cup with a gold leaf design running around the rim and was about to pour in the coffee when she felt a hand touch the small of her back. She turned.

'Hello, I'm Alice Knight. You must be Mark's sister.'

Up close she was even more striking. A quote about Marlene Dietrich floated into Sam's head – *She had the body of a woman but had never read the instruction manual.* Alice Knight didn't look like the sort of woman to bother with manuals. She could have made man, woman or beast consider sleeping with her. Sex, Sam thought, was obviously very high on her agenda. Or power. Alice Knight would flirt with a donkey if she wanted a free ride at the beach. Right now, it seemed, Sam was the one with the long furry ears and she had no idea why.

'High table has a certain timeless quality. I saw you had the joys of Richard Whitman.' She smoothed down a skirt that was only fractionally short of indecent, leaned towards Sam and whispered, '*Such* a blabber mouth, *such* a considerate conversationalist – how *does* one get a word in?'

Sam laughed, and as she did so, had an image of the Provost doing exactly the same. Who had Alice been poking fun at then? She couldn't help feeling that with Alice Knight humour always came at someone else's expense. Mark joined them.

'Mark, darling.' Alice offered her cheek to him and he kissed it. 'One of the pleasures of being here is renewing acquaintances with old friends. Of course, this must all seem very familiar to you.' She gestured round the room. 'The whole Oxford thing.'

'Not any more,' Sam said. 'I haven't lived here for a while.'

'Fled the ivory towers?'

'Cotswold stone last time I looked. And I think I just called it something mundane like moving to London.'

'It must have been strange being brought up inside one of these.'

The truth was that strange didn't begin to describe it, but Sam wasn't going to allow this woman to place her in a box marked 'freak'. 'Everyone thinks that their childhood is normal. That's all we knew.'

Alice turned to Mark. 'You didn't move far at any rate, did you, darling? It's lovely for a term, but I don't think I could stand this indefinitely. I need a bit of the real world. You've never really left home, have you?'

Mark blushed.

'Reality is over-rated,' Sam said sweetly. 'It certainly isn't the preserve of London or lawyers. Unless, of course, you're confusing reality with being stressed and rich.'

Mark burst out laughing and Sam sipped her coffee.

Alice Knight smiled a smile that was never going to make it to her eyes. 'So, what brings you to Oxford? A social call on your brother?'

Sam was enjoying herself now. 'Absolutely.'

'I hear you're a private investigator?'

'I wonder who on earth from?'

Alice didn't reply.

'Another cup of coffee?' Sam asked.

'Thanks.' Alice drained her cup and handed it over.

'Cream?' Sam said.

Alice nodded.

'Sugar?'

She shook her head.

Sam handed back the cup.

'Thank you.' Alice took it and stirred in the cream. 'Are you up here on a case?'

'I'm afraid I can't discuss that.'

She smiled. 'Of course. I heard about the case you were involved with recently. It must be a terrible thing to find a dead child. How on earth do you cope with that?'

'I decided not to try,' Sam said, and looked her straight in her pale green eyes.

No one spoke and Alice broke eye contact first, directing her attention to sipping her coffee. Mark ground his sugar in the bottom of his cup. The silence seemed to extend outwards to the rest of the Senior Common Room. It was Alice who spoke first.

'Well, I must be off. Lovely to meet you. I hope we bump into each other again.'

I hope you rot in hell, Sam thought, watching her glide

elegantly from the room, the eyes of every man there burning into her back.

Sam blew out her cheeks. 'Christ,' she said.

'You see what I mean?' Mark said.

'She is ghastly.'

'I'm glad you think so. Sometimes I think I'm going mad. Other people just love her, the Provost included. I've never been able to stand the woman.'

'I could do with some fresh air to clear the sulphur from my nose.'

Mark laughed. They strolled down shallow wooden steps into front quad. Sam inhaled deeply. The air was damp; in Oxford it always was.

'She pokes away, doesn't she? I think I've got a few bruises here, just under my ribs.' Sam raised her left arm and felt her side.

Mark rested his arm across the top of her shoulders and they strolled across the uneven flagstones towards his rooms.

Sam sat back in Mark's deep leather armchair and hugged her knees. 'Did you tell her I was a private investigator?'

Mark frowned. 'I don't think so, no. I try to have as little contact with her as I can.'

'Then who did? For a woman whose primary interest is quite obviously herself, she seemed remarkably interested in me.'

'You've been in the press, Sam. It's not a secret. Did you notice the whole "You haven't left home" bit? Like I'm some stunted adolescent who can't cope with reality and just stays in an Oxford college all his working life, covered in cobwebs and ivy, complaining about Governing Body and the chef.'

'Now you come to mention it, I think I can see something green just beginning to curl over the top of your ear.'

Mark laughed. 'She always did have the uncanny ability to wrongfoot me. Trouble is, recently, I've been thinking along the same lines.'

Sam frowned. 'What do you mean?'

'That it might be time to move on.'

'From *here*?' Sam couldn't keep the surprise from her voice.

'I've been feeling restless, like I could do with a new challenge. I've been thinking of doing VSO.'

'God.'

'Got all the forms and everything.'

'Well . . .'

Sam was shocked. Her brother had always lived in Oxford. It's true she didn't come down here that often but she liked to know that he was relatively nearby. She had been the one to move; he had stayed. 'The job you do here is as valid as any other. Teaching is a very important thing to do.'

Mark laughed. 'You sound like one of those ads for teachers. You know, the ones which are failing to recruit anyone with any sense of self-preservation. Try that one with a bit more conviction next time.'

'To be honest, I can't imagine you anywhere else. You've always seemed so happy here.'

'That's what lots of people say and I don't think it's a particularly good sign.' Mark shook a cigarette out of a packet and lit it. 'Please try to see Mum while you're here.'

Sam groaned. 'Not this again.'

'She says you never phone her.'

'She's right.' Sam rested her chin on her knees.

'She says she feels silly to keep phoning if you don't reply.'

'I keep waiting for the moment I feel like it.'

'And the moment never comes?'

'No.'

Mark pushed his glasses back up his nose. 'Perhaps you should just do it anyway.'

'Why? To make you feel better?'

Mark smiled. 'That's a perfectly good reason.'

Sam laughed. 'She been giving you grief, then?'

'Of a sort.'

'I don't phone her because I don't know what to say to her. We have nothing in common.'

'Lots of people have nothing in common with their parents. That's life. You just have to get on with it.'

'But you manage OK with her, with them, don't you?'

Mark shrugged. 'It's easier for them to get their heads round what I do for a living. That's all. I'm part of their world.'

'Yes, but that's quite a lot, when there's nothing else.'

Mark stood up and flicked his ash into the fireplace. 'Just phone her then, Sam. You don't have to visit.'

'She hates me. I've always thought that. I don't know why but she does.'

Mark began to protest but Sam held out her hand to stop him. 'No, just hold on a minute, Mark. She could never get to grips with me fighting and she can't get to grips with what I do now. She's never accepted me and I don't see why I should put myself in a position to be undermined by her again. And they never came to see me fight. Not once in all those years. Not even my World Championship Finals. They were completely indifferent to the things that mattered to me.'

'She doesn't *hate* you. It's just that you remind her too much of Dad.' Sam didn't say anything. 'You look like him, you even fight like him. Of course she didn't want you fighting. Look what happened to him. She couldn't stand the violence of it. She was always worried you'd get hurt. Especially the *way* you fought. You always took such risks.'

'It's what I was meant to do. You know that.'

'And the investigating?'

Sam shrugged. 'I fell into it. It's a way of making a living.'

'A dangerous one.'

'Not particularly.'

'Liar.'

'If it had been you and you'd decided to go into the army

she'd have been fine about it. It's because I'm a woman. She doesn't think it's ladylike.'

Mark frowned. 'I don't think she'd have been fine at all if I'd gone into the army. She'd have hated it. Anyway, you should just laugh her off.'

'You try laughing off someone who thinks the key to your happiness is finding a nice man to settle down with and starting a family.'

Mark blew a smoke ring into the air above his head. '*I'm* more likely to do that than you.'

Sam rolled over and grabbed her alarm clock. Four o'clock. Something had woken her. She was lying on Mark's floor. The mattress was thin and she groaned as she sat up. It was cold and she shivered as she walked over to the window and looked out into back quad. A large stone lion sat high up on top of the library opposite. Sam was sure she'd heard voices but there was no one visible. Perhaps she'd been mistaken. Then she heard it again, the sound of laughter. She pulled on her clothes, grabbed her coat and let herself out of Mark's rooms and down into the quad. Out here it was drizzling and the lion seemed hunched and miserable in the wet. The noise was clearer now and coming from the covered passage, which ran past the chapel door and under the bell tower, and linked back and front quad. Sam walked quietly round the edge of the quad towards the noise and poked her head round the corner.

Alice Knight's skirt was now well above her hips, her red fingernails clawing a blue-coated back. The man's trousers were round his ankles and something silver gleamed at his feet, maybe the buckle of a shoe. The noise was no longer giggling, it was much more distinctive, more rhythmic. Alice's head was thrown back against the chapel door, her throat white in the darkness. One breast hung loose from her shirt. A hand was clamped across it, squeezing.

'Fuck me,' she groaned. 'Yes, that feels so good. Fuck me – hard. Harder.'

The man in the blue three-quarter-length coat, whose head was turned away from Sam and buried in Alice Knight's shoulder, seemed to be having no trouble complying.

CHAPTER FIVE

Sam took a deep breath and stared up at the golden stone façade of the Oxford police station. Why is it, she thought, that life brings you back unerringly to the very place to which you had hoped never to return? Your nose pressed up against the wall of your avoidance. Life could be just too bloody neat that way, as if someone was pulling the strings. It was so annoying and unnerving that it was almost enough to make you believe in God. Or was that the Devil? She exhaled loudly and pushed open the door. Attack. If you don't want to do it, attack it. It was a policy she had used in training. If you attacked, it would be over sooner, or that's what her coach, Tyler, had said. It hadn't worked very well then either, especially not when sprinting up Headington Hill in the rain. And sure enough, the first person she saw as she let the door swing to behind her was Phil. He was wearing black Doc Martens, off-white chinos and held a brown leather jacket slung over his shoulder. There were a few more lines round his eyes, and a couple more pounds round his waist.

'Hi,' she said, putting her hands in her pockets. 'How are you?'

Phil ran his hand over a haircut that made the average five o'clock shadow look positively hippy-like and smiled. 'Yeah, OK, last time I checked.' He took a couple of steps towards her, bent down and kissed her awkwardly on the cheek. As he did so, she brought her hand up to touch his arm and hit his hand, which was trying to do the same to her. They grappled for a few moments.

'Still trying to throw me?' he asked.

'Sorry,' she said.

'You're looking good.'

'Yup,' she nodded, and had an image of a toy dog waggling its head in the back of a car, a gormless grin fixed on its face.

'So, you're after the O'Connor file?'

'Yes. I really appreciate you letting me see it.'

'No body, no life insurance?'

She shrugged. 'Was she covered?'

Phil frowned. 'He didn't tell you that?'

'I told him I'd read the file and get back to him. He probably figured I'd find all that in there.'

'I don't know what he thinks you might do that we didn't.'

'God nor do I,' she said and he smiled.

'Come on, let's see if there's a room free.'

Sam followed him along a green linoleum-covered corridor, through several swing doors. She found herself staring at his arse. She still fancied him and wished she didn't. She always had, but it didn't mean it could work out. It had never meant that in the past, so why should it be any different now? They had always shagged all night and argued all day. Lust, said Sam to herself, that's all it is. Lust is not love. Lust is lust. Lust is what Alice Knight had been up to against the chapel door last night. Sam could feel it, though, between her legs, in her stomach, in the back of her throat. She coughed. Lust is lust. Keeping away from him had always been the only remedy. That's why she'd left. It had been impossible to be friends. Phil stopped abruptly and Sam, trying hard not to think about lust but failing, ran slap into the back of him. They both jumped apart as if stung.

'Sorry,' she said. 'My mind was elsewhere.'

He opened the door and handed her the file.

'Thanks,' she said.

'You can stay until we need the room.'

Sam repressed the impulse to ask him for a drink and he closed the door.

The file didn't hold many surprises. The police had obviously pursued a line of questioning and investigation, which assumed John O'Connor had something to do with his wife's disappearance and had come up with absolutely no evidence to suggest that he had. Sam winced as she read through the transcripts of the interviews with him and thought of the thin white lines she had seen on his wrists the first time she met him, the scars he had tried to cover by pulling at his cuffs.

Interview of John O'Connor
Date: 3 October 2002
Present: Detective Sergeant Howard and Detective
Sergeant Rowland

PH: How long have you been married, sir?
JO: Seven years.
PH: Would you say you were happily married?
JO: Yes, yes. We have our ups and downs like any couple but generally speaking yes, I'd say we were happy.
PH: Were, sir?
JO: Are. We are.
PH: Any reason you can think of why she would have gone missing?
JO: No, Obviously I've been racking my brains since it happened but I can't think . . . of anything.
PH: There was nothing that had been upsetting her? Was she moody or depressed? Had anything unusual happened in the weeks leading up to her disappearance?
JO: No, she seemed cheerful enough. She was enjoying

life, getting more reviewing work than she had
been. It was easier because both the boys were in
school.

PH: Every marriage has its problem areas, sir. There's
no shame in that, is there?

JO: Of course not.

PH: What would you say yours were?

JO: Sharing of domestic responsibilities – childcare, who
should take out the rubbish. I don't know, the usual
trivia.

PH: Were you having an affair, sir? After all, they do
talk about the seven-year itch, don't they?

JO: No, no, I wasn't.

PH: Perhaps she was and she's run off with another
man? Perhaps you argued and things got out of
hand. Did you slap her around a bit? Hit her a bit
harder than you intended? Accidents can happen
especially when you're angry.

JO: No, nothing like that. She wasn't, I'm sure I'd have
known. And I've never touched my wife – violently.
Never. I never would. I'm not a violent person.

PH: But that's not strictly true, is it? Didn't you try to
kill yourself? Slitting your wrists is violent, isn't it?

JO: That was a long time ago. I've never been violent
towards another person.

PH: You're sure she wasn't having an affair? I'm sure
you find with your clients that it's amazing how
often people don't know. Refuse to see, perhaps I
should say. Denial, isn't that the word you use for
it? Is there anything you'd like to tell me, sir?

JO: I wasn't having an affair and neither was she. I've
never hit my wife. I don't know why she's gone
missing.

PH: The thing is this, Mr O'Connor; people don't just go

	missing for no reason. There's always a reason.
JO:	They do if they're abducted or murdered.
PH:	That's in a tiny percentage of cases. But is there any reason to think that's what's happened here?
JO:	Well, no.
PH:	Why do *you* think she's missing, sir?
JO:	I've told you I don't know. I wish I knew. I want my wife back. I want my life back.
PH:	Do you love your wife?
JO:	Of course I loved her.
PH:	Loved?
JO:	Love. I want her back. She's the mother of my children.
PH:	So you only want her back for their sake?
JO:	That's not what I meant. You're twisting my words. I want her back.

Using a big hammer to crack a small nut. And obviously he had cracked because there was a note: *Interview terminated due to ill health of Mr O'Connor*. And one of the last questions before that happened: *Do you love your wife?* His answer: *Of course I loved her ... Love ...*

Sam flicked rapidly through the rest of the file, taking down details of people the police had interviewed: neighbours in Oxford, work colleagues, family members, and also neighbours in Fulham. There was a note saying they still hadn't managed to interview the man who lived in the flat above Meg's, a Mr Hicks. This was all ground she'd have to go over again. At the back of the file was a letter from Allied Life Insurance confirming that Meg O'Connor was covered by a Life Insurance policy, which was to pay out £500,000 to her family in the event of her death; half a million pounds just sitting there, waiting for a body.

Sam shivered. It was unlikely, she felt, that Meg O'Connor would turn up alive. Maybe this miserable dank, damp city was getting to her. Maybe it was that bloody letter from God knows who, but whatever it was, she didn't like the feeling she was getting about this, she didn't like it one little bit. She heard people in the corridor outside and Phil poked his head round the door.

'Sorry,' he said. 'Time's up.'

She closed the file, put her notes in her bag and stood up. 'Well, nice to see you again, Phil.'

'I'll see you out.'

As they walked back to the front of the building, a uniformed police officer swung through the doors into reception, escorting a young lad with a shaved head and wearing a bomber jacket, khaki on the outside and bright orange on the inside. Phil moved Sam over so that he was between her and the young man. As they all drew level, the young man spat in Phil's face and he ducked, raising his arm too late.

'Fucking cunt!' the man shouted. 'I'll never forget your fucking face. No place you can hide. No fucking place.'

'Sorry, sir,' the escorting officer said.

Phil leaned against the wall and sighed, saliva trickling down his cheek.

'Joys of the job,' Sam said, handing him a tissue.

'I sent down his older brother a few months ago. GBH, out in Blackbird Leys.' He took the tissue and wiped his face. 'Think I'll go to the Gents and tidy up a bit.'

'Sure.'

'How long are you down for?'

'I'm getting the bus back in the morning.'

He nodded. 'What are you doing later?'

'I've got to see O'Connor then I'll be back at Mark's.' She turned to go, her hand was pushing against the door; it had swung a few inches and she'd almost escaped.

'Sam?'

She sighed and let the door swing back. 'Yup?'

'I'm going for a drink after work at the Red Lion. If you've got any questions, about the case . . .'

'Sure,' she said. 'Maybe I'll see you there, later.'

'It would be nice to catch up.'

She nodded, pushed open the doors and stepped out into the dank street.

Catch up? Well, that was one way of describing it. Who on earth did they think they were kidding?

Sam could have caught a bus in St Giles but in the end she decided to walk; she had always preferred walking to waiting. At least if she was walking she could think, whereas when she was waiting, all she could focus on was whether the bus would turn up or not. She dodged between the cars, buses and bikes jamming the top of the High Street and cut through the covered market, past the second-hand bookshop and along the front of Hedges, a proper sawdust-and-straw-hat butcher. When she was a child, rabbits and pheasants had hung from metal hooks above the shop, dripping blood on to the sawdust below, but today the only thing hanging up was the body of a headless boar, split open along the line of its belly. Sam turned right past Palms, the delicatessen, walked through the centre of the market and then turned left. The strong smell of coffee, wafting in the air around Cardew & Co, made her hanker for freshly ground but she didn't have time to stop. If she stopped she'd be late for O'Connor. She stepped out into Market Street and turned left into the Turl. Her mother had always shopped in the market, preferring the array of different shops and stalls it offered to any supermarket, and Sam had often gone with her to help carry the shopping home. Sam shook her head; the past again, setting the bees swarming. Concentrate on now, she said to herself. You are here now, not in the past. The trouble was no one could set foot in Oxford without thinking about the past; the whole place reeked of it.

A brisk twenty-minute walk up Parks Road and into the Banbury Road brought Sam to the turning into Park Town, where John O'Connor lived. Park Town was an eighteenth-century crescent, which looked as if it had been airlifted out of Bath by aliens, wanting to show the residents of the sturdy, Victorian mansions of north Oxford exactly what they were missing in style and elegance. It was smart, very smart, but Sam already knew that because this was where her mother and stepfather now lived. She took the four stone steps leading to O'Connor's front door in one jump and rang the doorbell, then turned and squinted anxiously at one of the houses on the opposite side of the crescent. Fortunately, there was a large garden containing a huge monkey-puzzle tree between her and where her mother and stepfather lived. There couldn't be enough trees as far as Sam was concerned. One thing was certain; if O'Connor lived here he was hardly short of a bob or two.

Hearing the door opening behind her, she turned, her eyes dropping from adult head level down to that of a small, brown-haired boy.

'Hi,' she said. 'I've come to see your dad.'

He stood there staring at her until O'Connor appeared behind him. 'Come in, come in. This is Bill. He's been feeling poorly today so he's off school.'

'I'm sorry, I should have phoned to check—'

'No, no, don't be silly. You're here now and Bill wanted to meet you.' He ruffled his son's head. 'Didn't you?'

Bill stared at Sam but didn't say a word.

O'Connor took her coat and hung it on a row of pegs attached to the hall wall.

'Let's go into the kitchen. Bill's been doing some drawing and we can have a cup of tea.'

Sam followed him into an open-plan kitchen, which was about the same size as her entire flat. There was a huge Rothko-type painting, in different shades of yellow, hanging over the fireplace.

O'Connor saw her looking at it. 'Do you like it?'

'Yes,' Sam said.

'One of Meg's,' O'Connor said. 'She's a great believer in the healing properties of colour. She's got paintings in the local hospitals.'

Sam nodded and, while O'Connor made the tea, she sat down at a large, circular wooden table covered in pieces of paper. She picked one up and looked at it. It was a stick-figure depiction of a family: man, woman, two smaller figures, obviously children, all drawn in different colours. A black crayon had been used to scrub out the face of one of the children; the crayon had been pressed so hard into the paper it had torn. Tension started building in Sam's head. Bill sat opposite her, doodling. She got up and walked round to his side of the table.

'So, what's happening here?'

A stick figure with a bright red body was standing in a door; behind the figure were stairs and railings, one of which was red like the body of the figure.

Bill pointed at the red figure. 'Daddy's getting the milk.'

Sam pointed to the red railing. 'What's that?'

'Daddy's dressing-gown thing.'

'What's it doing there?'

The little boy shrugged. 'Just was.'

A crayon rolled off the table and fell on the floor. She bent down to pick it up but it rolled away from her, and she got down on her hands and knees to get it. As she reached it, Bill slid out of his chair on to the floor beside her.

'Do you know where Mummy is?'

'No, I—'

'But you're going to find her. That's what Daddy says.'

'I'm going to try.'

'Why did she leave us? Did we do something wrong?'

Sam saw the scrubbed-out face of the stick-figure child. 'No, you—'

She heard something being put on the table above her head.

'What are you two up to down there?' O'Connor asked. 'Secret powwow?'

Sam crawled out backwards from under the table and sat down. 'Yes,' she said. 'Secret powwow.' And Bill smiled shyly at her.

'How do you like your tea?'

'Milk no sugar.'

He poured the tea and handed her a cup. Bill slid from his chair and walked towards the door.

'Where are you going?' O'Connor asked.

'Video.'

'OK, but when Ian comes in, it goes off.'

Sam sipped her tea. 'Do children always blame themselves?'

'Did you?'

Anger jolted through Sam so strongly she felt winded. When she spoke, she tried to keep her voice level but she couldn't altogether keep it from shaking. 'I'm not your client. I was simply asking you a question.'

O'Connor eyed her over the top of his glasses. 'Sorry, old habits, you know. Always turn the question back to them. Get them to find their own answer.'

'I'm not your client,' Sam repeated. 'And I'm certainly not looking for a therapist.'

'No, a lot of people are suspicious of us.'

Sam looked at him.

'Bad experience?'

She sighed. 'After my father died, I started getting into fights at school.'

'You must have been very upset.'

She ignored him. 'The school suggested I see a behavioural

specialist. Some mad American woman, who made me jump through hoops like a fucking circus pony. Know what she said?'

O'Connor shrugged.

'That I shouldn't be allowed to play with the other children during the breaks, that I was a danger to them. I had to stay with the teacher on duty, trailing around after her like a right idiot.'

'They didn't tell you to take up judo to channel your aggression?'

Sam laughed. 'You're joking. They just made me feel like something was the matter with me. This woman kept going on that it wasn't ladylike to fight. She was like something out of the Victorian era.' Sam shook her head. 'I mean – ladylike! For heaven's sake.'

'So, what made you start judo?'

'After my father died, we moved down from Hereford to Oxford. Mum got a nursing job. This was before she met my stepfather. She rented rooms out to postgraduates and one of her students, Akemi, was Japanese, doing a Ph.D. on the relative merits of the Japanese and British car industries. She was a black belt and suggested to my mother that I should come along to her club. And that was that.'

'And what was it like?'

Sam shrugged. 'Well, I was a natural. All the things I was being told were problems at school weren't problems in judo. I was a natural fighter. They picked me out quite quickly for special coaching and things went from there.'

'What did you like about it?'

Sam sipped her tea. 'It was the first time I'd been told I was any good at anything, that had a large part to do with it. For the first time since my father died I felt safe.'

O'Connor frowned. 'Your father made you feel safe?'

Sam narrowed her eyes and didn't reply.

'Sorry,' O'Connor said. 'You were saying judo fathered you?'

Sam stared at him. 'I didn't say that. What judo did was teach me respect.'

O'Connor picked up a biscuit and broke it in two. 'You know, a lot of therapists are complete idiots. You wouldn't want them anywhere near someone you cared about. Or near anyone vulnerable.'

'No,' Sam said. 'You wouldn't.'

'Anyway, to answer your original question, yes, children often do blame themselves. Children are little narcissists. If something happens – death, divorce, abuse – they always tend to think it's down to them. Couldn't be any other reason.'

'Bill asked me if he had done something wrong. If that was why his mother had gone missing.'

O'Connor winced and picked up one of the drawings. 'These help because I can get to see a bit of what's going on. It's a way of him telling me how he's feeling. At least it's visible, you know, not all just trapped inside him, hurting and poisoning.'

He picked up the tray and took it over to the sink. 'He keeps being sick, says he can't go to school, but really I think he's worried that when he comes back, I'll be gone, just like his mum. Basically, he doesn't want to let me out of his sight. As a parent I so much want to protect him from pain but as a therapist I know it's part of the human condition.'

The tension in Sam's head had ratcheted up a couple of notches. She put the palms of her hands to her head and pressed her temples. As she took her hands away she saw John O'Connor's brown eyes watching her. *Enough warmth for two.* She massaged her jaw; the pain always ended up there, in her teeth, as if there was a needle being jabbed into every nerve ending at the same time.

'Toothache,' she said. She reached for her bag and searched inside for her Nurofen, popped two out of the silver foil, and chased them down with some lukewarm tea.

'If ever you want to talk,' he said, 'casually, you know, nothing formal, as if I were a friend . . .'

'You don't think I have any?'

'That's not what I meant. I just want you to know the offer is there. That you can call on me at any time. I'm very fond of your brother. I owe him and you're helping me out here.' He turned towards the sink and picked a set of keys off a metal hook attached to the wall. 'Anyway, you came for the keys to Meg's flat.' He handed them to her. 'Did you have any questions arising from the police file?'

Sam put the keys in her bag. 'When they interviewed you at the station, what happened at the end?'

'Is that relevant?'

Sam shrugged. 'You don't have to tell me.'

O'Connor sat down at the table. 'They were accusing me of murdering my wife. I knew what they were doing, obviously. I could see why they were doing it and that they had to do it. Spouses are always the prime suspects but they were bullying me and accusing me and I was very upset. When they asked me if I loved her it was the last straw. I said, of course I loved her. And because I spoke in the past tense, as if she were dead, I felt it. All of it. How upset I was, how much I missed her, how frightened I was and confused. Up until then I'd just been numb with the shock, holding it all together for the children, thinking that she'd just turn up any day and there'd be a perfectly obvious explanation. I started to cry and couldn't stop. I hadn't cried since she'd gone missing and it was like a dam going down. The whole bloody awful hopelessness hit me all at once and I had difficulty breathing, so they brought the interview to a close.'

'I see.' Sam stood up. 'I'm sorry.'

'That you asked or that it happened?'

'That it happened. You're paying me to ask questions.'

He nodded. 'I should thank them really.'

A key scraped in the lock of the front door and voices filled the hall.

'That'll be Ian. Once it was over, I felt much better, more human. Before, I'd just been sleepwalking through it all, numb with shock.'

'I should be going.'

'Afterwards, I felt as if I'd got my life back. At least I could be of some use to the boys.'

In the hall O'Connor handed Sam her coat. 'Where do you go from here?'

'I want to visit her flat and interview a few of the people mentioned in the police file. There's Zandra Dodds for a start and the man who lives in the flat above Meg's. It seems he's a bit shy of the police. Maybe he'll speak to me. It's going over ground they've covered but sometimes people will tell private investigators things they won't tell the police.'

He nodded. 'I can understand that.'

'Actually there is one thing.'

'Yes?'

'Did you know about the amount her life was insured for?'

'No, I had no idea. She dealt with all the finances. That kind of thing has never really interested me. The police wanted to know all about that. Husband kills off wife for life insurance. But if there's no body, there's no payout, so if I'd been motivated by money you'd think I would have had the good sense to leave the body around to be found.'

'Were you surprised, when you found out the amount?'

'Yes and no. She was . . . is very good with money. Careful, you know, good planner. So the fact she had done that didn't surprise me. The amount did. But I don't need the money.' O'Connor gesticulated to indicate the house. 'What I want is the mother of my sons back.'

Sam nodded. 'I'll keep you informed of any progress.'

The door closed behind her and Sam stood for a moment,

looking across the crescent at the house opposite. The painkillers were starting to kick in; she could still feel the shape of the headache but the pain was receding. Even so she couldn't face crossing the road. No, not even for Mark. It would have to wait. She ran down the steps and set off at a brisk walk for the centre of town.

Sam squeezed her way through a crush of people to the bar of the Red Lion and waved a twenty-pound note vigorously in the smoke-filled air.

'Well, well, if it isn't the Oxford Strangler, returned to town.' A meaty, red-faced man reached across the bar, grabbed her cheek between finger and thumb, and squeezed hard enough to bring tears to her eyes. 'It's a long time since we've been honoured by your presence, Champ.' George Ryan, landlord of the Red Lion, let go of her cheek, wrapped a large hand around the left side of her face and beamed at her.

Feeling like a child, Sam beamed back. 'Hello, George, how are you?'

'All the better for seeing you, short-arse. We've still got you on our wall.'

He gestured behind him and Sam saw a fading photo of herself in a blue *judogi*, a gold medal hanging round her neck. Next to her was a photo of George's favourite racehorse.

'Couldn't have done it without you, George. There was no lottery funding for me when I started, just pub raffles.'

'Sure you could, love,' George said. 'Champions rise to the top, come what may.'

'The money you raised for me to train in Japan made all the difference. After a year there, I was an entirely different fighter.'

'We've missed you.'

'I've missed you, George. How's business?'

George blew out his cheeks. 'You know, love, since September the eleventh we don't get the Americans like we used to. And you?'

'Struggling, to be honest. Seems to involve a weekly conversation with the bank. Each time with a different person and each time I have to make up a different set of lies concerning my likely income.'

George laughed. 'Work bring you up?'

Sam nodded.

'I'm sorry about that little girl, love. Read about it in the papers. Must have been rough.'

Sam scratched the side of her nose.

'Saw they had the memorial service.'

Sam nodded again. The family had invited her but she couldn't bring herself to go to a service for a murdered four-year-old child. Who could? She was trying to block it all out, but it was impossible when the papers and the television were all full of it. It had been a job, she kept saying to herself, just a job. There was no need to get personally involved. All very well in theory but hopeless in practice. The discovery of Jenny seemed to have cracked open a door in Sam's mind and all kinds of things were pouring out, images and flashbacks that made no sense to her at all but had one thing in common – they all terrified her.

'You all right, love?'

Sam rubbed her eyes. 'Sure, George. It's been a long day, that's all. Is Phil here?'

George pointed behind her. 'In the corner. What'll you have? The usual?'

'Pint of Guinness,' Sam said. 'I'm no longer in training.'

'Looking trim, though.'

'Still my fighting weight.'

'Wish I could say the same, love.' George patted his paunch and nodded at Phil. 'That one must be pleased to see you. He's never been the same since you left.'

Since I strangled him, you mean, Sam thought. She turned and looked at him. The truth was that in this light, he didn't look great. There were dark rings under his eyes and the lower part of his face seemed bloated, like he was drinking too much. George placed two pints on the bar. Sam tried to pay him but he waved her away. She thanked him, picked them up and walked over to where Phil was leaning against the wall, watching a game of pool.

She nudged his arm, 'Here,' she said, and handed him a pint.

He smiled. 'Cheers.'

'So,' she said, pointing at the men playing pool. 'Who's winning?'

'Gerry. He always does by a mile.'

'He always did.'

'Find out anything from O'Connor?'

She shrugged.

'Visit your mum?'

She winced. 'Give me a break, Phil, you sound like Mark.'

He smiled. 'Still the same old Sam.'

Sam bit her tongue and counted to ten. There was nothing more annoying than ex-lovers placing you in the same judgemental boxes that had caused the relationship to end in the first place. She couldn't think of anything to say that wouldn't initiate some old tit-for-tat pattern. They drank in silence for a few moments.

Phil glanced sideways at her. 'I read about Jenny Hughes in the paper.'

Sam nodded and sipped her pint.

'CID couldn't work out how you did that.'

'Well, that makes two of us,' Sam said amiably.

'Someone tell you where she was?'

Sam shook her head. 'I'm sorry, Phil – it's nothing personal but I just don't want to talk about it.'

Phil drained his glass. 'Same old blabber-mouth Sam, filling in all the gaps.'

Sam watched him walk over to the bar. What on earth was she

doing here? Every opening conversational gambit seemed fraught with danger. Even 'How are you?' suggested she wanted to know, that she was interested. And she wasn't sure she was. Did she care? If she cared wouldn't she just end up getting dragged back in? She watched Phil laughing with George at the bar.

'Oi, Sammy.' She felt something tickle her neck and turned round to find herself eye to eye with the chalked end of a pool cue.

'Gerry,' she said. 'Still shafting the unsuspecting?'

''Course. What you doing in town?'

'This and that.'

'Oh, yeah, I've heard it called all sorts but never this and that.' Phil returned, holding another pint.

'You up to a bit of this and that, Phil?' Gerry leered.

Phil glanced at Sam and raised his eyebrows.

Sam patted Gerry on the shoulder. 'Go back to your coloured balls, little boy, and leave the grown-ups to conversation.'

Gerry moved a blonde curl away from Sam's forehead with the end of his cue.

'Still so mean and moody, Sam, so dominating. Still strangling your lovers, are you?'

Sam moved the cue away from her forehead and smiled sweetly. 'Still an arsehole, Gerry? Funny how the years don't change some things.'

Gerry blushed.

'First lesson for arseholes,' Sam said. 'Learn to take what you give out.'

'Could never see what you saw in this dyke, Phil. Maybe you just love being dominated by butch women.'

Phil took a step towards him and Sam laid a restraining hand on his arm. She laughed. 'Ah yes, the ultimate playground insult, the dyke. Ever since I started fighting I've had to handle that particular one. So, I've had lots of practice. I actually take that as

64

a compliment. I've been called it so many times I deserve to be an honorary dyke. Please don't tell me, Phil, that you're going to defend my honour, that would just be too – retro.'

Phil laughed and allowed Sam to lead him to an empty table on the other side of the pub.

'Why'd you hang out with him, anyway?' Sam asked.

'I was just watching the game. Wasn't hanging out with anyone.'

'Gerry and his mates are idiots. Always have been, ever since I was at school with them.'

'So, do you think you're going to find Meg O'Connor?' Phil asked.

Sam shook her head. 'What do you think about John O'Connor?'

'You know the statistics. If she's dead, statistically it's down to him.'

Sam nodded. 'What did you think when you interviewed him?'

'You read it. He got very upset, started wheezing and hyperventilating. Had to bring the interview to a close.'

'Did it seem genuine?'

Phil shrugged. 'He's a shrink, isn't he? He must know how to replicate the signs. Knows what to do in an interview.'

'And the last question before it happened—'

'I know. "Did you love your wife?"'

'Yes,' Sam said. 'I noticed that.'

'The breathing thing could have been brought on by the stress of lying. I thought he was lying about something. I just couldn't quite figure what it was.'

Phil picked up their glasses.

'Another?'

Phil's face contorted as he came and he slumped across her. Thank God for that, Sam thought. She'd come first and for the last fifteen minutes she'd been lying there, wishing he'd hurry up, but making the odd encouraging noise or two. In this particular case the drink had provoked the desire but definitely taken away both their performances. The only noise in the dark was Phil's ragged breathing. As he slid out of her, their bodies made a soft squelching noise. Like a limpet coming off a stone, Sam thought. And I'm the stone. Phil propped himself up on one elbow and looked at her.

'Where did you go?' he asked.

'I'm here, aren't?'

'Barely, I'd say.'

She shivered and pulled up the sheet. 'I came before you. Timing was a bit off. That's all.'

'You were long gone before then. You've been gone all evening.'

'Gone? Well, you've been pissed so give me a fucking break,' she snapped and swung her legs over the side of the bed. 'Anyway, what have you become all of a sudden – Mr Sensitive?'

She stood up and started putting on her clothes.

'Where are you going?'

'Out.'

'You used to be a fighter, Sam.'

'What the hell does that mean?'

'You never used to run away.'

'Maybe I wised up,' Sam said, pulling on her jeans.

'Bullshit.'

She bent down to lace up her trainers. 'Look, this was a really bad idea. I'm sorry, Phil, it's my fault. I should never have—'

'Where are you going?'

'Gloucester Green – I need to get out of this bloody place. I should never have come back. It's like my brain grows mould here. I can't think straight. I make mistakes.'

'But it's one in the morning.'

'I know what time it is. The coaches run all through the night.'

'I'll come with you.'

'No, I need to clear my head.'

She stood in the bedroom doorway. 'Sorry, Phil. Like I say, my mistake.'

He shook his head and turned away from her. She went downstairs and let herself out of his front door. For a moment she stood on the doorstep and inhaled deeply. A fox screamed somewhere off to her right and she jumped.

Why the hell had she done it? What a bloody mess. She'd wanted something familiar and reassuring and what had she ended up with? Bad sex. And that wasn't familiar at all because sex between them had always been good. She let herself through the metal gate into Walton Street and set off towards the bus station. A few seconds later a shadow detached itself from the shop front opposite Phil's house and followed her.

CHAPTER SIX

A bowl of strawberries stands on a wooden table. Sam sits staring at them. A needle is being stabbed through her upper lip.

'This won't take long,' the voice says.

She is immobilized. She tries to raise her hands from her sides but they refuse to move. Salty blood trickles into her mouth.

'That's all the way through, now for the lower lip. We'll soon have you all stitched up.' Sam tries to scream but can't. She feels the pressure pulling the stitch together. 'And then you'll never say another word.'

She turns and sees Jenny Hughes laughing at her. The child picks up a jug and drowns the strawberries in cream, then puts a spoon into the bowl and lifts a strawberry to Sam's lips.

Sam jolted awake and looked at her alarm – five o'clock. She'd got in at four, had only been asleep an hour. The smell of strawberries filled her nostrils. She'd always hated them. Even the smell could make her sick. Frank Cooper's paw pressed against her mouth. Two emerald orbs stared at her out of the darkness. She was sweating and her heart was pounding in her ears.

'Jesus Christ, Frank,' she gasped, removing his paw carefully from her mouth. Then she heard it. Frank had heard it too, because Sam felt his body stiffen and his tail lash against her side, then he bared his teeth and hissed. Wooden planks on the scaffolding outside her window creaked. Sam listened. The workmen left empty cans and bottles out there and sometimes, when the wind rolled them up and down, it could sound like a person moving about. A black shadow loomed against the blinds.

Someone was on the scaffolding, hands scrabbling at her window.

For a second Sam froze, then she jumped off the bed and sprinted across the room. She banged hard on the glass and shouted, 'What the fuck do you think you're doing? Get the fuck off the scaffolding or I'll call the police.'

She heard feet running away to her left, past the outside of her study and the kitchen. She ran through the flat, hoping to catch sight of whoever it was, but by the time she reached the kitchen, they were off the scaffolding and she heard footsteps in the street below. Adrenaline coursed through her veins. She looked down into the street and saw a man jump on a motorbike, rev its engine and screech out of Cristowe Road in the direction of Putney. She grabbed a pen and scribbled down the number – LT02 NBA. Frank was head-butting her shins. Sam scratched the top of his head. Her hands were shaking as she scooped the meat out of the can on to a saucer. She bent down and stroked the cat as he guzzled down the food.

She woke later to the noise of the phone ringing. She rolled over and grabbed her alarm clock – seven-thirty. She put her hand to her mouth and felt her lips. No, that had been a dream. The answerphone picked up and she heard Edie's voice.

'You there, babes? It's me. Are you there? Pick up. There's something on the scaffolding.'

Sam grabbed the receiver. 'Yeah, it's me.'

'There's something ... you better come and have a look, babes.' And the phone went dead.

Sam slung on a dressing gown, shuffled on a pair of shoes and stepped out on to the landing.

'Did I wake you?' Edie asked as she opened her own door.

'Bit of a rough night,' Sam said. 'There was someone on the scaffolding outside my bedroom window.'

'Cheapskate sod Crozier. You should write—'

Sam cut her short. 'What is it, Edie?'

'Take a look for yourself.'

They let themselves out of the front door and walked round to the side of the building. A small crowd of people had gathered on the pavement, directly under her bedroom window; they were looking up at something hanging from the scaffolding. The first thing Sam registered was orange fur.

'Frank?' she gasped and turned to run back into the flat. But hadn't she seen him just now? Wasn't he sleeping on the end of her bed?

Edie's fingers dug into her upper arm. 'No, dear, it's not Frank. It's a fox.'

The fox hung by its neck, its head at right angles to the rest of its body. Blood dripped from its engorged tongue.

'I mean, who'd do such a wicked thing?' Edie said, eyeing Sam.

Big Neil, who worked in the motorbike shop opposite, crossed the road and joined them. He was still wearing the leathers he came to work in. He'd once lent Sam a pump after her tyres had been let down by the local kids. He pulled off his helmet and ran his gloved hand over his gleaming head. 'Want me to cut it down, love?'

'It's OK,' Sam said. 'I can do it.'

'Let him do it, babes,' Edie said. 'You don't look fit for much.' She touched Neil's arm, 'Would you, love?'

Neil climbed the ladder and strode along the wooden walkway, the planks bending impressively under his weight. He lifted the fox's neck out of the noose and carried the body carefully down to ground level. He laid the fox on the pavement and a small crowd formed around it. Sam stared at it. Who would do such a thing? She reached out to touch its fur but felt a hand on her shoulder, pulling her away from the crowd.

'This was in its mouth,' Neil said, holding out a bloodstained envelope. It was addressed to her.

Sam didn't take it. He wiped the envelope on his leathers and held it out again. She looked up at him and then at the envelope.

'Sorry, love. I can just bin it if you want.'

Edie had detached herself from the group round the fox. 'I'll take it,' she said and snatched it out of Neil's hand. 'Come on, babes,' she said to Sam. 'Make me a nice cup of tea. You look like you could do with one as well.'

'We can't just leave the fox in the street,' Sam said. 'What about the children on the way to school?'

Neil pulled off his leather gloves. 'I've got a bag in the shop. I'll get it.'

The crowd had now dispersed; only Edie and Sam were left. Sam bent down and ran her hand along the side of the fox, felt the harshness of the fur and the fear of touching something wild, even if it was dead. The body seemed unharmed. It was just the neck that was broken. She heard Neil behind her rustling a bin liner and stood up.

'We can't just put it out with the rubbish,' she said.

'I'll deal with it,' Neil said.

'But what will you—?'

'Come on, babes, let him deal with it,' Edie said. 'Where's my cup of tea?' She took hold of Sam's arm and led her back to her flat.

'You going to open it, then?' Edie's beady little brown eyes had moved all over Sam's flat, like an auctioneer assessing the value of a particular lot. Finally, they had come to rest on the stained envelope lying on the kitchen table. Frank Cooper sat in Edie's lap or rather Edie held him there. Her small hands dug deep into his fur. He knew better than to struggle. Sam ripped open the envelope and unfolded a piece of paper.

Now we know where you live. Fucking bitch. This is what happens to those who meddle. It starts with animals. It can end in human blood. Don't go meddling in stuff you don't know nothing about.

Sam dropped it on the kitchen table and Edie picked it up.

She read it and frowned. 'You in some sort of trouble? You know if you are, you only have to tell me. I know some people . . .'

Sam was sure she did. According to Sam's gran, Edie had, in her youth, had a spell in the entertainment business and one of those she had been rumoured to entertain was Rachman's bodyguard. She still had the odd gentleman caller from the old days, although now, as far as Sam could work out, the trade seemed to be strictly brandy and tobacco.

'You're not going to phone the police, are you? Don't want them too near my baccy.' Edie nodded to her flat next door.

'They couldn't do anything anyway. He hasn't done anything yet.'

'You look done in, love,' Edie commented.

'Yeah,' Sam agreed. 'And it's only eight o'clock.'

Later that same day Sam sat in the pub watching the swollen Thames run under Putney Bridge. Alan was picking up their food from the bar. She looked across the room at him with affection. He was a great bear of a man with a reassuring or threatening physical presence, depending on his mood.

Sam had first met Alan one evening two years ago. She was clearing up after a women's self-defence class she taught in a Hammersmith gym and she turned and found a man-mountain hovering in the doorway. She let him hover while she packed up and then asked him if there was anything she could do for him. He said nothing at first, just turned red and looked as if his head was about to explode and then quite suddenly burst into loud sobs. Sam was shocked. Obviously she didn't think that big men didn't cry, but there was something about his size combined with his obvious upset that made him appear more vulnerable than if he'd been a normal size. She took him by the arm, sat him down on one of the benches that lined the wall of the gym and told him to wait there while she sorted out some paperwork with the office. When she came back, he was gone.

But then a couple of weeks later there he was again.

'Hello again,' Sam said.

'Hi, I'm sorry about last time.'

'Fine.' She waited for him to speak.

'It's just . . .' He paused and swallowed. 'A friend of mine . . . last week was ill. He was in hospital so I was upset. My nerves were shot . . .'

Sam nodded and continued rolling up her belt.

'The thing is . . .'

'Yes?'

'I see you're teaching a self-defence class for women.'

'Yes.'

'I wondered how you felt about men?'

Sam rolled her eyes. 'What?'

He groaned. 'Sorry, that came out wrong. I didn't mean to imply that you didn't . . . I mean, I didn't mean to suggest you were . . .'

Sam was starting to feel thoroughly pissed off. 'What *exactly* do you want?'

Alan sighed and his large chest rose several inches. 'I want you to teach a self-defence class for gay men.'

'You look perfectly capable of teaching them yourself.'

'I could but I don't want to. There are complications.'

'Such as?'

'I'm ex-police. There's a lot of suspicion of the police from the gay community. Also I think it would be better if it wasn't a man.'

'Why?'

'If it's a man there could be a lot of sexual competition. It could turn it into something else.'

'So, if they're not thinking of shagging me they'll concentrate on technique.'

He laughed. 'Something like that – yes.'

'How many people could you get?'

'Ten to fifteen. Maybe twenty if I strong-arm them.'

'That many?'

'We've had some queer-bashing going on. That's what happened to my friend. Gangs have been picking on gay clubs.'

'How is he?'

'He's in a coma. His skull was fractured. They don't know if he's going to be all right.'

'I'm sorry.'

'So, will you do it?'

'I'll see if I can get a slot next term.'

'The thing is some of them might have muscle but they need to be told what to do with it.'

'The short answer to that is lose it.'

Alan stared at his own chest and looked mortified. 'That won't go down well.'

'Too much muscle and you lose flexibility. You lose speed. It's a lot of weight to carry if you want to run fast and it can play havoc with your joints.'

Alan patted the tops of his arms. 'Bye-bye, babies . . .' He sighed. 'I can't tell you how long it took to get these.'

'It's the bulk you need to lose.'

'Excuse me! It's the bulk I've worked to put on.'

'Lean and strong. But muscle for the sake of it – I can't see the point.'

'Never heard of Adonis, the body beautiful?'

Sam grimaced. 'Doesn't do anything for me. It looks freakish and artificial. You're never going to look like that naturally. The aim of self-defence is to enable you to disarm your opponent and run away. It is not about a fight to the death. Or winning. It is about protecting yourself and getting to a place of safety. It is not about being macho. If you get macho you always put yourself in danger.'

'You're a bit stern, aren't you?'

'I have to be. You get too many idiots, mainly men I'm afraid to say, attracted to this sort of stuff because they fancy themselves as the next Jackie Chan. Look at him. Tiny man but strong as steel hawsers. You get people who are completely unfit, who turn up and complain if they're not performing flying kicks in the first session. But if you let them do it, you know their groins are never going to be the same again. And there's only one person they're going to blame.'

Alan laughed. 'God, they'll go ape-shit.'

'It depends what you want. A body beautiful or a lean, mean fighting machine.'

'But suppose, for argument's sake, someone stuck a knife in my chest. My muscles would protect me. The knife would have further to go to reach anything vital.'

'True. But if you were lighter and faster, maybe he wouldn't get the knife near you to start with. Also the easiest people to throw are those overloaded with muscle because they're top-heavy, easy to topple.'

'You could throw me?'

Sam didn't even bother looking at him. 'Oh yes,' she said, picking up her bag and walking out of the gym.

The classes had started the following term and the muscle versus strength debate continued to rage. At first Sam and Alan's relationship had been confined to the classes but after one particularly raucous New Year's Eve party when the class had insisted on taking Sam out clubbing, it had slipped into something else and gradually their friendship had blossomed. Their working relationship had started in a random manner. Despite what Sam said in their first meeting, there were times when she could use some muscle and, much to Alan's amusement, she had started to use him. Alan had spent ten years in the police before a canteen culture, which equated gays with child molesters or transsexuals, had got to him and he had decided there had to be an easier ways of making a living. Sam discovered that entirely separate from any police training, Alan had a Graham Nortonesque ability to extract information from people and she had begun to use him on a part-time basis.

Alan came back with the two plates he had picked up from the bar and they ate in silence for a few minutes.

'So,' he said, putting down his knife and fork and pushing the plate away. 'You were saying you wanted me to go through your old files.'

Sam dipped a bit of fishcake into some mayonnaise. 'Yes.'

'And look for what, exactly?'

'Anyone who might have wanted to hang a dead fox on the scaffolding outside my window in the middle of the night and send me this.' Sam pushed the letter across the table towards him. Alan picked it up and read it.

'Christ!'

Sam ran her finger through the condensation on the outside of her pint. 'Please don't look so worried.'

'Aren't you scared? I'd be fucking paranoid.'

Sam didn't reply. Some silly quotation ran through her head. *You have nothing to fear but fear itself*. It wasn't true.

'I've also received this.' She handed over the letter claiming to have come from her father.

Alan frowned as he read it. 'My God . . . do you think they're related?'

76

'I don't know what to think. Last time I heard a fox I was in Oxford. Look at the postmark on that letter.'

'Anyone else hear it?'

Sam paused a moment, thought of Phil and then discounted him. 'I don't think so.'

'The tone of the letters couldn't be more different,' Alan said. 'This one, well, it's very loving, isn't it?'

Sam didn't say anything but stared down into the bottom of her pint.

Alan glanced at her. 'But this one is – well, pretty mad.'

Sam nodded.

Alan studied her bowed head. 'How is Home Sweet Home?'

'Oxford's not a home,' Sam exploded. 'It's a place that allows you to shrivel in its shadow, until you develop enough strength of character to get out. When I'm there, it's like I'm underwater. I can't think straight. I make terrible mistakes. I don't even recognize myself in the mirror. I feel all blurry round the edges.'

'Isn't that called going home?'

'Do you get that?'

Alan looked smug. 'Born and bred in London – I never left. That's the best way to manage it.'

'The thing is, I was trying to think if there was someone I'd pissed off enough to do something like that. And also someone who knew.'

'Knew what?'

'Something about my father.'

'He is dead, right?'

Sam shrugged and flicked the letter. 'We buried something.'

Alan whistled. 'SAS. Mad bastards, aren't they?'

'I was wondering if you'd take a look through my files. See what you think? It's difficult for me to have much perspective on my own files. I'd appreciate an objective eye.'

'What? Who you might have pissed off enough to start killing foxes? I can think of plenty.'

'That's what I love about you, Alan, so reassuring. Such a comforting presence.'

He laughed. 'Have you told the police?'

Sam shook her head. 'All I've got are these,' she pointed at the letters, 'and a dead fox. There's not much they can do with that, is there? Also the letter says to tell no one. I don't want to go blabbing to the police, especially when we both know they'll do nothing.'

In her pocket was the number of the motorbike. She could give it to Alan; he had contacts in the police he could use. She fingered the piece of paper and thought of Phil. Perhaps she could ask him and use it as an opportunity to apologize.

Alan looked around the pub. 'This isn't bad for a breeders' hang-out.'

'You get to call us breeders and we can't call you—?'

He leaned forward and kissed her lightly on the mouth. 'You, darling, can call me absolutely anything you like and I'll still adore you because you pay me – sometimes.'

Sam winced and picked up their empty glasses. 'You know what they say?'

'Hmm?' Alan was looking at a large man, dressed in green-and-pink Lycra shorts, who had just entered the pub. A few minutes earlier he'd been rowing past the pub.

'The cheque is in the post.'

'Battle about to commence with the bank?'

Sam waved the empty pints in the air. 'After one more of these.'

The following afternoon, Sam stood in the front room of Meg O'Connor's Fulham flat, which occupied the ground floor of a white-fronted two-storey house. A large, coral-coloured sofa filled one side of the room. Over the fireplace hung a painting similar to the one in the Oxford house, but this time in red. Sam looked at it and frowned. The red seemed oppressive, almost violent. The flat smelled stuffy. No one had been living here since Meg went missing. The bay window at the front of the house looked on to green dustbins and a beech hedge, which was high enough to keep out the gaze of passers-by. Out the back a bedraggled lawn ran ten metres or so. Sam sat on the sofa and looked around.

'So,' she said sliding her hand down the side of the sofa. 'Who are you, Meg O'Connor, and why have you gone missing?'

The room didn't reply and her hand came up holding a slightly sticky two-pence piece and a crumpled tissue. She spun the coin in the air and caught it. She was met with silence and dust motes spiralling in the autumnal sunshine. She stood up and went over to the mantelpiece and picked up a photo. Meg and John O'Connor somewhere that looked like Greece, behind them Mediterranean blue skies and sea. She was dressed in a white sleeveless vest and light blue cotton skirt; he just in khaki shorts.

She put the photo back and walked through to the bedroom, which contained a large double bed, built-in white wooden wardrobes and cupboards, a small dressing table and a wooden chest of drawers. The wardrobe was only about a third full, containing a few dresses, jackets and skirts. She checked the pockets of the coats and jackets, but they were filled with the usual bits of paper that London life threw up; bus tickets, tube tickets, cinema tickets and receipts, and the invitation to the Tate Modern exhibition – nothing out of the ordinary or remarkable. Feeling like a pervert, Sam opened the chest of drawers and ran her hand through the bras and underwear, the T-shirts and jumpers. Again, nothing. Sam sat on the bed and looked at the pile of books on the floor – a mixture of self-help books, modern novels and a couple of academic psychology books. She opened the drawer of the bedside table: a bottle of evening primrose oil, an alarm clock, a couple of pens and a notebook containing lists of reminders.

Sam got up and walked back into the living room, tried a few keys before finding one that fitted the back door and stepped out on to the patio. From the flat upstairs came the smell of frying bacon. She walked across the soggy lawn and turned round at the bottom of the garden to look back at the house. A man's face peered from an upstairs window and then vanished. So, he was at home. Time to visit the neighbour. She walked round the side of the house and rang the upstairs flat's bell. After a few minutes, a man opened the door. He was in his sixties and wore a dirty white T-shirt stretched over a prominent beer belly. His right hand moved nervously up and down the side of a grubby pair of black polyester trousers. A nose like a tiny purple cauliflower dominated his face, the kind of nose that could put you off spirits for life.

Trying not to stare too obviously at his nose, Sam held out her card. 'My name is Sam Falconer. I'm a private investigator looking into the disappearance of Meg O'Connor. I wonder if I could have a moment of your time?'

The man took her card and peered at it carefully, then looked her up and down. 'No,' he said, 'you can't,' and slammed the door in her face.

Sam stood for a moment, rubbing the dog tags back and forth between her fingers. God, she really did love this job. It was just great. She shrugged and walked back into the garden. Sometimes she envied the police. If she'd been from the police, that miserable old git would have thought twice before slamming the door in her face. Uniforms tended to intimidate. Private eyes had to use charm and Sam was never sure she had quite enough. She turned and saw the curtains upstairs twitch, saw the face of the man looking at her then disappearing behind them. What was he so worried about and why wouldn't he speak to her? Sam walked back into the house and locked the patio door behind her. She shivered and turned on the light. The sunshine had gone and the sky was darkening. This place wasn't giving up any secrets and the man upstairs was holding on to his. She let herself out of the flat into the hallway that served both the upstairs and downstairs flats. A metal mailbox was attached to the inside of the door to catch the post. She looked through the letters and took one addressed to Meg: a telephone bill. The rest of it was mainly junk mail addressed to Mr David Hicks. She scribbled his name on the back of her card and on it wrote, 'In case you change your mind. I'd be very grateful to talk to you.' She dropped it into the mailbox.

Outside Sam began working her way down the street, ringing on doorbells. Most of the houses were occupied and it took her over an hour to finish the street and obtain absolutely no useful information whatsoever. A couple of the occupants knew Meg by sight, but because she lived mainly in Oxford not many of them knew her to talk to. None of them had anything to say about the period of time around when she'd gone missing. By the time Sam had finished, raindrops were polka-dotting the pavement and she was soaked and bitterly cold.

She was just about to set off for home, when the front door of a house opposite where Meg lived flew open and a woman wearing a long fur coat, no tights and carpet slippers stepped out into the rain. This was June, one of the Fur Women of Fulham, so called by Sam because of their tendency to wear the kinds of coats that many furry animals had died to make. When she had first started living in the area Sam had admired the sheer nerve of these women who walked up and down in real fur coats, but then it had gradually dawned on her that most of them were dotty and probably didn't realize that their coats screamed *Spray me with red paint! Slash me with a Stanley knife!* There was also the fact that Fulham was hardly the natural home of animal rights activists.

June saw Sam and started to mumble to herself. The cigarette dangling from her lips waggled up and down and about an inch of ash dropped on to the wet pavement. One thing united the Fur Women of Fulham: they all thought Sam treated Frank badly. It was an unfortunate fact that all of them passed Sam's mansion block on the way to the Post Office to pick up their pensions and more often than not they found Frank yowling on the doorstep. June in particular viewed Sam with deep suspicion. One day she had come across Sam trying to pull Frank out of a spindly tree he had been chased up by a large, muscle-bound dog. Frank had been up there for several hours, howling at the top of his voice, and Sam had decided enough was enough. But when she tried to pull him out, Frank dug all his claws into the top of Sam's head. At the exact moment when Frank had applied his headlock and Sam was trying to tear him from her scalp, June had come round the corner and started to attack Sam with her handbag.

Sam sighed and, not expecting much luck, crossed the road. 'Could I have a quick word?' she asked.

'Piss off,' June said, and increased the speed of her shuffle.

'Look, I just wanted to ask you about the house opposite where you live.'

June's eyes narrowed. 'Why?'

'A woman's gone missing from the downstairs flat.' Sam took a photo of Meg out of her pocket and showed it to her.

June sniffed.

'Do you know her?'

'Slut!' June spat.

Sam wasn't quite sure whether June was referring to Sam herself or Meg.

'Who's the slut?'

'Piss off,' June hissed. 'Or I'll report you to the RSPCA.'

'How can he be that fat if I mistreat him?' Sam said to June's shuffling fur back.

But June ignored her.

Sam pocketed the photo and, since she was heading in the same direction as June, crossed to the other side of the road to avoid walking past her and set off at a swift jog for home. The rain was pouring down and the red hood of her sweatshirt, which she had pulled over her head, soon blew off. She ran as fast as she could, feeling the rain stinging her face and trickling through her hair. When she reached her block, Frank was sitting on the steps wailing. Sam uttered a silent prayer of thanks that she had got here before June. As she was letting herself into her own flat she heard the door of the basement flat open and the words, 'That you, Sam?'

Spence walked slowly up the stairs. Time had not been kind to him nor had all the drugs he had taken during his life. His face was the colour of overcooked veal, and the flesh of his face looked as if it had given up its grip on the bone structure underneath and was slowly abseiling towards his toes. He usually wore his dyed-blond, shoulder-length hair loose, but today he had a centre parting and two plaits, tied with the elastic bands that the postmen scattered up and down the streets. The overall effect was Heidi meets Keith Richards.

'Hello, Spence, how are you?'

Spence sucked on his teeth. 'That cat of yours, screeching like the world was ending.'

Sam shrugged. 'He's all right. Doesn't like wet pavement under his paws.'

'What do you think about all of that?' Spence gave an airy gesture to indicate the scaffolding.

'Well, he does it every year, doesn't he?'

'Did you get the rent stuff?'

'Yes.'

'I'm not being funny but I don't see why I should pay for your new boiler.'

Sam sighed. 'You're not going to have to. They only take that into consideration in assessing *my* rent. It has nothing to do with yours.'

'Oh?' Spence didn't sound convinced.

'How are things with you?'

'Well, this weather . . .' He petered out.

Sam had never known exactly what it was that Spence did, although Edie had once mentioned window dressing. All she knew for certain was that he was in a lot, he was quiet and he rarely answered his front door if you knocked. Oh, and he was always skint. Edie's door opened a crack. Spence was always trying to bum cigarettes off Edie but he would never buy a whole sleeve and he certainly wouldn't pay the whole amount all at once. Mean bastard, was what Edie called him. Wouldn't give you the drippings off his nose. But she was convinced he had money stashed away. Cheques came for him in the post. Edie had seen them. Edie and Spence's relationship was somewhat fraught. Spence let Edie feed his fish when he went away to Italy or down to his mum's in Devon, but he had the good sense to lock up his wig stands. Edie wanted one of those stands but when she asked for one, Spence denied having any. So, battle-lines had been drawn. Fish, wigs and fags – hardly your average neighbourly dispute, but at least it was more interesting than loud music, crapping cats and barking dogs. The door to Edie's flat closed quietly.

'We should liaise about the rent officer,' Spence said. 'Will you phone him?'

'Sure,' Sam said wearily.

'Check the dates with me. I'm not always in.'

Who did he think she was – his bloody secretary? Sam let herself into her flat. The red light on her answerphone wasn't flashing; it had been that sort of day, no answers forthcoming from anywhere, but at least she hadn't been beaten up by an elderly woman in a fur coat.

CHAPTER SEVEN

Sam threw Meg O'Connor's telephone bill on to her desk and spun round in her chair. The office that she shared with Alan was remarkable for the extraordinary mess on Sam's side and the pristine order on his. As she spun round, a pile of blue files, which had been leaning precariously against her desk, toppled over and slithered across the floor. Sam swore but didn't move to pick them up. She had spent the morning phoning every number listed on Meg's telephone bill, talking to people and arranging to meet some, leaving messages for others, trying to find anything, any clue to Meg's disappearance.

Sam knew from experience that a significant piece of information often didn't look that way at first sight. Often it required something else to make it gain importance. At the moment she was trying to hold all the data she had received in a loose soup in her mind, not concentrating on any one thing over the other, trying not to be sidetracked. And then, up through the soup, floated something entirely unrelated to Meg O'Connor: *Don't wait until you feel like it or you'll never do it*. Well, she certainly wasn't going to phone her mother. She phoned Phil and apologized.

'Forget it,' he said, but his voice didn't sound like he would.

'It's Oxford. It addles my brain – does something to me. Makes me lose my manners, anyway.'

'How would you feel if I did something that pissed you off and blamed it on a city?'

85

Sam laughed. 'I wouldn't be impressed, unless of course it was Oxford and then I'd understand.'

Silence. He wasn't allowing himself to be schmoozed – not today.

'Well,' she said, 'that's what I wanted to say.' She didn't have the neck to ask him about the number plate. She'd have to try that one on Alan.

'You ever read that Mars Venus book, Sam?'

'*Men are from Mars, Women are from Venus*?'

'Well, you're completely Martian.'

'Oh?' she said politely. 'And what does that make you? Little Miss Muppet.'

'Got to go,' he said.

'Well, I'll probably see you next time I'm down.'

There was a grunt and the phone went dead.

I don't need a bloody book to tell me that, Sam thought. Mars was the god of war, after all.

As a fighter, Sam had been famous for never knowing when to quit. She simply would not stop fighting; she would not surrender. Even in *randori* she fought as if her life depended on it. However much Tyler shouted 'Eighty per cent' at her, one hundred per cent was all she ever produced. If her opponent wanted to win then Sam always made sure that she had to beat her. It had been obvious to those around her that she'd never willingly retire. There would be no conscious decision made. It would be forced on her by injury. She had always been utterly reckless with her physical safety.

In the penultimate round of the 1998 European Championship in Prague she dislocated her shoulder in the process of throwing her opponent. The shoulder was put back in and Sam insisted on fighting in the final. She still had one good arm and two good legs. After all, six years previously, in 1992 in Berlin, she'd won the World Championships for the second time with a fractured leg. A wounded animal is more dangerous, she said to Tyler; a wounded animal can have you, before you know where you are. It can eat you up and then crawl into a bush to recuperate. Tyler disagreed, but she insisted. But this time she had lost and the shoulder had separated again so badly that she needed an operation to pin it. She fought back from that operation, underwent a painful rehabilitation and then the first time she competed in a serious competition, exactly the same thing happened. It was obvious to those around her that her fighting days were over.

But to Sam, of course, it wasn't. Judo was what she had done since she was seven years old and had first stepped on to a mat with Akemi. It had been her whole life. That is who she was; a champion fighter. Take that away and she didn't have a clue.

For a while she hung round her old club in Cowley, watching the training, trying to stay involved, persuading herself that she could make a comeback, that the shoulder just needed a rest and then she would be as right as rain. But the longer she couldn't train the more depressed she became, until she was struggling to get out of bed in the morning, drowning in inactivity, with the horror of an Oxford summer stretching ahead of her. Oxford was a cruel place to be in the summer. During the dog days of August, it was devoid of the energy that undergraduates injected into it and filled with American tourists standing in forlorn groups in Radcliffe Square, looking around them and asking where the university campus was.

It was George Ryan who had rescued her. George knew all about retirement. He'd seen enough ex-coppers sitting at his bar, drinking away their retirement because they didn't know what to do with themselves, finding the golf course and daytime TV an inadequate substitute for a working life. Looking at Sam, he saw someone going through the same withdrawal but at a much younger age. It was then that he had suggested that she work for his brother and sister-in-law, David and Diane Parker. They ran a firm of private investigators based in Putney. Their factotum,

Jill, was due to go on maternity leave, and they needed someone to take calls, do some filing and generally help around the place. It was in London but their office was close to where Sam's gran lived. She could walk to work, it would only be for a few months and then she'd be fit and ready to train again. Or that's how George sold it to her anyway.

Sam hadn't been so sure. But one thing she did know was that she needed to get out of Oxford. Another Oxford summer would be the end for her. It was only a matter of time before her mother would ask the question to which she had no answer: What are you going to do with the rest of your life?

Before the interview, Sam assumed that David was ex-police and that Diane was involved in the administration but it quickly became apparent that this was not the case. The interview did not get off to a particularly good start.

'George has told us about the judo,' Diane began. 'And frankly it rather worries me.' Sam didn't reply and Diane continued. 'We get a lot of macho types attracted to the job. Ex-coppers are the worst. Think they can throw people up against a wall and beat the information out of them, forget they don't have the badge any more, always being done for assault and trespass, don't adapt well to civilian employment. I hope you don't have any of those sorts of ideas?'

'First, I'm not ex-police. Second, when I fight, I fight in competitions on a judo mat. I'm a sportswoman. Just because my sport involves physical contact doesn't mean I'm aiming to solve every argument violently. Third, I haven't touched anyone off a judo mat in anger since I was about seven years old. In fact there's probably much less chance of me doing that than your average member of the public because I am all too aware of the damage I can do. Anyway, the impression George gave was that you wanted me to help round the office. I'm hardly going to have a violent dispute with a filing cabinet.'

'Oh, I don't know – I have.' Diane pointed to the battered bottom drawer of a dark green one.

Sam laughed and the atmosphere thawed slightly.

'I used to be in the police, you see,' Diane continued. 'I left when I became pregnant. In my day that was it, they booted you out. It was before the Sex Discrimination Act. And I'm fed up to the back teeth with ex-coppers thinking they know better than me, and bringing inappropriate attitudes to this kind of work. Mind you, women can be even worse, wanting to out-macho the men.'

'Just because I'm a fighter doesn't mean I behave like a man. I'm a woman. I fight. That's it.'

'Well, so long as that's clear. And I don't know what George told you but we don't want some glorified secretary. Jill had a case load and we want you to cover it.'

'But I've no experience.'

'Just a matter of keeping them ticking over until she's back. She's left you notes.'

'But George said—'

Diane looked at her watch and stood up. 'Look, I don't care what George said. Do you want it or not? Otherwise we've got other people to interview.'

Sam thought of Oxford in August. She thought of groups of Japanese tourists photographing beautiful, empty buildings. She thought of spending a summer pulling pints for George in the Red Lion, waiting for her shoulder to mend, waiting for autumn to come, for a change of season, wondering if she'd ever fight again.

'I want it,' she said.

'Good. You better look at these, might as well jump in at the deep end.'

And that is exactly what Sam had done. Jill had not come back from maternity leave. Sam's shoulder had not healed properly. And Sam had stayed, retaining Jill's caseload, specializing in missing persons. Two years later, Diane was dead from breast cancer and David no longer had the heart for the work. With some money that her gran had left her and with a hefty loan from the bank, Sam had bought the business and changed the name to Gentle Way Investigations.

The door opened and Alan came in. He rested his arm on top of the green filing cabinet.

'When are you going to get rid of this thing?'

'I'm fond of it. Reminds me of Diane.'

'It's so tatty, so battered . . .'

'I know the feeling,' Sam said. 'Maybe it makes me feel at home.'

'But—'

'Look, you're not going to have one of those *feng shui* conversations with me, are you, Alan? I'm not in the mood. For the record, I'm never going to be in the mood. I know how you feel about this office block. I know you think it suffers from sick-building syndrome or whatever it's called, and that you feel ill when you work here. I know half the offices aren't let and that's bad *feng shui*. But, in its defence, we get a great view of the river and the park and we get to use one of the empty offices to interview our clients in because I bribe dear dodgy Greg, our beloved receptionist, with Edie's contraband tobacco. So long as that man smokes, it's worth us being here. So don't tell me there aren't some advantages.'

Alan laughed, took off his coat, threw it over the filing cabinet and sat down at his desk. 'Actually, I was not going to have the sick-building conversation with you. I was wondering how you are?'

'Fine.'

'Hey, girl, it's me, your old friend Alan.'

Sam groaned. 'Oh God, Alan, I always forget you actually want to know and it makes it so much more complicated.'

'That's the one.'

'Well, finding it difficult to concentrate on the O'Connor case, to be honest. Been covering her phone bill, following up the last calls in the weeks before she went missing. Got a few appointments for the afternoon.'

'Good. Good.'

'Then I've been sitting here thinking about how on earth I got involved in this business in the first place. It's such a mess of a job. Fighting, judo was so straightforward.'

'You've got four planets in Scorpio, girl, that's heavy-duty shit to live with.'

Sam groaned. 'Come *on*, Alan. Give me a break.'

'I'm just telling you. Four planets in Scorpio – that's major attraction to the dark side. Real underbelly stuff.'

'So who am I? Darth Vader.'

'I'm just saying.'

'I know, Alan – four planets in Scorpio. You always know how to cheer a gal up. I wish I'd never given you my time of birth.'

Zandra Dodds threw herself backwards into an overstuffed armchair with all the practised petulance of a toddler. 'So, she still hasn't turned up?'

'No.'

Sam lowered herself carefully into a sofa, which she knew would require the upper-thigh strength of Arnold Schwarzenegger to extricate herself from. This woman was definitely into plush furnishings. 'Could you run through exactly what happened that evening?'

'I've told all this to the police already.'

'I appreciate that and I'm sorry to take up your time, but it would be a tremendous help for me to hear it from the horse's mouth. If you'll pardon the expression.'

'Fine. But I'm not going to talk with that on.' With a fat white finger that looked like a sausage about to split out of its skin,

Zandra indicated the tape recorder Sam had placed on the coffee table. 'I'm afraid they just give me the creeps.'

'No problem.' Sam turned it off and put it back in her bag. 'I usually concentrate better with it off, anyway.'

'I'd prefer it if you left it out on the table so I can see it isn't on.'

Sam took the tape recorder out of her bag and placed it back on the table.

Zandra Dodds folded her hands over her purple-velvet-covered stomach. 'We were both at the press preview and agreed to go round it separately and then meet up and have supper in the restaurant. You know, the one at the top of Tate Modern. We discussed the exhibition, gossiped a bit, then she said she was tired and went home. That was it.'

'Do you know how she got home?'

'I assumed the tube – Embankment because she lives on the District line.'

'That's quite a walk.'

'Yes, but it was a mild night and it wasn't raining and there were lots of people about. Also it wasn't that late.'

'How long have you known her?'

'Meg? We first met ... at the Warhol, I think. It must have been when she first started reviewing. We both disliked him, you see, wrote very similar pieces and then the next time we met, we sort of bonded. It's a small world, that of the art critic, small and vituperative. We're all too happy to eat our own – makes for one less competitor. So if you happen to find someone you get on with, it's a relief.'

'Was there anything that night that struck you as unusual or at all out of the ordinary? How did she seem?'

'Well, tired I suppose, but that's hardly unusual for a working mother with two children.'

'Did she say anything out of the ordinary?'

'No. We talked about the exhibition mainly, chatted and made our way home.'

'There was nothing that stood out from the conversation?'

'We aren't *really* that close. It's a relatively recent friendship. She wouldn't necessarily confide in me about personal matters. It's more a work relationship than anything else.'

'Could you tell me what she's like?'

'What's that got to do with anything?'

'It helps me to build a picture of her. Different people have different impressions of people. One impression may give me a clue as to why she's gone missing, while another—'

'Well, funny, sharp. Sassy, as they say in America.'

Sam nodded.

'She was brought up all over the place – New York, Paris. Her dad was something in the diplomatic. She's got that sort of polish and a very wide frame of reference for things. It's why she's such a good critic.'

'Would you say she was stable?'

Zandra barked a short, sharp laugh. 'Stable? God, who do you know who's *stable*?'

Sam smiled. 'I mean, was she impetuous – the kind of person you can imagine just disappearing? Walking out?'

She shrugged. 'Anyone can, can't they? Isn't it the quieter ones you need to watch? Not the ones emoting all over the place.'

'Is that what she did?'

'Not usually, no.'

'She had red hair.'

'If you don't mind me saying so, that's rather a facile thing to say. She has red hair so she must be a screaming loony. I don't think that one holds up, frankly.'

'Did she have a temper?'

'Not that I ever saw. But like I said, I was seeing her in a work context, so—'

'And there's nothing else you can think of that might be of any significance?'

She shook her head. 'I'm afraid not.'

Sam levered herself out of the sofa, which had all the resistance of quicksand. 'Thank you for your time.'

'Is that it?'

'Yes. I'll leave you my card in case anything else comes to mind.'

'You said that you'd been hired by Mr O'Connor?'

'Yes.'

'So he wants her back?'

'He has hired me to find her or to find out what has happened to her.'

Zandra Dodds heaved herself upright and escorted Sam to the front door.

Sam opened the door and then turned. 'One last thing. What did she phone you about the following morning?'

For a moment Zandra Dodds's mouth gaped like a fish. 'I don't—'

'The phone bill lists a call to you around twelve o'clock that day. It was the last contact she had with anyone before she disappeared.'

'I don't recall that . . . but she may have phoned me to confirm some details of the exhibition.' Zandra Dodds gestured towards the white wooden bookshelves that lined the hall. 'I have a very extensive library and she was away from hers, wasn't she?'

Sam smiled and held out her hand. 'Thank you again for your time.'

The hand she shook felt like moist dough. Sam barely squeezed it, resisted the impulse to shudder and ran down the stairs to pavement level.

Sam stood on the top floor of Tate Modern looking across the

Thames at St Paul's. She wasn't sure how she felt about modern art but the view was fantastic.

'You want to talk with me?'

Sam turned and saw a dark, angular, good-looking young man standing in front of her.

'Jean-Louis?'

'Yes.'

'Thank you,' Sam said. 'Did your boss say who I was and what I wanted?'

'Something about one of the shifts I was on?'

'I'm investigating the disappearance of a woman who is an art critic.' Sam held out a photo of Meg and he took it. 'She came to the preview at the beginning of October and then ate here in the restaurant with another art critic called Zandra Dodds. This was on the day before she disappeared. Apparently you were on the evening shift that day.'

Jean-Louis nodded. He took the photo from Sam and frowned. 'I don't remember her. We serve many people. I try not to look at them all.'

Sam laughed. 'She was with another woman.'

'This other woman. What did she look like?'

'I don't have a photo but she's very big and loud. Probably wore bright colours. I just left her and she was wearing a purple mohair cardigan that came to her knees, purple velvet trousers and a bright orange scarf.'

Jean-Louis wrinkled his nose. '*Mon Dieu! C'est impossible.*'

'Does it ring any bells?'

'The customers, they blur. It is a defence mechanism, you know, when dealing with the public. They would only stand out if they were very nasty or very nice.'

'Or big tippers?' Sam suggested.

'Perhaps. Yes. You have no picture of this other woman?'

'No.'

'I don't think I can help you.' He looked at his watch.

'I don't want to hold you up,' Sam said, 'but it's just occurred to me that Zandra Dodds might have written a book which the shop stocks. There might be an author's photo. Would you come downstairs with me for a second? If you see her you might remember.'

He shrugged. 'Sure. You talk to my boss, I come with you.'

Down in the bookshop it didn't take Sam long to find the relevant book, a monograph on Matisse. She flicked to the back inside page of the cover and there was an unrecognizably glamorous picture of Zandra.

Sam groaned. 'I'm not quite sure how they got her to look like that. This isn't really very helpful.'

But Jean-Louis had snatched the book from her and was hissing through his teeth in a decidedly Gallic manner.

'Her!' he said, flicking the photo savagely with his finger. '*Salaude!*'

'Oh yes?' Sam said.

'I should have known it was her. The wonder is no one has thrown her in the river.'

'Really?' Sam repeated.

'Now then, that evening. Yes, I remember now, it was the night you are asking about.'

He put the book back on the shelf and they began walking towards the lifts.

'She did not complain. Usually all the time she complains. The meat is undercooked; it has to go back. The wine is not chilled. The bread is stale. It is all rubbish. On and on she goes. She does not want ice in her water; she has to have unsalted butter. But that evening she was not like that. It was very remarkable. I was shocked.'

'So what was she like?'

'She was nice.'

'Sorry?'

'For the first time ever. And I have served her many, many times.'

'Do you know why?'

'The other woman. She was very upset. So, this Zandra, she could not make the big fuss. She was looking after this other woman. For once it was not all about me, me, me.'

'In what way upset?'

'It was obvious.'

'How?'

'Tears, of course.'

'She was crying?'

He nodded.

'Did you overhear the conversation?'

'The other woman, she was upset, so I gave them a lot of time. You know, I am discreet.'

'You don't remember anything that was said?'

He shook his head. 'She was upset. This Zandra, she was not the bitch from hell she usually is. These are the things I remember.'

'Thank you,' Sam said. 'You've been very helpful.'

'You think you will find this woman?'

Sam shrugged. 'I don't know.'

Jean-Louis returned to work and Sam walked out of the museum and across the bridge towards St Paul's. If Jean-Louis was correct, then what had been making Meg O'Connor so upset that she was crying in a public restaurant the day before she went missing? And more significantly, why had Zandra Dodds lied to her? The phone call to Zandra the next day had been made after Meg O'Connor e-mailed her editor with her review, so whatever the content of the conversation, it couldn't have related to the contents of the article as Zandra had said.

CHAPTER EIGHT

Sam looked up at the London Eye, turning slowly against a grey sky. The big wheel had transformed this whole side of the river. People were selling souvenirs: union jacks, T-shirts of the Tower of London and postcards. They were twisting metal into names, offering caricatures in twenty minutes and bungee jumps in front of the old City Hall. The smell of chestnuts and peanuts mingled with sausages and onions. A long, slowly moving queue snaked from the bottom of the wheel. Across the river the Houses of Parliament sat in gothic splendour, managing to look impressive even in light drizzle; something Sam had never managed.

She rested her elbows on the stone parapet and watched a boat nudge its way downstream towards Greenwich. The tide was out and a man dressed in waterproof trousers and jacket, and wearing a sheepskin hat with earflaps, was inching his way across the riverbed with a metal detector. She was early; she always was.

A hand on her back turned her attention away from the muddy green Thames.

'Want one?' Alan held out some chestnuts.

Sam shook her head and turned back towards the river, trying to get away from the smell.

'Do you think they ever find anything?' she asked, pointing at the man.

'Yup, Roman coins a few months ago. It was in the papers. This river is old, love, and things have been thrown into it for centuries.'

Sam nodded. The man had stopped and was poking in the gravel bottom with a stick.

'Ready for your birthday treat?' Alan asked.

'I suppose so.'

Alan eyed her. 'Well, you're looking particularly cheerful today.'

'I've just turned thirty-two, the same age my father was when he was killed.'

'Well, there's a jolly thought for a cold wet day.'

Sam looked up at the wheel and touched the dog tags in her pocket. What would he look like after all this time if he were still alive? Would she even recognize him if she saw him? She shook her head and let go of the tags. He was dead. She was just indulging in sentimentality.

'So,' Alan said. 'He liked *The Third Man*?'

'Apparently he could quote it line by line.'

'It's one of my favourites. Especially the whole cuckoo-clock scene.'

'Apparently, he had an ancient record of the zither music, and after every mission, when he came home, it was the first thing he'd put on.'

Alan started to hum it. 'I think it's playing down the way.' He pointed in the direction of the NFT. 'We should go.'

Sam wasn't listening to him. She was looking at the tickets. 'We need to start queuing now.'

The door to a capsule opened and people who had just completed their trip poured out. Alan and Sam were the last ones in and stood looking east, towards St Paul's; gradually the ground began to drop away from them. A little boy had discovered he was frightened of heights and began to scream. His mother held him down on the wooden bench in the middle of the capsule and tried to placate him with sweets, while the father stood away from the family group, binoculars trained at the horizon, trying to pretend it was nothing to do with him. Sam sympathized.

'The way I look at it,' Alan said.

'Yes.'

'As in the people you may have pissed off.'

She nodded.

'Well, there are the Hugheses.'

Sam frowned. 'I don't think so, Alan. The grandparents hired me because they were suspicious of their son-in-law. They thought he'd done it and they're not going to blame me for what happened. They wanted Jenny found. I found her. That was it so far as they were concerned. What I did just confirmed their worst fears.'

'Yes, but the discovery of Jenny's body confirmed Andrew Hughes had killed his own daughter. No body, no case. And *you* found the body.'

'The only person I can think of who would want revenge on me is Andrew himself and he's in prison awaiting trial.'

'What about his wife, Anne?'

'Makes no sense, Alan. Jenny was her daughter. However much she loved Andrew and "not much" is my guess, she's not going to have an axe to grind with me. It wasn't me who killed her child.'

'True, but there may be people who blame you, who think he's innocent.'

'Who? No one thinks he's innocent. Everyone knows he's guilty. All the evidence points to him having done it. He'd accessed all those child pornography sites on his computer and there were semen samples all over Jenny's dress.'

Alan shrugged. 'OK, well, that seemed the most obvious one to me because that case had the most publicity. It's also recent. Before that there were the pub cases. You pissed off a fair number of landlords with all that undercover work you did last year. Those cases are due to come to court in the next couple of months and they're relying on your evidence. There's a few who might want to put the frighteners on you about that.'

'But would they know who I was or where I lived? I was fairly careful about changing my appearance.'

'Sure but then after you found Jenny you were splashed all over the papers. They could easily have read about you, seen your picture and put two and two together.'

'Fucking papers,' Sam said. 'It's just what you want, as a private investigator, fucking publicity.'

'Publicity's OK. We could have done without the photos. But if you will insist on solving such high-profile cases, what do you expect?'

'I was happy for the police to take all the credit.'

'I know you were, but "Police Solve Missing Child Case" is hardly good copy, is it? On the other hand, "Fighting Falconer Discovers Body of Murdered Child" is what I call a story.'

The capsule had reached the top of the wheel. Alan and Sam had moved and were looking west towards Buckingham Palace and St James's Park.

Sam shuddered. 'Hanging a dead fox outside my window's so . . .'

Alan put his arm around her. 'It's not a nice business, Sam. You know that.'

'It's actually the letter that's doing my head in more than the bloody fox. So much of my life's been built on my father's absence. On the story of his death.'

'What was he like?'

'That's the thing, I can't really remember. I was four when he was killed. And Mark and my mother have always been quite reticent. They don't talk easily about him. I've got pictures, of course, and cards he wrote. But when we moved to Oxford we left behind the army connections, people who had known him. I think my mother wanted to get as far away from the whole thing as possible. And when she remarried that was all forbidden territory. I mean, you can't get further away from the SAS than an Oxford college. We weren't supposed to talk about it. We weren't even supposed to go and visit his grave. Didn't stop me, mind. There was my godfather, Max, but I haven't seen him since the funeral.'

'So you don't actually know what he was like?'

'No, but I've always identified with him because of the fighting. I felt it was my destiny. He was a fighter, I was a fighter. It was important to me. I always felt it was up to me.'

'What was?'

'To honour his memory. To live up to his reputation. That I had no choice. I always believed that. Maybe I had it more than Mark because I couldn't remember him. I had no memories to hang on to. You see, he never really seemed human – more like a god.'

'One of the immortals?'

'Someone I could ask for things, pray to. It was a bit like that. When I was fighting, the last thing I'd touch before setting foot on the mat was his dog tags. Every time. It was a touchstone. I always felt he was out there and on my side.'

'Are you sure he's dead?'

'They told us he was dead. We buried him.'

'They buried Harry Lime – twice.'

'And he turned out to be a sewer rat.'

Alan laughed. 'Where was he killed?'

'They didn't tell us at the time. "On active service" was the extent of the information. But I've read the histories. The SAS were in Oman at the time of his death and they had casualties there.'

'Oman? North Africa – right?'

Sam shook her head. 'It's in one of the southernmost nations in the Middle East. In the south-east it borders the Arabian Sea and its north-western border faces Saudi Arabia and the United Arab Emirates.'

'Ever thought of being a geography teacher?'

Sam smiled. 'It's amazing how interested you can get in a place if you believe your father was killed there.'

'So, what was going on?'

'Yemen, which lies to the west of Oman, was a Marxist state and the Yemeni government was supplying weapons and ammunition to rebels inside Oman. If the rebels had won, that would have left communists controlling the Gulf of Oman, the entrance to the busiest and richest sea-lanes for the world's oil tankers. It would also have meant that they had Oman's own oil supplies.'

'Oil,' Alan said. 'I wonder how many people have died because of it.'

'The SAS presence there was a secret at the time. No one knew about it. If he was killed there we wouldn't have been told.'

'Have you told your family about the letter?'

'Mark but not my mother. Why upset her if it's a hoax? It's got to be, hasn't it?'

'Don't you think she has the right to know?'

But Sam wasn't really listening to him. 'One thing's clear from the photos: I'm the spitting image of him. Mark's tall and dark like my mother. I'm short and blonde like him. There's practically no crossover whatsoever. Mark's all hers, I'm all his.'

'His? Hers? Aren't you forgetting someone?'

Sam raised her eyebrows. 'You getting clever on me, Alan?'

'You, for example.'

Sam smiled. 'Yeah, yeah. You're beginning to sound like O'Connor.'

'I wasn't intending to.'

Sam sighed. 'Everyone's allowed a little fantasy, aren't they?'

'You won the fights, Sam. You were World Champion four times, European Champion five times. It was you who snapped a dislocated finger back into place and went on to flatten Nomura. It was all you. I mean, look at your hands?' He tugged one of her hands out of the pocket of her red fleece, held it in his much larger hand and tapped each finger. 'How many times?'

And Sam answered, 'Three times, once, can't remember, four, I think.' She pulled her hand away. 'Poor, bloody fingers,' she said, flexing her swollen joints. She remembered holding her gran's hand in hospital, shortly before she died. Their knuckles hadn't looked that different.

'It was you,' Alan continued. 'If you place your triumph at the door of some mythic father it diminishes the achievement; it's not even true.'

'Oh, I know I did it,' Sam said, leaning her forehead against the glass walls of the capsule and staring out at a drizzle-covered London. 'Every morning I drag myself out of bed my body reminds me of *that*.'

They sat in the bar of the Royal Festival Hall nursing two bottles of beer. Behind them a string quartet was tuning up.

Sam took a piece of paper out of her pocket and put it on the bar between them. 'I wonder if you could see what you can do with that.'

Alan picked it up and looked at it. 'What's this?'

'Number of the bike I saw riding away on the night of the fox.'

Alan frowned. 'For God's sake, why didn't you give this to me before?'

'Thought I might get Phil to give me a hand but the conversation didn't end in any condition for a favour to be asked.'

'So, tell, tell.'

She shook her head. 'There isn't anything to tell.'

'Yes, there is.'

'How can you be so certain?'

Alan folded his arms and looked at her.

She sighed. 'Well, I could hardly avoid him, could I? He's

working the Meg O'Connor case. Do you find it difficult not to sleep with exes?'

Alan laughed. 'Depends which ex you're talking about. Some I find all too easy to avoid. So, did you?'

'I did, but I shouldn't have. The sex wasn't even that good. He just seemed comfortable and familiar. I suppose I was upset about the letter. Oxford actually, I blame Oxford. Whenever I go back there it's just such a mess. It's like I lose all sense of who I am. It's a muddle, too many memories. I lose the ground under my feet and then try to re-establish it with sex.'

'Did it work?'

'Well, what do you think?'

He laughed. 'So, what happened?'

'Well, I slept with him and then as soon as we'd done it, I thought, God, that was a big mistake and left.'

Alan whistled between his teeth. 'Very smooth. Highly sensitive. Very *Yang*.'

Sam groaned. 'It's this bloody case. I should never have taken it on. I can't stand Oxford. I hate therapists and there's all this nonsense going on with my dad.'

'O'Connor seems OK.'

'It's not O'Connor in particular. But you know, they look at you in *that* way. And they're always prodding and poking away at you and saying, How *are* you? And you can't help feeling completely paranoid that they know things about you that you don't know yourself. Things you've been working really hard all your life never to know about yourself.'

'He's very attractive.'

Sam frowned. 'Is he?'

Alan rolled his eyes. 'You know, in that crumpled linen jacket, academic sort of a way.'

'He's too furry on the inside for me. Recently, I feel as if I checked my libido into a cloakroom and lost the ticket. Anyway he's a client. End of story.'

'Not with Phil, you didn't.'

'What?'

'Lose the ticket.'

'No, with Phil the ticket is always there, fluttering in front of our bloody noses. Mind you, he accused me of being from Mars.'

Alan laughed. 'Hardly makes him Einstein, does it?' He picked up the paper with the number on it. 'Talking of exes, I'll give Gary a ring. See if he can help with this.'

'Thanks.'

'You know, I was thinking perhaps you should get in touch with the SAS, let them know what's going on. Maybe they'd have some ideas. I mean, if this person is stringing up dead foxes outside your window . . .'

'I don't think they're the same person,' Sam replied. 'And in the letter he says tell no one.'

'I know, but suppose for argument's sake they are the same person. It is your dad and he's nuts, you know, swinging between mad psycho, hence the fox, and loving Daddy, hence the letter. Don't you think you should tell someone?'

'I suppose I could tell my godfather.'

'Who's he?'

'Mad Max Johnson, a friend of my dad's. They were badged at the same time.'

'Have you had much contact with him?'

'You're joking. I remember him at Dad's funeral, but that's about it.'

'I don't know why people ever make heterosexual men godfathers, it's a big mistake. Gay men are perfect. They always remember birthdays, love to go shopping, adore a good party and they'll probably die rich and childless and leave all their money to little Amy.'

'How many have you got?'

'Six – and I could tell you all their ages and all their birthdays, so there.'

'Six! Christmas must be hell.'

No one had ever asked Sam to be a godmother, much to her relief because she didn't believe in God, and she wasn't sure she believed in mothers either.

The string quartet had finished tuning up and begun to play. Alan and Sam turned round on their stools to listen.

CHAPTER NINE

The following morning Sam paused and looked up at the marble and glass façade of Max Johnson Security Ltd. The client's first impression – your building and how much rent you were paying to impress them. Quite a lot, by the look of this place. Sam pushed through the door and walked into the foyer. The second impression – your receptionist. In this case, blonde, blue-eyed, and big-breasted. Sam felt flat-chested and rather grubby in jeans, trainers and sweatshirt. She shifted her rucksack off her shoulder and held it down by the side of her legs in a slightly furtive manner. The woman's eyes had scanned her as she came through the door and then returned to her desk. Not important enough, Sam thought. She probably thinks I'm a courier. She stopped in front of her and waited for her to look up.

'Yes?' she said, marking the sentence she was reading with a well-manicured nail.

'Sam Falconer. I've got an appointment to see Max Johnson.'

The woman's eyes returned to her desk and a large appointments diary. 'Ah, yes, twelve o'clock. I'm afraid Mr Johnson is running a little late. Would you take a seat? I'll let him know you're here.'

Sam nodded and sat down on one of the large black leather sofas opposite the receptionist's desk. Glossy brochures were scattered across a low glass table. She picked one up and the first picture to greet her was of her godfather, free-falling at altitude; he was wearing an oxygen mask and doing the thumbs-up to camera. Others followed: Max, white-water rafting; Max with

Michael Schumacher; and finally Max in pinstripe suit and tie, corporate and branded. *Whatever your security needs, let us take care of you.*

That would be nice, Sam thought.

The lift door opened and Max Johnson himself stepped out into the foyer. He looked at Sam and his head snapped back on his shoulders, as if he'd just been on the receiving end of a Lennox Lewis jab.

'My God, I had no idea. You're the spitting image of him.'

Sam stood up and smiled.

'Look at you, you're like his twin. Smaller, of course, and you're a woman. I've seen your photo in the paper so I knew there was a similarity, but all the same . . .'

He strode towards her and engulfed her in an awkward bear hug, awkward because he was about a foot taller than Sam, which placed her face level with his armpit.

'Paula,' Max said to the receptionist. 'This is my goddaughter. A world champion in karate.'

'Judo,' Sam corrected.

A smile formed instantly on Paula's lips. Her hand left the pages of the magazine and reached out towards Sam. 'Very nice to meet you.'

Sam took it and smiled back, feeling slightly less grubby.

'I've been the most terrible godfather.'

Sam shrugged. She could hardly deny it.

'I can imagine,' Paula said.

'The last time I saw you was—'

'Dad's funeral.'

'Yes, of course it was.' He tugged at his ginger moustache. 'Let's go upstairs. I was very surprised to hear from you.'

He put his arm round Sam's shoulders and she was engulfed in a cloud of aftershave that made her think of a pack of testosterone-fuelled dogs. He ushered her towards the lift. 'How's your mother?'

'Haven't seen her for a while.'

He frowned. 'Married some brainy bastard, I heard.'

'Yup, that just about describes him.'

'So,' he said, when they were sitting in his office. 'What can I do for you? Thirty years' worth of birthday and Christmas presents?'

Sam laughed. 'No, there's no need for that.'

'A job? We can always use women protection agents. Some of our clients don't like men that close to their women. There are cultural concerns, especially among the Saudis. Can you shoot?'

Sam shook her head. 'No, it's nothing like that. I've been getting letters from someone claiming to be my father.'

Max frowned.

Sam took the letters out of her rucksack and handed them to him. There was silence as he read them.

'If it were just a case of the letters, I wouldn't be so concerned. But the second letter was in the mouth of a fox, which was hung on the scaffolding outside my bedroom window.'

Max jumped out of his black leather power chair and began pacing up and down behind his desk.

'The thing is,' Sam said, 'I wondered if you could let them know.'

'Who?'

She shrugged. 'Whoever you think should know – SAS, military police. You see, I don't know if there was anyone with a grudge against my father that might have transferred to me. If someone might have been away, come out of prison. I mean . . . I'm assuming my father *is* dead. That bit of it is correct?'

She paused, but he didn't fill the silence that followed or answer her question.

'Max?' she said.

Max had stopped and was staring out of the window. He turned back into the room. 'I don't like this at all. Not one bit.'

Sam felt as if a hand had reached into her guts and made a fist of her entrails, as if she had just described physical symptoms to a friend and they had turned white and reached for the phone to make her a doctor's appointment.

Max shook his head. 'Killing *animals* . . .'

'I suppose it could have been road kill,' Sam said feebly.

Max stared blankly at her.

'You know, scraped off the road. There are lots of urban foxes these days, especially round where I live.'

'Can I keep these?' Max indicated the letters.

'Sure, if you could make me copies.'

'I'll make some calls.'

'Thanks.'

'A fox,' Max muttered.

'I've got an orange cat – I presume it was meant to frighten me.'

He looked her straight in the face. 'Did it?'

Sam blushed and then felt furious. 'Why do you think I'm here, asking a favour from a man I barely know?'

Max looked away from her. 'Why a fox?'

'I was in Oxford on a case and I heard one. I presume it was meant to let me know they were following me. Unless it was a coincidence.'

'Anyone else hear it?'

'No-o,' Sam said hesitantly. 'It was late – just me, the fox and an empty road. Or so I thought.'

'No one else there?' Max asked again.

Sam thought of Phil and then ruled him out. 'No.'

Max ran a finger through his moustache and frowned.

Sam continued. 'I've been looking into my cases, seeing if there's anything there but there's nothing that stands out.'

'You found that dead child, didn't you?'

Sam blinked once as if someone had shone a flashlight in her eyes and glanced down at the floor.

'How did you do that exactly?'

Sam didn't reply.

He looked at her with renewed interest. 'Sure you're not looking for a job?'

'I've never been one for bosses.'

'Your dad never liked authority. Anyway I'll make those calls.'

'Thanks.' Sam stood up.

He walked her to the door. As she touched the handle, his hand touched her arm. 'You got someone to watch your back, Sam?'

'Do I need someone?'

'Might be a good idea until this situation resolves itself.'

'I've always minded my own back. You'll let me know if anything turns up?'

'They'll probably be in touch themselves.'

Sam nodded. 'I appreciate it.'

As she walked out through the foyer, Paula looked up and smiled. 'Goodbye, Ms Falconer.'

Sam smiled. 'Goodbye, Paula,' she said, and pushed her way out through the revolving door into the street.

From the top of the number 22 bus, Sam watched lunchtime shoppers thronging down Piccadilly. Max's words were echoing in her head: *How did you do that exactly?* Good question, Max. She wished she knew the answer. She wiped the condensation from the inside of the window, wishing she could clear her memory in the same way, that she could remember. But the truth was she had little recollection of the events leading up to her discovery of the body of Jenny Hughes. Bits and pieces had come back in nightmares and waking flashbacks, but in no particular order, in nothing approaching an accurate time-line. It was as if substantial periods of the day had been erased. She couldn't remember how she got there, although she knew she must have driven. She didn't remember why she stopped where she did, or even walking through the woods. What she did remember was looking down at the place where Jenny was buried and knowing in every cell of her body that the child was there. She rang 999 from her mobile but when the police asked her where she was, she couldn't tell them – in the middle of the woods, standing over the body of a murdered child was the most she'd managed. She returned to the road and flagged down a passing motorist, handed him the phone and asked him to give directions to the police. Then she sat in her car, gripping the steering wheel to stop herself shaking, waiting for the police to turn up.

After she had shown them the place she walked back to the road, not needing to see what happened next. She knew the wet earth would be carefully scraped back to reveal a foot, a lock of brown hair, the blue dress with the strawberries on it. She knew they'd find the body. Jenny was the same age Sam had been when her father was killed. It might as well have been me, Sam thought, I died then, too. I've just been walking round pretending to be alive. Afterwards she had tried to numb it all out, to close the door. But who was she trying to kid? The door was ajar, the nightmares and flashbacks were coming closer and closer together, and mixed up with them was something else, something that didn't have an exact shape but filled Sam with terror, something that had nothing to do with Jenny Hughes and all to do with Sam. It was as if the discovery of Jenny had lit a match in a darkened room. A room Sam hadn't even known existed. But the more Sam looked, the less she could see; the match always went out just before she could see who was in there and what they were doing. And now she had a bloody therapist as a client.

The police had taken her in for questioning; suspicious of how she had known, assuming the murderer must have told her and that she was protecting him. But no, she couldn't remember why she had stopped at this part of the road and she didn't know why she had walked to this precise spot. Sorry, she just didn't know. She had nothing to tell them. They hadn't believed her. Well, you wouldn't, would you? She could have said: 'I felt someone walking next to me. I saw a picture in my head of the site, clear as a bell, as if the images had been transmitted straight to me.' She could have said: 'Every bone in my body knew.' She could have said all this and still it wouldn't have satisfied the police. It didn't satisfy her. What it did was frighten and disturb her.

The simple truth was that something had led her into the forest and stopped her where Jenny was buried and she had no idea how to explain it. The police had pressurized her. They thought she was lying. They stopped when they found her sitting in the corner of the interview room, hugging her knees, rocking backwards and forwards. 'Don't touch me,' she'd said. 'Don't come near me.' They hadn't. They'd called a doctor who'd given her a sedative and sent her home. She stuck to her story and then when the forensic evidence had tied the father, Andrew Hughes, to the child, they had backed off; body found, murderer in custody, end of case. But it hadn't been the end of the case for Sam. She was left trying to explain what had happened to her. Worrying over it like a cat with a dead mouse.

Of course Sam knew about the power of the mind; she'd used visualization techniques her whole fighting career, seen herself executing the perfect *ippon*, the perfect strangle, standing over her opponent, arms raised in triumph. She had felt the weight of that gold medal around her neck long before it actually hung there. She had imagined it and it had happened. But that was different. She had generated the pictures herself. She knew she had. But in the case of Jenny Hughes the pictures had been flashed from outside – very directly, very clearly.

The trouble was, Sam didn't believe in outside. Not if outside was God. She hadn't believed in God since her father died. After all, if God allowed her father to be killed then God wasn't to be trusted. But after she found Jenny Hughes she had visited All

Saints, a local church, and lit a candle and looked hard into the flame. Then she'd walked out of there disgusted with herself. Who did she think she was? The atheist who turns to God on discovering a lump in her breast? She didn't even know who she was lighting the candle for. The dead child? Herself? Or whatever had led her into the woods that night?

The bus turned left by Harvey Nichols and accelerated down Sloane Street. Sam took a picture of Meg O'Connor out of her bag and looked at it. She had a nice, open face, curly auburn hair that stopped level with her shoulders, and friendly blue eyes. Sam felt a mixture of anxiety and fear. She didn't want what had happened with Jenny to happen again. She wanted to find Meg O'Connor the usual way, using the logical investigative techniques that Diane had taught her.

The only person that Sam told about what had happened to her was Edie. She didn't know why exactly. She asked her in for a cup of tea shortly afterwards and it just spilled out of her. Edie had been entirely matter-of-fact about it.

'Oh, yes, your gran had that. Whenever one of the cats went missing she'd always tell me where he was, if they weren't coming back. She always knew. It's probably inherited. You know, like your eyes. You just got a different sort of sight.'

'But I've never had it before,' Sam said. 'How come it just turns up now out of the blue with no warning?'

'There's no point in questioning it, babes, that's what Rose said. She used to say it came and went like a cold in winter.'

And Sam had thought that was as good a way of looking at it as any. If it had just been a question of receiving the pictures, that would have been upsetting enough. But what she didn't want, what she dreaded, was the feelings that went with them. Standing over Jenny's grave, she had felt her terror and panic, the feeling of being about to die. First, the numbing blow to the back of the head and then the hands around the throat. Sam had not just found the child's body, she had died the child's death. And then seen someone smooth back Jenny's hair and straighten her dress, pick up a handful of earth and pour it into her mouth, before burying her.

The bus lurched to a halt and Sam jumped off and walked the short distance to her door. She should be concentrating on finding Meg O'Connor, not paddling around in the murky waters of the past. The phone was ringing as she opened her front door and she picked it up.

'Hey, sis.'

'Mark, how's the play going?'

Mark groaned. 'Come down for the opening night and see for yourself?'

'Doesn't sound very inviting.'

'Sure. Well, I don't blame you.'

She heard the disappointment in his voice. 'Look, tell me when it is and I'll definitely come down.'

'Will you? Really?'

'Definitely.'

'Excellent! It's tomorrow actually, is that too short notice?'

'No, fine.'

'But that wasn't the reason I was phoning. It was about Alice Knight.'

Damn, Sam thought, I could have got away with less. 'What about her?'

'Well, she knows you're involved in the O'Connor thing—'

'Did you tell her?'

'No, I haven't said a word. But she does know and she wants to talk to you.'

'What about?'

'She didn't say, but she was very insistent. Asked me to get in touch and ask you to phone her.' He read out two phone numbers. Sam wrote them down.

'I can't see what she has to do with it.'

'No idea, that's for you to sort out. I'm just the messenger here. Do what you like. Phone her. Don't phone her. I don't care. Can't bear the woman. Any more news about that letter?'

Sam thought of the fox hanging outside her window and the note in its mouth.

He was her older brother but she had always been the one to protect him.

'No,' she said. 'Nothing more on that. Maybe it was just some crank. You haven't received anything?'

'No – he wouldn't get in touch with me.'

'Why not?'

'Oh, no reason. Look, I'll see you tomorrow. It's at the Cranmer Rooms – starts at seven-thirty.'

'Sure.'

Sam put down the phone and stared at the two numbers Mark had given her, a mobile and a landline, then dialled the mobile.

The following evening Sam knocked on the glass window of St Barnabas's lodge. This time it wasn't Jack but a younger man Sam didn't recognize. He looked at her suspiciously. Porters were like policemen, Sam thought. They were skilled at inducing feelings of guilt.

'Sam Falconer – I'm here to see Alice Knight.'

He scribbled her name on a piece of paper and glanced at a board behind him. 'Front Quad, staircase three, second floor.'

She turned left past a noticeboard covered in flapping pieces of white paper. Ahead of her walked a group of men in dinner jackets. Dinner jackets could make the most unpromising of individuals look like catwalk models but one man in particular required no such assistance. Sam eyed him appreciatively. He was in his fifties, over six foot tall and broad-shouldered with a good head of grey hair, cut close to his head. Good hair for television, Sam thought, then remembered that was where she had seen him, on a late-night cultural review programme. She slowed her natural pace and gently stalked him round the quad until he disappeared through an arch with his companions. Sam had been so entranced by him that she had missed Alice Knight's staircase. Retracing her steps, she found the correct one and took the shallow wooden stairs three at a time.

Sam smelled Alice Knight's perfume as she heard the inner door open. By the time the solid oak outer door was opened, she was sneezing loudly.

'Bless you,' Alice said. 'Come in, come in. Excuse all this.' She gestured at the full-length crimson velvet evening dress she was wearing. 'There's a gaudy tonight so I'm dressed to kill.'

'I saw the penguins were loose in the quad,' Sam said.

Alice smiled. 'Yes, the most unlikely of candidates end up looking semi-respectable for once. Please take a seat.'

Sam sat down. Even though she was only going to be teaching for a term, Alice Knight had managed to obtain a larger set of rooms than Mark's and had taken the trouble to make herself feel at home. Two green and red Turkish rugs covered the worn carpet and a fake wolfskin cover had been thrown over the battered leather sofa. In the far right-hand corner of the room were a modern desk and blue office chair and against the side of the desk was a teetering pile of files. A large black leather briefcase sat next to the files wedging them upright. A laptop sat open on the desk, its screen blank. On the walls were several non-figurative paintings but above the fireplace was a portrait that looked remarkably like the man Sam had followed round the quad.

Alice noticed Sam looking at the portrait. 'You may know him from the television,' she said.

'Did I just see him out in the quad?'

'You could have done. He's here as my guest for the gaudy. He's my husband – Tony Ballinger.'

'You were taught by him, is that right?'

Alice smiled. 'Oh yes,' she said. 'All sorts of things.' She walked over to a table covered with bottles. 'I'm very grateful to you for seeing me at such short notice. I wasn't sure your brother would contact you. I fear he doesn't think much of me. I don't altogether blame him for that. I'm sure I was thoroughly obnoxious as a student.' She gestured at the bottles. 'Can I get you anything?'

'Straight tonic is fine.'

She poured some tonic into a glass for Sam and then poured the rest of the bottle over a large amount of vodka for herself. The hand that passed the glass to Sam was shaking slightly.

'Have you told John you're seeing me?'

'Mr O'Connor?'

'Yes.'

'No,' Sam said. 'I haven't.'

'I'm not sure what you know.'

'Perhaps you should just tell me why you've asked me here and then we can go from there.'

'I'll presume John hasn't told you, then?'

Sam thought Alice Knight appeared to be enjoying herself. She said nothing and waited for the game-playing to end. The silence extended. Alice jiggled the ice back and forth in her glass. Sam poked at the lemon in hers.

'What is it you want to tell me, Ms Knight?'

'Alice, for God's sake, call me Alice.' She brushed her hair away from her forehead with her hand. 'The thing is, John's been refusing to answer my calls. We've only spoken once since Meg went missing. He said that he couldn't cope with any pressure, had to focus on the children, on everything that was going on, which I understand, of course. So I don't know what he's told you. I didn't want to go to the police because I didn't want to land him in hot water. I really don't want to make any trouble but I felt I had to tell someone and you're it.'

Sam sat forward in her chair and held her glass of tonic in both hands.

Alice Knight tossed her hair off her face. 'We're having an affair.'

Sam nodded.

'You don't seem surprised.'

She shrugged. 'People do it all the time. Did Meg know?'

Alice shook her head.

'Oxford's a small place.'

'Of course it is. But I hadn't told her and John certainly hadn't. He was very anxious to keep it all under wraps. He had more to lose. Was very worried about losing the children.'

'Had you told your husband?'

Alice laughed. 'We have an open relationship.'

'How long had the affair been going on for?'

'Couple of months. Since I came down here. We bumped into each other in Blackwell's and it went from there.'

'Do you think Meg could have found out?'

Alice Knight drained her glass and jiggled the ice some more. 'It's certainly not beyond the realms of possibility.'

Sam nodded. 'Do you think this has to do with her disappearance?'

'If she had found out, she might have had some kind of crisis or breakdown. I believe there had been something of that kind in her past.'

'So why have you contacted me?'

'I thought you should know.'

'Why?'

'What?'

'Mr O'Connor, for whatever reason, has not disclosed your affair to either me or the police, presumably because he doesn't think it's relevant, or to protect you, or himself, or his wife. Now, here you are telling me. Do you want to tell me why? Or is it simply a way of forcing him back into contact with you?'

Alice picked up a packet of cigarettes from the table, shook one out into her hand and lit it. She inhaled deeply and threw back her head. 'I'm afraid this may appear somewhat melodramatic but since she disappeared I have felt worried about my personal safety.'

Sam frowned. 'Has anything happened?'

'My car has been broken into and I have been receiving calls in which someone rings, I hear breathing and then they hang up. They never say anything, there is just this silence.'

'What was taken from your car?'

'That was the thing that worried me most. At first I thought nothing had been taken. The passenger window was smashed but the radio wasn't stolen. I couldn't think of anything that had gone. But then I remembered that when I went to work that morning I'd been in a hurry and I'd picked up the post and left it on the front seat. I'd taken anything interesting into the office with me, but I'd left the junk mail and a telephone bill. All of them were gone and they had my address on them. So now whoever it is knows where I live and my telephone number.'

'Last time I was down I was reading in the *Oxford Mail* that there's been an increase in drug-related robbery and theft. Maybe it was a junkie. Has anything else happened?'

'Nothing actual. I mean nothing in reality. It's just that I feel under threat. In danger. I've been trying to tell John that. Of course, I realise I could be projecting my guilt about the affair onto an avenging angel who is coming after me. I have no proof and I am aware it must sound rather daft . . .'

'You could go to the police.'

'I know that. But if he hasn't told the police about us, it'll land him in it. I wanted to tell someone. I thought another person should know the true situation. After all, it does have a bearing on the case.'

'If she knew,' Sam said.

'Yes, yes, of course, if she knew.'

'If she didn't know, you're still looking at a disappearance with no apparent reason, aren't you?'

'Yes,' Alice said. 'I suppose you are.'

'If you genuinely feel under threat,' Sam said, 'I strongly suggest you tell the police.'

'I've already told you why I don't feel in a position to do that.'

'I'm not in a position to protect you and I'm not going to tell the police. All I'm going to do is talk to Mr O'Connor.'

Alice laughed. 'I realize that. I just wanted someone involved with the case to know. In case.' She stubbed out her cigarette. 'Well, anyway, now I've told you, so you know.'

'Yes,' Sam said. 'Now I know.'

The two women considered each other in silence.

Sam was the first one to move. She glanced at her watch. 'I must be off. I'm going to see Mark in *Romeo and Juliet*.'

'Isn't he a little old for that?'

'He's playing Friar Lawrence.'

'Ah yes, I can see that. He has an other-worldly quality.'

'Could I use your bathroom?'

'Be my guest.' Alice pointed towards a door leading off the main room.

The bathroom smelled strongly of perfume and Sam started sneezing straight away. She sat on the lavatory puzzling over why Alice Knight had wanted to talk to her and came to no obvious conclusion. Her nose was streaming; she grabbed some lavatory paper and blew her nose. The trouble was she didn't like Alice Knight and so she found it hard to see her clearly. She washed her hands and then looked for somewhere to chuck her snotty tissues. There was a small white plastic bin with a lid under the sink. She took off the lid and was about to throw the tissues in when she saw the packaging of a pregnancy kit. She took it out and looked at it, tapping it backwards and forwards against her hand, then threw it and the tissues away and put the lid back on.

Alice turned away from the window as Sam came back into

the room. 'Thank you for coming,' she said. 'I really appreciate it.'

'You're welcome,' Sam said. 'I'll talk to O'Connor.'

She started to walk towards the door. As her hand touched the doorknob she turned. 'Is there anything else you want to tell me?'

For a second Alice looked startled, then her composure returned. 'No – I've said everything I wanted to. Perhaps you could ask John to return my calls.'

As Sam reached the bottom of the stairs and turned into the quad she heard steps behind her. She turned just in time to see a man in a dinner jacket step through the entrance she'd left seconds before. She didn't seen his face, just his back. She glanced at her watch, swore and began running towards the front of the college.

CHAPTER TEN

By the time Sam reached the Cranmer Rooms, the play had already begun. She showed her ticket and slid into a seat on the back row. The actors babbled away on stage but Sam felt uninvolved because she was sitting far away from the action, and had missed the beginning. She only really focused when Mark was on, so she'd have something to comment on afterwards. Half her childhood had been spent being dragged to dire student productions, usually sitting outside, bum going numb on wooden boards, a rug wrapped over her knees and an umbrella over her head to ward off the miserable Oxford summers. There was only one play she remembered with any affection, a production of *As You Like It* in Merton, when squirrels had hopped over the feet of the performers.

At least this was indoors, that was the blessing of plays put on during the Michaelmas term. It was stuffy and dark. Sam folded her arms, rested her chin on her chest and dozed. *Romeo and Juliet* was only ever going to end one way. If it had been *Coriolanus* or *Macbeth* it would have had more chance of holding her attention. Fighters she understood; she wasn't so sympathetic to the suicide of the lovelorn.

As the first ripple of applause broke out, Sam jolted awake, stretched and rubbed her eyes. Mark stood on the stage beaming and bowing with the rest of the cast. As the audience began leaving, Sam remained seated, waiting to go backstage to congratulate him. And then, to her horror, she saw someone

124

bearing down on her whom she had not expected to be there and did not want to see – her mother, Jean.

Sam's mother was tall and dark like Mark, with the same brown eyes and long dark lashes. She had a nose that would have given Virginia Woolf a good run for her money; it was very long with a slight kink in the middle. Jean always said that the kink ran in her family but Sam had never seen it in any of the old family photos. It seemed to her that the kink was her mother's alone and it was the only disorderly aspect of her appearance. Jean was the personification of groomed and elegant femininity. Her daughter, Sam, who had spent a large part of her life in tracksuits and *judogi*, had always been a sore disappointment to her.

'Sam, darling. What a surprise. Mark didn't mention . . .'

Sam stood up and braced herself to endure her mother's look up and down.

'No, he didn't mention to me either.' Of course he hadn't, knowing full well that if Sam had known her mother was going to be there, she would never have agreed to come.

'It's lovely to see you, darling.'

Sam smiled weakly and glanced anxiously behind her mother. 'Is Peter—?'

'No, no – he had a committee meeting that ran over, otherwise of course . . .'

'Of course.' Thank God for committees, Sam thought. Her mother *and* her stepfather, with no prior warning, that would have been too much to endure; one at a time was borderline.

'How are you, darling?' Her mother moved a curly strand of hair away from Sam's forehead and tried unsuccessfully to tuck it behind her ear.

Sam had an uncontrollable urge to scream. She swallowed it, produced a strange clenched-teeth smile, dug her hands deep into her pockets and took a small step backwards.

'Fine, thanks.'

'I was worried about you after,' her mother lowered her voice, 'you know, the whole child business. I did phone.'

Sam nodded. She hadn't talked to her mother about that. From experience she knew that she couldn't because every conversation would end the same way with her mother suggesting she quit and do something else. After she had first started working for Diane she had made the mistake of going home for a few days. She had been exhausted and monosyllabic, and her mother had used the opportunity to suggest she was in the wrong job and shouldn't she think about settling down and perhaps starting a family. Sam didn't know how many times she had told her mother that she had no intention of having children, but she was exhausted and didn't have the energy to argue. She'd just left and vowed that she would never again call where her mother lived home. It wasn't. It wasn't a safe place. It wasn't a place where she was accepted. She was an adult, for heaven's sake. She had her own home in London. If it happened to involve an overweight cat with an ugly disposition and a cigarette-smuggling pensioner, so be it. It was infinitely better than anything else that was on offer. At least she didn't expect Frank and Edie to understand her.

Before she was required to plunge into the murkier waters that existed beyond 'fine', Mark appeared behind Jean, still in costume.

'Hello,' he said, putting his arm round his mother and kissing her on the cheek. 'How are my two favourite women?'

'Fine,' Sam said again. 'Great show.'

'Yes, darling. Wonderful. Well done.'

'Good, good. Has she told you?' he said to Sam. She looked at her mother. Mark continued. 'Mum and Peter are giving a party for the cast at home.'

There was that word again. 'Ah,' Sam said, as if opening her mouth to receive root canal treatment.

'You must come,' Mark said. 'Got to.'

'OK,' Sam said, feeling completely pissed off. 'I will.'

Mark looked at her anxiously, his eyebrows joining in a dark caterpillar across the top of his eyes.

Fucking family, Sam thought. Fucking family, fucking with my fucking head.

'I just need to get out of this gear,' Mark said. 'I'll meet you both out front.'

'I'll come with you,' Sam said, pushing him towards the stage. Under her breath she whispered, 'You can't leave me alone with her.' Out loud she said, 'Never been backstage before – the glamour, the greasepaint. See you out front in a bit, Mum.'

A couple of people were leaving the dressing room as Sam and Mark entered it.

'You coming to the party, Patrick?' Mark asked.

'Free booze and food? You bet we are,' Patrick replied.

'See you there, then.'

As soon as they were alone Sam punched Mark hard on the upper arm. 'You bastard. You might at least have warned me.'

Mark rubbed his arm and winced. 'If I'd told you she was going to be here, you wouldn't have come.'

'I might have surprised you.'

Mark sat down in a chair and started covering his face with white make-up remover. 'No, you wouldn't. I'm fed up being the one stuck in the middle, bearing the brunt from both of you.'

Sam grabbed a tissue from a box on the table. 'Here,' she said. 'Let me.' Rather roughly, she began to wipe the cream off his face. 'I never say anything to you about her.'

'I know, but she does and I'm tired of defending you. Watch it, will you? There's skin under here. Anyway, from now on you're on your own.'

Sam took a deep breath, wiped a bit of cream out of Mark's hair and threw the tissue in the bin at his feet. 'Fine.'

'And I expect you to come to this party.'

'Right,' Sam said.

'And, Sam, for God's sake, try to stay longer than ten minutes.'

Sam folded her arms and pulled a face.

'Haven't seen that one since . . . yeah, you were about five.' She laughed.

'Turn round. Me taking these tights off is not going to be a sight you want to see.'

'I thought you said it was going to be in modern dress.'

'Turns out the director's added schizophrenia to his list of mental illnesses.'

'You should do *Twelfth Night* next, those legs'd look good in yellow – a sort of Yellow Brick Road.'

'Shut up.'

'I can't stay that long, I need to see O'Connor.'

'Well, he's a neighbour, isn't he? I think Mum's invited him. Actually, I thought he might have come. Did you see him?'

'No,' Sam said. 'I didn't.'

Sam sat in the back of Mark's car looking out of the window as they drove up St Giles and thought about Peter Goodman. When she was feeling charitable she attributed her stepfather's personality, or lack of one, to the fact he was a mathematician. He liked the purity and beauty, the logic of numbers. When she wasn't feeling charitable, she thought of him as a control freak from hell, lacking one iota of passion. The only time she'd ever seen him behaving spontaneously was when he'd pushed a cork into a full bottle of expensive claret and sprayed a fine pink mist all over himself and the newly painted, pristinely white walls of the dining room. Then, he had completely lost it, and gone up in Sam's estimation about a hundred per cent. Mark turned right into Park Town. Sam felt trapped. When she was with her family she always felt short of oxygen. She wound down the window and heard a babble of voices floating from her parents' house into the cold night air. She shivered.

One thing Peter had never been able to handle was Sam's fighting. It simply wasn't logical to him that a girl, or a boy if it came to that, would want to fight. Somewhere along the line they had agreed to differ but only after a lot of arguments – and many things being said that would have been better left unsaid. At least he had always been consistent. When she started winning, he had never jumped on the bandwagon and said he had always known she had it in her and how marvellous it was. Sam respected him for that. His stance had not shifted at all.

And now here he was, standing in the doorway to his house, without a hair out of place, looking like a neatly balanced equation.

'Ah, he's back,' Mark said, turning off the engine.

Sam caught her mother's eye in the mirror, wound the window back up and pushed open the passenger door. She was never quite sure how to greet Peter; sometimes they kissed, sometimes they shook hands. Sam held out her hand, which hung in mid-air as he leaned forward and kissed her on the cheek. She then tried to kiss him on the other cheek but by that time he had pulled back and Sam ended up falling towards him and kissing air in front of his shoulder. Peter was one of the few people who could throw her completely off balance.

'It's very nice to see you,' Peter said in a voice that sounded as if he was reading from an autocue, and stood aside to let her in.

The living room was already full of people, a mixture of cast, friends and neighbours. The actor and actress who played Romeo and Juliet were locked in a torrid embrace on the sofa. Sam spotted John O'Connor in the corner, grabbed a glass of wine and elbowed her way through the throng towards him. He looked terrible; the bags under his eyes had deepened and his eyes were red and puffy. The skin of his face seemed stretched even more finely over his high cheekbones.

Sam touched his arm. 'Sorry to interrupt. Can I have a word?'

'I wondered if you'd be here.' He turned to the young man he was talking to. 'Excuse me, will you? Good luck next year.'

'Shall we go out on the balcony?' Sam suggested. 'It's stifling in here.'

They stood on a small, iron balcony looking out into a garden lit by a number of patio lights.

'Alice Knight contacted me.'

John sipped his drink and shivered. 'Oh, did she?'

'And I wanted to check out with you what she said to me.'

He was silent, looking straight ahead.

'She said you were having an affair.'

'Did she say that?'

'Yes, she said it had been going on for several months.'

O'Connor looked into the bottom of his glass.

'She said that Meg didn't know—'

He turned suddenly. 'Why did she get in contact with you? Did she say?'

'She said she feels under threat, in danger. Her car was broken into and nothing was taken other than some junk mail and a bill, which had her address on it. She's been receiving anonymous phone calls and said she wanted someone to know, in case—'

'God, she always was melodramatic. Liked to be the centre of attention. But this is quite extreme, even for her. I suppose Meg going missing has meant that she has to push herself forward, place herself at the centre of things. Contacting you is a way of getting at me.'

'Perhaps. She said she didn't know what you'd said to the police, that she didn't want to land you in it.'

He laughed. 'That's very considerate of her.'

Sam took hold of his arm. 'Perhaps you should tell me the truth, Mr O'Connor, before something happens that could easily be prevented. Lying isn't going to do anyone any good and it's not going to help me find your wife.'

'Do you never call anyone by their first name?'

'Not someone I'm wishing to maintain a professional relationship with.'

'Ah.' He swilled the remains of his red wine in the bottom of his glass. He looked up. 'Do you never lie?'

'This isn't about me.'

Sam waited but he said nothing.

O'Connor stared out into the garden. 'You think it's as easy as that, do you? Just tell the truth.'

'I don't assume anything's easy,' Sam said. 'I think sometimes there's a choice to be made. For example, you could choose to trust me with information you would rather I didn't know, knowing that I will treat that information with complete confidentiality. According to the waiter who served your wife on the night before she disappeared, she was visibly upset, crying. Do you know what that was about?'

O'Connor frowned. 'She seemed fine when I spoke to her in the morning.'

'Could she have found out about the affair?'

'I—'

'Was it true that you were having the affair?'

Before he could answer, the door to the balcony swung open behind them and Sam's mother took hold of her arm.

'Oh, there you are, Sam, darling. I'm sorry, John, but there's someone I'd like her to meet.'

'Mum, I'm just—'

'You can't spend the whole evening on the balcony. You have to mingle, darling.'

And before Sam could say anything, her mother had whisked her into the middle of the party and placed her in front of someone who looked as if he had even fewer social skills than Peter. Fortunately, Sam's hopeless conversational attempts with one of her stepfather's more socially maladjusted research students were brought to an abrupt halt by her mobile going off.

'Sorry,' she said, and smiling apologetically at her mother, who was glaring at her from across the room, she slipped out into the hall.

'Babe, babe, is that you?'

'Edie?'

'The Bill have just left.'

'Police?'

'Yeah, yeah, it's what I'm saying – the Bill.'

'About the tobacco?'

'What, love?'

'The cigarettes, Edie. Was it Customs and Excise?'

Edie laughed. 'No, love, they wasn't here for me. It was you they was looking for.'

'Sorry?'

'They came for you, banging on the door. Rang on my bell to ask questions.'

'The police, looking for me?'

'Yes, babes, that's what I'm saying. Thought it was for me at first, but then why would they bother with a small-timer – don't make sense.'

Sam felt thoroughly confused. 'Let me get this straight, Edie; the police came to my flat, looking for me.'

'Yes, love.'

'Did they say why?'

''Course not. Said they wanted some help with their enquiries, usual shit.'

'Did you let them in?'

'No love. Told 'em you wouldn't let anyone have your keys. Made out I didn't like you, that you were a snooty, standoffish sort.'

Sam laughed. This was probably a fairly accurate description of what Edie actually did think of her. 'Thanks, Edie.'

'Big bastard leaned on my filing cabinet, you know, the one I got from downstairs. Didn't know what was in it, mind.' Edie laughed loudly. 'This takes me back to when Jack went AWOL and the MPs came calling. We stuffed him in a trunk that time and sat the kiddies on it while they went round and round.'

The front-door bell went and Sam started backing towards the kitchen.

'Edie, I've got to go. Will you feed Frank for me?'

She didn't wait to hear the reply but snapped the phone shut and slid into the kitchen just in time to see Peter open the door.

'Samantha? Yes, she is here, Officer. Come in.'

Sam watched just long enough to see Peter usher two men into his study and then re-enter the room where the party was now in full swing. Then she ran past tables covered with silver trays containing canapés, quiches, sandwiches and vol-au-vents, and clattered down the metal staircase that descended into the garden. From there she took off, climbing through bushes and scrambling over fences towards the Banbury Road. Once out on the street, she set off swiftly towards the centre of town. She decided against getting the bus at Gloucester Green; that was the first pick-up point and if the police were looking out for her that's where they'd be. Instead she headed down Park's Road, turned left into Holywell and then followed the road round until it came out into The High. From there she jogged over Magdalen Bridge and past the roundabout until she reached the bus stop in St Clements. Once again she thanked god for the frequency of the Oxford to London coaches. As she was checking the timetable, her bus loomed into view and Sam stuck out her hand and climbed on board.

Sam stared at the headlamps of the oncoming traffic, running through in her mind why the police might want to speak to her. Perhaps it was something to do with Jenny Hughes? Andrew Hughes was locked up in Rampton, so that wasn't it. No, she thought, it must have something to do with O'Connor and Alice Knight. Maybe Meg had turned up dead. She thought of Alice Knight resplendent in crimson velvet, of Tony Ballinger and of whoever had turned into the staircase behind her as she was about to leave St Barnabas's. Rain lashed against the windows of the coach and behind her the snores of a fellow passenger rose and fell. Sam tried to remember exactly what O'Connor had said. She could remember what he hadn't said. He hadn't confirmed he was having an affair with Alice. If only she'd had a bit more time with him, but her mother had put paid to that. Mind you, at least it had given her an excuse to leave the party. Sam rested her head against the cool glass of the window and closed her eyes.

A couple of hours later Sam stood outside a tower block in Hammersmith and pressed the intercom of a flat on the twenty-sixth floor. She'd phoned Alan several times on the bus journey back to London but hadn't been able to get hold of him. At last an angry voice answered.

'What the fuck—'

'Alan, it's me. Let me in.'

'Sam, it's not really—'

'Please, Alan, just do it.'

After a brief ascent in a urine-smelling lift, Sam stood outside Alan's front door. She knocked. He opened the door with a towel round his waist.

'Look, Alan, I'm so sorry. I've been trying to get hold of you all night.'

'Sam, what the—'

'I know, it's just I need somewhere to stay for a while.'

Alan pulled her into the flat. 'The reason you have not been able to get hold of me,' he hissed, 'is because I have been shagging like crazy for hours.'

Sam smiled. 'God, I'm sorry. But I'll be no trouble.'

'What the hell's happened? Why can't you go home?'

'The police came calling.'

'Why?'

'I don't know. But according to Edie, they were round my place this evening asking questions.'

'You don't know why?'

Sam shook her head. 'I need a bit of a breather. I also need to talk to O'Connor before I talk to the police.'

'Talk about a passion-killer,' Alan said.

'Look, just go back to what you were doing and I'll curl up on the sofa.'

Alan left and came back holding a sheet and a duvet. He threw them at her and retreated to his bedroom. Sam kicked off her shoes, curled up on the sofa and turned off the lights. Alan's red and purple lava lamp undulated in the darkness. She watched it until she fell asleep.

CHAPTER ELEVEN

Sam lay on the sofa pretending to sleep and allowing Alan to say goodbye to his lover without being observed. The front door banged shut and Alan walked into the room and kicked the back of the sofa.

'Rise and shine,' he shouted.

Sam rolled over on to her back and groaned. Her body felt stiff and in need of a bath.

'Sleeping on a leather sofa is not to be recommended; it squeaked like a piglet every time I turned over.'

'Piglet doesn't recommend you either.'

'God, you look unbearably pleased with yourself. Why doesn't sex work that way with me?'

'Because you overcomplicate it all.'

'No shit, Sherlock.'

'Coffee?'

'Now you're talking sense.'

Sam stood up and walked to the window. Alan's flat was on the twenty-sixth floor. The sun was rising over London and down below, traffic was nose-to-tail on the Hammersmith fly-over. Alan handed her a mug that was decorated with rabbits in a number of different sexual positions.

'So,' Sam said after she'd looked at all the different combinations, 'which of these did you do last night?'

Alan had opened his mouth to reply when her mobile went off.

'Sam?' It was Mark.

'Oh, hi.'

'Don't "Oh hi" me. Where the hell did you disappear to last night?'

'Needed a bit of a breathing space. Sorry, but I really had to go.'

'I presume you know what's happened?'

'All I know is the police turned up at my place in London looking for me, and Edie phoned to warn me. Then the police turned up at the party and I decided I should get out of there.'

'Alice Knight's been murdered.'

'Oh my God.' Sam stood up and walked out on to Alan's balcony and looked down at the traffic. She shivered violently.

'And according to the police, you were one of the last people to see her alive.'

'I see. Where was she found?'

'In her rooms in college.'

'And how was she murdered?'

'They weren't going to tell us that, were they?'

Sam didn't know what to say. She thought of the man going up the stairs to Alice Knight's rooms after she'd left.

'The police were extremely pissed off that you'd done a runner and frankly so were Mum and Dad.'

'He's not my dad,' Sam said.

'Give it a rest, Sam. I can call him what I bloody well like.'

'How can you call that stick insect "Dad"?'

'Because he was there, Sam. He wasn't off getting killed and leaving his family in the shit. That's why. He's the only real dad we ever had. The other one exists purely between your two ears. He's a fantasy.'

Sam decided a diplomatic silence was her best option.

'You still there?' Mark snapped.

'Yup.'

'They kept grilling us about where you were. As far as we

137

knew, you were at the party. You could have said something before you went.'

'I'm sorry but I didn't have time. And if I'd said something, it would have made it much more difficult for you. As it was you didn't have to lie.'

'No, we just looked like complete fucking idiots.'

'I'm sorry if I ruined the party.'

'Don't flatter yourself. The party was just fine without you. Takes more than an invasion of policemen to ruin a cast party. Incidentally, Phil was there.'

Sam grimaced. 'Oh, shit.'

'He wasn't that happy either.'

'No.'

'You need to get in touch with them.'

'I can't, not yet. I have to speak to O'Connor. I was just about to, when Mum whisked me off the balcony and told me I had to talk to some research nerd of Peter's.'

'Mum's fault again – well, that's useful. When are you going to start taking responsibility for your own fuck-ups?'

Sam considered smashing the fucking bunnies mug against the wall but then remembered it wasn't hers to smash.

'You're a suspect, Sam. They need to cross you off their list. They want to know what you were talking to her about.'

'Obviously. It's just I don't want to tell them, yet. I can't.'

Mark sighed. 'You were never any good at keeping out of trouble, so I don't know why I'm wasting my breath.'

'Look, Mark, thanks for phoning. I will contact the police but I need to talk to O'Connor first, otherwise I may land him in the shit. And he is my client.'

'Fine, well, talk to him then and you'll get the police off our back.'

'Just tell them I haven't been in contact. You've no idea where I am.'

'Yeah, I think I can just about manage that.'

Sam winced as the phone went dead. She looked up at Alan. 'That's one pissed-off brother.'

Alan refilled her cup. 'Want to tell me what's been happening?'

So she told him.

'The trouble is my bloody mother whisked me away from O'Connor just before he could confirm or deny. I can't go to the police and tell them what Alice said without landing O'Connor in it. He lied in a police interview. Said there was no reason for his wife to go missing and that he wasn't having an affair. Then Alice Knight turns up saying they were and that she feels under threat. If I tell the police, at worst it makes O'Connor prime suspect in his own wife's disappearance and Alice's murder. At best he's exposed as a liar.'

'But isn't he the prime suspect anyway?' Alan said.

'I need to know what he has to say for himself before I talk to the police. He is my client. I can't just hang him out to dry.'

'But what about you? You're one of the last people to see her alive. You've got information relevant to a murder enquiry. I mean, she told you she felt under threat and if you don't come forward, the longer you're out there the more they'll suspect you.'

'Tough,' Sam said.

'Will the police link O'Connor to Alice Knight?'

'Eventually, yes. There must be phone calls between them. But not at first. If they get me, they'll get that link. At the moment there's nothing to tie the two together.'

'Unless Knight had told someone else about the affair.'

'True. And then they'll get to O'Connor eventually anyway.'

'Was Knight married?'

Sam frowned. 'Yes, to Tony Ballinger. He was there – I saw him in the quad, dressed up for the gaudy.'

'The what?'

'Gaudy – Oxford's name for a big feast. Usually involves graduates of the college.'

'You'd better try to get hold of O'Connor,' Alan said.

Sam picked up her mobile and dialled. No response and after a few rings the answerphone clicked on. Sam didn't want to leave a message. She tried his mobile and again got an answering service. This time she did leave him a message to call her urgently.

'So,' Alan said when she'd finished. 'Want to know what I found out while you were haring round Oxford?'

Sam threw her mobile in her bag and stretched. 'OK.'

Alan tossed a piece of paper on to the table in front of her. 'Name and address of a certain bike owner.'

Sam smiled. 'Gary came up with the goods, then?'

'In remembrance of good times past.'

'You old rascal.'

Alan smiled broadly. 'Just spare me the helmet and truncheon jokes.'

'It's too early in the morning for that.' She picked up the piece of paper, read the address and groaned. 'I bet it's not a part of Hoxton that Damien Hirst and Tracy Emin frequent.'

'Shall we go visit? There's not much you can do until you speak to O'Connor.'

'Sure,' Sam replied. 'Why not?'

Alan and Sam stood in Hoxton Street looking up at a flat above a bargain shop that was selling everything from lava lamps to loo rolls, from spider plants to spanners. It was raining. Even in bright sunshine Hoxton Street would have looked miserable; in the rain it made suicide seem an attractive option.

'I like that one,' Alan said, pointing at a purple and red lava lamp.

'Of course you do, you've got one in your living room.'

The lamps looked as if they'd only just been switched on. The wax was sluggish and barely moving inside the glass. Sam knew the feeling. The bell to the flat was in a doorway next to the shop front, which was filled with old fish and chip papers and smelled strongly of piss. Sam wrinkled her nose and rang it.

A window was pushed up and Sam and Alan stepped backwards into the street and looked up as a young woman with a pale face and lank black hair poked her head out.

'Stop leaning on the fucking bell,' she hissed. 'I've only just got her down.'

'We're looking for Bernie,' Sam said.

'So?'

'Does he live here?'

'Who're you? Old Bill? Council? What's he done now?'

'Can we come in?' Sam asked.

'No. Last time I did that they took the telly.'

'He's been left money in a will,' Sam said. 'We've been asked by a solicitor to trace the beneficiaries.'

The young woman laughed. 'Fucking liar. Left money in a will? I don't think so, love, not Bernie. Must have the wrong bloke.'

She began to pull down the window. The thin wail of a baby's cry could be heard somewhere in the flat.

'Now look what you bloody gone and done.'

'Any idea where we might find him?' Sam asked.

The woman seemed to relent. 'He didn't come in last night. Probably slept over at Joe's. He'll be down the Nelson, for the hair of the dog. If you find him, tell him to come home.' She slammed the window shut and ducked her head under the dirty white blind, which banged down flat against the glass.

'We passed it as we walked up,' Alan said, and they turned and made their way back along the litter-strewn street, past puddles of oily water and gutters filled with detritus from the fruit and veg stores lining the street.

Sam paused on the threshold of the pub. It reminded her of some of the rougher places she'd worked undercover in; pubs where all sorts of things had been going on – counterfeit money being passed through the tills and drugs being sold in the loos. The only smart thing about this pub was Lord Nelson himself as depicted on the newly painted sign.

It took time for their eyes to adjust to the dinginess of the interior; then they saw there were only a handful of people leaning on the bar. All of them turned and watched as Alan and Sam walked towards them.

Sam nodded at the barman. 'All right?'

The barman didn't say anything. Sam turned to Alan. 'What'll you have?'

'Pint of Guinness,' Alan said in his most macho voice.

Sam couldn't help smiling. It was hardly his drink of choice.

'Two of those please,' she said. As the barman picked up a glass and began to pour their drinks, Sam looked round the pub. The man they wanted wasn't there. Not yet anyway.

The knuckles of the hands that placed the pints in front of Sam proclaimed 'love' and 'hate' in blue tattooed letters. They took their drinks and sat down at a table near the door.

'Not here yet?' Alan asked quietly.

'No, although the man who owns the bike and the man who uses it could be different.'

'Do you think you'll recognize him?'

Sam shrugged. 'When he got off the scaffolding he wasn't wearing a helmet and I got a pretty good look at him. His bike was parked right outside my flat and under a streetlight. I should know him.'

Alan put the glass to his lips and wrinkled his nose. 'The things I do for you. And I haven't had much sleep.'

'Don't drink it if you don't want to. It's too early for me, anyway.'

The pints stood untouched in front of them.

The door opened and a man of medium height wearing a dark brown leather jacket, jeans and trainers came in. Police, Sam thought, as soon as she saw him. He glanced at Sam and Alan, got himself a pint and sat down opposite them, on the other side of the door. He took a newspaper out of his jacket, folded it twice and then took out a pen. His pint also stood untouched in front of him.

'Feels like *High Noon*,' Alan whispered.

' "Do not forsake me, oh my darling," ' Sam murmured.

'Of course not,' Alan replied.

Sam smiled. 'Who's Gary Cooper?'

'Bloke opposite, I reckon. Seems the patient type.'

The man looked up at them and then returned his gaze to the paper.

'What do we do if this bloke doesn't show?' Alan asked.

'Ask at the bar?'

'You're joking, aren't you?'

'In judo you can get penalized for passivity. You can lose a match if you don't attack.'

Alan rolled his eyes. 'Ask that question of this lot and all you'll get is "love" on your nose and "hate" in your solar plexus.'

Sam laughed.

'God, if we stay here much longer I'm going to have to drink this out of sheer bloody boredom.' Alan picked up his glass and raised it reluctantly to his mouth. He had just dipped his upper lip in the head of the pint when a man came into the pub and walked over to the bar. Alan glanced at Sam and she nodded and stood up. The man had his back to them.

'Bernie?' Sam said, and the man turned round.

'Who wants to—?' But then he caught sight of Sam. He grabbed a pint glass, threw the contents at Alan and the glass at Sam, and bolted for the door. Alan swore, shook the beer out of his eyes, and set off after him. Sam followed.

The rain was coming down in sheets now. All three of them ran straight down the middle of the road, jumping over boxes of fruit and veg and barging pedestrians out of the way. The man reached the bottom of Hoxton Street and turned right into Hoxton Square. Alan was ahead – Sam a few paces behind. They had just entered the square, when Sam heard footsteps running behind her and felt two arms close around her, pinning her own arms to her sides. She went limp and then feeling the grip relaxing, thrust out her arms, jabbed her elbow hard into his ribs and threw him, over her right hip, hard on to the pavement. She jumped over the body and set off again in pursuit of Alan. She was horrified to see him running back towards her.

'Are you all right?' he said, looking over her shoulder to where the man she had just thrown was picking himself up off the pavement and beginning to run slowly out of the square. But Sam had only one thing on her mind; finding the man who had run from the pub.

'Fine. I'm fine.' She pushed Alan out of the way and continued running.

But it was too late. As they ran into Hoxton Market, there was no sign of the man they'd been chasing, and three routes he could have taken out of there. Sam stopped and bent over trying to catch her breath.

'Fuck,' she said, gasping. 'We lost him.' The rain dripped down the back of her neck. They were both soaked to the skin. 'Why the hell did you do that?' she snapped.

'I saw that bloke grab you.'

'For God's sake, Alan, you know I'm perfectly capable of looking after myself. Give me some credit.'

'Sorry, I thought—'

'No,' Sam said. 'You didn't think. It's just that same old macho shit. Protect the woman. It's the argument they always use to stop women from fighting in the armed forces. That men will protect women fighting at their side and put the entire operation at risk.'

Alan blushed.

'And now we've bloody lost him. Just so you get to play St George and rescue the fucking damsel in distress.'

'Turns out the *fucking* damsel's the *fucking* dragon,' Alan shouted. 'And by the way, if you'd been a bloke, I'd have done the same.'

'No, you wouldn't.'

'Yes, Sam, I would.'

They stared at each other, breathing heavily. Sam looked away first.

Alan coughed and spat into the street. 'Who the hell was that who grabbed you, anyway?'

Sam ducked under a canopy, which stretched out over the front of a restaurant.

'No idea, assumed it was someone from the pub.'

'Know who it looked like?'

Sam wheezed in the negative.

'Looked like the bloke sitting opposite us doing the crossword.'

'Gary Cooper?'

'Yes.'

'Well, he'll have some pretty sore ribs tonight,' Sam said. 'That's for sure.'

Sam had a snapshot in her head of the man hitting the pavement. He hadn't landed like a sack of potatoes; he'd known how to break his fall. In fact, now she came to think of it, he'd landed like an expert.

CHAPTER TWELVE

That evening Alan went out for a drink, leaving Sam in no doubt that he was unlikely to be coming back to the flat later that night. He was still pissed off with her and Sam couldn't decide whether he was justified or not. She stood on his balcony, holding a bottle of beer and looking down at the traffic. If I lived here, she thought, that's probably all I'd do – stand here watching cars crawl from one place to another. The sight of it was soothing as was the thought that she wasn't down there, trapped in all that aggravation. Just like Oxford. There was nowhere these days you could go to escape traffic jams.

Sam had a car but rarely used it in London. Parking was a nightmare and she always ended up getting a ticket, however careful she was. She had at one time thought of ditching it for a motorbike but you couldn't undertake overnight surveillance sitting on a bike; you'd freeze your arse off. You needed somewhere you could sit that gave protection from the elements. The trouble was public transport held its own nightmares. The buses couldn't get through streets clogged with roadworks and the Tube was underfunded and plagued by strikes. The city was gradually grinding to a halt.

Sam sighed. She wanted to be back in her own flat with Frank howling to be fed and Edie up to no good next door. She felt restless. O'Connor hadn't phoned and the events of the day had got her no closer to finding out what the hell was going on with those letters. She held the ice-cold bottle up to her cheek and breathed in deeply, coughing as the pollution surrounding the tower caught in her throat. Waiting had never been her forte. A wave of sadness washed over her. The first letter was so tender, the fox so brutal. No father would string up a fox outside his daughter's flat unless that father was mad or sick. There was no way this had anything to do with him. He was dead, as dead as he'd been since she was four years old and stood slipping on the artificial grass covering the side of his grave, looking down at his coffin. She had allowed hope to cloud her better judgement. But if he were dead, who would write such a letter? Perhaps it was better that she was away from her flat. After all, whoever was stalking her knew where she lived. No one knew she was here except Mark. The doorbell sliced through her thoughts like paper through a finger.

She walked into the hall and stared at the intercom phone, which linked the flat to the entrance downstairs. She waited. Perhaps it was someone ringing the wrong number. It happened all the time where she lived. The intercoms in the flats broke and people would push all the bells in turn, trying to find one that was working in order to gain access to the block. Perhaps it was someone for Alan. It rang again, longer and harder this time, as if the person was getting pissed off or more frantic. Sam didn't move. Fear and indecision fixed her to the spot. Then her mobile rang and she unfroze, walked into the living room and grabbed it off the sofa.

'Sam, you're there. Thank God. It's John.'

'Where have you been? I've been trying to get hold of you all day.'

'I know. I'm sorry, will you let me in?'

'Sorry?'

'I'm downstairs. It's me ringing the bell.'

'But how did you know—?'

'Mark told me where you were.'

'I see.'

'We need to talk. Will you let me in?'

'Hold on a minute.' Sam cut the line and phoned Alan. His messaging service clicked in. 'Alan, I've got O'Connor downstairs and I'm going to let him in. I just wanted you to know . . . Anyway, he may be here when you get back.' She'd said 'when', not 'if'. Alan had said he had no intention of coming back but if he picked up this message she hoped he'd change his mind. She walked over to the intercom and buzzed O'Connor up.

O'Connor dropped a black hold-all on the carpet of the living room and groaned as he straightened his back.

'Can I get you something to drink?' Sam asked.

'That'd be nice.' He pointed to the empty bottle of beer on the table. 'I've just dropped off the children with my sister for the weekend. I thought it'd be good for all of us to get out of Oxford for a bit.'

Sam walked into the kitchen, took a beer out of the fridge and walked back into the front room. She snapped the cap off the bottle and handed it to him. 'You know I've been trying to get hold of you all day?'

O'Connor grimaced. 'Sorry – I seem to be only able to focus on one thing at a time at the moment. I think it's the stress. I thought I'd get us to London and then when the children were settled, come and see you.' He slumped down on the sofa and ran his hand through his hair. 'God, I'm exhausted. How on earth are you supposed to live with it when someone goes missing? How do you handle that?'

Sam sat down in a chair opposite the sofa. 'As best you can, I dare say.'

He flicked the bottle of beer with his fingernail. 'I've been trying to steer clear of this. It's just too tempting at the moment. But just one can't do any harm, can it?'

Sam didn't reply. She was hardly going to lecture him on drink. He was the therapist.

'You know Alice Knight has been murdered?'

He nodded and looked down at the bottle he was holding.

'I need to know if what she told me was true.'

He rolled the bottle back and forth between his hands then placed it carefully on the glass table in front of him and wiped his hands on his trousers.

'Mr O'Connor?'

He cleared his throat and looked up. 'Sorry?'

'Were you having an affair?'

'Oh yes, we were.'

Sam groaned in exasperation. 'And you didn't think that was a reason for your wife to go missing? She finds out about the affair and she disappears? You didn't think that was an important thing to tell me or the police?'

'But the boys, I can't believe she would just abandon them.'

'She hardly abandoned them. They were at school. They weren't going anywhere. She knew they were safe.'

He shook his head. 'All the same, I just can't—'

Sam cut across him. 'Did she know?'

'I hadn't told her.'

'Had Alice?'

O'Connor frowned. 'But why should she?'

'To break up your marriage. To force you to leave your wife. I don't know ... because you agreed she would.'

'Alice knew how important the boys were to me. She wouldn't have. I can't believe it of her. I never told her I was going to leave Meg and she hadn't asked me to either. Neither of us knew what it was anyway, it was complicated by the past.'

'Why did you lie to the police?'

'I didn't think it was any of their business. And I didn't want to land Alice in it. That way I kept her out of it. She didn't want the embarrassment of it.'

'Why would it be embarrassing? Surely it's more embarrassing for you than her?'

'She was married as well. She was a very ambitious woman. She was very conscious of appearances.'

'Oh, I see.' Sam couldn't quite keep the sarcasm out of her voice.

O'Connor got up wearily and walked over to the window. He rested his forehead against the glass. 'Amazing view.'

'She told me she had an open relationship.'

'Yes, I believe Alice had always been open about her affairs. She liked to discuss the details of such things.'

'So you weren't protecting Alice by not saying if Tony already knew.'

'If Meg turned up I didn't want her knowing about Alice. I lied at the beginning because I thought she'd come back and there'd be some perfectly logical explanation for her absence. Then the longer it went on – I didn't want to admit I lied. I knew the police suspected me. If they knew I'd lied I thought that would increase their suspicions.'

'When Alice spoke to me she said she was feeling under threat. Had she told you that?'

'I hadn't had much contact with her since Meg went missing. I was too confused and needed to be there for the boys. I couldn't . . .' He paused. 'I didn't have the energy.'

'Who do you think she might have been feeling threatened by?'

O'Connor turned away from the view and leaned against the glass door that led out on to the balcony. 'I honestly don't know. Perhaps she wanted to force me back into contact with her. By getting in touch with you. By saying she was frightened.'

'But she was killed, so presumably she was right to be frightened.'

O'Connor didn't reply. He sighed and walked back to the sofa and sat down.

Sam tried again. 'So, you have no idea who she might have felt threatened by?'

'No, I haven't.'

'Meg, perhaps.'

O'Connor's gaze snapped on to Sam. 'You think she's still alive?'

Sam shrugged. 'I don't know, but if she is she would have a motive, wouldn't she?'

He nodded.

'*You* hadn't threatened her in any way?'

'Me?' O'Connor laughed. 'What with?'

Sam had a sudden craving for a cigarette. She walked over to where her denim jacket was slung over the back of the sofa and patted its pockets. She usually carried a packet, just in case. She found one but couldn't find a lighter, shook a cigarette out of the packet and said, 'I'll see if he's got a light in the kitchen.' But in the kitchen there was no sign of matches. Next door she heard the zip of the hold-all being pulled. When she turned round O'Connor was standing in the doorway and the kitchen seemed to have shrunk in size. She picked up the bottle opener.

'Another beer?' she asked.

'Sure.'

She opened the fridge, took out two bottles and gestured towards the living room. 'Shall we go back?'

O'Connor nodded and turned round, and Sam, breathing a sigh of relief, followed him. She put one bottle on the table in front of him and one next to her chair and sat down.

'No luck,' she said, holding up the cigarette.

'Oh, sorry,' he said. 'That's why I came into the kitchen.' And he held out a yellow plastic lighter. 'Do you mind if I join you?'

Sam pointed to the packet lying on the table. 'Help yourself.'

He took out a cigarette, lit it and handed the lighter to Sam. They smoked in silence for a few moments. It was O'Connor who spoke first.

'How did you handle your father going missing?'

'I was four and so far as I know, he didn't go missing. He was reported as dead.'

'What about other people you've worked for?'

'Well, I think the tendency is to veer between "they must be dead" and "of course they're alive". The knack seems to be occupying both possibilities at once. Like balancing on a child's seesaw. Keeping level is the hardest thing to do. Because the truth is you just don't know. You don't know until they walk through your front door or until they turn up dead. Sometimes neither of those things happens and people just have to come to terms with the fact they'll never know.'

'But surely the longer it goes on the more likely it is they're never coming back.'

'But you still don't know. That's the truth. You don't know if they're alive or dead. It's still the same thing. You don't have a body to mourn or bury.'

'I'm swinging about all over the place.'

Sam nodded. 'I'm not surprised.' She looked appreciatively at the glowing red end of her cigarette. 'How long had your affair with Alice Knight been going on?'

'Couple of months. She'd moved to Oxford to set up a new office here and we bumped into each other. There were unresolved issues from our past, which complicated matters.' O'Connor leaned forwards and stubbed out his cigarette. 'I was in love with her at college. She was really the first person I'd ever fallen in love with. You know that whole "I will never be happy, my life will not be complete if I don't have this person" fantasy. But she was having an affair with Tony, although I didn't know it at the time. So at college it never moved beyond the platonic. It was a tortured mess – or rather I was. But then when I saw her again it was still there, as strong as ever – the attraction. I was always incredibly turned on by her. It would be difficult not to be. So then there was this chance to see if ... well, to put the fantasy to the test.'

'And did it match up?'

O'Connor was staring into the middle distance. 'I'm sorry, what did you say?'

'The reality, did it live up to—?'

'Oh, God, yes. That was the trouble. The sex lived up to every bit of my fantasy. More than I could possibly have hoped for. That's what made it so difficult. That's why the affair was continuing. I couldn't get enough of her. I mean, I was trying to separate but the truth is I was addicted to her, to how she made me feel when I was with her, to the sex we were having.'

Men, Sam thought.

O'Connor scanned her face. 'You probably think I'm one sad fucker.'

'Of course not,' Sam lied.

He smiled. 'Some of my clients are better liars.'

Sam ignored him. 'Who do you think killed her?'

He shrugged, picked up the bottle of beer and raised it to his mouth.

'The police haven't contacted you?'

'No.'

'They almost certainly will. They'll trace you to her in some way. You realize I'm going to have to tell them?'

'But—'

'I was apparently one of the last people to see her alive and I have to tell them what she told me, apart from anything else, to remove myself from suspicion. It means they'll tie you to her and realize that you lied to them. I think it would be best if we went in together and talked to them.'

'But that will put me under suspicion as well.'

'You'll just have to tell them what you told me. That you thought Meg would come back and you didn't want her knowing about Alice. That you didn't want to land Alice in it. The police will get to you anyway. It would be much better if you offered the information voluntarily.'

O'Connor rested his forehead in the palm of his right hand. 'I'm so tired at the moment I just can't think straight. I can't decide what the best thing is to do.' He looked up suddenly. 'You're not going to jack in the case, are you? You're the only . . .' He stopped. When he resumed, he sounded as if someone had him by the throat. 'You must help me find out what's happened to Meg.'

'If the police tie Alice Knight's murder to your wife's disappearance then you'll become part of the murder enquiry. I'd understand if you didn't want me involved any more.'

'No, no, I do. I trust you.'

'Well then,' Sam said.

'I was wondering if I could lie down for a few minutes. I haven't been sleeping much and I keep getting these waves of exhaustion.'

'Sure, there's a room through there on the right you can use.'

'Thanks.' He picked up his bag. 'I think my head will be clearer once I've slept.'

A couple of hours later, Sam jolted awake to find a menacing-looking Alan standing over her. She swung her legs off the sofa and groaned. Alan was waving his hand in front of his nose and holding the saucer with the fag ends in his hand. He didn't say anything, merely raised his eyebrows.

'Sorry,' Sam said. 'I got a craving.'

'Well, keep your cravings to your own home,' Alan snapped. He walked over and opened the door to the balcony. 'Is he still here?'

Sam nodded. 'He's lying down next door.'

Alan took the saucer into the kitchen and then quietly closed the door of the living room. 'Are you completely mad? I couldn't believe it when I picked up your message.'

Sam shrugged. 'I needed to talk to him. It was late. That's why

I left a message on your phone. I thought you'd come back if you picked it up.'

'Bit of a big if – especially after our conversation in Hoxton.'

'But you came, didn't you?'

'You're an idiot. No way you should have seen him by yourself. His wife disappears and his mistress turns up dead. Who's the common link? And you know about the affair. You had the conversation with Alice and you haven't told the police yet.'

'All right, but he *is* my client. It's not your life that's been put on hold. You're not the one the police are looking for. You're not the one who can't go home and feed her cat. I needed to talk to him.'

'Your trouble is you have too strong a sense of decency for your own good. I'd have shopped him to the police.'

'No, you wouldn't. Anyway he's an old friend of Mark's. The job came through him. He saved him once when he tried to commit suicide. I can't imagine he'd kill me. And I'm not stupid; I kept my eye on him. I'm perfectly capable of looking after myself.'

Alan shook his head in exasperation. 'For God's sake, Sam, I'm not saying you're not, it's just an unnecessary risk . . .'

The door opened and O'Connor appeared, wiping his glasses on his shirt.

'Sorry,' Sam said. 'Did we wake you?'

'No, I don't think so.' He tugged at his hair, trying to flatten it, and looked back and forth between Sam and Alan. 'I'm sorry, I hope I'm not disturbing—'

'No, no,' Alan said. 'It's fine.'

O'Connor slumped on the sofa next to Sam. 'These days I end up feeling worse when I wake up than before I go to sleep. I keep having nightmares. Not surprising really.' He smiled fleetingly. 'I keep having a nightmare that Meg is out there and has killed Alice. I see her standing over the body but then the body changes. It's Meg and then it's Alice and then I look down and see I'm holding a knife. I've killed them both and then I turn and see Bill and Ian and begin to walk towards them and they start to run . . . my own children frightened of me, thinking I'm going to cut their throats . . .'

He stood up abruptly and walked over to the window. His back was to both of them. Sam and Alan glanced at each other but neither moved. Sam made a shooing motion with her hand to suggest Alan go over to him but Alan just folded his arms and stared at her. They waited.

Sam sighed. Was O'Connor going to cry like he had at the press conference? She had such a strong physical reaction to men crying that it was all she could manage to just stay in the same room. She could feel it now, stark terror and an agonizing tearing in her stomach and her chest. She looked at Alan again and put her hands together in a praying gesture but he shook his head and pointed at her. However much she tried to maintain her distance and be professional there always came a point in each case where the boundaries blurred, where there seemed to be no choice but to cross the line. People in pain: that was always what forced her to take that step. It wasn't one she took at all willingly. O'Connor brought his hand up to his face. Here we go, she thought. She couldn't just leave him. She forced herself to her feet and walked over to where he was standing. She placed her hand on his back. He kept his face turned away from her. She stood there, waiting for him to regain his composure. His shirt was drenched in sweat and she could feel his back burning through the material of his shirt. *Enough warmth for two*, Mark had said. Maybe more than two. As the thought entered Sam's head, she stepped abruptly away from him.

'Can we get you some water?' she asked rather brusquely.

He nodded. Alan went into the kitchen and came back with a glass of water, which he handed to O'Connor.

O'Connor turned round and drank from the glass. 'I'm

frightened. That's partly why I brought the children up to London. I felt frightened to leave them in Oxford.'

Sam frowned. 'Has anything happened?'

'Nothing specific. It's difficult because I've been under so much stress. I could be imagining things. But I don't feel safe in Park Town any more. Even before what happened to Alice.' He drained the glass of water. 'I feel like I've entered some sort of hell. When I'm asleep I'm having nightmares and when I'm awake I'm living one. There's no escape.'

Sam placed the palm of her right hand against her left. She must have been imagining it, but her hand was still burning, as if she could still feel the heat of his body, as if she'd put her hand on an electric plate, not a man's back.

'Are you getting any help?' she asked.

'Sorry?'

'Don't you need to be under some sort of supervision if you're a practising therapist?'

O'Connor looked at her in bewilderment. 'I didn't think you believed in therapy.'

She shrugged. 'But if you do then surely it's because you have an experience of it helping to make a difference. And if that's the case, aren't the present circumstances exactly the time to use it?'

'It's been difficult recently because of the children. I've let my appointments lapse. But you're right, I should sort that out.'

Alan yawned. 'You'd best spend the night here. You can have the couch or the spare room.'

'I'll take the couch,' Sam said.

O'Connor smiled. 'It's all come a long way since Freud, you know.'

'It couldn't come far enough, so far as I'm concerned,' Sam replied.

'I'm knackered,' Alan said. 'I'm off to bed.'

Sam rolled over and looked at the clock on the front of the video.

It was three o'clock. She got up and walked through to Alan's spare room and pushed open the door. O'Connor was muttering in his sleep – just noises, no words – horrible, strangled sounds. She turned on the light and he sat upright, squinting at her.

'Where?'

'You're at Alan's. You were shouting in your sleep.'

'Sorry.'

'Is there anything I can do for you?'

O'Connor held out his hand to her. She folded her arms and remained standing in the doorway. The boundaries might have temporarily blurred earlier but now they were firmly back in place. His hand dropped to the bed.

'I'm so grateful for your support. I can't tell you what it means to me.'

'You haven't seen the bill yet,' Sam said.

He smiled. 'Do you always do that?'

Sam raised her eyebrows.

'Reject people's acknowledgement.'

Fucking therapists, Sam thought. 'Not always,' she said. 'It depends whether I think it's deserved or not.'

O'Connor turned on to his side and rested his head in his hand. 'And you don't think it is?'

Sam unfolded her arms and then, not sure what to do with them, decided the best thing to do was to fold them back up again as tightly as possible.

'I know how hard you find it to reach out to people who are upset, Sam.'

'No, you don't,' Sam said. 'You've absolutely no idea.'

'Thank you, anyway.' He wasn't wearing his glasses and his gaze was particularly direct. Sam wished he'd put them back on. She wanted as many barriers between them as possible.

'You realize I have to go to the police tomorrow?'

'Yes, yes. I see that you're in an impossible situation.'

'Do you have an alibi?'

He stared at her blankly. 'Sorry?'

'They'll want to know where you were when Alice was murdered. I left her at about seven-fifteen. Can anyone confirm what you were doing between that time and when you arrived at the party?'

'I had to go out to a client.'

'I didn't know you did house calls.'

'It was an exceptional case. I'd been treating a woman for post-natal depression. Her child died and there was the suggestion that she had killed it. It can happen in severe cases but it hadn't in this one, I'm glad to say. But she had tried to kill herself and been committed to the Warneford in Headington. I went up to the hospital to see her and brief the doctors who were treating her.'

'And there would be people who can confirm that?'

'Yes, the psychiatrist, Dr Rowe and her husband James Arnott.'

'And then you came to the party?'

'Yes. Will they arrest me?'

'It depends whether your alibi checks out.'

O'Connor sat up in the bed. 'How could I have killed her, Sam? I'd been in love with her since college.'

'It's not me you need to convince. I'm just saying you need to be clear in your own mind before you see the police.' She turned to leave the room. 'Shall I turn out the light?' He nodded. She left him staring into the dark, hugging his knees.

Back in the front room Sam phoned Phil. His answerphone clicked on and Sam groaned. 'Phil,' she said. 'It's me. Pick up if you're there.'

She heard Phil fumbling for the receiver and then a sleep-blurred voice said. 'For Christ's sake, Sam, where the hell are you?'

'Look, don't get arsy. I'm phoning to say I'm coming in with O'Connor tomorrow.'

'What the hell do you think you're playing at? You were one of the last people to see her alive.'

'Doesn't mean I murdered her.'

'I'm not saying that but you're doing yourself no favours by playing silly buggers. You're interfering with a murder enquiry. This isn't a game.'

'I know that, Phil. That's why I'm telling you I'm coming in with O'Connor tomorrow.'

'Sam, wait.'

She had been about to put down the phone but the concern in his voice stopped her.

'You know how she was killed?'

'No.'

'She was strangled.'

'Well, women hardly ever strangle.'

'But you can see why they're eager to talk to you?'

'So, I'm capable of strangling someone. So are you.'

'But I wasn't in Alice Knight's rooms just before it happened. What were you doing there anyway?'

'It was to do with the O'Connor investigation.'

'And what's it got to do with him?'

'I'll see you tomorrow, Phil.'

'Sam?' There was the same urgency in his voice. 'This O'Connor, be very, very careful.'

'He hired me to find his wife, Phil.'

'I know but it could be a cover. Makes him look like the devoted husband when in fact . . .'

'Come off it. You hire an investigator to cover the fact you've got rid of your wife? Don't you think that's a bit risky? I might actually find her.'

'Maybe he doesn't rate you.'

'Oh, fuck off, Phil.'

'No, hold on. If he withholds relevant bits of information, he can keep you going round and round in circles. He's a shrink, he knows how to fuck with people's heads, doesn't he?'

'His job is to straighten out people's heads.'

'Yes, but if he can do one, can't he do the other? Don't let him get too close. That's all I'm saying. Is there any other weird stuff going on?'

Sam thought of the fox and the letters. Phil had been there; he must have heard the fox.

'No,' she said.

'Well, watch out, Sam, that's all I'm saying.'

Sam put down the phone. She looked behind her and saw O'Connor standing in the doorway. 'God, you made me jump.'

'Sorry – I wanted a glass of water.' He nodded towards the kitchen. She had no idea how long he'd been standing there.

'I was telling the police we'd be in tomorrow.'

O'Connor shook his head. 'God, I must be losing my touch. I could have sworn you were talking to a lover.'

CHAPTER THIRTEEN

The following morning Sam and O'Connor picked up Ian and Bill and drove back to Oxford. After they'd dropped the children off at O'Connor's neighbours, they drove to the police station.

O'Connor hesitated on the pavement outside. 'Any advice?'

'Stick to your story. Be polite and helpful.'

'I can't imagine you doing that.'

'Giving advice and taking it are two entirely separate things,' Sam said. She looked up at the cloudless bright blue sky. This was no day to spend in a police station. She blew out her cheeks. 'Might as well get it over with.' She led the way up the wheelchair ramp to the entrance.

Sam stood in front of the desk sergeant, waiting for him to raise his eyes from his paperwork. When he didn't, she said, 'Sam Falconer and John O'Connor – it's about the murder of Alice Knight.'

That got his attention. It wasn't long before Phil and another police officer, who introduced himself as Detective Sergeant Rowland, appeared and she and O'Connor were taken off to separate interview rooms.

'Tell me again,' DS Rowland said.

Sam sighed and shifted in the blue plastic moulded chair, and ran a mantra that she had been running with increasing desperation for the last couple of hours: *Always be polite to the police. Losing your temper won't help*. Her eyeballs were aching from the flickering strip lighting above their heads, and the whirr of the tape recorder on the metal table in front of her was getting on her nerves. She pressed her eyes with her fingers and started again.

'I told you. Alice Knight asked me to meet her. You can check that with my brother Mark. He gave me her number and asked me to ring her. She told me she was having an affair with Mr O'Connor. She said that she felt under threat. She didn't want to go to the police because she wasn't sure what O'Connor had told you and she didn't want to create difficulties for him. Since his wife had disappeared he wasn't answering her calls. She told me her car had been broken into and that some of her post had been taken, also she had been receiving phone calls in which someone phoned, didn't say anything and then hung up. I told her I wasn't going to do anything until I'd talked to O'Connor but I strongly advised her to go to the police.'

'And what time did you leave?'

'Like I said – seven-fifteen. I then walked to the Cranmer Rooms and arrived there late, so sometime after seven-thirty. You can check with the person who was taking tickets.'

'And no one saw you?'

'I've told you. Someone went up the stairs behind me as I left but I didn't see his face. He was wearing a dinner jacket. Also, the porter may have seen me leave. He certainly saw me arrive.'

'There were approximately one hundred men in dinner jackets in the college that evening for the gaudy.'

'Well, I can't help that. After I'd left the college I walked fast and didn't stop to do anything or talk to anyone.'

'You saw absolutely no one?'

Sam shook her head.

'Are you in love with him?'

Sam was bewildered. 'Who?'

'O'Connor – are you protecting him?'

Sam laughed out loud. 'He's a client. I have a purely professional relationship with him.'

'He's a good-looking man.'

'Your type, is he?' Sam said, and immediately regretted it. She set the mantra running in her head with a slight variation this time: *Always be polite to the police. Always be polite to the police. Do not accuse them of being homosexuals.* 'Sorry,' she said. 'But he doesn't do anything for me.'

DS Rowland interlaced eight stubby fingers, bearing nails bitten to the quick and placed them carefully on the table. 'Why didn't you come straight to the police?'

'As I said, I needed to check out the facts with my client. I didn't know if Alice Knight was telling the truth. I suggested she go to the police. She obviously didn't have time.'

'Why did you run away?'

'That's your interpretation of what I did.'

'And what's yours?'

'I was buying myself time to talk to my client. I needed to know O'Connor's side of the story. I'd like to point out that as soon as I had done that I told him to come here and speak to you and came myself.'

'Think you're clever, do you?'

Sam sighed. 'I know I'm not. I've spent too much time around very clever people to labour under that particular illusion.'

He stared at her and Sam stared back.

A man came into the room and whispered in Rowland's ear; he got up and left the room.

'Bundle of laughs, isn't he?' Sam said to the uniformed officer left sitting with her.

He didn't say anything, just sat back in his chair and folded his arms. Sam pulled a packet of cigarettes from her denim jacket and shook one out of the packet. Then remembered she didn't have a lighter.

'Got a light?' she asked.

He shook his head slowly backwards and forwards. 'No smoking,' he said.

'Right, better try to find one for myself then.' She stood up abruptly and headed for the door. 'Hold it . . .' she heard behind her.

But before she could reach it or he could reach her, the door opened and Rowland's substantial girth blocked her exit.

'Ah,' Sam said. 'Just the person I'm looking for.' She waved her cigarette in the air. 'Got a light?'

'Sit down, Miss Falconer.'

There was no option other than to comply. She sat but waggled the cigarette in the air. Rowland looked across at his colleague. 'Oh, get her a light, Thomas, for God's sake.'

The man got up and left the room.

'Not been at this game long, have you, love?'

Sam didn't say anything.

'No background in the work, have you? Bonking a copper doesn't quite fit the bill.'

Sam took a deep breath and set her mantra running fast and furious: *Always be polite to the police. Losing your temper won't help.* She stared at the end of her unlit cigarette.

Rowland sat back in his chair and folded his arms. 'Just another amateur fucking it up for the rest of us.'

Still she didn't say anything. The other officer came back into the room and threw a lighter on the table. Sam picked it up, lit her cigarette and placed the lighter back on the table. She inhaled deeply and blew the smoke straight up into the air above her head. Edie would be pleased with her; her smoking was steadily increasing. She smoked and waited.

'Could you kill, Miss Falconer?'

'What do you mean?'

'It's a straightforward question.'

'No, it's not,' Sam said. 'Do I have the technique, the physical skills? Yes, I do, as I'm sure you know. Do I have the temperament or predisposition to kill? No, I haven't.'

Rowland leaned forward on the table. 'You would know how to strangle someone?'

Sam nodded.

He pointed at the tape recorder. 'Please speak your answer, for the record.'

'Yes, I would know how to strangle someone. I could demonstrate if you like on your colleague here. It might wake him up a bit. Depriving him of oxygen could do wonders for him.'

'Did you kill Alice Knight?'

'No, of course I didn't.'

'Who do you think did?'

'I've absolutely no idea.'

'Did you like her?'

'No, not particularly. She didn't strike me as a very likeable woman but that doesn't mean I killed her.'

Rowland opened his mouth to speak but Sam cut across him. 'Look,' she said, stabbing the air with her cigarette. 'This is complete and utter bullshit. I've told you everything I can. I didn't kill her. I was one of the last people to see her alive, that's all. I have absolutely no motive for killing her. Charge me or let me go. I'm not answering any more of your fucking stupid questions.'

She plunged her cigarette into a white plastic cup, which two hours ago had contained tea, and the smell of melting plastic filled the room.

Sam stood outside the police station and stared at the Crown and County Courts on the other side of the road. A white flagpole on top of the building stood out against the blue sky. She inhaled deeply. There was nothing like being in a police station to make you want air in your lungs. Police interview rooms were not for the claustrophobic. She felt grubby and sweaty and her stomach was growling hungrily. She had told the police everything she knew again and again and again. The trouble was that the period of time they were most interested in was the time it had taken her to walk from Alice Knight's rooms to the Cranmer Rooms. A period of time during which she had not stopped to talk to anyone, not even a *Big Issue* seller. She had been late and she had walked quickly, stopping off nowhere.

Sam turned as she heard someone come out of the door behind her. It was Phil.

'You still got O'Connor in there?'

He nodded, took out a cigarette and put it between his lips.

'Going to let him go?'

He shrugged. 'They're checking out his story. Having trouble getting hold of Dr Rowe, the psychiatrist at the Warneford. If that checks out he'll be released.' He took a drag on the cigarette. 'You managed to get under Rowland's skin good and proper.'

'Stupid fat fuck,' Sam said viciously. 'He got under mine and all.'

'There's no point in antagonizing him, Sam. You'll just end up making your life more difficult.'

Sam sighed. 'I know. That's what I tried telling myself.'

'And?'

She laughed. 'It seems I won't be told.'

'Promise me you'll be careful, Sam.'

Sam groaned. 'Don't start on this again, Phil.' She shifted her rucksack on to her shoulder. 'We went over it all on the phone.'

'Has anything else been going on? Anything distracting that's been keeping your focus off the case? Anything unusual?'

'No, I told you before.'

'I don't believe him. He's devious and manipulative. He lied about Alice Knight.'

'That's hardly a crime. Most men lie about their affairs, don't they? And anyway, he lied because he was worried his wife would turn up and then she'd find out.'

'Look, I know I'm not the best person to say this to you. I know that. But setting the past aside would you try to listen to what I'm saying to you? To take care?'

Sam relented. 'Sure I will. I always do.'

'No, you don't, Sam. You never took any care of yourself when you fought.'

'That's why I won,' Sam said.

'Yes, but life's different to a judo mat. You could get badly hurt.'

Sam flexed her swollen knuckles. 'Well, I'm hardly a stranger to that.'

'He doesn't want his wife found. I'm sure of it. Why didn't he tell us about the affair in the first place? He lied, Sam, and if he thinks you're getting close . . .' He dropped his glowing cigarette butt on the pavement and stood on it.

'Well, I'm not getting close,' Sam said. 'Nowhere near. All the same, maybe I should bill him before he kills me.'

'It's not a joke, Sam.'

'No, I know. Don't worry, I'll keep an eye out.' She patted Phil's arm. 'I'll be at Mark's. Time to make it up to my older brother. Last time we spoke he was pissed off as hell with me.'

Phil kissed her on the cheek and watched her stride up St Aldates towards Carfax.

Sam looked over Mark's shoulder and picked up an essay lying on the desk in front of him. On the last page was written, 'Sloppy plagiaristic rubbish C+.'

'Ouch,' Sam said.

'He's bright but lazy. Thinks he can read the introductions and conclusions of the books on the reading list, patch them together and that I won't notice. Sometimes this kind of thing,' he pointed at what he'd written, 'can shame them into working harder. If they work harder they enjoy it more. If he doesn't he'll be in trouble come the summer.'

'So he won't just curl up and die of shame when he reads that?'

Mark laughed. 'This one's much too arrogant about his own abilities.'

'You care about them.'

'Of course I do. I realise there's more to this university than studying but they have to do something.'

Sam dropped the essay back on the desk. 'Look, Mark, I'm really sorry about the other night. I didn't know what else to do.'

Mark took off his glasses and put them on his desk. 'Sometimes I just wish you could be involved with the family and I could feel that you weren't there under some sort of protest. Even when you are there you've always got some excuse to be going. It's like seeing a wild cat in a cage.' He picked up his glasses, tugged out his shirt and began to rub them clean. 'Frankly, I just wish you could be nice and uncomplicated, that you could come to a party or visit and it not involve some huge melodrama. It always ends up being about you.'

Sam walked over to the window, which looked down into the quad and pondered the 'N' word for a while. 'The thing is Mark, I'm not nice. I don't think I ever have been. You don't see it because you're my brother. And I've never been at ease in the family – ever.'

'No,' he said. 'I know. But sometimes you do yourself no favours with Mum and Dad. You make it so easy for them to disapprove of you and judge you.'

'They've done that since I was little. I can't see that anything I do now is going to change that.'

'Maybe that's true but behaving like a bolshy teenager doesn't help. If you could just be a bit more diplomatic about it sometimes.'

Sam didn't know what to say so she fell back on the stars. 'Apparently I've got four planets in Scorpio.'

'For heaven's sake, Sam. Give me a bloody break.'

'According to Alan, it means all kinds of trouble.'

'Please tell me you're taking the piss?' Mark said.

'Of course. Don't think I believe all that nonsense, do you?'

Mark laughed. 'Idiot. I suppose I could try that on Peter – see what he says.'

Sam grinned. 'I'd love to see what his logical brain did with astrology. Do you mind if I have a bath?'

Mark gestured to the door behind where he was sitting. 'Help yourself.'

'Police stations,' Sam wrinkled her nose. 'I just feel as if I want to wash it all off me.'

'Sure.'

Sam set the bath running and then returned to the main room. 'I'm exhausted.'

'I won't tell Mum you've been arrested.'

'I wasn't. Technically, I was helping the police with their enquiries – voluntarily.'

'Did they fingerprint you?'

'I was in her room before she died. They had to do that to rule out my prints.'

'Are they convinced you didn't kill her?'

Sam sat down and hugged her knees. 'If they've got any sense. There's no motive. They wanted to know what I was doing there, what I was talking to her about. They've still got John. They're checking out his alibi.'

'How's he coping?'

She shrugged. 'He was having an affair with Alice Knight.'

Mark groaned and pushed the essay he was looking at away from him. 'Oh God, you're joking, aren't you?'

'Old passions die hard.'

'Sometimes it seems they don't die at all.'

Mark got up and walked into the bathroom. The noise of running water ceased and he came back into the room.

'You met her, Sam. She was a highly combustible woman – the kind of woman men wreck themselves against.'

'A rock?'

'A very jagged one. She would destroy the people around her and walk out of a terrible situation that she had created without a backwards glance.'

'Do you think he tried to kill himself over her?'

'At the time I thought it was because of his dad. Maybe it was a mixture of factors.'

'But this time she's not walked away unscathed, has she? This time she's the one who's dead. So one part of the triangle's been removed. What's the point of therapy anyway? You'd think O'Connor would have more sense.'

'I think that's a bit simplistic, Sam. Lots of people I know have had counselling. They find it helps. It's not about making them perfect human beings.'

Sam stood up slowly. 'I'm sorry about the hassle you've had. Hopefully now we've gone to the police you won't be bothered. They may want you to confirm that Alice asked you to get in touch with me. But that's all.'

'I wish you did something else,' Mark said.

'You sound like Mum: You used to say that when I was fighting.'

'Well, I didn't like that either. I was always worried you'd get hurt.'

'I always *was* getting hurt.'

He laughed. 'I know.'

She took off her jacket, slung it over the chair and walked into the bathroom. She took off her clothes and inhaled the steam, then slid under the water. She watched large bubbles drift across her body.

An hour later she woke to banging on the door.

'You still alive in there?' Mark shouted.

'Yes, yes.'

'You haven't drowned, have you?'

'Just snoozing.'

'Get out of there before you turn into a prune.'

The ends of Sam's fingers looked like walnut shell. 'Too late,' she shouted, and used her big toe to pour some more hot water into the bath.

A few minutes later the banging resumed. 'Sam – it's John on your mobile.'

Sam got out of the bath, wrapped a towel round herself and walked next door. Mark handed her the phone.

'How's it going?' she said.

'I'm still here.' O'Connor sounded exhausted. 'They've not been able to confirm my alibi. I was wondering if you could do me a favour and try to track down either Doctor Rowe or James Arnott, my client's husband. The police don't seem to be having any success. I don't know if it's deliberate or not.' He gave her the telephone numbers and addresses.

'Have they told you how long they're going to hold you?'

'No, but I think if you could get hold of either of these two it might speed things up a bit.'

'Sure.' Sam looked at the details on the damp piece of paper in her hand. 'I'll see what I can do.'

An hour later Sam stood in front of an overgrown privet fence, outside a detached, three-storey-Victorian house. Two bins oozed rubbish into the front garden. Stockmore Street was within spitting distance of where Sam had lived when her family first came to Oxford. As she rang the bell for the ground-floor flat, a group of boys, who had been playing football in the street, stopped and watched her. There were no lights on in the house and no windows open. In fact there was no sign of any occupancy other than the dull thud of a bass coming from the back. More ringing on the bell produced no response.

Sam walked round the side of the house, but was stopped by the presence of a padlocked, wooden door. Here, the music sounded even louder. She looked at the wooden door, assessed its height, then turned and walked away from it back towards the street. The group of boys watched as she sprinted towards the door, jumped up and caught hold of the top and pulled herself up. Balancing for a second, she waved at them and then dropped down into the garden.

The house was in darkness. She cupped her hands round her eyes and peered through the back window. Someone was lying on the sofa. She banged on the glass but he didn't move; the banging was no competition for the music. To her surprise, when she tried the back door it opened and she let herself into a room smelling strongly of alcohol. Turning on the lights produced no response from the sleeping man but when Sam turned off the music, he jolted awake and stared at her.

'Who the fuck—?'

Sam started to talk quickly. 'Mr Arnott, my name's Sam Falconer. I'm working for John O'Connor, your wife's therapist. He asked me—'

But Arnott was on his feet now, reeling towards her. 'Fucking bastard . . .' He staggered a few more paces. 'Get the fuck out of my house.' He was a tall, strongly built man, but he was also very drunk and not wearing any shoes. Sam could have stamped on his toes and stopped him easily enough but she felt sorry for him and also wanted his co-operation, so as he swung at her, she ducked under his arm, came up behind him and caught him as he toppled sideways. She lowered him on to the sofa, smelling his sour body odour. She stood back and looked at him. His eyes were closed and he was breathing heavily. Sweat glistened on his forehead and he looked as if he'd slept in his clothes.

'I'll get you some coffee,' she said. She walked through into the kitchen and put on the kettle. The sink was full of unwashed dishes, congealed dirty plates and mugs with brown stains in the bottom. She found two cups and washed them up, then opened cupboards until she found some tea; they didn't seem to have any coffee. She opened the fridge, wincing at the pictures of a baby attached to the door, and sniffed at a bottle of milk. The kettle clicked off and she poured the water over the tea bags, added the milk and walked back into the living room. Arnott was sitting upright on the sofa, staring into space. The pallor of his face had taken on a greenish tinge. She put the mugs down on a table, cleared a chair of some magazines and sat down.

He looked at her as if he were seeing her for the first time. 'What are you doing here?'

'I'm a private investigator working for Mr O'Connor.'

He didn't say anything and Sam continued. 'He needs you to confirm that he was in the Warneford on Friday evening.'

'Too fucking right he was. And whose fault was that? He was supposed to be keeping her safe. Her and the baby. The baby's dead – she tried to kill herself.' He stopped and looked at Sam. 'Where is he?'

'He's at the police station. He just needs you to confirm that he was at the Warneford that evening. Would you be willing to do that?'

Arnott grabbed his trainers, shoved his feet into them and stood up. 'Let's go.'

Sam was taken by surprise. 'Don't you want your tea?'

'Tea? What the hell are you talking about? Do you think tea makes a fuck of a difference?'

Sam was of the Tony Benn school of thought when it came to tea. She patted the steaming mug regretfully and followed the shambling figure of James Arnott from the room.

As they entered the station, Sam saw O'Connor sitting opposite the desk sergeant. She nodded to him and he stood up and walked towards them. He held out his hand to Arnott.

'I appreciate you coming in, James. I know it's not an easy time right now.'

Arnott stared at the extended hand but did not take it, and O'Connor let it drop to his side.

'Are they letting you go?' Sam asked.

He nodded. 'They tracked down Doctor Rowe. With James's confirmation that should do it.'

'Good . . .' Sam saw O'Connor's eyes widen.

'Jesus . . .' he began and grabbed Sam's arm, pulling her towards him.

Sam turned and saw the metallic flash of a knife in Arnott's hand.

'You fucking bastard.' He took a step towards O'Connor. Sam was standing in front of him, her eyes fixed on a knife she had last seen on James Arnott's kitchen table. She took a step backwards, pushing O'Connor behind her.

'James . . .' O'Connor said.

'You killed my baby. You killed her. You almost killed my wife. You think you can get away with that? You think you'll just walk out of here. All those hours. All that money and all that pain and what's the result? One dead child.'

His voice had risen to a scream. He lunged forward and Sam knocked his hand to one side, grabbed his wrist and applied an arm lock. He yelped in pain.

'Drop the knife, Mr Arnott. I do not want to have to break your arm.' The knife fell to the floor and Sam kicked it out of the way.

'Fucking bitch,' he spat. 'Fucking interfering bitch.'

Phil had appeared behind Arnott and Sam handed him over to him, stepping smartly away. He pushed one of James Arnott's arms up his back and walked him away from Sam and

O'Connor. 'Come on, sir,' he said. 'That's not going to bring your baby back.'

Arnott looked as if someone had slapped him in the face. His body sagged and he allowed himself to be led to a chair. Phil let go of his arm and Arnott dropped into it and put his face in his hands. O'Connor took a step towards him. Sam put her arm out to stop him.

'No,' she said. 'Leave him to Phil. There's nothing you can do for him right now.'

O'Connor said nothing; his face was white and there was a tremor under his left eye.

'You can go, right?' Sam asked.

O'Connor nodded.

As they began to leave the station, Phil shouted, 'Sam!' She turned and raised her eyebrows. He looked from her to O'Connor. 'Remember what I said, will you?'

She nodded and followed O'Connor outside.

O'Connor shivered. 'What did he say?'

'Oh, this and that,' Sam said. 'You know, policemen are always full of good advice and they do insist on giving it to you.'

'You know the difference between us?' O'Connor said.

'I feel sure you're about to tell me.'

'I find it easier to step towards a man who is crying and you find it easier to step towards a man wielding a knife.'

'Backwards,' Sam corrected tersely. 'It gave me more room for manoeuvre.'

'But the crying man frightens you more than the knife carrier?'

'Too bloody right he does,' Sam said.

CHAPTER FOURTEEN

Sam spent the night at Mark's and got an early coach back to London in the morning. By ten o'clock she was back in Fulham. She knocked on Edie's door and as the door opened, Frank waddled out on to the landing.

Sam had never seen Frank Cooper so fat.

'God, Edie, I'm going to have to rename him Barry White.'

Frank was rubbing his head on Edie's flowery slipper in a disgustingly servile manner and seemed reluctant to leave Edie's flat.

'He's had nothing but the best, babes. Fish, chicken – all fresh, mind. I wouldn't feed them on any of that canned nonsense. Or those biscuits. For a full-grown cat!'

'But it's supposed to be good for his teeth, isn't it?' Sam said weakly.

Edie snorted.

'Come on, Frank,' Sam said. Frank walked slowly into Sam's flat and tore grimly at her rug.

'How much do I owe you?'

'No, love. Do me a favour sometime.'

'But Edie—'

'No,' Edie said firmly.

Sam sighed. She preferred to pay, otherwise she knew Edie would call in the favour: a couple of trips to the supermarket or a lift to the train station. In the past she'd taken Edie regularly to the shops but then there'd been a series of incidents involving missing purses. Edie always had a long explanation about what had happened and who she thought had done it. Sam had come to the conclusion that Edie was going shopping for more than pork pies, beetroot and minestrone soup, and had stopped taking her. Edie's door slammed, ending any chance of further conversation.

It was good to be back home, even though she'd only been gone a couple of days. The flat smelled musty. She opened the kitchen window and Frank stood on the window sill, sniffing at a pot of paint left on the scaffolding by the workmen. Sam made herself a cup of tea and then walked back into the hall to listen to her answerphone. The first, second and third messages were all from her godfather, each one becoming progressively more urgent and frustrated. Sam picked up the phone and dialled.

'Christ, about bloody time,' Max growled. 'Where the hell have you been?'

'A case turned a bit nasty. You could say I was helping the police with their enquiries or you could say I was sitting on my arse waiting for them to check out my alibi.'

'Well, I've spoken to the powers-that-be about the letter and they're looking into it.'

'What does that mean?'

'They're looking into it,' he repeated.

'I also spoke to someone who was in D Squadron and in Oman with your dad in nineteen seventy-three. He says—'

Sam slammed the phone down. She stood staring at it for a few seconds and then pressed redial. Her hands were shaking as she picked up the phone. 'Sorry, Max,' she said. 'We got cut off.'

But Max wasn't buying it. 'What the hell's the matter with you?' he snapped. 'I can't get hold of you for days and then you cut me off.'

'Look, if I want any more details about my father, I'll ask you. At the moment I don't want to hear.'

'Has anything else happened?'

Sam told him about Hoxton and the man they'd chased.

'So you lost him?'

'Some mate of his grabbed me and then Alan thought I was in trouble and turned round and then, yes, we lost him.'

'A mate?'

'There was a bloke who came into the pub after us. He'll have some sore ribs, mind.'

'Broken – two of them.'

'What?'

'You broke two of his ribs. He's a bit pissed at you, and at me for not warning him that you could look after yourself.'

'He was one of *yours*?'

'I asked him to keep you out of trouble.'

Sam was speechless.

'Look, Sam, the general idea was to keep you out of harm's way.'

'I do not need a bloody minder. I did not come to you for *protection*. I came to you to pass on information. That idiot got in the way and prevented us from finding someone who might have told us something about who hung that fox outside my window. And I can look after myself.'

'So Chris tells me. But there's no shame in having someone mind your back. It doesn't make you weak. Why do you think the SAS always work in four-man units? Much safer.'

'You have absolutely no contact with me for years. Then when I do come to you, you put a minder on me. And you don't even tell me. Don't you think it's over-compensating? Couldn't you have just sent me a bloody teddy bear when I was younger?'

'If I'd told you, you wouldn't have agreed to it.'

'Aren't you the clever one?'

'Only a fool thinks they're stronger alone, Sam.'

'Call him off or I won't be responsible for my actions,' Sam snarled. 'Next time I'll break more than his bloody ribs.'

'You know, your father – he was arrogant. Don't make the same mistake—'

'Fuck off!' Sam shouted. 'Just fuck off!' and she slammed down the phone.

Frank stood in the hallway listening to the sounds of Edie hoovering next door. He looked up at Sam, then at the front door and began to howl. 'And you can do the same.' Sam said. 'You're on a diet – starting now.'

Was she arrogant? Of course she was. You don't become a World Champion in any sport without thinking you're the best. And you have to think you're the best before you have the record to prove it. Which came first, the chicken or the egg? But Sam wasn't so foolish as to think she had done it alone. There was Tyler, her coach, and fitness trainers and dieticians. There was in fact a whole team. Even George at the Red Lion had played his part, raising money, which had enabled her to go to Japan and attend the best training camps. But setting all that aside, when Sam set foot on a judo mat and bowed to her opponent, there was no one to help her. If her opponent looked like Rambo, was four inches taller and substantially heavier, Sam was the one who had to get on with it. It was all down to her and how much she wanted it. And she had wanted it a whole damn lot.

When she started fighting as a child she had motivated herself by telling herself that if she did well it would bring her father back. Win this fight and he'll walk through the door. Win that and he'll be outside in the car park waiting for you. But of course he hadn't been. Then, she had to rejig it a little. He wouldn't bother with minor competitions, he'd only come back for the big one; the National Championships and the Europeans weren't big enough. He'd only come back for the biggest one of all – the World Championships. If she won that, he would be there waiting for her. It was simple really – with every fight she won, a small part of Sam believed she was raising her father from the dead.

And the first thing Sam did after holding her arms aloft in triumph over the prostrate body of Mi-Jeong Moon that night in 1990 in Paris, the night she first became World Champion, was look for him. She scanned the audience but he hadn't come. No one had jumped out of the audience to embrace her. The tears that then coursed down her face had not been tears of joy but tears of sorrow. Now she knew that no amount of fighting or success could resurrect her father. If he wasn't there at the World Championships he was never coming and her moment of greatest triumph had turned into her moment of greatest desolation. She had become World Champion but she had lost her father for good. No amount of bouts won would bring him back. Or that was what she had believed until she had received a letter saying that he had been there all the time, watching, just as she had always thought.

Arrogance? If she'd been a man, would her godfather have accused her of arrogance? If she'd been a man, he would never have given her a minder without telling her.

Sam opened her wardrobe and took out her blue *judogi*, the one she had worn when she first became World Champion. She ran her thumb over the Union Jack stitched into the front of the jacket. She had fought for her country; her father had died for his. In a shitty, secret little campaign in Oman that no one had known about at the time but in which twelve men had lost their lives. Sam wasn't particularly patriotic but the first time she had fought as part of the national squad she had been surprised at how proud she felt. It had changed her relationship to the Union Jack. The jacket was soft, tenderized by fighting. Sam sat on the edge of her bed with the jacket hanging over her knees. All that was over now. She was never going to fight competitively again. She should find someone to give this to. Perhaps Tyler had some baby champions in the making. Time to let go, to move on. The trouble was, she had no idea how to do that. Sam found letting go of a paperclip hard work. She lay back on the bed and pulled the soft blue jacket over her. She curled up on her side and slept.

Jenny Hughes walks towards her. The earth spills from her mouth. It dribbles down her chin and down the front of the blue dress with the red strawberries. She spits and coughs but still more comes. Her hands are outstretched towards Sam. When all the earth is out of her, Sam knows Jenny is going to speak and she doesn't want to hear what the little girl has to say. Sam tries to run away but her legs feel as if they are set in concrete. The child is coming closer and closer. Her eyes are open but there are no eyes in the sockets just empty holes. Sam puts her hands over her ears.

'This isn't mine,' she says. 'Don't tell me.'

Jenny coughs and a gout of blood so dark it's almost black spills into her hands. She pulls at it and more blood gushes from her mouth. She stretches out a bloodstained hand towards Sam. If she touches her . . .

'He's back,' Jenny says. 'He's back.'

The pitch of her voice rises steadily until she is screaming. Sam puts her hands over her ears to block out the terrifying noise. She tries to run but she can't. The child's hand reaches out towards her; long nails, like yellow claws, touch her leg.

'They grow,' Jenny says, her voice dropping now to a whisper, 'In the dark, underground, they grow. Even though I'm dead. And I can't stop them.'

Sam jolted awake to the sound of the doorbell. She sat on the edge of her bed for a minute, trying to clear the images from her head. She looked at her leg, expecting to see a print of a bloodstained hand, those long yellow nails. She could still feel the pressure of the child's hand. The last couple of nights she'd been free of nightmares. She thought they might have gone for good. The bell rang again. She opened the door to her flat and peered out at the main door to the block. Alan was standing there waving at her and she buzzed him in.

'You look like shit,' he said, bounding up the few stairs to her flat.

Sam groaned. 'Bad dreams,' she said, and stood back to let him in.

He looked at her. 'God, they must have been really bad.'

'They were. Jenny Hughes again.'

Alan stood looking round her front room. Sam stood in the doorway, rubbing her eyes. 'Don't do that,' she said.

'What?'

'It's what my mother does whenever she sees me. Gives me the once over.'

Alan laughed. 'You've done so much to the place since I was last here – all these changes.'

'Sarcasm will get you absolutely nowhere,' Sam said. 'This is exactly why I don't have people back here.'

'I'm good at DIY. If you want a plasterer, electrician, painter, carpenter, carpet layer ... I could go on.'

'Don't.'

'Well, it's up to you. If you want to live in an old lady's flat.'

'Well, it was an old lady's flat.'

'*Was*. You're thirty-two, Sam, not Miss Havisham.'

Sam threw herself down on the sofa. 'What exactly are you doing here, Alan?'

Alan walked over to the mantelpiece. 'Touching base.'

'Is that what you call it. I thought you were giving my interior decor, or lack of it, the third degree.'

He smiled. 'How was it in Oxford?'

'The police accused me of murdering Alice Knight in order to protect O'Connor, with whom, according to them, I have fallen in love.'

Alan frowned. 'He's not your type.'

183

'I know. And then a man attacked me with a knife. Well, he attacked O'Connor really and I just happened to be in the way.'

'Who was he?'

'Husband of one of O'Connor's clients – seems he had a dim view of O'Connor's therapeutic skills.'

'They let O'Connor go?'

Sam nodded.

'His alibi checked out, then?'

'Seems so.'

Alan picked up a couple of ornaments and blew the dust off them.

'You come here to clean up or what?' Sam said.

'Won't you offer a man a cup of tea?'

Sam shook her head. 'No milk.'

'Want me to get you some?'

'Alan . . .'

Alan sighed and sat down on the sofa next to her. 'I had an interesting chat with Bernie.'

'How did you manage that?'

'It was a question of waiting for last orders at the Nelson and following him home.'

Alan cracked a couple of knuckles.

'Poor Bernie,' Sam said.

'Turns out he was paid to put the frighteners on you. What he did was left up to him. Said he found the fox dead in the road, saw the scaffolding outside the block and thought it all up by himself.'

'Who paid him?'

'Seems the most likely candidate is Eddie Turner. Turns out his baby brother is landlord of the Blue Posts in Dagenham.'

'Alfie?' Sam remembered a skinny man with hooded, lizard-like eyes and a finger in every pie. 'The Blue Posts was a real shit-hole. All kinds of scams going on in there.'

'It's their way of letting you know they're not at all happy with you testifying against him. Case is due up in court in a couple of months.'

'Anything else likely to occur?'

'I encouraged him to tell me but I don't think he knew anything. He's pretty low on the food chain.'

'You can't get much lower than Alfie Turner,' Sam said. 'Lower than that and you'd be in a primeval swamp.'

Alan laughed. 'Sam . . .'

But Sam didn't allow him to continue. 'Don't, whatever you do, tell me to mind my back, Alan. That'll really piss me off.'

'No, I wasn't going to say that. You're welcome to come and stay with me.'

Sam thought of Alan's neat, minimalist flat with the lava lamp undulating in the corner and the perfect black leather sofa and cream carpet. 'I can't leave Frank.'

'Edie'll look after him, won't she?'

'I can't leave him with Edie, she'll feed him until his liver explodes. He's already more football than cat.'

'Bring him.'

Sam saw Frank sharpening his claws on Alan's sofa. 'No, he's used to going out. He'd go stir crazy, probably leap from your balcony in protest and end up as a pile of hairy jam on the concrete below.'

'For heaven's sake, Sam, don't you think your safety's more important than a bloody cat?'

'No,' Sam said firmly. 'With a pet, it's like marriage. For better or worse. In sickness and in health. There are responsibilities.'

Frank barrelled into the room and jumped on to Alan's lap. Alan picked him up like the proverbial bag of shit and placed him carefully back on the floor. 'God, he's gross. What's that dirty patch on the back of his neck?'

'He's so fat he can't reach round to wash it.'

'That's disgusting.'

'Well, so are lots of spouses. Anyway, I'm not going to be frightened out of my own home. Then the bastards win, don't they?'

'These are not nice people, Sam,' Alan said. 'They're vicious, brainless thugs. I remember them from my time on the job.'

Sam wasn't really listening to him. 'If Eddie Turner is responsible for the fox via Bernie, then the letter from my dad must be unconnected to the fox. That's too close to the bone. That's from someone who knows me, someone who knows exactly how to upset me. The Turners wouldn't write a letter like that – not their style at all.'

'O'Connor know about that?' Alan asked.

'What?'

Alan raised his eyebrows. 'Does he know about your dad?'

'Well, yes, he does, he's friends with Mark.'

'He'd know it would upset you, right? He's a shrink, he knows about that kind of stuff.'

'Come on, Alan, you hardly have to be a shrink to realize that.'

'Who do *you* think wrote it?'

'I think it may be very simple,' Sam said. 'What's the answer we're not considering?'

'That your father wrote it?'

'Yes,' Sam said. 'He wrote it. He's out there. He was never killed.'

'You must remember you don't really know him, Sam.'

She saw the pity in his eyes and couldn't bear it. 'Don't lecture me, Alan,' she snapped. 'Not about this.'

He put both hands up, as if she'd pointed a gun at him, and said nothing more.

After Alan had gone, Sam stood looking out of her front window. On the other side of the road a white car was parked. Not a stalker. This was one of Edie's gentlemen callers, Denis.

He bought Edie's cigarettes and sold them at the bowls club down the road. Boring bastard, is what Edie called him. 'There's no life in him,' she complained. Poor Denis was diabetic and had a heart condition and didn't respond when Edie put on Ricky Martin and pumped up the volume. He refused to get up and dance with her. He didn't respond to much really. He came every Wednesday, regular as clockwork, and always parked in the same place. Then he sat with Edie, watched the lottery draw and made his way home with the cigarettes. Occasionally, he brought Edie food, which he got from his son who worked for a supermarket. Trouble was the food was always well beyond its sell-by date. Edie called him 'plastic shoes' because of his light grey plastic footwear. 'You'd think he'd stretch to a bit of leather when he comes calling,' she said.

There were no other cars parked out there or people. Sam shivered and let the blind bang down against the window. What was she going to do about the Turners? If she testified, they knew where she lived and she'd have to spend the rest of her life watching her back and worrying they were going to string up Frank. If she didn't, they got away with it one more time and lived to prosper another day. Sam wasn't going to be frightened out of her own home by a bunch of thugs. Frank head-butted her shin. He was fat but she loved him. She didn't know what she was going to do.

CHAPTER FIFTEEN

The following afternoon Sam sat with her feet up on her desk, watching the sunset bruise the sky over Bishop's Park and thinking about the gumshoeing she'd been doing that morning. First there had been Meg's editor, Ian Bruce, whom Meg had spoken to on the morning of the day of her disappearance. The offices of the *Modern Art Review* were at the top of an old building in Soho's Dean Street. Sam had found Ian Bruce doing what all editors have a tendency to do – tearing his hair out. He was a small blond man, much too young for the bow tie that adorned his neck. Although on further consideration, Sam thought it had probably been round his neck when he slithered, young-fogeyish, from his mother's womb.

'Frankly, I don't see why we couldn't have done this on the phone,' he said.

'Sometimes,' Sam said. 'I like to see the whites of the eyes of the person I'm speaking to.'

Ian Bruce looked up sharply from the piece of paper he had in his hands and then dropped it on his desk. 'It's very inconvenient to lose a critic. It's damnably hard to find ones that are any good. Any idea when she's coming back?'

Sam shook her head. 'It's not altogether clear that she will be coming back.'

'I really don't see how I can help you.'

'Could you tell me if there was anything in that final conversation that you had with her that might have made you think that she was distressed or likely to go missing. Did she say anything to you that stands out?'

Ian Bruce ran his hand over his bald patch. 'No, no, nothing at all. It was a purely professional conversation. I needed to make a few cuts. She usually wrote to a set number of words but I'd had a piece in unexpectedly early that I wanted to include and it involved reducing the size of her review. I have found from bitter experience that it's always best to consult the writers if you possibly can, otherwise they can get very offended.'

'Yes,' Sam said. 'I can see that. So your conversation was purely about the article?'

'Yes, exclusively.'

'Was she a good critic?' Sam asked.

Ian Bruce was standing over a fax machine ripping a sheet of paper from it. He looked up. 'Yes, she was passionate about art and she had the knack of writing about it with a complete lack of pretentiousness. A knack that this particular writer,' he waved the piece of paper in his hand, 'certainly *doesn't* have.'

After that Sam caught the number 22 bus from Piccadilly, got off at Parson's Green and walked through to Laburnum Street, which ran south-east off the Fulham Road. This was where Nicole Hardy lived. Her telephone number had been on the bill that Sam had taken from Meg's flat. The woman who opened the door of the brick-fronted, terrace house was in her forties, wearing a loose white shirt and trousers and flat black Chinese slippers. Her long brown hair reached halfway down her back. She led Sam into a spacious, sun-filled kitchen situated at the back of the house.

'Thank you for seeing me,' Sam said, sitting down at a battered wooden table.

Nicole didn't reply but handed her a cardboard box full of herbal teas. 'I'm afraid I only have these. Would you like to choose one?'

Sam peered into the box and tried to find one she thought might be drinkable. In the end she decided on lemon and ginger.

Nicole smiled. 'A good choice.'

She boiled the kettle, tore the paper sachet from the tea bag, dropped the bag in a cup and poured water over it. Sam wrinkled her nose as the smell wafted towards her. Nicole placed the cup in front of Sam and joined her at the table.

'You know that Meg has gone missing,' Sam said.

Nicole nodded.

'Can I ask you how you knew her?'

'We were old friends from her London days – before she was married and moved to Oxford. I'm a shiatsu practitioner amongst other things. When I was first training I used to work on her and once I'd qualified I'd massage her once a month. Less frequently once she'd moved to Oxford, but still on the odd occasion when she was feeling particularly tired or stressed.'

Sam checked in her notebook. 'The call I'm interested in is the one you had with her on the sixteenth of September, a couple of weeks before she went missing.'

Nicole nodded but didn't say anything.

'Can you remember what was said?'

'Nothing much, she just made an appointment.'

'Did she keep it?'

'Yes, she did.'

'Could you tell me the date?'

Nicole walked out of the kitchen and came back a few moments later carrying a blue diary. 'Here we are.' She showed Sam the entry. The date was the day before Meg had disappeared.

'And how was she?' Sam asked.

Nicole sighed. 'I have a real problem with this.'

Sam picked up her tea, brought it halfway to her lips and then changed her mind. 'Would you tell me what that is?'

'Confidentiality – she was a client as well as a friend.'

Sam nodded. 'I understand that – but I want you to know that I'll keep anything you say to me absolutely private.'

Nicole stared at the table. 'It wasn't really anything she said as such. It was more how she felt as I worked on her.'

Sam frowned. 'What do you mean?'

'There was this great sadness and exhaustion in her body. She'd never felt like that before. This is going to sound silly.'

'No,' Sam said. 'I'm sure it won't.'

'Well, after she'd gone, I felt sad and at first I just thought it was the emotions I'd absorbed from treating her. You know, you pick up these things from clients. But later I thought, no, it wasn't that. I felt sad because I was never going to see her again.'

Sam stared at her.

'I told you it was going to sound silly.'

'You mean you had a premonition?'

'I suppose so, yes. When I saw John on the TV it didn't surprise me.'

'Have you experienced anything like that before?' Sam asked.

She shook her head and her hair fell across her face. 'No, and I hope I don't again; it frightened me.' She swept her hair off her face. 'Do you understand what I'm talking about?'

'Yes,' Sam said. 'I do. Is there anything else you could tell me?'

'No, that's it I'm afraid.'

'Well, thank you for your time,' Sam said and stood up.

Nicole smiled and looked at Sam's untouched cup. 'Sorry,' she said.

'I've tried them before, you know. But I never seem to get on with them. The first whiff of strong coffee or tea and I relapse.'

Nicole walked Sam to the door. Sam shrugged on her coat and picked up her bag. 'You think she's dead, don't you?'

Nicole shook her head. 'I don't know. All I know is that she felt dead under my hands and I've never felt that in my life before.' She turned away and closed the door.

Sam knew exactly what Nicole Hardy had meant. It was what she'd experienced the first time she met Andrew Hughes. She'd felt death all around him. Although in that case it hadn't been his own, but the death of the daughter he had murdered.

The telephone on Sam's desk rang, jolting her from her thoughts about the morning back to the present; she dropped her feet to the ground and grabbed the receiver. It was O'Connor. She told him about her morning, omitting Nicole Hardy's premonition. Why worry him when there was no evidence or proof that Meg was dead?

O'Connor sounded exhausted. 'The police pulled me in for questioning again.'

'But Arnott and Dr Rowe confirmed your alibi, didn't they?' Sam said.

'I know,' O'Connor's voice was monotone. 'But now they keep banging on about how I could have stopped off at the college, either on the way there or the way back and done it then. They started in on all the same old stuff. They say my prints are all over her college rooms.'

'But you were having an affair with her. Why shouldn't they be?'

'They said I never mentioned going to her rooms. Anyway, I don't think I can take much more of this. You don't think I did it, do you?'

Sam was silent for a moment. 'If I thought you were a murderer I'd be foolish to keep working for you, Mr O'Connor. They can't place you in the college at the right time. No one saw you there.'

'Because I wasn't there.'

'Well then, they've got no case unless you confess or unless forensic evidence ties you to her body in some way.'

'They said I murdered Alice because she threatened to go to the police and that she would have revealed me to be a liar.'

'We all lie, Mr O'Connor, to varying degrees. I'm sure you

find that with your clients. I would think that lying to cover up an affair is par for the course.' Sam stretched her back.

'Are you ever going to call me John?' When she didn't reply he continued. 'They've told me not to leave Oxford without telling them.'

'If they had enough evidence to pin the murder on you they would have arrested you.'

His voice cracked. 'I keep thinking the boys would be better off without me.'

Sam lost patience. 'Don't talk rubbish. In my experience children are not better off without their father. They just aren't. You're doing fine in extreme circumstances.'

'Have you forgiven him?'

Sam didn't have any idea what he was talking about. 'Sorry?' She was spinning a yellow pencil round and round, using her thumb and first finger.

'Your father – have you forgiven him?'

The pencil clattered on to her desk and fell on the ground. 'Like I said before, I'm not your client, Mr O'Connor.'

'We think it keeps us powerful, that it protects us but it's quite the reverse. Resentment holds us in thrall to the people we resent. He'll have the power over you. More power than you can possibly imagine. Holding ill-will takes tremendous energy.'

Sam jumped to her feet. 'Why do you insist on doing this?' she snapped. 'I have never once intimated to you that I want your advice on my life, my father – anything. And yet you insist on giving it. Have I ever invited your professional opinion? I am not looking for a therapist. You are *my* client. If you're not happy with me sack me.'

There was silence on the end of the phone.

Eventually O'Connor spoke. 'I don't find it easy.'

'What?'

'Being helped. I'm used to doing the helping. Being in that

position. I'm used to being the one with the power. It's difficult to accept a change of role.'

'I don't *have* any power,' Sam said in exasperation. 'You hired me to do a job.'

'But to do that job you have to have access to my life, my private life. And you have been helping me.'

'Not very much at the moment. I'm no closer to finding out what happened to your wife.'

'But neither are the police. It's difficult for me. I see things. I know I can help to make things easier. You have no idea how much forgiveness can transform your life. When I forgave my father—'

'Back off,' Sam snarled. 'You've no invitation.'

He was silent. Sam could hear him breathing. She felt defensive, angry. In some way diminished and wrong-footed. She heard him sigh.

'I've talked through some of these things with Mark.'

'I don't care if you've talked them through with the Pope. You're *not* talking to me in this way.' She was about to slam down the phone.

'Sam, hold on.'

She paused.

'The reason I called.'

She waited for him to continue.

'Tony Ballinger phoned and asked if you'd meet him.'

'He *phoned* you? How was *that* conversation?'

'Not particularly comfortable.'

Sam let out a low whistle under her breath.

'But the thing is, you were the last person to see Alice alive. He wants to see you. I told him I'd ask you. He is my old tutor and I owe him a lot. I'd really appreciate it if you would.'

'What am I supposed to say to him?'

'What she said to you? I don't know, whatever he wants to hear. He lives in Islington.'

'OK,' Sam said. 'Give me his details.'

After she finished the call she walked over to the floor-to-ceiling window that made up one wall of her office. The sky had turned a pale turquoise green. She pressed her hands against the cool glass. God, O'Connor got under her skin. So, the route to freedom was forgiveness, was it? Shame that. Sam wasn't the forgiving type. Her route to freedom had always been through fighting. Next time round she'd probably come back as a dung beetle. Next time round! Sam hoped she was never coming back; one life was quite enough to endure. She turned and looked at the square, tear-off calendar on her desk. She lifted that day's date and looked underneath – 1 November. Tomorrow she'd be heading north to Hereford, looking for answers where there were none, as she had done every year since she was old enough to travel on a train by herself. She had to go – she always had.

Military graveyards are always beautifully looked after. The SAS plot in the graveyard of St Martin's, Hereford was no different. There wasn't a weed to pull out of the grave or a leaf to brush away. Sam ran her hand over the top of the gravestone, then crouched down and patted the grass. As if she could touch him, as if she were any closer to him by doing that. In some ways it might have been easier if there had been some tidying to do. But because there wasn't she touched the headstone and the grass tenderly.

Who or what was down there? What had they buried? She placed her hand flat on the grass as if feeling for vibrations. As a child she had looked down on to the brass plate on his coffin:

Sergeant Geoffrey 'Hawkeye' Falconer
Born 24 August 1942,
Died 1 November 1974, aged 32

The same age as Sam. Every day now took Sam beyond the age

he had lived. O'Connor's voice drifted through her head. *Have you forgiven him?* What was there to forgive? He had died for his country. He had died a hero, hadn't he? Surely that was a source of pride? Sam's recollection of the day of the funeral was hazy – a sandy beret sitting on the coffin together with a set of medals, the red sashes round the chests of some of the soldiers, the legs of the soldiers who carried the coffin. Sam's eyes had been level with their knees and she remembered the stiff creases in their trousers and the way their shoes shone, then gunshots ringing out over the coffin and the rooks flying up out of the trees in an explosion of black, flapping wings.

Her mother had never been that keen to visit the grave and neither had Mark. And after her mother remarried she had stopped coming altogether, understandably trying to draw a line under the past, identifying her new life with her new husband, Peter Goodman. But it hadn't been understandable to Sam, who was a confused and volatile teenager. Her mother might have been ready to let go of the past but Sam certainly wasn't. She hadn't wanted her mother to remarry and she definitely hadn't wanted to move from their home. She always insisted on going to Hereford on the anniversary of his death. But more often than not she had gone alone. Sam looked up at the sky as she heard the whirring wing beat of a flock of geese flying overhead in formation, a black triangle against a grey and lowering sky.

She stood up and began to search the ground around her. Not finding what she wanted in her immediate vicinity, she walked back to the path leading into the graveyard. Finding a stone that satisfied her she walked back to the grave, rubbing it clean against the front of her trousers. She touched the stone to her lips and placed it on top of the gravestone. She knew it was a Jewish custom and her father wasn't Jewish and neither was she. But she liked it and always did it. The stone had marked her visit in some way, it wasn't like flowers that would wither and die. She stood up and stretched. In the far corner of the graveyard was a young woman with two small children. It could have been her and Mark. Large drops of rain began to fall from the sky.

Forgiveness. If she forgave him, she'd have to let him go. Sam had an image of talons gripping on to a dead rabbit, blood dribbled from the rabbit's mouth – an image of ferocious attachment. No one could tear those talons from the rabbit without inflicting terrible damage, without leaving gaping wounds. She heard Alan's voice in her head. *You got four planets in Scorpio, girl, you let go of nothing*. It was one of the things that had made her such a good fighter – her grip. Sam had a visceral, physical memory of holding on to her father etched deep in her bones. She had to hold on or something terrible would happen. This memory was an integral part of her and it had been a vital part of her fighting. It was something she accessed in competition. Once she had hold of an opponent, it was as if they became a single unit that would only separate in victory for Sam and in defeat for her opponent. Somewhere in her was a memory of holding on with all her might and it being a matter of life and death, a question of survival and not just hers. How on earth could she get rid of that? She wasn't sure she even wanted to. Her hands were clenched in her pockets. She took them out, forced herself to uncurl them, turned her palms upwards to the skies and threw back her face to meet the driving rain.

At ten o'clock the following morning Sam stood in the living room of a large house in Islington's Canonbury Square, a house she presumed was more a consequence of Alice Knight's legal career than Tony Ballinger's academic one. At first sight Tony Ballinger did not look like a grieving widower, Sam thought. But her instant dislike of him was perhaps generated by the fact he reminded her of her stepfather, Peter, not in looks but in manner.

Above the gas-generated fire was an enormous portrait of Alice. Sam couldn't help but stare at it. It dominated the room.

Alice was wearing a low-cut summer dress, which emphasized the swell of her breasts. Her lips were slightly parted and she looked straight out of the portrait directly at the viewer. Her gaze carried the direct sexual invitation of a mini-skirted hooker.

Tony Ballinger stood in front of it wearing jeans held up by a black leather belt with a silver tip. His white shirt was linen and open at the neck, showing the hairs on his chest. He was no hairy-eared, dandruff-covered academic; rather the academic version of the gold medallion man. He had looked stylish in a dinner jacket and he was certainly charismatic on television but in the flesh he was a disappointment, seedy rather than sexy.

'Thank you for seeing me at such short notice,' he said.

'Mr O'Connor asked me to.'

Sam walked across the room towards a chair.

Ballinger's eyes tracked her. 'So, you're Mark's sister. You're very unalike.'

She nodded and sat down. Sunlight filtered through the window to Sam's right and lit up Ballinger's face. Closer to him now, Sam could see that there were signs of strain there. His eyes were red-rimmed and his hand strayed to a place under his left eye as if the flesh was pulsing there and he wanted it to stop.

'How is he? I don't see much of him these days.'

'He's fine. I'm very sorry about your wife,' she added.

Ballinger did not seem to have heard her but Sam saw the muscle in his jaw tighten. He checked his watch and sat down on a brown leather sofa. 'I'm sorry but we're going to have to keep this short. I'm afraid I have an appointment.'

'You wanted to see *me*.'

'Yes, of course.'

'What do you want to know?'

'Could you tell me what she said to you?' He crossed one long, elegant leg over the other and placed both his arms on the back of the sofa. His shirt opened even further. Sam wished he had done up one more button – all that grey chest hair was distracting. He and Alice had obviously been well matched. Although the position of his body was one of openness and relaxation, his face was etched with tension.

'She said she felt threatened. That was the gist of it. Her car had been broken into and she felt threatened.'

'Was anything stolen?'

'Only some bills and junk mail she had left on the passenger seat. But one contained her telephone number and address. I told her not to worry, that it was probably opportunistic – a junkie who thought there might be something more interesting in the car. But she seemed worried that Meg might be coming after her. The expression she used was avenging angel.'

Tony frowned. 'She mentioned Meg?'

'Yes.'

He seemed puzzled. 'Was that the only reason she wanted to see you? Just to tell you that?'

'No, I think the real reason she wanted to talk to me was to see if I knew about her affair with O'Connor.'

'Did you?'

'No, I didn't. She was also concerned about going to the police with her fears because she didn't want to land O'Connor in it. She didn't know what he had said to them about their affair.'

'I see.' Tony's foot was bouncing up and down, as if someone was pulling an invisible string attached to his big toe.

'Had she talked to you about O'Connor?'

He swept his hand across his face. 'To be honest, we had been living relatively separate lives for some time. She had moved to Oxford a few months ago and I was living here. It was frankly a relief. It was only a matter of time before we got divorced. I think we both realized it was over.'

Sam was surprised. 'Really?' Her eyes strayed to the painting of Alice above the fireplace.

He saw her looking at it. 'I need to take that down. It's convenient because it fills the space.'

'So you knew about the affair?'

'With John? Oh yes, she delighted in telling me of her affairs in great detail. That one in particular ripped off a few old scars in a way that seemed to satisfy her.'

Sam frowned.

Tony cleared his throat. 'I'm afraid we no longer cared for each other. We were at the picking-wings-off-each-other stage of the relationship. It was actually a relief that she had moved to Oxford; her viciousness was becoming rather tiresome.'

'Can you think of anyone who would want to murder her?'

'She was very ambitious and very clever, but not a particularly easy woman and she had her fair share of enemies, I'm sure. But I've told all this to the police. She would pick people up, anyone who took her fancy, really. Maybe she just struck unlucky. There was nothing else she said to you?'

'No, I've told you the gist of it.'

He nodded and looked at his watch again.

'Were you surprised by her affair with O'Connor?'

'It was history. They'd been at college together. No, it didn't surprise me that she would do it. Testing her powers. But I'd have thought he'd have more sense. He's a shrink, isn't he? So that bit did surprise me. But she liked to mess with people's lives and I suppose because of the past he was relatively easy to reel in; he had been infatuated with her at college.'

Sam thought of the man in the blue coat. 'So far as you knew, she was only having the one affair?'

He laughed. 'Alice was a very attractive woman in all sorts of ways, and a very predatory woman. It wouldn't surprise me if there had been others.'

'There wasn't anything that happened recently that was out of the ordinary?'

He stood up. 'I'm afraid I need to—'

'Of course. Just one last thing – did you know Meg O'Connor?'

'No, why should I? Before I spoke to O'Connor the other day the only contact I had with him was when he wanted a reference from me to do his psychotherapy course. He didn't take his degree so they needed some kind of academic evaluation from me. He was clever. Not as clever as Alice, but then Alice was exceptional in all kinds of ways. Anyway, what I said about him must have satisfied them because he got on to the course and did the training. I heard about her going missing, of course. There was all the publicity about it. I saw him at the press conference, poor bugger. She didn't pick up her kids, did she? Have they found her?'

'No, not yet.'

'Any leads?'

'I'm sorry I can't discuss that with you.'

'No, no, of course. I understand.' He walked over to where she was sitting.

She remained seated, even though he was standing over her in a way which made her want to place as much distance between them as possible.

'You really can't think who might have been threatening her?'

'No, I told the police that.'

'Do you think she was telling the truth?'

'What about?'

'About feeling threatened.'

He blinked. 'Why would she lie? It's true that she was always very good at fantasy – although in rather a different context.'

Sam stood up abruptly and followed him out into the hall. 'If anything else occurs to you that might be significant...' She handed him her card, which he glanced at briefly before sliding into his shirt pocket.

'I appreciate you coming,' he said before closing the door.

That afternoon Alan and Sam sat in a coffee shop on Putney High Street, peering into their coffee cups with just about equal levels of dissatisfaction. They had been warned by Greg that the landlord's agent, Paul Adams, was due to visit the offices and since Sam's last rent payment had bounced and she had no idea when she was going to be in a position to pay it, she decided it would be diplomatic for her and Alan to be out when he came.

Sam dropped her spoon with a clatter into the saucer. 'He seemed remarkably unperturbed by the murder of his wife. I mean, I know academics can be cold fish but all the same, you'd think that there'd be some sort of upset.'

'Yes, but if she were a promiscuous old slapper who was tormenting him, he's probably relieved to have got rid of her.'

'Perhaps. But he ran this whole line about how they were going to get divorced and no longer cared for each other. But he had this huge portrait of her hanging over his mantelpiece, like an icon. Like something he was worshipping. Do you do that if you don't like someone?'

Alan shrugged. 'Maybe he hadn't got round to taking it down.'

'Maybe, but it didn't fit with what he was saying.'

Alan scooped the froth off his coffee and dumped it in his saucer. 'Jesus Christ,' he said. 'This fucking steamed milk. Out of ten, this is a three.'

'That's being generous,' Sam said, doing the same.

'The search for the perfect cappuccino on Putney High Street goes on.'

'Until hell freezes over.'

'How was Hereford?'

Sam sighed heavily. 'Hereford was Hereford.'

'And you?'

She shook her head. 'I don't know, Alan. Why visit a grave? Why do I do it?'

'To remember . . .'

'He's not there.'

'No . . .'

'Mark and Mum would never do it. They let go of him ages ago. But not me. Heaven forbid. I keep trudging up to Hereford every year and what for? Especially this year, with everything that's been going on.'

Alan opened his mouth. Sam held out her hand.

'If you're going to say anything that relates to Scorpio or four planets, I'll fire you.'

'Sometimes you're just no fun.'

Sam sipped her coffee and then licked the chocolate from her upper lip. 'O'Connor told me I should forgive him.'

Alan frowned. 'What for?'

'Oh Christ, I don't know, dying on me, I suppose.'

'Fucking nerve. Where does he get off telling you to forgive your father?'

'I've told him I'm not looking for a therapist – I don't know how many times. I should never have taken this on. I knew it was a mistake. I mean, a therapist based in Oxford. It's like a photofit match from hell for me, Alan. Why did I ever agree to do it?'

Alan began counting off on his fingers. 'One, because he came via Mark who you adore. Two, you were a basket case after Jenny Hughes and needed to keep busy. Three, you were in no financial position to turn down work.'

'But not in Oxford, not with a therapist. I must have been mad.'

Alan smiled. 'I'd never risk saying that to your face but—'

'Shut up,' Sam said. 'Or I'll shake your hand.'

Alan laughed. 'Do you think Tony killed her?'

'He was there at the gaudy. He had the opportunity. But he doesn't bother to disguise his dislike of her.'

'Would he risk slagging her off if he'd killed her?'

Sam tapped her spoon on her saucer. 'Double bluff?'

'But you said they were going to get divorced.'

'Maybe the motive was money. She was a lawyer; perhaps he

thought if they divorced she'd fleece him. I wonder what her will says. If it's the usual one, he'll stand to benefit, won't he?'

'Could be.' Alan picked up a packet of sugar and shook it.

'Or,' Sam continued, 'maybe the O'Connor thing got him going and he couldn't bear it.'

'But from what he says he was glad to get rid of her. He didn't want her any more.'

'I wonder what Alice told O'Connor about the state of her marriage?'

'Yes,' Alan said. 'I wonder.'

A heavily pregnant woman made her way past Alan and Sam's table.

'God,' Alan said. 'She looks like she's about to drop.'

Sam looked up from the table. 'What?'

Alan nodded at the woman. 'I said she—'

'Oh shit!' Sam said. 'I forgot . . .'

'What's the matter?'

'There's was a pregnancy test kit in the bin in Alice Knight's bathroom,' Sam said. 'I completely forgot.'

'You *forgot*?'

'Well, yes, I did.'

'Have you told anyone?'

'No, I forgot. How could I tell anyone?'

'For God's sake, woman! Call yourself a private investigator? Anyway, it probably doesn't matter now, they'll have the results of the post-mortem. If she was pregnant, they'll know that by now.'

'So, was she pregnant and if so who by and had she told them *and* what was she intending to do and how did they feel about it?'

'That's a whole lot of questions,' Alan said. 'How old was she?'

Sam shrugged. 'Contemporary of Mark's, so that would make her about forty.'

'Biological clock could have been giving her grief. It happens.'

'Does it?' Sam said. 'I never hear mine.'

He rolled his eyes. 'Why doesn't that surprise me? Ears stuffed with cat fur.'

Sam ignored him. 'How much did we pay for these?' she asked, scowling at their coffee cups.

'Even if it was a penny it'd be too much,' Alan said, shoving the cup away from him in disgust.

Sam picked up her mobile and phoned Greg. 'Has he gone?' she asked.

'Yes, love, Elvis has left the building. To be precise, he left it about fifteen minutes ago. He was most regretful that you weren't here.'

Sam laughed. 'You sure he's not lurking about?'

'Absolutely bloody positive. Saw him screech out of the car park with my own peepers.'

'Thanks, Greg. See you in a bit.'

Back at the office Sam picked up the phone and put in a call to O'Connor.

'Could you tell me what Alice said to you about the state of her marriage?'

O'Connor was silent for a few seconds. 'She didn't really tell me much about it.'

'Did she give you the impression it was over?'

'No,' O'Connor said slowly. 'She didn't do that.'

'Had she told Tony about you?'

'Yes, she had. That became obvious when I spoke to him on the phone.'

'She didn't tell you she had?'

'No.'

'Was she pregnant?'

Silence.

'Mr O'Connor?'

'What on earth makes you ask that? Have you spoken to the police?'

'No, I saw a pregnancy kit in her bathroom.'

She heard O'Connor clear his throat but he said nothing.

'She hadn't said anything to you?'

'The police want to DNA-test me and Tony. Apparently the post-mortem identified that she was pregnant.'

'Were you using contraception?'

'She said she was on the pill.'

'Did you see her take it?'

'No. When you're having an affair there are lots of things you don't necessarily see.'

'Were you using condoms?'

'No.'

'So you were relying on her telling you the truth.'

'Yes.'

'Did you ever discuss children with her?'

'In what way?'

'In any way.'

'She'd fallen pregnant with Tony as an undergraduate. That was partly why they got married but then she lost the child.'

'And they didn't try again?'

'It had been an accident so—'

'But by then they were married?'

'Yes, they were.'

'She never said she wanted to have children?'

'No, and frankly I think she and Tony were far too narcissistic. It wouldn't have suited their lifestyle.'

'So, if she were pregnant, what do you think she would have done with it?'

'Got rid of it, I presume.'

'I thought having children was the ultimate narcissism,' Sam said. 'You produce lots of little replicas that remind you of you.'

There was a resounding silence on the end of the phone.

'Sorry,' she said after the silence had extended for an uncomfortable length of time. 'That was rude.'

'No, that's fine,' O'Connor said. 'I was just thinking about what you'd said.'

That evening back in her flat, Sam had just begun tucking into a prawn korma she'd ordered from the Indian takeaway down the road, when the phone rang. She swore, wiped her mouth and grabbed the receiver.

'What?' she said.

'Depends. What you offering?' a man's voice replied.

'Sorry?'

'What's in it for me?'

'Who *is* this?'

'You leave me your card and don't know who I am. Not much of an investigator, are you, girlie?'

'I leave my card with lots of people.'

She waited for an explanation to be forthcoming and watched anxiously as Frank sniffed around the edges of her curry.

'You were at the door a week back. Left your card. Asked about that bird who's gone missing at number thirty-seven.'

Now she had him. The man in the flat above Meg's: a pot belly, a purple nose and a hand shaking against black polyester trousers.

'What do you want?'

'Isn't that the wrong way round?'

Sam sighed and waited for the game-playing to end.

'Bottle of Bell's.'

'Right.'

'Time's ticking, girlie. Bring it over and I'll talk.'

The phone went dead. 'You really are Mr Charm, aren't you?' Sam said into the silent receiver.

She looked at her watch. The shop down the road would still be open for her to buy the whisky. If it wasn't she could probably try Edie. She looked longingly at her curry, then put the cardboard lids back on the foil containers and took it all through into the kitchen. She picked up a bag of rubbish she'd been meaning to take down for days and headed for the door. Frank Cooper trotted ahead of her as she walked swiftly round the mansion block and down the stairs to the bins.

Sam picked up the heavy rubber lid of a dustbin, found it full and let it drop back down again. The next one she tried was empty other than for a few broken shards of glass, covered in oily, rank-smelling water. She heaved her rubbish bag into the bin and dropped the lid back down. The area around the back of the mansion blocks was disgusting. Everyone used it to dump things they couldn't be bothered to take to the tip: unwanted boxes they hadn't broken down into a size the bin men would take, pieces of broken glass, car batteries, rolled-up pieces of matting and old mattresses. The six-monthly turnover of tenants in the rented flats in the block meant that there were often rich pickings for Edie, who examined the bins carefully each morning before she went to the Post Office to get her three papers: the *Daily Mail*, the *Mirror* and the *Sun*. Edie had found all sorts out here: a nice pair of black and white Minnie Mouse ears (good for parties), a three-drawer filing cabinet with keys in which she kept her tobacco, and once a serviceable portable colour TV that she now had in her bedroom.

Sam wasn't beyond a bit of rummaging herself. She stood over a bin, which seemed to have been stuffed with a lot of perfectly acceptable men's shirts. How could people throw things like this away when there was a charity shop less than five minutes' walk away? She was just contemplating whether she had the energy to take them there herself when she heard a noise behind her. Frank, she thought – and then the blow fell.

Perhaps she had known it was coming and was moving instinctively away, because the blow didn't hit her flush on the head, it glanced off the left-hand side of her skull, hit her ear and crashed on to her left shoulder. She staggered and began to turn, but the following blow was harder, more direct. As she fell forwards on her hands and knees she had an image of Alfie Turner's lizard eyes. The dog tags, she thought, have I got them? She took one hand off the ground and tried to check her pocket but as soon as she did, her other arm crumpled under her and she pitched forward. The last thing she saw before her face hit wet concrete was Jenny Hughes reaching out long yellow nails towards her.

CHAPTER SIXTEEN

Sam regained consciousness in darkness. Her eyes were blind-folded, her mouth bound. As she moved the muscles of her face, she felt her eyebrows, eyelashes and her hair all pulling against sticky tape. Something had been stuffed into her mouth and it pressed against the back of her throat, making her gag. She tried to move her arms and legs but couldn't; she was paralysed. She felt something tight round her wrists – more tape. She sucked in air through her nose and felt the pain explode in her head. Wriggling her fingers produced more pain. She tried to sit up but groaned as an excruciating spasm ran down her neck into her shoulder. Breathe, she said to herself. You must breathe. Concentrate on that, on not being sick. If you're sick you'll die on your own vomit. She focused on her breathing, dipping in and out of consciousness, but each breath dragged up the nausea from her stomach. It was only a matter of time. She passed out.

Petrol. She smelled it first, then heard liquid being sloshed around in a can. She was wide awake now, terrified, her feet scrabbling for a foothold on the ground. Liquid was being poured over her body and thrown in her face. She was being soaked. The petrol caught at the back of her throat. A match was struck. Something light hit her body.

She attempted to scream but the noise was muffled. She tried to wriggle out of the way but where had the match landed? Which bit of her body? She heard laughter. She wanted to cover her face, but her hands were tied tight behind her back. Soon she would be alight, incapable of movement, screaming and burning down to the bone. And all the time she was thinking: Who is doing this to me? Who could hate me enough to humiliate me, to kill me? Who wants to frighten me this much? Because she was terrified, more scared than she'd ever been. She wanted to pass out but she couldn't. She wanted the safety of oblivion, but there it was again, that soft laughter. She lay still and waited.

The smell of burning. God, was that her? She couldn't protect her face. She wanted to cover her face at least. She had to roll, isn't that what they told you to do? To roll over and over to put out the fire. So she started rolling but everything was hurting: her shoulder, her head and her hands. And still she felt no heat. But it must be coming, mustn't it? Something was alight.

A hand grabbed the front of her jacket and pulled her into a sitting position.

'Tell him to come in. Tell him if he doesn't want to speak to us we'll be speaking to you.' The man was well spoken with no trace of any identifiable accent. It certainly wasn't one of the Turner brothers.

Sam tried to speak but couldn't. A hand scrabbled at her mouth and tore the tape off. She gagged and felt the cloth pulled out of her mouth. She leaned forwards and heaved out her stomach contents. She retched and retched until there was nothing more to bring up. Then she was babbling, the words tumbling out of her.

'Who are you talking about? I don't know . . . ?'

A slap rocked her head back on her shoulders.

'Shut up. You know who we want. We know he's been in contact. Find a way of getting hold of him or we'll be talking to you again.' A hand patted the side of her face. 'Real soon. You think this is bad? I tell you, this is nothing.' The gag was shoved back in her mouth and the tape stuck back over the top. A hand pushed her to the ground.

She didn't know how much time had passed. All she knew was

that she was still alive, that she was not on fire. There was no laughter. She heard feet running, then voices.

'Jesus Christ, is she all right?' The voice was familiar. She felt hands on her head. 'It's best I do this fast, I'm afraid.'

The tape tearing off her face stung like crazy. She tried to open her eyes, flinched and closed them – then peeped them open again. All she could see was shapes and shadows. Then someone did the same to the tape over her mouth. Her hands and feet were free now but she couldn't stand, just bringing her hands forwards to the front of her body hurt. She couldn't feel her feet. Hands came up under her arms.

'You have to walk to get the feeling back.' But it was like walking on numb blocks. She took a step and stumbled. Took another and began to fall. Someone caught her but they wrenched her damaged shoulder and she cried out.

'We've got to take her to hospital,' she heard.

'No hospital!' she shouted. 'No fucking hospital. I'm fine. Take me home.' She turned and focused on the person holding her upright. It was Gary Cooper. 'Sorry,' she said. 'Your ribs. I didn't know. Max . . .' *Do not forsake me, oh my darling*. But she had been, forsaken, hadn't she? She put her face in her hands and started to shake. She couldn't stop, and the more she tried, the more she felt she was holding a pneumatic drill.

'It's all right,' he said, and put an arm round her shoulders.

'Don't touch me,' she snapped, shaking his arm from her shoulder. The last thing she heard before she lost consciousness was his laugh.

She woke screaming. It was dark and she thought she was back there; she could smell the petrol. She flung out her arm and something fell to the ground. She felt sheets. Light flooded the room and Max stood in the doorway.

'How are you?'

Sam tried to sit sideways on the bed but it hurt too much,

everything hurt too much, and she fell back against the pillows. She flexed her hands and feet, rotated her shoulders; every bit of her ached.

'Where am I?' she asked, but her throat was so dry it came out as a croak. She reached for the glass by her bed and drained it.

'At my place. Hospital didn't seem to grab you. So once we'd checked nothing was broken we brought you here.'

'*I* feel broken.' Sam looked down and saw that she was wearing a huge yellow and black striped rugby shirt that came practically to her knees. She looked at Max and raised her eyebrows.

'Sorry, but we had to undress you. I got Paula to help me. Your clothes were wrecked so we threw them out.' He sat on the edge of her bed. 'You've got some pretty nasty enemies.'

Sam didn't say anything. Nausea was sliding up and down her gullet like a big snake. She concentrated on not being sick. The water had helped. 'Can I have some more?' she asked, holding out the glass.

He came back with a full bottle of water and handed it to her. But when she tried to pour it, her hands were shaking so much she started to spill it all over the table.

'Here,' he said, and took the bottle from her and poured the water into her glass. She swallowed more water on to the head of the snake; for the moment it lay still.

'They seemed to think Dad's alive,' she croaked.

Max frowned. 'This was about him?'

She nodded. 'Told me to tell him to come in or they'd be paying me another call.'

'But you haven't even seen him, have you?'

Sam shook her head. 'Who do you think they were?'

Max shrugged. 'You better get some rest. You can stay here as long as you like.'

'What were you doing there?'

'Getting you out of a shitload of trouble.'

Sam looked at him. 'You didn't call him off, did you?'

'Get some rest,' he said. 'I'll leave you to sleep.' He turned out the overhead light. She turned on the one next to her bed. She didn't want to sleep in the dark. She never wanted to sleep in the dark again.

Later she woke and had a bath. Under water, her body looked a mess. She couldn't have the water as hot as she usually did. It hurt too much. She lay in the lukewarm water counting her welts and bruises, flexing her toes. Her face wasn't much better. She had a large abrasion across her forehead, which she had picked the grit out of. She'd swabbed it with witch hazel and it stung like hell. There was a cut across the top of her nose and to cap it all, half her eyebrows seemed to have come off with the tape. She had two bumps on the back of her head and her left ear was a mess. She could move no individual part of her body without the whole lot hurting, one hurt connecting to another, and then to another. Her body was a map of sore places. She dropped her head back in the water and tried to loosen the blood caked into her hair. There was a knock on the door.

'You all right in there?' Max asked.

'Yes,' she lied. 'Fine.'

'There's food when you're ready.'

She did not want to get out of the bath, it hurt too much to bend and stretch. Everything hurt. She prodded her scalp and felt a large crusty scab above her left ear. She didn't think she'd be able to eat. She wondered if she would ever stop feeling sick, if she would ever stop smelling petrol. Gingerly she put on Max's dark blue towelling dressing gown. It brushed the top of her feet but probably came halfway down his muscular calves. She slid her feet into a large pair of sheepskin slippers with broken-down backs and shuffled through to where she could smell cooking.

'Fry up,' he said. 'Always my best attempt at cooking.'

'Fine,' Sam said, and lowered herself carefully on to a straight-backed wooden chair. Max put a plate down in front of her: fried eggs, toast, bacon, and fried potatoes. The surface of the eggs had that slimy, jelly-like look. She swallowed the salty taste that rose up in her mouth.

'You must eat,' he said, firmly.

'Yes,' she said, and picked up her knife and fork. She sniffed. She could not get the smell of petrol out of her nose. The taste was still there at the back of her throat.

'Tuck in,' he said, gesturing to the plate of food with his fork. She slashed through the top of the egg and watched it bleed yellow over the pink bacon.

Afterwards she did feel better. At least she felt better until he picked up his cigarettes and struck a match; then she was running from the kitchen to the bathroom and her head was down the toilet and she was violently sick.

She sat on the edge of the bed, crouched over, hugging her stomach.

'Sorry,' she said.

'What is it?'

She said nothing, leaning over, rocking back and forth.

'Sam?'

'They doused me in petrol, they struck a match. I thought they were going to set me alight.'

He flinched. 'Sorry, I didn't think.' He sat down next to her. 'I need to talk to you about your father.'

She felt the tears sting her eyes and blinked them away. Oh no, she thought, not now, not when I feel like this. I don't have the strength to make him stop and there's no phone I can slam down this time. So she said nothing, just pinched the top of her nose.

'I talked to one of the blokes out in Oman with him.'

'So he *was* in Oman?'

'Yes, he did two tours out there.'

'According to the histories they lost twelve men. We weren't told but I always assumed.'

Max nodded. 'This guy was out there with D Squadron in his first five-month tour. He said on the first tour your dad was fine, nothing much happened, relatively straightforward, but that weird things started happening on the second tour. He said your dad came back from leave acting really odd. Saying it was all up for him, that he knew he was going to cop it this time round. He said it was as if he'd lost his nerve, as if he'd decided to die. But the strange thing was that he thought he was putting on an act. He said your dad had never been like that. Always gung-ho for action and a bit of a joker, then here he was and it was like he was a different person altogether. Like something had happened on leave. They were worried about his mental condition, said he was introverted and very quiet. All he said was negative shit that was getting on their nerves.'

'Did he see him killed?'

'No, that's the thing. He said they'd gone out on patrol and your dad stayed behind in the sangar. When he and the other guys came back, they were told that a sniper had got him. But there was no sign of any hit. They'd lost a couple on the last tour and that had been through mortars and a rocket. Things that really mess you up. You get hit by a mortar, place ends up looking like an abattoir. There's nothing left. But in this case he said there was no sign of anything having hit the sangar. No damage at all and no sign of your dad; all his stuff was gone, no blood, no sign of action. They were just told he'd been killed. They all thought it was a set-up. They thought he might have cracked up or gone AWOL and they weren't being told. But that was all that happened. They were told he was dead. Nothing else.'

'So no one actually saw him killed?'

'No.'

'So, what happened? The SAS killed him? They wanted him to appear to be dead? He went AWOL? What?'

'I don't know but this same bloke served later in Northern

Ireland. He was working on the border, grabbing members of the IRA as they crossed over from the Republic into Northern Ireland. It was their job to act on intelligence received and capture people, then hand them over.'

Sam stared at him as he scratched the back of his head. 'And?'

'Sometimes they handed them over to the authorities – RUC.'

'Yes.'

'Other times they were ordered to hand them over for ... disposal. He swears your dad was in one of these abduction and assassination squads. He'd grown his hair and a beard, but he said he was sure.'

'He saw him?'

'Yes, he says he did – on several occasions.'

'When was this?'

'Nineteen seventy-five.'

'Did he approach him?'

'He did, but when he said something your dad just said he must have the wrong bloke. Made some joke about having a twin. Just shrugged it off. Also these occasions were not times for small talk. They were handing over people to be killed. So everyone was pretty jumpy. But he was fairly certain. And he said he'd never been convinced that he'd been killed in Oman. So it made sense to him that he was still alive.'

Sam straightened up and looked at Max. 'Did he die in Northern Ireland?'

'I don't know.'

'Why would we be told he'd died if he hadn't, Max? Why do something like that?'

Max shrugged. 'To protect you. To protect him. Maybe it was the only way to secure the situation.'

'You're saying he could be alive. Is that what you're saying?'

'Yes.'

'Who did you tell about the letter?'

'The SAS.'

'And who would they have told?'

Max shrugged. 'They'd probably have passed it on to Special Branch or MI5.'

'Did they do this to me?'

Max frowned. 'What . . . ?'

'Did they do this to me, the people you told?'

Max's face turned bright red. 'No, Sam. Why would they?'

'To flush him out. Were you watching to see if he'd appear? Did you have me set up as bait, Max?'

'No . . .'

But she saw a flicker of doubt in his eyes.

'If you were watching me, why did it take so long for you to get to me?'

'He took you out the other side of the block. My man was expecting you back in Cristowe Road after dumping your rubbish but then when you didn't come out he went round the back and saw the guy dragging you up the other side.'

'I see.'

'One thing's for sure, Sam. No one's going to find your dad if he doesn't want to be found. That just won't happen. Escape and evasion – it's what we're trained in.'

'I thought you were trained to kill.'

He shrugged. 'That too.'

Sam put her head in her hands and swore as she touched the mess on her forehead. She groaned and straightened up and looked Max in the eye.

'What was he like?'

He broke eye contact at once. 'Well . . .'

Did she imagine it or was he looking distinctly uneasy?

'I don't think this is the time—'

But now she was interested. 'You didn't like him, did you?'

He shook his head. 'That's not it,' he said. 'You must get some more sleep. This isn't the time for this.'

'What happened when he was on leave? Did something happen? Tell me.'

Max didn't reply to her question. 'Go to sleep. We can talk about this later.'

'What a fucking mess,' she said.

'Sleep. You're in no fit state to think straight.'

'No.' But somehow she didn't think that sleep alone would make any of it any clearer.

'You want something to help you sleep?'

Sam nodded. He left the room and she heard him opening a cabinet in the bathroom. When he came back into the room, she was sitting up in the bed. He handed her the pills and she took them.

'Tell me these provide dreamless sleep,' she said.

'Absolutely. Why do you think I take them?'

'Max?'

He turned.

'If that's what you were doing, thanks for watching my back.'

He frowned. 'I'm really sorry we didn't get to you sooner, Sam.'

She shrugged. 'At least you got to me – that's what counts.'

CHAPTER SEVENTEEN

Sam woke to a silent flat. The first thing she thought of – after how much her body still hurt – was the expression on Max's face when she asked him what her father was like. It had been an expression of extreme reluctance. She levered herself upright and walked slowly into the kitchen. On the table was a note.

Sorry, had to go out. Make yourself at home. Stay if you want. Help yourself to food. I've left some clothes out for you on my bed.

Sam grimaced. Well, the conversation about her father was going to have to wait. Part of her felt relieved. She walked through into his bedroom and looked at the clothes: jeans (way too big), a belt, a T-shirt, a blue jumper and a pair of trainers. The trainers actually fitted her and so were obviously not Max's. Sam looked round the bedroom, saw signs of female occupation and presumed the shoes must have belonged to Paula.

She picked up the phone and called Alan.

'Where the fuck have you been?' Alan said. 'I've been going mental.'

'I'm at my godfather's.'

'Where the hell have you been?' he repeated.

'Don't give me grief,' Sam said tersely. 'Got beaten up. Got rescued.'

His tone of voice softened. 'You're joking, right?'

'No.'

'You all right?'

'No.' Sam heard the crack in her voice and stopped talking. 'Sam?'

'I thought they were going to set me on fire.'

There was a low whistle on the other end of the line. 'The Turners?'

Sam was silent. At least Max wasn't here and Alan couldn't see her. She gave up the struggle for control and allowed the tears to course down her face.

'Sam?'

It was a while before she could speak. 'I feel like shit, Alan. Like shit. It wasn't the Turners. Someone was looking for my dad.'

He waited for her to regain some control. Then: 'What did they want?'

'Said they wanted *him*. That if they didn't get him they'd pay me another visit.'

'But you haven't even met him. You're not even sure he's alive. You *can't* deliver him.'

'They weren't interested in that particular point of view.'

'Well, I hate to heap trouble on trouble, but O'Connor's going completely mental.'

'What's been happening?'

'He got a note. Scared the shit out of him. Says it threatens his children. That Meg is out there somewhere and is coming after the children. I can't make head nor tail out of the note either. Seems bland as hell but it definitely means something significant to him.'

'Sounds like he's lost his marbles. Why on earth should she? She might come after *him*, I suppose, if she's pissed off about the affair, but not the children. It doesn't make any sense. Has he gone to the police?'

'Yes, but he says they're not taking him seriously and meanwhile he's terrified.'

'Well, try to calm him down.'

'OK, but he's desperate to talk to you. Says he'll be up in town the next couple of days and wants to see you.'

'It's going to have to wait, Alan, we've got some business to attend to.'

After telling him what it was she put down the receiver and stared at the clothes. She still felt dirty, could still taste petrol at the back of her throat. Even though she'd had a bath last night she needed another wash. She walked into the bathroom and stared at the shower. It needed to be quick, so that would have to do. She took off the rugby shirt, stepped inside the cubicle and got the water running. What she really wanted to do was scrub off the feelings of vulnerability and helplessness, of terror. Using a pungent bar of Max's soap, she scrubbed every bit of her that didn't hurt too much and then patted herself dry and put on the clothes Max had left out. The trousers were the main problem. She had to turn them up by about a foot and even with the belt done up as tight as it would go, they sagged dangerously low on her hips. Never mind, she thought, at least hipsters were in fashion.

That afternoon Alan and Sam stood outside Meg O'Connor's Fulham flat and looked up at the grimy net curtains, which hung in the windows of the upstairs flat.

'Very nice,' Alan said.

'Unlike the occupant.'

Sam had felt too fragile to do this by herself and had asked Alan along for moral support. She rang the doorbell and waited. Eventually Hicks came to the door wearing blue tracksuit bottoms and a grubby red cable-knit jumper. His nose was as purple as she remembered it.

'You took your bleedin' time.'

'Something came up.'

'Forty-eight hours' worth? Was it a wall then? Walk into a

door, did you? Women drive you bleedin' mad, don't they?' He nodded to Alan, seeking confirmation.

Sam didn't respond. Feeling Alan starting to close in on the man, she put a restraining hand on his arm. They weren't going to get any information from this tosser by getting into arguments on domestic violence.

'Who's he?' He nodded at Alan.

'A colleague.'

Hicks looked Alan up and down. 'That's what they're calling them these days, is it?'

'You want to tell me anything or not, mister? If not I've got better things to do with my time.'

'You got the Bell's?'

Sam lifted the blue plastic bag she was holding in her left hand and felt her shoulder throb in protest. He turned and walked up the stairs to his flat. Sam and Alan followed.

The flat stank of old cooking oil, damp and unwashed clothes. They followed him into a room with a battered sofa covered in brown nylon and two armchairs with floral covers. The carpet was brown like the sofa and worn. He sat down in the armchair closest to a three-bar electric heater, set into the wall. His head dropped back against a black greasy stain on the back of the chair. The flat was bitterly cold. Sam and Alan sat carefully on the edge of the sofa, hugging their coats round them.

'So what do you have to tell me?'

'Can't think with my throat this dry.'

She took the bottle out of the plastic bag and placed it carefully on top of a newspaper showing a Page Three girl with very large breasts. He grabbed the bottle and twisted off the lid.

'Now that's what I call a real woman,' he said, staring sullenly at the photo and then at Sam's chest.

Sam decided she had had enough of playing it reasonable. She snatched the bottle out of his hands, took the lid off and tipped it upside down. Whisky poured on to the carpet and the smell filled the room.

He scrambled to his feet.

Sam straightened the bottle. 'Got anything to tell us? Or we're leaving and this is leaving with us.'

'Fucking bitch,' he said.

'Manners maketh man,' Sam said, beginning to turn the bottle upside down again.

He began to speak quickly. 'The bloke were carrying her. She were legless.'

Sam righted the bottle. 'Who?'

'Woman you're interested in.'

'Meg O'Connor downstairs?'

He nodded and sat back down, his eyes fixed on the bottle. 'When was this?'

'Day before the police were crawling everywhere.'

'The day before she went missing?'

'Dunno when she went missing, do I?'

Sam nodded to the TV. 'Can you remember what was on that?'

'Watch a lot of that,' he said glumly.

'What time was it?'

'Late – they woke me up.'

'Late? You mean twelve? Three? What?'

'Later. Noise woke me up. Got up, looked out of the window and there they were.'

'What sort of noise?'

'Shouting, carrying on.'

'Had you seen the man before?'

'Not as I remember.'

'Was it her husband?'

'Don't know what he looks like.'

Sam remembered the photo of O'Connor and Meg in the flat downstairs. She turned to Alan. 'Could you go downstairs and

224

get the photo in the living room?' She dug in her pockets and handed him the keys. Alan nodded and left the room.

'Did you get a clear look at the man?'

'It was dark. He had a hat on, one with the long brims they all wear these days.'

'A baseball hat?'

He shrugged. 'They all wear them.'

'And he was carrying her into the house?'

'Didn't say that, did I?'

'What then?'

'Other way round.'

'Out of the house?'

He nodded. 'Putting her into his car.'

'Did they say anything?'

'She was out of it – wasn't going to be saying much.'

'Did you tell the police this?'

He looked hard at the electric fire. 'Don't like the police. Me and them don't see eye to eye.'

'You're sure it was her?'

He nodded. 'Recognized her dress. Seen her wearing it.'

'Did you get a look at the car?'

'Car's a car.'

'Colour?'

He shook his head; his eyes were fixed on the bottle in Sam's hand. 'Told you – it were dark.'

'And you're sure you'd never seen this man before?'

Again he shook his head. Sam put the bottle back on the topless woman and he grabbed it, put it to his lips and then placed it down by the far side of his chair, out of Sam's reach.

Alan came back into the room with the photo and handed it to Hicks. He looked at it and frowned. 'Don't think it was him.'

'But if you didn't see him properly . . .'

'Too young – this bloke was older, taller.'

'Are you sure?'

He shrugged. 'No.'

Sam looked at a black-and-white photo of a girl and boy dressed in forties style, which was on the mantelpiece. 'Sweet-looking kids,' she said.

He stood up and turned the photo face down. 'That's all I've got for you.'

Sam stood as well. 'Thank you. I appreciate your help. If anything else occurs to you, phone me.'

'It won't,' he said, and sat down heavily, his face turned away from them.

They let themselves out. It was dark and beginning to drizzle and Sam shivered and hunched herself down in her jacket. Alan did the same. Sam looked across the street and thought of what June had said.

'Alan? How do you fancy exercising a bit of your famous charm?'

'Why do I have a bad feeling about what you are going to ask me to do?' Alan replied.

Sam nodded across the road. 'In that house lives June. Perhaps you could ask her about Meg. I tried, but she hates me so I didn't get very far.'

'Why does she hate you?'

'She thinks I torture Frank.'

Alan laughed. 'So what's the catch?'

Sam tried to arrange her facial features in a pattern of complete openness and innocence.

'Don't do that,' Alan said.

'What?'

'Whatever you're doing to your face. It's unnerving.'

'She's a bit dotty, that's all.'

'How dotty?'

Sam patted his arm encouragingly. 'She'll love you. The thing is last time I showed her a picture of Meg she said "Slut" and I thought she was insulting me. But perhaps she saw something and she meant Meg. Do you see?'

'Vaguely,' Alan said.

'I'll wait for you at the end of the street.'

A few minutes later Alan returned.

'Well?' Sam said.

'Nice old thing. House is in a terrible state. Newspapers piled practically up to the ceiling. Bit like yours.'

'Shut up,' Sam said. 'Did she see anything?'

'It's a bit difficult to tell. But I think she saw what Hicks saw. Says whoever it was, it definitely wasn't her husband. She knows him. O'Connor's probably the type to talk to her, isn't he?'

Sam nodded. 'Any description of the man or the car?'

Alan shook his head. 'She's hardly interested in cars, is she?'

They began to walk back to Sam's flat. With each step Sam felt some part of her body protest.

'Christ, that was depressing.' Alan said. 'Do you think that's how we're all going to end up? Like Hicks and June?'

'Don't be silly,' Sam said. 'Do you think he was telling the truth?'

'Why should he lie? Doesn't look like the sort who would welcome visitors.'

'I think he's fine about visitors, provided they're carrying bottles of whisky.'

'Do you think she was dead?'

'I don't know if she was then. But my guess is she definitely is now.'

'If you had a dead body and wanted to dispose of it, where would you take it?'

Sam and Alan looked at each other. 'The river,' they both said simultaneously.

'I had a friend,' Alan said, 'who committed suicide by jumping off Chiswick Bridge with stones in his pockets. The police said then it could take up to six weeks for the body to turn up and they were right on the money. In the end he turned up barely a hundred metres from where he'd jumped.'

Sam shivered. 'If that's what happened, she could turn up any day now.'

Alan nodded. As they reached Sam's flat, two men got out of a car parked directly in front of the block. One was Max. The other Sam had never seen before. He had prominent pale blue eyes and long fair eyelashes.

Max nodded at Sam. 'How you feeling?'

'Rough,' she said, not taking her eyes off the other man.

'He'd like a word.' Max nodded to his companion.

'Would he?' Sam stared at him and the man stared back. But Sam wasn't up to sustained eyeballing and she broke contact first. 'You better come in, then.' She put her key in the front door and they entered the block. Sam looked at Edie's spy-hole. If she was in, this would be too much for her to miss. She winked at the hole and then let them into her flat. The three large men stood awkwardly in her front room.

'I'd prefer to see you on my own,' the man said, eyeing Alan.

'You see me with him or not at all,' Sam snapped. 'He knows the situation anyway.'

The man was silent and then obviously deciding it wasn't worth the argument, sat down. His eyes took in Sam's front room.

'You got a name, some ID?' Sam asked, and his eyes flicked back to her.

'I've got him,' the man said, nodding at Max. 'He can vouch for me. You don't have to know who I am. It's for the best.'

Sam laughed. 'I've always hated being told what's best for me.'

'We wanted to know if you had been contacted again by someone purporting to be your father.'

'No, just the letter, which I presume Max showed you.'

He stared at her. 'Nothing else. No contact whatsoever?'

Sam looked at Max. 'Did you tell him what happened?'

He nodded.

'If you are contacted again, we would very much like to know. We need to talk to him.'

'Is he alive?' Sam snapped.

'I'm not at liberty—'

'So, why should I do *you* any favours?'

The man sat back in the sofa and adjusted the front of his jacket. 'It would really be in your own best interests to co-operate with us, Ms Falconer.'

'Why doesn't it seem that way to me?'

No one spoke. Max was the first one to break the silence. 'Sam . . .'

Sam held out her hand to stop him speaking. 'No, let's get something straight here. If my father's still alive, we've been lied to. So why the fuck should I trust this arsehole? You don't get any favours from me without some information.'

The man ran his hand over a shaved head. 'The truth is we don't know if your father is alive or not.'

'Did he die in Oman in 1974?'

'No, he didn't.'

'Was he in Oman?'

'Yes.'

'Was he in Northern Ireland?'

The man's eyes darted towards Max.

Sam saw herself squatting next to her father's grave, running her hand over the grass. She thought of the stone she had left. She jumped to her feet. 'What did we bury?' she shouted. 'What the fuck did we bury?'

The man didn't say anything. No one said anything.

'Get the fuck out of here,' Sam said. 'Just get out. How dare you come here asking me for favours when you've fucked up my head with your lies.'

Alan stood up. 'Time for you to leave.' But the man looked at him impassively and remained seated.

'I understand you don't feel disposed to trust me. But we are concerned for your safety as well.'

'No, you're not,' Sam said. 'Even if you are, it's too bloody late, isn't it?' She pointed to the large abrasion on her forehead. 'The only reason I wasn't fried like a chip in a pan was because of Max here.'

He sighed. 'These people want to get at your father through you.'

'What, people like you, then? Did you ever pour petrol on someone and threaten to set her alight? Was it you softening me up prior to this little visit? Getting me nice and scared and pliable ... Well, fuck you.'

He didn't answer her but opened his briefcase. 'Here's a number to call in case your father contacts you.' He handed her the card but she refused to take it. He dropped it on to the sofa and stood up. He offered her his hand but she turned away from him. She didn't feel very polite.

'Get out!' she shouted.

The man stood up. 'You coming?' he asked Max.

'No,' Max said. 'I've got some stuff to pick up from Sam. I'll be along later.'

The man nodded and let himself out of the flat.

'Fucking arsehole,' Sam hissed as the front door slammed. She rounded on Max. 'And what the hell are you still here for?'

'Sam, it's not Max's—' Alan began.

'It's fine,' Max said. 'I thought we had a conversation outstanding. Maybe my timing's a bit off.'

'What are you talking about?'

'Yesterday you asked me what your father was like.'

The colour drained out of Sam's already pale face. The abrasion on her forehead stood out a startlingly vivid red. Sweat pricked the palms of her hands and her heart raced so fast she had difficulty catching her breath.

Alan glanced at Sam. 'I'll make you some tea,' he said.

Sam sat down heavily. 'No milk.'

'I'll get some. Give me your keys.'

Sam dug into her pocket and handed her keys to Alan.

He nodded to Max. 'Back in a minute.'

The front door banged behind Alan. Sam looked at Max.

He folded his arms. 'The thing is, Sam, you've had a rough enough time of it as it is. I don't want to upset you but I don't see how I can do this without that happening.'

Sam's heart rate jumped up a notch. 'You better just spit it out,' she said. 'The more you talk like that the more frightened I'll become.'

He nodded and cleared his throat. 'Well, your dad had a violent and unpredictable temper. Didn't show itself in the stuff he did for the SAS but it did show itself in his family life. Your mum or Mark ever talk about it?'

Sam shook her head slowly.

'He was mainly fine with his mates and on ops, but at home ... Thing is, he knew he could get away with it. If he'd pulled that shit with us he'd have been RTU'd just like that. Also he'd have met with a bit more resistance.'

'He beat up my mother?' Sam's voice sounded distant to her own ears.

'Not just your mother. It was well known in the regiment. He got around a bit before he settled down with Jean. The other girlfriends and wives knew his reputation. He wasn't liked for it but ... it's tolerated unless it crosses a line and becomes regimental business.'

'And what line is that?' Sam's voice was heavy with sarcasm. 'When someone dies?'

'After his first tour in Oman, when he was on leave, he crossed it. There'd been a couple of casualties. He'd seen a friend of his blown to pieces in front of him and when he came back he was all over the place. Last night of leave he went out and got completely hammered and went looking for a fight in town. When he didn't find one he went home . . .'

The door to the flat opened and Sam jumped. Alan stuck his head round the door. 'Tea on the way.' But when he saw Sam's face he closed the door quietly behind him.

'What happened then?'

'I got a call from Harry, who'd been out on the piss with him. He said I should get myself over to your place because he didn't like the look of your dad. He was worried what he might do.'

Max took a deep breath.

'Well, when I got there, he was sitting on the doorstep crying. He was holding you and saying you were the only one who was any good. You always were some sort of talisman for him. He couldn't stop crying and I couldn't get you away from him. When I tried, you latched on to his dog tags and started screaming so much you frightened me. It wasn't the first time he'd done something like that. I think that was the last straw for your mum.'

'What had he done?'

Max stood. 'Well, he'd gone berserk in there.'

'Did you go inside?'

He walked over to the window. His back was to Sam. 'It was shortly after that he went back to Oman for his second tour of duty.'

'I don't remember any of it,' Sam said. Her teeth were chattering now; however tightly she clenched her jaw she couldn't keep them still.

'I'm not surprised,' Max said. 'You were so little.' He stroked a finger through his ginger-grey moustache.

'Are you not going to tell me?' Sam asked.

'Well . . .' He started to speak, then stopped, then started again. 'Sam, I don't know what to do. I really think you should talk to your family.'

Sam laughed. 'They've said not one word of this for the last

232

twenty-eight years and now suddenly they're going to start blabbing to me? I don't think so. My mother is never very chatty at the best of times. The stiff upper lip is her preferred *modus operandi*, not the confessional.'

'No,' Max said. 'I remember your mother as a quiet woman but if she and Mark realize you know something they may change their minds. If you get no change from them then I promise you I'll tell you everything I know.' He picked his coat off the back of the chair and placed it over his arm. 'I'm really sorry, Sam.'

She tried to shrug. 'Reality check.'

He nodded. 'I know, but all the same.'

'It's best I know what I'm dealing with.'

'I think so too. Things seem to be coming to a head.'

After he'd left, she went into her bedroom and grabbed her jacket. She walked into the kitchen where Alan was reading one part of the *Evening Standard* and Frank was sitting on the other.

'I have to go out,' she said. 'Let yourself out when you want.' And she turned and ran back through the flat and down into the street. Behind her she could hear him calling her but she didn't stop. There was something she had to do.

Sam would have run all the way if she could but her body was too bruised by the battering she'd got, so she half ran, half walked along the New King's Road towards Putney. Her shoulder ached each time her foot hit the ground. She cut down the passage that ran to Putney Bridge tube and then followed the road around and walked up the stairs on to Putney Bridge. She leaned on the stone parapet and reached into her pocket. A perfect D-shaped moon glared from behind a ragged tear in the night sky. It was clear but bitterly cold. She held the dog tags out over the black river and tried to open her hand. But again that feeling overwhelmed her, that visceral feeling of holding on. Max said he'd tried to get her away from her father and that she'd screamed so much it had frightened him. She'd only been four years old. She tried again. Her knuckles stood out white in the moonlight. Her nails dug into the palm of her hand. Sam had an image of the nails passing through her palm and coming out through the back of her hand. A train ran over the bridge opposite, lights from the coaches rippled over the surface of the river. Her whole arm was shaking; she could not let go. Sam looked at the blue neon lights cascading down the front of a newly built building next to the church at the bottom of Putney High Street and willed herself to open her hand.

'Sam?'

She turned round to see Alan standing next to her, breathing heavily. 'You can't half move when you've a mind to.' He took hold of her arm and pulled it down to her side and placed his hand round her balled-up fist. He didn't ask her what she was doing. 'Come on, girl, let's get you a drink.'

Sam didn't move.

'Come on,' he said again. 'You look like you could do with one.'

He put his arm round her shoulders, pulled her to him and led her across the bridge.

Sam and Alan sat in a tapas bar at the bottom of Putney High Street with a large jug of strawberry margaritas in front of them. Sam's clenched right fist rested next to her glass. She had just finished telling Alan what Max had said about her father.

Alan pointed at her fist. 'You're going to have to let go in order to drink.'

Sam relaxed her hand, dropped the dog tags on the table and seized her glass. 'I'm going to get really drunk.'

Alan glanced at the dog tags. 'How did you end up with them?'

'Max gave them to me at the funeral.'

'Why didn't he give them to Mark? He was the eldest and a boy.'

'I've no idea. Maybe after what he did to him, Mark didn't want them.'

'What do they mean to you?'

'Good luck. Protection.' Sam twiddled a bright pink cocktail umbrella round and round. 'Or maybe that's what they *did* mean. Now I'm not so sure. If my father was a violent bully who beat up his own family, I don't know what they mean any more, but I can't demystify them just like that. I can't throw them away.'

'I'm not surprised,' Alan said. 'You've got twenty-eight years' worth of belief in them as a lucky charm.'

'Yes,' Sam said. 'Belief in a myth, in a fucking myth. My father, the dead hero.' She stabbed the sharp end of the cocktail umbrella savagely into the table until it snapped. 'How deluded can you be?'

'You're being unfair on yourself. How were you to know what he was like?'

'I could have asked, couldn't I? Instead I just allowed Mum and Mark their silence. I never really bothered to find out. I preferred my own myth to anything as sordid as reality.'

'Well, that's no crime,' Alan said.

'No, it's not a crime, it just makes me feel pretty damn stupid. Let's get another of these,' she said, tapping the side of the empty jug.

'They're quite strong, you know.'

'I know, Alan, that's why I want more of them.'

Alan went to the bar and came back a few minutes later with another jug. He filled their glasses and sat down. 'It wasn't as if you had any incentive before to find out about your father. I mean he was dead, wasn't he? So it wasn't as if what he was like mattered much.'

'But now it does,' Sam said. 'If he's come back, it matters a whole damn lot.'

They stayed until closing time, until they were both very

drunk. Alan insisted on walking Sam home even though he was so pissed he'd hardly have been any use even if help were required. They parted outside Sam's flat.

Sam hugged him. 'You're the only friend I've got,' she slurred. 'I'm hopeless with friends.'

'You've got that ugly cat,' Alan said.

'Oh yes, thank God – one friend and an ugly cat. So I'm all right then?'

'You're laughing, love.'

Sam staggered up the steps to her flat, and after fumbling with her keys let herself in. She threw down some food for Frank, tried to drink a bit of water to ward off the hangover she knew was beckoning and then collapsed, fully clothed, on her bed.

The following morning Sam sat in her office, waiting for the Nurofen to kick in. She wasn't sure what ached more, her head or her body. Last night, several jugs of margaritas had seemed like the best idea in the world; this morning it seemed like the worst. She reached for a can of Coke that Alan had thumped down on her desk half an hour ago and sipped cautiously. Alan was sitting at his desk with his head in his hands, emitting the odd moan or two. The phone on Sam's desk rang and Alan groaned even louder. Sam picked it up.

'Thanks, Greg. Send him up. Is it OK to use the empty office? Thanks.' She put the phone down. 'O'Connor's here,' she said.

'Whatever you do, don't bring him in here,' Alan said.

Sam laughed, stood up, walked out of the office and went to meet the lift. The doors opened and O'Connor stepped out. He stopped suddenly when he saw her face.

'God, what happened to you?' he asked, staring at her forehead.

Sam pressed the area with her fingertips; it had scabbed over and was starting to itch. She looked like a Klingon. 'It's my preparation for the next *Star Trek* convention.'

He stared blankly at her.

'I can see that one went over your head,' she said, and began walking towards the empty office.

'Is that why I haven't been able to get hold of you?'

'Partly.'

'Are you all right?'

'To be perfectly honest, I feel like I've been trampled on by buffaloes and I've got the hangover from hell.'

'Right.'

They entered the office and Sam closed the door behind them and sat down. 'Alan told me you'd received a message or something?'

O'Connor dropped a piece of paper on the desk. 'It's this.'

The note was neatly typed on white paper:

He stood bending over the kettle, with his watch in his hand, timing the eggs so that his back was turned...

Sam struggled to keep a straight face. She had been expecting something menacing. This was about as menacing as a Delia Smith recipe. 'This means something specific to you, I presume?'

O'Connor picked up the note and started walking up and down. 'She's coming for them. She's coming for the children. It's a direct threat.'

Sam followed him with her eyes as he paced back and forth, the note scrunched in his hand, and tried again. 'These words mean something to you, then?'

'Mean something? It's from the most depressing book in the English language.'

Sam tried to think of a witty retort, failed, and waited for him to spit it out.

'*Jude the Obscure* – that bloody awful book.'

'I haven't read it. What's the significance?'

'Significance! First, it's set in Oxford. Second, all the children kill themselves. Third, Jude, the father, dies.'

'Oh. And this bit?' She pointed at the note.

'This is just before the bodies of the three children are found. She's coming for the children. I know she is.'

'She?'

'Meg.'

Sam thought of Meg O'Connor being carried from her flat in the dead of night and doubted it. 'I just don't think that's likely. It doesn't make any sense. If she were coming for anyone, surely she'd be coming for *you*. And she has no history of violence, has she?'

O'Connor put his face in his hands. 'This is all my fault. I started the whole thing off by starting the affair with Alice. This is *all* my fault.'

The Nurofen didn't seem to be having the required effect and Sam was tiring of his histrionics. 'Have you met David Hicks?'

He took his head out of his hands and looked at her. 'Sorry?'

'Man who lives in the flat above Meg's.'

'Oh,' he said, and the 'Oh' was heavy with significance.

'What do you know about him?'

'Alcoholic – was living there with his sister until the authorities took her away.'

Sam thought of the black-and-white photo of the boy and the girl on his mantelpiece, how he'd turned the photo over.

O'Connor continued. 'Turned out they were having an incestuous relationship. He started drinking more and more.'

'So that's why he's shy of the police. Anyway, he says he saw Meg being carried from the house by a man and being put in a car the night after she went missing.'

O'Connor was staring at Sam. 'Did he recognize him?'

Sam shook her head. 'Maybe he was holding out on me – I don't know.'

'Have you told the police?'

She nodded. 'I told Phil this morning. The police may get more out of him than I managed.'

'Do you think he was telling the truth?'

Sam shrugged. 'He's weird but I can't imagine he'd make it up. Doesn't seem like the imaginative type. Also the woman across the road saw the same thing.'

O'Connor stopped pacing. 'You think she's dead, don't you?'

Sam sighed. That was exactly what she thought, but it seemed exceptionally brutal to say it.

He placed his hands flat on the desk and leaned towards Sam. 'Tell me the truth.'

She looked at him and wished she wasn't hung over. Sensitivity wasn't exactly her strong point even when she was completely sober. 'Look, John—'

'You do, I can tell from your expression.'

'It doesn't matter what my expression is or what I think. We still don't know. That's the truth and we both know it.'

'No,' he said, straightening up. 'The truth is we both think she's dead and she probably is.'

CHAPTER EIGHTEEN

Derek Moss had walked through Bishop's Park twice a day since his wife, Ruth, had died two years earlier and the dog walking had fallen to him. He hadn't wanted a dog. Had been dead against it from the start. Especially not the one she brought back. If he had to have one he wanted a proper man's dog: a Labrador or an Alsatian. But his wife had been insistent. They couldn't have a big dog, not in a flat without a garden. It was unfair and they were too old. She'd looked into it and decided on a pug. Embarrassing, Derek thought. Looked like a pig, with its squashed nose and big, bulging eyes. Looked as if the eyes would pop out on to the ground if you hit the back of his head too hard. No, Derek hadn't liked it one bit. Ruth said he would walk the dog and it would be good for his blood pressure but Derek suspected she just wanted him out from under her feet. He was recently retired and he knew he was driving her mad, hovering about the place, not knowing what to do with himself.

A month after they'd got Toby, his wife died suddenly from a heart attack, leaving him with a puppy that wasn't housetrained and still crying for its mother. He'd thought about giving him to Battersea Dogs' Home; he'd even thought about just throwing it in the river in a sack. That's what his father would have done. But then his father had been a brute. And in the aftermath of Ruth's death he found Toby a welcome distraction because he had to be walked and that's what got Derek out of bed in the morning, got him washed and out in the world. Walking the dog created a structure to his life in those first months when the days stretched ahead of him, punctuated only by visits to Putney Vale cemetery, where Ruth was buried.

Derek liked to walk early, when the park first opened, before the rollerbladers, the joggers and cyclists flooded in. He wasn't too steady on his pins any more and having people brushing past him at speed made him feel off-balance and frightened. It was all rush, rush, rush and people jabbering away on mobile phones. Also, if he came early he felt he could let Toby off the lead and he could have a good run around. Derek liked a peaceful park. If he'd still been able to drive he would have gone to Richmond but his eyesight wasn't up to it now and after Ruth died, he sold the car.

On this particular morning, Derek had gone all the way to Craven Cottage before he realized Toby wasn't snuffling at his heels. Usually the dog never went far away from him, rooting around in the bushes or galloping a bit ahead and then turning round and barking at him. Derek turned and whistled but there was no response. So, instead of stopping as usual and leaning on the green metal railings and watching a few planes descending towards Heathrow, he walked back the way he had come, calling for his dog. He found Toby on the stone steps leading down to the river. He was barking and nuzzling something – white legs sprawled in a position that no one alive would adopt. A floral dress was up around the upper body. Derek had to call the dog repeatedly before it left the corpse and came reluctantly to his side.

A man was jogging towards him. Derek waved him to a halt and the man slowed reluctantly to a walk.

'Got a phone, mate? There's a body. Got to call the police.'

The man looked, then looked again. 'Jesus . . .' he said, and an expression of fascination and revulsion crossed his face. He fumbled in the pouch round his waist, took out a phone and punched 999.

Derek listened to him give their location. The man put the phone away.

'They told me to wait but if I do I'll be late for work.'

'It's OK,' Derek said. 'I'll stay.' He watched the man jog away down the path. He bent down and clicked Toby on to the lead. He wished he could cover the woman or at least pull the dress back down over her legs but he knew he shouldn't touch the body. By the look of her she'd been dead a long time. But at least he could stop people coming along the path – warn them. Ten minutes later, that's how the police found him, standing sentinel on the path, his dog wheezing at his side, and a small group of people trying, not very subtly, to look over his shoulder at what lay beyond him on the wet stone steps.

Sam sat waiting for O'Connor to come out of the toilet. It would have been easier, she thought, if she could have viewed Meg O'Connor's face as having nothing to do with a human being. It was only when she tried to think of it as a human head that the nausea began to crawl up her stomach and into her throat. O'Connor had thrown up violently and suddenly under the metal gurney and that hadn't helped much either. Sam sat waiting for him and battled with her own sickness. She was sipping from a bottle of water but the water seemed to have taken on the smell of the place, and the more she sipped the sicker she felt. She hadn't wanted to come. She knew some sights stayed with you for the rest of your life. She knew that there were certain things she didn't ever want to see. It hadn't taken much imagination to realize that a body six weeks in the water was one of them. But O'Connor had asked her to come with him. He was frightened, he said. He wanted someone there with him. What could Sam say? Sorry, you're on your own, mate? Maybe next time she'd have no qualms in doing that. The door to the toilets swung open and O'Connor walked unsteadily towards her, running a damp handkerchief over his forehead and across the back of his neck. He sat down next to her. He was shivering uncontrollably.

'You all right?' Sam asked.

He shook his head. 'God,' he said. 'I didn't think it'd be as bad as that.'

Sam nodded and stretched out her legs in front of her. 'You were certain?'

He nodded. 'Even with all the damage, it's definitely her.'

'I'm so sorry.'

'I thought, you know, that it would be a relief, that at least I'd know where I stood. I could tell the boys and we could get on with our lives. God, how stupid can you get?'

Sam didn't say anything.

'How am I going to tell the boys?' He looked at her. 'Sam? How am I going to tell them their mother's dead?'

He covered his eyes with his hand and began to cry. I'm no good at this, Sam thought, as she placed O'Connor's coat over his shaking shoulders and patted his back. I'm no good at this at all. Alan would know what to do. He would be affectionate and warm. He would know how to comfort someone. I just want to get as far away from him as possible. The most that she could manage was not running from him. She sat there in silence, feeling agonized and embarrassed, sipping her water that smelled of a six-week-old corpse, patting him on the back, and waiting for him to stop, hoping to God he'd stop soon.

In the end she brought him back to her office and made him a cup of tea. It was a cliché, she knew, but it made *her* feel a whole lot better. Greg wasn't in reception and the office she normally used for clients was locked, so there'd been no alternative but to bring him into her own office. O'Connor had calmed down but he was still shivering violently.

'Do you think she could have killed herself?' Sam asked.

'No, absolutely not – her sister had done that as a child and

243

Meg had seen the effect on her family. She'd always said it was something she'd never contemplate, however bad things became.'

'We'll have to wait for the post-mortem but it'll almost certainly say she was murdered.'

'By the man in the baseball hat?'

'Perhaps. It'll be a full-scale murder enquiry so it's really the end of the case for me. I'll pass on all I know to the police and—'

'But what about the note I received?'

'The police would be best for that.'

'But the police suspect me. They're not interested in the notes.'

'There are a few loose ends I want to tie up. I want to visit Zandra Dodds again and see if I can get anything more from her. But other than that—'

'I want you to stay on until it's clear who murdered her.'

'But—'

'Look, bill me for the work so far and then we'll take it from there.'

'OK, if that's what you want.'

'It is. One more thing, Sam.'

'Yes.'

'Would you come to Alice's funeral?'

Sam frowned. 'You're going?'

He nodded.

'When is it?'

'Tomorrow afternoon.'

'If you're sure.'

'I am.'

O'Connor sipped his tea and looked around her office, a bit like Edie, Sam thought, but without criminal intent. He caught her watching him.

'Sorry – old habits. People are reflected in their environment. Therapists rarely get to see their clients in their offices or homes.'

'And?'

'I like the chaos,' he said eventually. 'You always seem so orderly, so in control. This is a relief, it actually makes you seem more human.'

Sam pointed to the scab on her forehead. 'I can assure you, I'm all too human.'

'Also, I was thinking you have nothing in here that relates to your judo. How many times were you World Champion? European Champion? A lot – right? But there are no photos, no certificates and no medals. It's like it never happened.'

'That was then,' Sam said. 'You can't live in the past. Off past glories.' But even as she said it, she thought, I do, that's exactly what I do.

'It's unusual. Usually people have signs of their status in their offices. It's like having your power on display. You're saying, This is who I am. This is what I've achieved.'

'Sad fuckers,' Sam said. 'For men it's like having your dick on the table, isn't it? Anyway, that's not my style.'

'No,' he smiled. 'I can see that it isn't. I have certificates on my wall. I'm proud of them.'

Sam opened her mouth and then decided the best thing to do was to close it again. O'Connor smiled and sipped his tea. She was saved from further embarrassment by a knock on the door. Alan poked his head into the room. 'Can I have a word?'

'Sure.' Sam followed Alan outside and closed the door behind her.

'I bumped into Phil in reception. He was down to see the body and talk to the post-mortem boys. Do you want to see him?'

'I'll just finish up with O'Connor.'

O'Connor gave Sam the details of the church where the funeral was taking place and they arranged a time to meet the following day.

'So,' Phil said as he came through the door, 'these are your offices.' Then he caught sight of Sam. 'God! What the hell happened to you? Are you all right?'

Sam shrugged. 'Joys of the job. You know how it goes.'

'How did it happen?'

'I don't want to go into it. It happened. I'm recovering.'

Phil took out a packet of cigarettes, shook one into his hand and reached into his pocket.

Sam smelled petrol and heard a light being struck. Her heart started pounding and sweat trickled down the side of her body. She was going to have to get over this or she was never going to be able to have another smoke in her life. She looked at the lighter in Phil's hand and saw flesh melting down to the bone. 'God, sorry, Phil, but I'd rather you didn't.'

He frowned, shrugged and put the cigarette back in the packet. 'Are you sure you're all right?'

'Fine,' Sam lied. She got up and walked over to the window. She had a sudden need for fresh air. She opened the window and inhaled deeply before turning back into the room. 'So, you've seen Meg O'Connor?'

He nodded. 'Not a pretty sight.'

'Murder or suicide?'

'They don't know yet. My bet would be murder.'

Sam nodded her agreement. 'You talked to Hicks?'

'He's proving elusive.'

'You know about his sister?'

'Local station updated me on that.'

'O'Connor told me Alice was pregnant.'

Phil nodded. 'Six weeks.'

'You're DNA-testing them both?'

'Yup, we should get the results in a couple of days.'

'There was a pregnancy testing kit in her bathroom bin.'

Phil frowned. 'I don't think the crime scene boys came up with that. I'll check.'

'It was definitely there when I left. Mind you, the identity of the father isn't going to tell you anything, is it? You know about the affair after all.'

'Oh, I don't know. It's something to ask about in interrogation.'

'According to her husband, Alice slept around a lot and enjoyed telling him about it in detail.'

'Yes, I know, that's what he said to us but we haven't been able to trace any other lovers and he couldn't give us any names other than O'Connor's. If she was such a whore of Babylon you'd think there'd be more evidence of the fact.'

Sam thought of the blue coat she had seen covering the back of the man who was pressing Alice Knight up against the chapel. Perhaps it was his. 'A week earlier when I was staying with Mark I saw Alice Knight having alfresco sex with a man up against the chapel door.'

'Did you tell Rowland that?'

'No.'

'Why on earth not, Sam? She was killed ten days ago, for heaven's sake.'

'I didn't like him,' Sam said. 'And then I got distracted.'

'God, you can be such a nightmare sometimes.'

'Sorry, Phil. To be honest I've had a lot of other things on my plate recently, unrelated to the O'Connor case.'

'Like what?'

'I don't really want to go into it.'

'Can I take you to lunch?'

'Sorry?'

'Can I take you to lunch?'

'Oh God, Phil, I'm not sure. I've got—'

'Whatever, I just thought . . .'

Sam looked at him and had a sudden wish for the oblivion that sex brings, for something to make her forget everything that was happening. He was always coming forwards and she was always rejecting him. She was fed up with it. She felt a surge of affection for him. She stood up and walked round her desk towards him. 'Come back to my place,' she said. And it was clear from her hand on his face, that she didn't mean for lunch.

The sex was better this time, gentler and slower. Perhaps being sober helped. Phil moved over her body, frowning and kissing the multiple abrasions and bruises. They made love affectionately and afterwards Sam did not want him to leave, which was progress of sorts. Yes, the sex had definitely been better.

'Sometimes, you know, I forget why we split up,' Phil said, running a finger lazily across her belly.

Sam tapped the scab on her forehead. 'I strangled you and then you behaved like an idiot.'

'Oh yes,' he said. 'That was it.'

She laughed. 'How do you see it?'

'About the same.'

'Do you?'

'What can I say? My pride took a battering. I was hurt. You know what the canteen culture's like. The boys were always teasing me about it. You always seemed so sure of yourself. It was frightening. You didn't seem to need me at all, to need anyone, come to that. You didn't seem to have any respect for anyone.'

'Needs,' Sam repeated slowly. 'No, I've never been particularly happy with those. Ever.'

'And respect?'

'Perhaps I lost track of that. It's easy to lose track of that over time.'

'How did we ever get together?'

'There was the judo.'

'Yes.'

'And your arse.'

Phil smiled. 'Ditto.'

'Maybe the sex covered over our mutual incompatibilities.'

'Which were?'

Sam didn't really want to go there. What was the point? She rolled on to her back, linked her hands behind her head and looked up at the large stain on the bedroom ceiling, caused by her neighbour's leaking washing machine, and wondered how long it would be before the vibrations from the spinning made the plaster fall on her head. 'God, I miss the fighting. Sometimes, I don't think I'm ever going to get that kind of buzz again. You know, that's going to be as good as it gets.'

Phil frowned. 'But you've got your work.'

'Yes,' she said. 'There's the work – but it doesn't come close.'

'Are you happy?'

She laughed. 'You are joking, aren't you, Phil?'

'People are though, aren't they?'

'Sure they are.'

'You sound like you've given up hope.'

'Hope,' Sam repeated. There was no hope for Jenny Hughes or Alice Knight or Meg O'Connor. She thought of her father, of the things Max had said. She thought of what had taken place in that house, of a conversation she still had to have with her mother and Mark. 'Life's too complicated.'

'I've really missed you, Sam.'

'What? The rows, the arguments, the slammed down telephones ... being strangled?'

'Well, no, obviously not that. I don't miss that.'

'There you go then. Beware a selective memory.'

Sam had a bad feeling about the way the conversation was going. She jumped off the bed and pulled on a dressing gown. 'Anything from the kitchen?'

'I thought I'd just had lunch,' Phil said.

'Ha, ha,' Sam replied.

He smiled. 'What you got?'

She frowned. 'About an inch of milk beginning to turn to cheese, one unopened jar of pesto sauce, a two-hundred-year-old, rock-hard piece of Parmesan, three small pieces of rancid butter and a freezer containing four packets of fish fingers with two fish fingers in each, although they're really Frank's. He likes a fish finger or two for his supper provided the batter is removed . . .' She drew breath as if to continue.

'Stop,' Phil said. 'I'll take you out to lunch.'

Sam looked at the clock on the table next to her bed. 'Pretty late lunch.'

'Well, let's get on with it then,' he said, beginning to pull on his trousers.

'There's an Italian down the road – just opened. I've been meaning to try it.'

'Fine.'

They sat under a film poster of *The Godfather* in a restaurant called, rather unconvincingly, Cosa Nostra. Phil folded a slice of pizza and placed it in his mouth. 'This place is OK.'

Sam nodded and pushed her empty plate away.

'You seeing anyone at the moment, Sam?'

Sam considered lying but then shook her head. 'You?'

'Nothing serious – I was seeing someone. It ended.'

Oh no, she thought, here it comes. Any minute now he was going to say it and she wouldn't be able to stop him with a horrifying description of the contents of her fridge.

'I was wondering . . .' He looked at her and laughed. 'There's no reason to look so terrified.'

'How do you know?'

'We could get back together.'

Sam shook her head. 'I don't think so, Phil.'

'Why not?'

'We live in different places for a start.'

'I could get a transfer.'

'You always said you never wanted to work for the Met. It was difficult enough and we never even lived together.'

'We wouldn't have to live together.'

Sam tried another tack. 'I'm in no fit state for a relationship.'

'Isn't that a bit of a cop-out?'

'No, not at the moment, it isn't.'

'Could you tell me why?'

Oh shit, Sam thought, they had loved each other once. Why don't I just tell him? Tell him all of it. It can't be Phil. For a while she had thought it might be. He had after all heard the fox. He must have done, it was practically under his window, and God knows he had a good enough reason for wanting revenge. But now that was down to the Turners. It had just been coincidence. It couldn't be the behaviour of the man who had made love to her so tenderly, not that man. He wasn't out for revenge – quite the reverse. So she told him all about the notes, her father, and the fox and all about the beating she had taken and the things that Max had said. By the time she had finished, worry was etched across his face.

'Christ, Sam. Have you reported it?'

She shook her head. 'I think it would complicate things, don't you? I've told Max and he's told whoever . . .'

'Do you think it's him – your father?'

'I don't know what to think any more.'

His large hand covered hers. 'I'm worried about you.'

'Well, worrying about me won't do me much good.'

'And they're saying he could still be alive?'

'Between the lines and saying nothing at all, that's exactly what they're saying, yes. So, you see, I have rather a lot on my plate at the moment.'

'Yes, I see that. What are you going to do about the Turners?'

'I'm not sure yet. I'm assessing my options.'

'Which are?'

'Well, testify against them and spend the rest of my life looking over my shoulder.'

'Or?'

'Tell them I'm not going to.'

Phil nodded. 'But you don't have to deal with all this alone, you know.'

Sam looked at him and simply didn't believe him. It was *her* past. *Her* history. They wanted revenge on *her*. She had been pretty much alone when they poured petrol over her and threatened to set her on fire. She *was* alone with it, whatever he might say. That was the truth. She had to settle it herself. No one was going to find out the truth about her father or get the Turners off her back other than herself. She waved at the waiter and asked for the bill, making domino dots with crumbs while she waited for him to bring it.

'You know what we were talking about before?' Phil said.

'Yes.'

'We're older, wiser.'

Sam laughed. 'Speak for yourself.'

'You know, I thought, perhaps we could make it work – this time.'

Sam looked at him. Everything was running backwards. It was as if she were standing on one of those moving walkways you get in airports. There she was, with the same baggage she'd always had, but travelling backwards, instead of forwards to new destinations.

'Work doesn't sound much fun,' she said.

He smiled. 'We had some good times though, didn't we?'

The waiter brought the bill and Sam grabbed it, glanced at it, threw a card on the saucer, mentally crossed her fingers and handed it back to him. Did we? she thought. Are you so sure? Increasingly, she couldn't remember. Wasn't it just having sex on tap that men liked? Sex and no commitment. Thinking about it, wasn't that exactly what she had wanted just now? But Phil had actually never been like that, he'd always wanted more from her than that. That was the problem.

'You need to find yourself a good woman,' she said. 'Settle down and do that whole domestic thing.'

'I thought I had,' he said.

The waiter came back and Sam scribbled her signature on the credit card slip. 'No,' she said, shaking her head. 'Even in my most deluded and drunken moments, I've never called myself a good woman.'

CHAPTER NINETEEN

The following morning Sam stood on Zandra Dodds's doorstep in front of the glowering art critic.

'Sorry,' Sam said. 'I've been leaving messages for you but I haven't been able to get you on the phone. This seemed the only way.'

Zandra Dodds did not move her substantial turquoise-velvet-covered body one inch backwards from the doorway. 'I've been *very* busy and it really is *most* inconvenient at the moment. I'm having to file copy by . . .' She looked at her watch. 'Well, I should have done it by now.' She began closing the door.

Sam placed the palm of her hand flat against the door, 'I'll only take up a second of your time, and it really is very important. I presume you'd prefer to explain to me why you lied rather than the police?'

Zandra Dodds twirled round and flounced down the hall, leaving Sam to close the door behind her and follow in the wake of a powerful perfume trail. It should be Poison, Sam thought. Zandra Dodds stood with her hands on her hips, leaning up against the fireplace. Sam was not invited to sit.

'Well?'

'Meg O'Connor's body's been found. It was pulled out of the river not far from her Fulham flat.'

Zandra Dodds's face flushed and her hand came to her mouth. 'God, how awful,' she said eventually.

'Could you tell me again what happened on the press night at Tate Modern?'

'I already have.'

'What was she talking to you about when you ate together? What was she upset about?'

'Who says she was upset?'

'I asked the waiter who served you. He said Meg was visibly upset.'

'My, my, you are thorough, aren't you?'

Sam didn't say anything. Dodds sighed and sat down. 'Someone phoned her and told her that her husband was having an affair. Meg was very upset. In shock, really. So far as she was concerned, they had both been faithful during the course of their marriage.'

'Did she believe the caller?'

'Oh yes, it fitted with certain behaviours of her husband over the last few months.'

'Did she tell you who had phoned her?'

'She didn't say who it was.'

'Did she suggest she knew the person?'

'No. It was a man. He had asked her to meet him.'

'Did she say what she was going to do?'

'She wasn't really thinking straight at all. I don't think she knew.'

'Why didn't you tell me this before?'

Dodds's eyes narrowed. 'Why should I? It's none of your business. You've been hired by her husband, haven't you? He wants his property back, I suppose.'

'You didn't think that it was suspicious that she had disappeared?'

'Look – that phone call you mentioned. She wasn't phoning about the article she was writing. She phoned to apologise for the state she'd been in the night before. Not that she needed to. She said she might disappear for a few days to try to get her head round it. She was absolutely furious and wanted to punish him. I thought she was getting him good and worried and that then she would turn up again.'

'Punishing who?'

'Her husband, of course. And anyway I told her I wouldn't tell anyone. I promised and I always keep my promises.' She looked at her watch again. 'Now, I have to get on.'

'Did she seem suicidal to you?'

'Absolutely not. Upset, certainly, and shocked, but not suicidal. I think she mentioned castration, mind you.' She paused. 'Was she murdered?'

Sam nodded. 'It seems so.'

'Oh God, how awful. Poor Meg. What did she ever do to deserve that?'

Sam remained silent.

'He probably did it,' Zandra snapped.

'Who?'

'The husband, of course. He dotes on the children, from what she said. Probably thought it was the only way he could keep them. Kill the mother, move in the other woman, isn't that how it works?'

'Did Meg think she was under threat from him?'

Zandra Dodds shook her head. 'She didn't mention that but there doesn't have to be a history of violence for someone to murder. Surely not if there's a strong enough motive.'

'And you think his fear of losing his children would be that?'

'Oh yes, he's besotted with those boys. She said the boys were more important to him than she was. She said it was his way of getting rid of his past. You know who his father is, I assume?'

Sam nodded.

'Having his own family was his way of wiping the slate clean. He'd had a miserable childhood. He disapproved of the way his father had behaved towards his mistress and their child.'

'Did she say she was going to confront him with it?'

'She didn't, but wouldn't you? It's the obvious next thing to do. Now you really must go.' She moved towards Sam with the same inexorable motion as an ocean-going oil tanker.

Zandra Dodds's front door slammed behind her and Sam shivered in the biting wind blowing along the front of the mews houses. She raised her collar, touched the dog tags in her pocket and set off for the tube. Children as redemption – she wondered how that worked exactly. Max had said that her father regarded her as a talisman. He hadn't been able to tear her away from him because she had started screaming; but was that because he was holding on to her or because she was clinging to him? But if that's what you believed, and you thought you were going to lose them, then what? But to kill for it? For Sam, redemption had come in the form of fighting. It had saved her. And without it? She didn't know the answer to that yet. Without it, life was certainly more complicated, happiness more elusive. She was always looking for the thing that was missing.

That afternoon Sam stood on the steps of St Michael's church, Islington, holding a cigarette in one hand and a lighter in the other. She flicked the lighter then let the flame die, flicked it again. Her hand shook. She took a deep breath, put the cigarette in her mouth and touched the flame to its tip. It was fine if *she* did it, if *she* was controlling it, but not if other people did it. Anyway, it was a start and she desperately wanted a cigarette. After all, if you couldn't smoke at a funeral, when could you? Traffic was queuing nose-to-tail along Upper Street. She looked at her watch. Presumably the hearse was stuck somewhere in the immense traffic jam caused by a burst water main at the Angel. London wasn't content with just making getting to work on time a trauma for most of its inhabitants; now it didn't even allow them to be buried on time. Alive or dead, the traffic held you up. Pigeons hobbled around Sam's feet, pecking at the grimy shreds of confetti that covered the steps.

Sam had only been to two other funerals in her life: her

father's and her gran's. She thanked God this was a funeral of someone she didn't really know. Those were the easy ones. She'd been surprised O'Connor was going to this one. Did you go to the funeral of your mistress? She wasn't sure what the etiquette was but then therapists probably didn't set much store by such things. He had said he had cleared it with Tony, so here she was, waiting for him to turn up. He was presumably stuck, along with the hearse, in the traffic. A number 19 bus edged forward and Sam saw the hearse pull up outside the church. She took a last drag on her cigarette and flicked it into the bushes. A pigeon, suspecting it might be edible, fluttered after it. There was still no sign of O'Connor but deciding she couldn't wait for him any longer, she stepped into the church. It was only slightly warmer in there. Sam sat in a pew halfway down on the left-hand side and waited.

The coffin was carried in and the service began. About halfway through O'Connor edged his way into the pew beside her. 'Sorry,' he said. She shrugged. It was his funeral, so to speak. It was up to him whether he turned up on time or not.

The service droned on. Sam liked churches. She liked the stained glass, the flowers, the candles and the smell – but she didn't like religion. She thought of the artificial grass on the edge of her father's grave, of being frightened that she might slide in on top of him, and be buried as well. She wasn't sure what she wanted to happen when she died. She liked the idea of a wicker coffin – something that would rot. She didn't mind being eaten by worms. She had always liked the idea of being buried in the woods. Or she had until she had discovered the body of Jenny Hughes. Now she wasn't so sure. She wondered who would be there to arrange her funeral, if anyone would? That was the advantage of children; they ended up having to do all that stuff. She glanced at O'Connor, sitting next to her. His face was white but at least he wasn't crying. That's what therapy did to you, Sam thought. Made you incontinent with your emotions, incapable of restraint. *Earth to earth, ashes to ashes, dust to dust; in sure and certain hope of the Resurrection to eternal life.* The words cut through her thoughts. She remembered them from her gran's funeral. To be sure and certain of Resurrection, now that would be something. Sam wondered what it would feel like to have faith like that. She couldn't imagine it. Resurrection. To rise from the dead, but in order to do what? Why had her father come back? Somehow she doubted saving the world was on his agenda.

Sam watched as four burly men in black picked up the lily-covered coffin and hoisted it on to their shoulders. Tony followed behind it. He wore dark glasses but it wasn't the shades Sam was struck by. It was his long blue cashmere coat. That was what really got her attention. Sam stared at his back as he walked past her. The height was right and so was the coat. But according to Tony, he and Alice had been leading separate lives; it was all over between them. They were about to get divorced, not have alfresco sex. So why had he been making passionate love to his wife, late that night against the chapel door? Sam saw Alice's head thrown back, she saw his hand clamped across her white breast and, underneath the cashmere coat, she saw Tony Ballinger moving in and out of his wife's body. 'Fuck me, darling,' Alice had said. But why would she have been saying that if their relationship was over?

After the funeral O'Connor and Sam went back to Ballinger's house. The portrait of Alice had still not been taken down. Instead the mantelpiece underneath it had been cleared and covered in candles and nightlights. O'Connor stood stock-still in the doorway to the room when he saw it, a queue of people forming behind him.

Sam tugged at his arm. 'People are trying to get past,' she said. 'You have to move.' But he wasn't listening to her. 'John...'

'Oh, God, sorry.' He moved further into the room. 'It's just that portrait. I've never seen it before – it's a shock.'

Sam looked at it again. If anything, the eroticism of the portrait seemed to have intensified in the flickering light of the candles. O'Connor's face was drained of all colour. The candles in front of the portrait guttered and danced in the draft from the front door. Tony Ballinger stood in front of his wife's portrait, staring at them.

'I need a drink,' O'Connor said, and moved towards a table covered in wine glasses. As O'Connor set off for the table, Ballinger moved through the throng of people to intercept him. Sam followed in O'Connor's wake.

'John . . .' Ballinger held out his hand and O'Connor took it. 'Thank you for coming.'

Sam watched the two men shaking hands. O'Connor, she noted, was having a hard time holding Ballinger's eye.

'I'm so sorry to hear about your own wife,' Ballinger said, his eyes boring into O'Connor's.

'Yes, thank you.'

'Two murders,' Ballinger continued. 'So close together.'

O'Connor frowned. 'They don't know for certain that she was murdered.'

'Oh really, I'm sorry, I just assumed . . .'

'It's an extraordinary portrait,' O'Connor said.

'She was an altogether extraordinary woman. But of course, you knew about that, didn't you?'

O'Connor took a large gulp of red wine.

Ballinger glanced at Sam. 'I see you've brought your minder along.'

O'Connor frowned. 'Sorry?'

Ballinger nodded at Sam. 'For moral support, I suppose. Or are you fucking her as well?'

Sam didn't say anything. She'd been called worse things than a minder in her time and this was his wife's funeral after all. People were allowed to behave badly at funerals.

O'Connor blushed. 'No, I . . .'

Ballinger looked at Sam then back at O'Connor. 'Perhaps I should hire her to find out who murdered Alice. The police certainly don't seem to be making much headway. Although perhaps that would raise conflicts of interest.'

O'Connor put down his empty glass and reached for another.

'And you had made her pregnant.' The statement hung in the air.

'It could have been yours,' O'Connor said.

Ballinger shook his head slowly from side to side and lowered his voice. 'No. We both know that child was yours.'

Sam looked at O'Connor.

Ballinger leaned towards him and touched his upper arm. 'I'm surprised she settled on you. She always said you were rather mediocre, a bit of a weakling after all that suicide nonsense. She liked strong men. Maybe she liked who your father was. Perhaps she thought his success would skip a generation. It does sometimes, doesn't it? After all, you wouldn't be the first mediocre son of a talented father, there are lots of those. But she did say you were so easy to reel in. The domestic nature of your sex life made you pathetically eager for what she had to offer.'

O'Connor shook off Ballinger's hand and put his glass down quickly on the table, spilling a large puddle of red wine on to the white tablecloth. He then walked swiftly from the room. Ballinger was laughing in triumph. Sam watched as he turned and raised his glass to Alice's portrait.

That evening Sam opened her front door to Edie.

'This came for you when you were out, babes. Took it in. Save you the trip to the post office, won't it?'

'Thanks, Edie.' As Sam took the box, it tilted and she felt something heavy slide from one end to the other.

'Need any more baccy?'

Sam shook her head.

'Can bring you beer if you want? Spirits?'

Sam shook her head. She tried not to keep alcohol in the flat. If she had it she drank it, if she didn't, she couldn't. That was more or less how she liked it. And she had the recent memory of her margarita hangover from hell.

'No, it's OK, but thanks anyway, Edie.'

'You been in the wars, then?'

Sam gave up and opened the door wider for Edie to come in. 'Cup of tea?' she asked.

Edie stepped swiftly through the door into the hall. 'Thought you'd never ask, girl.'

Sam followed Edie into the kitchen, smiling at the wisp of fine brown hair, which always hung down from under Edie's black curly wig. When Frank waddled towards Edie, she sucked dramatically on her teeth. 'So thin,' she said. 'Turn sideways and you'd miss him, poor baby.'

Sam put the box down on the table. Edie sat down and crossed her short, fat legs.

'You should do this place up,' Edie said looking round the room. 'You've not touched it since your gran died, have you?'

'That's what a friend of mine just said.'

Sam looked at the wood-panelled walls, the stained sink, the fridge that was always icing up at the back, the oven that didn't close properly and needed a stool to wedge it shut in order for it to heat anything. That didn't matter anyway because she never cooked. As she filled the kettle, the tap screamed at her. Edie was right, everything was falling apart. The trouble was she liked things that were broken but continued to work. There was a sort of heroism in it. Sam recycled everything: papers, plastic, glass and even the cans from the cat food. She did not believe in throwing things out, she never had. If she bought a new fridge, this one would just end up on a fridge mountain and it was perfectly serviceable – so long as she kept her food at the front, got rid of the water that collected at the bottom and didn't mind the freezer door falling off now and then.

'I like it this way,' she said. 'I've never been fussy about things like that.'

Edie frowned. She was houseproud. She washed the inside of her windows once a week and was always going on to Sam about finding someone to do the outside. Edie believed in new things, in clean things. Edie nodded at Sam's forehead.

'What happened to you, then?'

Sam told her.

'God, girl.'

The kettle turned itself off and Sam threw a tea bag into a cup and poured in the boiling water. She squashed the tea bag against the side of the cup, threw it in the sink, added some milk and handed the cup to Edie. 'Have you seen anyone hanging around?'

Edie shook her head. 'I'm off on the boats, girl, aren't I?'

For a couple of years after Edie's husband died, she barely moved out of her flat. She looked out of the window, watched daytime TV and complained to Sam about the terrible state of her legs. Complained so much that in the end she made her doctor register her as disabled and got herself a home help from the council. 'There if I want her, girl. Before I need her.' But since Edie had discovered the joys of tobacco smuggling, she had been nipping around like Mrs Tiggywinkle on speed and there was no more mention of dodgy knees.

'Don't look out of the windows like I used to,' she said sadly, as if referring to a friend she no longer saw. 'It's a life on the ocean waves for me, now.'

'When you next off?'

'Tomorrow. Got pulled last weekend. Sniffer dogs – the lot.' Edie tugged at her own collar with finger and thumb. 'Seven hundred quid's worth.'

'God, Edie!'

She shrugged. 'I'm behind with me ordering. Need to bulk up.'

'But seven hundred pounds!'

'It's a risk of the business. They're not going to lock me away at the age of seventy-nine, are they? Waste of prison space. Just got pissed with Bert on the coach on the way back. He's atrocious but what can you do? Couldn't pretend I wasn't over me limit, could I? This is my last trip for a while. The Italians are off on holiday. I've got their cat for a week.'

'Would you keep an eye out for me? Anyone you're not used to. Anyone watching the block.'

Edie sipped her tea. 'Of course, love. Sure you don't need some baccy?'

Sam sighed. 'Why not?' At least she was actually smoking them these days.

'The usual then?'

She nodded.

'Back in a minute.'

Sam heard the front door slam and a few minutes later Edie returned with a sleeve of cigarettes. Sam handed over the money.

'I'll keep my eye out. Let you know.'

With Edie you never got anything for nothing. Well, maybe that was fair enough. Life had never dealt Edie any favours, so why should she deal any out herself?

Sam walked back into the kitchen and took a bread knife to the tape round the parcel Edie had handed her. There was a lot of it; as if someone wanted to make extra certain that the box wouldn't burst open accidentally. Inside, plastic bags had been scrunched round a central object, which was covered in bubble wrap. Sam pulled at the bubble wrap and then took the knife to the Sellotape, which was holding it together. The parcel unfolded like a flower and Sam saw two things; a worn, sand-coloured military beret and a case that looked as if it held a small pair of binoculars. She snapped open the popper on the case and looked inside. She frowned, put her hand inside and pulled out a small, grey, snub-nosed gun.

Sam had never held a gun of any sort. She put it down so quickly that she misjudged the distance and cracked her knuckles on the side of the table. She stood looking at the blood filling up the graze. Then she picked up the beret, turning it in her hands, looking inside it, twisting it. Not knowing what to do. She pulled the plastic bags out of the box to see if there was anything else, and found a cardboard box full of bullets and at the bottom, under all the bags, a note: *You are in danger. Learn to use it.* The writing was the same as the original note.

She turned the box over and looked on each side but there was no Parcelforce sticker, nothing to identify that it had been sent through the post at all. And suddenly it came to her. It hadn't been sent through the post, it had been hand-delivered. She put the gun back in the box and covered it with plastic bags, walked through the flat and out on to the landing. She opened the letterbox and whistled a couple of times so Edie would know who it was and waited for her to come to the door.

Edie looked puzzled. 'All right, love?'

'The parcel, Edie – who delivered it? Was it the postman?' Edie frowned.

Sam continued. 'I mean, was he in uniform?'

'No – just a sort of average bloke.'

'Because there were no markings on the parcel, no stamps or stickers. I think it was hand-delivered.'

'I heard the main door go and thought it was the post. Came out and he was bending over your door. When he saw me he straightened up. I said, "I'll take it in for you, love. You don't want to leave it there. Anyone might have it." But he wasn't that keen. I told him I knew you and it'd save you a trip to the post and then he handed it over.'

'What did he look like?'

265

Edie adjusted her glasses. 'Late fifties, I'd say, but fit-looking – shortish. Nothing special. Wouldn't stand out in a crowd.' She looked at Sam and frowned. 'Looked a bit like you, love – same shape of face and eyes. Yes, and your colouring.'

'Thanks, Edie.'

Sam closed the door to her flat and leaned back against it. He was coming closer. Slowly but surely he was coming closer. A man with a violent temper. A man who had been declared dead. A man who had done something so terrible to his family that he had had to disappear. Her father – Geoffrey 'Hawkeye' Falconer – a trained killer, back from the dead. Sam touched the dog tags in her pocket. Soon she was going to be face to face with the man who had worn them. Then she would know the truth.

CHAPTER TWENTY

At three o'clock that night Sam lay awake trying to decide what to do with the gun. From downstairs boomed 'The Wombles of Wimbledon Common' at full volume. Her neighbours had come crashing into the block five minutes earlier and slammed on the music. Sam found their choice bewildering to put it mildly. As far as she could work out, the flat was occupied by two men in their early thirties with the sort of thick necks that belonged in a rugby front row. Well, it took all sorts, Sam supposed. Hopefully they'd pass out soon and the CD would run its course. At least it wasn't 'God Save the Queen' and 'Abide with me', which they'd favoured during the Golden Jubilee.

Sam was certain of one thing – there was no way she was going to do what the note suggested; she wanted the gun out of her flat as quickly as possible. She hated the way it made her feel just to hold it in her hand. The strength of her desire to keep it horrified her. She couldn't put it out with the rubbish because Edie might find it; she always gave the bins a good going-over. Downstairs, the CD came to an end and silence followed. Sam reached a decision, curled up on her side and went back to sleep.

The following morning Sam phoned the only person she knew who had anything to do with guns: Max.

'I need to see you.'

'Aha.' In the background Sam could hear strange gibbering noises. 'Have you talked to your family yet?'

'No, it's not about that.' More peculiar noises came over the phone. 'Where on earth are you – the zoo?'

'Theatre,' he whispered. 'In rehearsal.'

'Given up the day job?'

'Not me stupid, a client.' He mentioned a famous Hollywood actress. Even Sam, who was hardly a fan of *Hello*! culture, had heard of her. She was over in London being paid £300 a week to slum it with the Brits, in return for the kudos of a London theatre performance on her CV.

Sam's curiosity was roused. She couldn't help herself. She asked the obvious question. 'What's she like?'

'Charming.'

She laughed. 'That's what they always say. Can I see you?'

'She's rehearsing. I'm with her all day. You better get yourself over here if it's urgent. I'm not supposed to leave her side. Come to the box office and ask for me.'

'Fine,' Sam said. 'Where are you?'

'The Donmar.'

'Look, he's Kylie Mailer's bodyguard,' Sam said. 'He's in rehearsal with her. Could you let him know I'm here?'

'I can't leave the box office.'

'Could you get someone to tell him, then?'

The man looked down an extremely long and elegant nose and picked up the phone with equally long and elegant fingers. He muttered something into it and put it back down; he didn't deign to say anything to Sam.

'So?' Sam said.

'Yes?' he said, as if seeing her for the first time.

Sam had had enough. She slammed on the glass, making him jump. 'Fucking bullshit,' she said. She walked further into the theatre and pushed open the doors to the stalls. Behind her she heard him shouting, 'You can't go in there, rehearsals are private.' It was dark and she waited a moment for her eyes to adjust before spotting Max and walking down the central aisle towards him. Behind her she heard a commotion and the actors on the stage stopped what they were doing and looked in her direction. Max turned round in his seat and stood up.

'One of mine,' he said. The actors' attention returned to the stage.

Sam sat down next to him. 'Busy morning?' she whispered.

'The things they do in rehearsal are downright weird. Director needs to see a shrink.'

'He says the same about you.'

'Probably. How are you?'

Sam dabbed her forehead. 'The Klingon effect is on the wane. Still feel stiff.' She shifted her shoulder. 'All over.'

'Body mends. It's the head stuff that stays with you. That's what you need to watch.'

She nodded. Yes, she thought, the head stuff. Well, at least she could light a cigarette without screaming. That was progress of sorts.

'Look, I'm really sorry about the other day. I'm still not sure I should have told you.'

She patted his arm. 'It's not your fault my father was an arsehole.'

'I know, but every kid wants their father to be a hero.'

'Well, I'm thirty-two. It's time to grow up and realise heroism's a complicated business,' Sam said, touching the dog tags in her pocket.

One of the actors turned to face the stalls. 'Hey, Max, quiet it down out there, will you? We're trying to work here.'

'Sorry,' Max said.

Up on the stage someone began hooting like an owl.

'Could we go to the back?' Sam suggested.

'Sure.'

They got up and made their way to the back of the stalls. Sam undid her rucksack and took out the beret, the note and the case containing the gun. 'I got sent these.'

Max held the beret in his hands and ran his thumb over the

badge of the winged dagger, then looked at the note. Sam handed him the case containing the gun.

'I don't want anything to do with this. Could you get rid of it for me? Do whatever you do?'

Max opened the case, looked inside and closed it again, looked up at her. 'Perhaps you should – I could teach you.'

'I want nothing to do with it,' Sam repeated. 'I am not going to start carrying a gun.'

'Perhaps he knows something you don't. If he thinks you're at risk you probably are. He's in the business to know.' He patted the case. 'Are you sure, Sam? It's a nice gun. I could take you through the basics.'

Sam shook her head. 'Absolutely sure. Will you tell the faceless ghoul who came visiting?'

Max shrugged. 'Do you want me to?'

'I'll leave it up to you.'

He nodded.

'Could I have those back?' She indicated the beret and the note.

'Sure.'

Sam held the hat in her hands. 'Is it really him, Max? Do you know?'

He shrugged again. 'I don't know. Not for sure.'

'You think it is though, don't you?'

'I never thought he'd died. Like I said, there were so many rumours at the time and his name's not carved on the clock tower in Hereford. The names of all SAS killed are on it but not your dad.'

'Are you sure?'

He nodded. 'I think they wanted him to appear to be dead so they could use him in Northern Ireland. If he were involved in assassination squads, they wouldn't have wanted that traceable to the SAS, army or the government. If you're using a dead man then you're using a man who doesn't exist. A shadow that leaves no trace. He couldn't have been doing those things because he was dead.'

'What did my mother know?'

Max shook his head. 'I don't know, but the way he treated her she'd have just been glad that he was gone.'

'What I can't work out is why he's poking his head above the parapet now?'

'Good Friday? Maybe he thought the climate had changed and he'd be safe. Maybe he was tired of hiding, of being on the run. Maybe he's just got older and wearier and is fed up with running away. Maybe he wants to come home.'

'Maybe he thinks he has nothing to lose.'

'He's put you at risk, Sam. That's plenty to lose.'

'If he gives a damn.'

'Oh, he gives a damn about you all right – always did.'

Sam grabbed his arm. 'But why, Max? Why me? I don't understand?'

'I don't know, Sam, he just did.'

'But I was only four when he died.' Sam shook her head. 'When he went . . .'

In sure and certain hope of the Resurrection. That phrase ran through her head again. Forgiveness? Redemption? What was he looking for?

'Why did you give me his dog tags?'

'What?'

'His dog tags – at the funeral. Why didn't you give them to Mark?'

'You were holding on to them, Sam, that evening he went mad. When I tried to get you away from him, your hands were gripping on to his tags. I just thought you should have them.'

'But . . .'

'Hey, Max, baby?' An American voice cut through the gloom. 'You there?'

271

Max waved. 'Over here.' He began walking towards the front of the theatre.

'Sure, I lost you there for a moment.'

Sam watched him talk to a woman immortalized in any number of films. She seemed tiny, both more ordinary and more beautiful than she appeared on the screen.

Max walked back towards Sam.

'Max, baby?' Sam mimicked.

He shrugged. 'Her lunch order.'

'Don't tell me, let me guess: Bacon, lettuce and tomato on brown.'

Max laughed. 'A hundred pounds' worth of sushi from Nobu.'

'A hundred quid? Anyway, what's that got to do with you?'

'We get it for her.'

'Can't she get it for herself?'

'That's not how it works, Sam. These kinds of people do nothing for themselves.'

'I wouldn't be any good at that – pampering prima donnas.'

'It pays well.'

Sam thought about the office rent she had failed to pay and the unopened white envelopes she had buried somewhere on her desk. She'd probably be able to stand it just fine if things got any worse. 'Anyway, I must go.'

He touched her arm. 'You know I'm serious about what I said. Just a couple of sessions would—'

Sam held out her hand in a stop sign. 'Save it for Charlton Heston. But thanks for taking care of that for me.' She nodded at the gun.

'Sure,' he said.

Alan stood in the doorway of the office holding two cardboard cups of coffee.

'Want to give these a whirl?'

'Only if it's black as death, hot as hell and sweet as sex.'

Alan laughed. 'If they were that, you wouldn't be able to get them away from me.'

'Come on, let's see.'

He handed her one of the cups and Sam peered into it, and then screwed up her face. 'Beige,' she said.

Alan sipped his. 'Maybe a four,' he said. 'Although that's being generous.' He sat down at his desk.

Sam opened a jar of instant coffee, tipped two spoonfuls into her cup and stirred vigorously. 'Phil phoned, said the details were in on the post-mortem on Meg.'

'And?'

'No water in the lungs, so she was dead when she hit the river. That rules out suicide. Apparently they're not sure of the cause of death. The flesh deteriorates in the water, so it's not so easy to see signs of bruising. But they think she was probably strangled and raped.'

'Phil have any joy with Mr Charming David Hicks?'

Sam shrugged. 'I don't know. He was proving elusive to interview.'

'So, we have a man in a baseball cap dragging Meg O'Connor from her flat in the middle of the night. We have no proper description of him and we have no details of his car. In fact we have next to nothing.'

'Actually,' Sam said, 'we do have something else. I'm sure that it was Ballinger who was having sex with his wife against the college chapel.'

'Really?'

'Yesterday, at Alice's funeral, he was wearing this long blue coat.'

Alan laughed. 'Look around, Sam. Lots of men wear long blue coats. We're a conservative lot – pink and yellow are usually out of the question.'

'It wasn't just that, he was wearing a belt with a silver tip to it. Do you know the sort?'

'Sure.'

'Well, I think that's what I was seeing on the ground when they were doing it. Something was shining at the time. I thought it was a shoe buckle but now I think it was the buckle of his belt.'

Alan frowned.

Sam rubbed her eyes. 'And if it was Tony Ballinger, then that's completely at odds with what he was saying about Alice. He told me that the relationship was practically over, that they were virtually separated and that he was indifferent to her affairs. But I tell you they were far from separated when I saw them. Alfresco sex is hardly the kind of thing you indulge in if your relationship is devoid of passion, is it? And also, it would make sense of the portrait. He hadn't taken it down because he was still in love with her.'

'So, how does this change things?'

'Well, for a start, it might make him a whole lot angrier about O'Connor and Alice having an affair. If he was splitting up with her anyway then so what, but if he wasn't then ... Also he seemed pretty keen to be as offensive to O'Connor as possible. There was nothing indifferent in his behaviour towards him after the funeral.'

'The green-eyed monster raises his head?'

'Absolutely.'

'So, what did he do? Murder them both? But why would he murder Alice if he was still in love with her.'

'Sexual jealousy and rage.'

Alan shook his head. 'Why hasn't he murdered O'Connor then?'

'Maybe he intends to.'

'By the way, O'Connor phoned earlier. He's got another note.'

Sam groaned. 'Not these bloody notes again. And this time?'

'Same as before – reduced him to a babbling idiot and completely baffled me.'

'Maybe Tony Ballinger's sending them to him. He intends to exact retribution on him and his children and wants to scare the hell out of him first.'

Sam's phone went. 'Probably him,' Alan said. 'Prepare for the babbling shrink.'

Sam picked up the phone. It was O'Connor.

'Oh, thank God I've managed to get hold of you. You heard about the autopsy on Meg?'

'Yes.'

'She was murdered.' O'Connor's voice sounded flat with shock.

'I'm so sorry, John.'

'I can't get my head around it. I mean, who on earth would want to murder her? It just doesn't make any sense. She was a wonderful person who never harmed a fly. She wouldn't even let me kill wasps.'

'I'm so sorry,' Sam repeated, acutely aware of the inadequacy of her words.

O'Connor sighed. 'Look, one of the reasons I called was that I wanted to ask you a favour. Could you come down and look after Bill and Ian? I have to go away this weekend. My father's been in a car accident and I need to go there.'

'Why can't you take them with you?'

'My mother's too old to look after them and I'm going to have to do some driving around. Also after all they've been through in the last few weeks I don't want them any more traumatised. Apparently they don't know if he's going to pull through.'

Sam didn't say anything. She did not want to go.

'Did Alan tell you I got another note?'

'Yes.'

'*Because we are too menny.*'

'What?'

'It's what the note said. "Many" is spelled M-E-N-N-Y. It's spelled that way in *Jude the Obscure*. It's the suicide note from the children.'

'I see.'

'It's a clear threat. The police say they're not able to offer any sort of security. All they'll do is send a patrol car past. They say I'm over-reacting but that's easy for them to say, it's not their children who've been threatened. I have to know that they're safe.'

'What about a babysitter?' Sam said feebly.

'Sam! I think my children are under threat. Their mother's been murdered. I'm not going to leave them with a bloody babysitter. Please. I need someone I can trust. I need someone who can protect them.'

'I don't know anything about children,' Sam said gloomily.

'You were one once.'

'A hell of a long time ago.'

'Please.'

'OK,' Sam said. 'Fine, I'll do it.' She scrunched up her cardboard coffee cup and threw it savagely at her bin. A jet of coffee spurted out and splashed against the wall.

'Thank you. I really appreciate it.'

Sam put down the phone and stared at the coffee trickling down the wall. It was time to go back. Time to talk to her family.

Sam arrived in Oxford during the late afternoon of the following day. As the coach reached the bottom of Headington Hill, Sam wondered what on earth she was going to do with O'Connor's kids? She wasn't the babysitting type. If she'd been doing anything in the evenings as a child it was judo, judo and more judo. What did you do with two small boys who had just lost their mother? The coach swung round the roundabout in the middle of The Plain, continued over Magdalen Bridge and ground to a halt in The High. Sam got off, glanced up at the cupola of Queen's, then set off one more time for St Barnabas's.

Mark opened the door. 'What the hell is that on your face?'

Sam hadn't told him. Why worry him after all? 'Oh nothing,' she said.

'Doesn't look like nothing to me.'

She slumped into a chair. 'Why did I ever take on the O'Connor case?' Tears pricked her eyes and she blinked them away. 'I can't think when I'm here. I feel numb, then upset. I feel . . .' She struggled for words. 'What's the matter with me? Why doesn't it do that to you?'

'I live here – it's my life, not just memories. I never left. If you never leave you don't have to come back home. You are home.' He looked at her forehead. 'What happened?'

After she had told him he didn't say anything for a while. She handed him the note and the beret.

'The gun?'

'Gave it to Max.'

He turned the beret over and over in his hands. 'They think it's him?'

'Max does. But what sort of man would send his daughter a gun? Who would do that?'

'Oh, he would all right.' Mark stood up and walked over to the window. 'You were young when he died. Well, when he went missing. Whatever he did.'

'What's that got to do with anything?'

'When you're young it's easier to idolize. That's all you have. The relationship you had as a child. You grow up, but the relationship stays the same. It can't develop. You can't.'

'You were a child too.'

'An older child, a much older child.'

'Max told me a bit of what happened. Then he told me to ask you and Mum.'

Mark shook his head and took a deep breath as if there was no

277

air in the room. 'Come on,' he said. 'I'm not going to do this sober.'

Do what? Sam thought as she picked up her bag and slowly followed him from the room. What's he going to do?

They turned right into The Broad and walked in silence to the *King's Head*. Mark got them two pints of Guinness and they settled into a window seat. Sam waited for him to begin.

'You were always so attached to him,' Mark said. 'It was as if nothing could come between you and your memory of him. You were so tight to each other. It never seemed the right time to have this conversation. I never thought he'd come back. I never thought we'd have to have it.'

Sam stared at her pint, fear fluttering in her stomach. 'Don't,' she said suddenly.

'I think I have to. He's coming closer. Even if it's not him, it's probably time.'

Sam wanted to get away. She wanted to put her fingers in her ears and scream. She saw herself jumping up and turning over the table, the pints crashing to the ground. She was out of the door and running past the Sheldonian. She was running for the bus that would take her out of here. From above she saw herself fleeing the city, like Lot's wife but never tempted to look back. The coach drove back up Headington Hill towards London where salvation lay, the future and her present life. But of course she didn't move; she couldn't. She sat rooted to the spot, turning her pint round and round on the dark wooden table, terrified of what he was going to say to her, waiting for him to begin.

Mark sipped his beer, swallowed and replaced his glass exactly on the beer mat in front of him. He cleared his throat. 'I never liked him. He didn't like me. You know what I was like as a child – all big knees and big feet, gawky and awkward. I couldn't kick or catch a ball to save my life. I couldn't even run. I was always falling over my feet. He couldn't bear it, I don't think. He couldn't bear me.'

'That's not true.'

Mark held up his hand. 'Just let me do this all the way through. Then you can say whatever you want. I just need to do this all the way through.' His voice was shaking. 'He bullied me mercilessly. He always said I couldn't be a son of his. I wasn't good enough. I was too soft—'

'But—'

'I hated him, Sam. He made my life a misery. He never gave me any reason to feel any other way about him. He was a bully. I've learned that bullies are weak men. They're cowards, and he was a coward. He picked on me and disowned me. It was always a relief when he was away and it was hell when he came back. I never wanted him to come back.'

'But that file with the cards. You kept those cards.'

'False sentiment,' Mark said brusquely. 'Mum probably bought them anyway. Probably forged his writing. I wish he'd been the kind of father who sent me cards. That's why I keep them but he wasn't. I should have got rid of them years ago. Burned them. It's taken me years . . .' Mark picked up his pint. 'John's been really helpful. You know he had a terrible time with his father. He's helped me see.' He stopped and looked at Sam. 'He's helped me admit the abuse.'

Sam stared at him.

'You don't remember.' It was a statement rather than a question. But was it the truth? She saw him pause, pull back from the brink, approach it again, pull back again. He couldn't meet her eyes. But he had said the word. The word could not be taken back. It hung in the air between them. Abuse.

Mark changed tack. 'I don't know what I'd have done without John. I still go to him when it's too much. When it all piles up on me again.'

He had said the word. Make it go away, Sam thought. Rewind it like a tape in her old video recorder. Back and back. She heard the whirring of the machine, the scream intensifying until it clunked to a halt, like a train hitting the buffers. She wanted to scream at Mark: Take it back. Take back that word. She felt sick and dizzy. She saw O'Connor's brown eyes watching her and remembered their conversation.

If ever you want to talk, casually, you know . . . as if I were a friend.

You don't think I have any?

That's not what I meant.

He knew what had happened but *she* couldn't remember.

'Get away from me.' She was shocked to hear that she had spoken the words out loud.

Mark put his hand on her arm. 'Sam, you were younger than me, perhaps—'

She pulled her arm away. 'What don't I remember?' she snapped.

Mark shook his head. 'No, nothing – I just meant, you know . . .' he petered out.

He was back-pedalling now and she knew he was lying. Now she knew there was something she didn't remember. This was why Jenny Hughes was haunting her dreams. A match flared in her mind but it always went out before she could actually see what was going on. Mark was evading her, backing off. He had come to the brink and drawn back, but the word, the word could never be withdrawn. The word was spoken for all time.

'You were younger,' he repeated quietly. 'Maybe—'

'And what does that mean?' Sam snapped. 'As if that makes any difference.'

'What I mean is your self-confidence never seemed to be affected.'

'Are you joking? Why do you think I had to keep winning? Why do you think I was so driven? Why did I fight with a fractured leg, dislocated shoulder, broken fingers . . .'

What don't I remember?

'Tell me,' she said. 'Tell me what happened when he came

home from leave after his first tour in Oman. Max said he went berserk.'

Mark turned his pint round and round and then looked up. 'You really want to know what happened?'

Sam nodded.

He smiled with half his mouth, turned to face her and swept his hair off his forehead to reveal the mesh of thin white scars. 'Well, this is what happened to me.'

Sam stared at him. 'But . . .'

'He picked me up by the foot and smashed me into a glass cabinet.'

Sam felt as if someone had kicked her in the stomach. Mark pointed at her empty glass. She nodded. He picked it up together with his own and walked to the bar. She watched his back. He had lied all these years to protect her and she always thought she was the one who protected him – punching the bullies on the top of the bus and, once, throwing out her arm to receive a cigarette burn meant for him.

Mark returned with the pints.

Sam picked up the glass. 'Why didn't you tell me before?'

'He was such a hero to you. I didn't want to be the one and you were always so ferocious in your memory of him. You guarded it savagely. Why break that?'

'And now?'

'If it is him, Sam, if he's coming, I want you to know the sort of man he was. Or the sort of man he was to me. I don't want you to go into this with any illusions. I want you to have some sort of warning.'

'You think it is him, don't you?'

'There were reasons for him to disappear, Sam. There were good enough reasons, totally separate from anything involving the SAS.'

'And now he's back, what's he looking for?'

'He's looking for you, Sam. He always adored you. You're the one he made contact with. It would always have been you that he approached. Not me or Mum.'

Sam tried to adjust her image of her father. Tried to shift him from hero to abuser, from hero to coward. She tried but couldn't. She didn't have those memories. She didn't think she did anyway.

'Why me?'

He shrugged. 'The luck of the draw, I guess. He'd fucked it up with me and Mum. There was no going back there. But you were new. Someone he could project his ambitions on to. He's got no reason to think you might hate him. You were young. Maybe he didn't harm you.'

'What does he want from me?' She looked at Mark. 'I don't understand what he wants.'

He didn't lift his eyes from the table. He knows, she thought, but won't say.

'Why send me a gun?'

'You must be careful. He's not thinking of you. He never thought of other people.'

She looked at her watch. 'Shit, I've got to go. I'm due at O'Connor's.'

Mark stood up and she hugged him, and felt the same savage protectiveness she had always felt, the same visceral and ferocious love.

Sam walked briskly up Parks Road and into the Banbury Road. She felt light-headed from the beer and the cold evening air didn't seem to be sobering her up, quite the reverse, in fact. She unwrapped a piece of gum and put it in her mouth, chewed it, trying to clear the beer from her breath. She didn't feel sober enough for O'Connor, so she continued beyond Park Town, walking the things that Mark had told her like dogs on a leash. Walking and walking and wishing that she could bend down and loosen the collars of her thoughts and slip free of them. But she couldn't; they stayed with her, walking obediently at her heel. When she thought she'd sobered up sufficiently she turned round, took a left into Park Town and knocked on O'Connor's door.

CHAPTER TWENTY-ONE

The children were already in bed. O'Connor poured her a glass of wine and placed it on the table in front of her, poured himself one and joined her. Sam wondered why she had bothered with the gum and the walk to clear her head.

'Today has been a better day,' he said.

'How are Bill and Ian?'

He shook his head. 'Upset, sad, confused.' He sipped his wine. 'Clinging to me like a lifeboat in the storm. I don't feel like a lifeboat,' he added.

Sam felt such a strong need to speak to him it was like a sickness, a pressure in her gullet that was growing and growing. She swallowed repeatedly. Perhaps if she could just swallow it back down. But the lump in her throat remained. She ran her finger through the condensation on the outside of her glass.

'You know you said . . .' Her voice was a whisper, a croak.

'Sorry?' O'Connor frowned, trying to catch what she was saying.

She cleared her throat, looked at him. Yes, she was going to do this. 'You know you said I could talk to you.'

He looked surprised. 'Yes, of course.'

She felt his focus shift, his attention coming on to her in a different way, like heat. He waited for her but she said nothing. Now she had begun she didn't know what to say. She didn't know how to continue. The silence lengthened.

He cleared his throat. 'Would it help if I asked you?'

She nodded.

'Has something happened?'

She nodded again. She hated feeling this vulnerable, this needy. She couldn't bear it.

'Sam?' She heard him from a distance.

'Sam?' Even further away this time.

She closed her eyes. She heard a chair scrape back and felt a hand touch her shoulder. 'Breathe,' she heard. Then she heard him closer and more urgent. 'Sam, take another breath.' She did. 'Take another.' She did that also. She opened her eyes. The voice was clearer now, closer. 'One more deep breath.' Here she was back again, exactly where she didn't want to be.

He sat back down. Brown eyes. *Enough warmth for two*: for me, for Mark, for Alice, for Meg. Two of them were murdered. He'd made love to them both.

'Tell me what happened?'

'Mark – he told me.'

'Oh.'

She fingered the dog tags in her pocket. 'He says.' She paused. 'He used the word abuse.'

O'Connor nodded.

'He said I didn't remember.' Sam looked at him. 'What don't I remember, John?'

He said nothing; she could see him thinking. He swallowed. 'John?'

'I don't think . . .' He twisted the stem of his glass between his fingers. Then he nodded as if in response to an internal conversation he was having with himself. 'I'm sorry but I can't discuss what Mark told me. I just can't. It was spoken in confidence to me in my capacity as a therapist. It would be a breach of trust.'

She repeated. 'What don't I remember?'

He shook his head. 'Look, we can do it this way. Tell me what you *do* remember.'

'Nothing.' But as she said it, she knew it was a lie.

'Tell me what you're feeling right now.'

'Nothing – just numb. Blank.'

'And if you look beyond the numbness, what is that protecting you from feeling?'

'Fear.' As she said it Sam felt pins and needles spark in her hands. The way she used to feel before a fight when the adrenaline was coursing.

'And what are you frightened of? What is the fear saying?'

'It says: Why did you start this? It says: Get away from him. It says: Don't look. You don't want to look.'

'And if you do?'

'It will destroy you.' Sam hugged herself.

'I'm sorry but I don't think this is a good idea. I think we should stop.'

Sam put her head in her hands.

'If I were your therapist it would be different. If we had that sort of relationship, there would be a place to deal with the issues raised. But I'm not. We can't continue. We could open a whole can of worms and you would have nowhere to take it. I can recommend someone. I'm sorry, Sam.' He reached across and touched her hand. 'I shouldn't have begun.'

She shifted her hand out from under his and flexed it. 'And in the meantime?'

'Sorry?'

'What the hell do I do?'

'Have you heard of ring-fencing?'

'Something to do with company assets.'

'Imagine putting all of it in one place and running a fence around it. Tell yourself that you will deal with those things in due course, that they're safe there. That you will come back to them.'

She nodded.

'But Sam, make sure you do. Don't leave it too long.'

'It won't be long now,' she said. 'It's all coming to a head.'

'But if you deal with it on your terms it'll be easier.' He flicked through a diary and wrote something on a piece of paper that he then handed to Sam; it had a name and number written on it. 'Phone Reg, he's a good bloke.'

She stood up and walked to the front of the house, pulled the curtains back and looked across the street. In that house was someone who could tell her the truth. 'I could ask my mother,' she said.

'You could. Perhaps it would be best to do that with someone else present.'

'You offering?'

He smiled but said nothing.

O'Connor left early on Saturday morning. The children were a distraction for Sam. She took them to the park, kicked the football around with them. Let them watch a video their father wouldn't have approved of. Let them play their music too loud and their computer games too long. In the evening she got takeaway food with lots of chips. And nothing happened. There was no threat to the children. O'Connor phoned and was reassured, phoned and was reassured again. The children woke in the night. She told them to get into her bed and they woke the following morning all sprawled over each other like kittens. She didn't know if it reassured them but it did wonders for her.

And as for the ring-fence – did it hold out? Well, in a manner of speaking, it did. There was the odd dart for freedom, a bit of tunnelling and wire-clipping. But when this happened she was firm. Yes, she said, I know you're there. Yes, I will handle you. I will deal with you. And they turned round in their tunnels, climbed down from the wires, got back into their huts and pulled their blankets over their heads. For the moment, anyway.

She must have looked at the piece of paper O'Connor had given her a hundred times. She liked his name. Reg was a no-nonsense sort of name. Not an airy-fairy name. Reg Ellison. By the end of the weekend the piece of paper was worn soft and creased. She went over the number again in biro. She touched it in her pocket and now it seemed more reassuring than the dog tags. The dog tags were losing their power. This is where she would go. This is what she would do. The demons inside the ring-fence wouldn't know what had hit them. Or at any rate that was what she thought on Saturday.

Sam stood in the kitchen on Sunday evening filling the dishwasher. She hadn't realized how exhausting children could be. How did parents have time for anything else? She unfolded the TV section of the paper to see if there was anything on. There was nothing. Nothing she could watch even in desperation. From upstairs came the noise of the boys playing computer games. She picked up the phone and dialled Phil. His answerphone picked up.

'Where are you? I'm at O'Connor's looking after the children. I could do with some company. Are you there? Do you want to come over? It'd be great to see you.'

She put down the phone. Well, she couldn't make it plainer than that. She felt restless and didn't know how to settle. Other people's houses did that to her. Nothing was where you wanted it to be. There was nothing to ground you but yourself. The music wasn't yours and the chairs weren't comfortable. Everything was awkward. Sam stood in front of O'Connor's bookshelves, picked a book out, glanced at it and put it back. So many books – too many in her opinion. She ran her finger along the spines. She took out a book and as she did so found another one tucked at the back, out of sight. She pulled it out. It was a cheap 99p edition of *Jude the Obscure*. She flicked through it; looking for the bits the notes came from. It wasn't hard to find. Two sections were highlighted in green marker pen. She turned the page and found another. *Things are as they are and will be brought to their destined issue.*

'Things are as they are.' Sam said the sentence, then shuddered at the fatalism. She flicked through the rest of the book. There were no other markings. Just those three highlighted sentences. But so far as she knew O'Connor had only received two notes. Why was the third one highlighted? The doorbell cut across her thoughts. Phil, she thought, he's got my message and has come over. She put the book down on the table and, still puzzling over it, walked through into the hall and opened the door.

She saw the silver tip of the end of the black leather belt first, then the blue cashmere coat. She was thinking about the quotation; she was thinking about Phil. For a few seconds she failed to respond because what she was seeing didn't match her thoughts. It was all the time Tony Ballinger needed. He stepped swiftly past her into the hall and closed the door behind him. She looked at his face, then down at the small, snub-nosed gun that had appeared in his hand. He smiled. My God, she thought, the fox has come for the chickens and I've opened the door to him. He leaned back against the door, his thumb hooked into his belt.

'Stay exactly where you are,' he said. She did as she was told. 'You move an inch and I'll shoot you, do you understand?' She nodded. 'Where are his brats?'

Her mind was whirring on exits and escape. Was there a fire escape out the back? Could they jump into the garden? Could they climb down the gutters? She didn't say anything but at that moment the children appeared at the top of the stairs. Their frozen faces were the last things she saw before Ballinger hit her hard on the side of her face with the gun and she passed out.

'Wakey, wakey.' Ballinger was slapping her awake. He slapped her again. Where was she? What was happening? Sam tried to open her eyes but could only open one; the other was swollen shut. She was propped up against the wall in the kitchen, his belt tied tight around her hands. Bill and Ian were nowhere to be seen. Ballinger waved a knife in front of her eyes and it had the same effect as smelling salts – all of a sudden she felt very wide awake. She knew how sharp it was: only an hour ago she'd been using it to cut up tomatoes. The tip of that knife was a centimetre from her eye. He dropped it down to her cheekbone, just below the socket and poked at the flesh there. She felt something cold then something wet trickle down her cheek and into her mouth. Her tongue tasted blood.

'You don't know how far I'm willing to go. Do you?'

He removed the knife from her face. She scanned the room with her one good eye. Where were the boys? Were they all right? The knife was being waved in front of her face. It landed on her face again, sliced. Get him talking, she thought, that's what you're supposed to do. Establish a relationship. It's more difficult for them to kill you. For God's sake, do something before he cuts off your face.

'You and then them. Them and then you?' He paused 'What shall I do? So many choices. I think I'll save you to last.' He caressed the belt that encircled Sam's wrists. Let his fingers stray on to her hands. 'Alice loved to be tied up. It really turned her on. She loved to be totally exposed. She liked it rough. How do you like it? Shall we find out? A little bit of sex education for the boys perhaps?'

Her eyes didn't leave his face. He was touching the belt as if it was alive. His thumb rubbed the silver tip. Sam was trying to work out how long she'd been unconscious. Had Phil got her message? Would he come?

'Why did you kill Meg?' she asked.

'Why? He'd taken everything from me. Alice was everything. And he thought he could start screwing my wife and there'd be no consequences. He thought he was safe. That I'd do the decent thing, step aside. Let it go on.' His hand squeezed her throat. 'Alice was everything to me. I gave up my job at Oxford for her. Do you know how difficult it is to get a fellowship in an Oxford college? I gave all that up for her.'

'But she'd had other affairs. Why was O'Connor any different?'

'She hadn't.'

'But you said—'

'I know what I said. I lied. Of course Alice loved to flirt. She was that kind of woman. It was easy to make you think she was promiscuous.'

'She was faithful to you?'

He nodded. 'Until O'Connor. He thought he could just start screwing my wife and that I'd be so polite about it, so middle-class. What did he think I'd do? Send him a fucking thank you letter? I wanted to give him a lesson. Actions have consequences. It's a simple lesson as old as time. An eye for an eye. A wife for a wife. In the Old Testament tradition. There's a certain dramatic symmetry to that, don't you think?'

'Did you kill her in Fulham?'

He nodded. 'I phoned and we arranged to meet in the White Horse at Parsons Green. Afterwards she invited me back to her place. I suggested a little revenge to balance things, but she was squeamish and had to be persuaded. Rather forcibly, I'm afraid.' Ballinger was tracing the knife down the side of Sam's neck. 'I might not have killed her if the silly little bitch had agreed to a quick fuck.'

'Then you took her to the river?'

'It was the easiest thing to do.'

He dropped the knife on the table, sat down and crossed his legs. His foot bounced up and down, up and down. 'And now here we are. I wasn't expecting you – an added bonus. I was hoping for O'Connor and his brats alone together. Where is he?'

'He'll be back any second – a take-away . . .'

He smiled. 'I doubt it.'

'And Alice?'

He frowned. 'Alice?'

'Why kill her? You loved her.'

He laughed. 'You think I killed her? Have you been listening to a word I've been saying?'

'You were there at the gaudy. You found her.'

'You really think I would kill her? You don't understand anything, do you? I loved her.'

'So you killed Meg but not Alice?'

He picked up the knife, touching the tip with his finger.

'You knew about her pregnancy?' Sam didn't care about the answer, she was just trying to stop him doing whatever he was going to do next.

His foot stopped moving; it hung quite still.

'Of course, she told me everything. That's what the O'Connor thing was all about.'

'Was it yours?'

He laughed. 'No, that's one thing I knew for certain.'

'How can you be so sure?'

He started to throw the knife back and forth from one hand to the other. 'I couldn't have them.'

'But she was pregnant. Wasn't that why you left Oxford? Why you married her?'

He looked surprised. 'My, my! Perhaps I should hire you to find out who murdered my wife. Although, of course, I don't have to because I know already.'

'So, surely the child could have been yours.'

'No, she lied about being pregnant in order for us to marry. She didn't think I'd do it otherwise. She said she had a miscarriage but later, when we tried, we couldn't. We had the tests and it turned out I couldn't. Then she admitted she'd lied, that she'd never been pregnant. It had all been a scam. She just wanted to marry me.'

'And you wouldn't have married her if she hadn't been?'

'At that time, probably not. I was never very keen on marriage. Alice liked the status, of course. My star was rising at that point and she was always in love with status.' He sighed.

'That's what the whole O'Connor thing was about for her – children. That's what she said anyway. She wanted a baby, couldn't have one with me and then she bumped into O'Connor in Blackwell's. She said it seemed serendipitous. She knew she could reel him in easily enough. It turned out it was his sperm she was after.'

'But if that's all it was, why did you have to kill Meg? I don't understand.'

'And how do you think it made me feel that my own wife was having to go to some weak-minded, blubbering little shrink to get some sperm?' He stood up. 'And now to unfinished business.' He walked towards Sam, bent over her and cut a curl from her forehead. 'A memento,' he said. She smelled his aftershave. 'I'll enjoy this.' He put down the knife and his hand moved to his fly.

The doorbell went. His hand covered her mouth. 'Who is it?' he hissed. 'Very quietly.' He released his hand from her mouth just enough for her to be able to speak.

She shook her head. 'I don't know.'

He pulled a handkerchief from his pocket and rammed it brutally into Sam's mouth, then drew back his hand and hit her hard in the face. She blacked out for a second and then pretended to be unconscious. He let go of her and moved to the front of the house, pulled back the curtain and looked outside. The bell rang again. It's now or never, Sam thought. He is going to kill me anyway, so I might as well go out fighting. She wriggled towards the wall and, leaning heavily against it, stood up. She had to be quick or Phil would be gone. The mobile phone in her pocket began ringing; Phil was trying to get hold of her. Ballinger turned round and saw Sam standing and began to move towards her. Sam launched herself at the thing she thought would make the most noise if it fell over – a small portable TV. Sam and the television crashed to the ground in a cacophony of breaking glass. She lay in the remnants of the television, covered in broken glass and bits of electric wiring. The doorbell was ringing continuously now.

Tony Ballinger stood over her. 'Stupid bitch,' he said. He grabbed the front of her shirt and pulled her towards him. 'Think you're so fucking clever, do you?' Sam heard the glass in the front door smashing. Better make it quick, she thought, or I'm dead. She felt cold steel against her throat. Too late. She closed her eyes and waited to die. *In sure and certain hope of the Resurrection*. She didn't think so, no. Dead was dead – unless it was her father. Her eyes were closed, she was expecting to feel the knife at her throat and feel her windpipe cut open. A deafening explosion. Her face was wet, sprayed with her own blood. But she'd felt no cut – she could still breathe. Another explosion. She opened her eyes and blinked. Tony Ballinger sat a couple of feet away; a red flower blossomed from his mouth, spilling on to the white linen of his shirt. Sam was soaked in blood. His eyes rolled up in his head and he fell backwards. The knife dropped from his hand. He's dead, Sam thought, and it should be me. But she didn't understand what had happened. She just didn't get it. He had put the knife to her throat but *he* had died.

Phil leaned over her, pulling at her clothes, at the handkerchief in her mouth. 'Where are you hurt?' All he could see was blood. His hands ran over her limbs.

'I'm not,' she said.

He went over to where Ballinger lay, and placed his fingers under his jaw, feeling for a pulse that wasn't there. Then he returned to Sam. 'You're covered in blood.'

Sam nodded. 'His mostly.'

Phil tugged at the belt tied round Sam's wrists.

'Did you do that?' she asked.

'What?'

She pointed at Ballinger.

He shook his head. 'I thought you had.'

Sam rubbed her wrists. 'With my hands tied?'

Phil returned to Ballinger's body. 'Bullseye,' he muttered. 'Straight through the mouth. The whole of the back of his head's missing.'

A dark red puddle was creeping from under the skull. The sweet smell of blood filled the room. Sam thought of the butcher's and the blood dripping from the rabbits' mouths down on to the sawdust and discarded pieces of meat.

'It wasn't me,' she said. Then she remembered. 'Christ, the children.' She tried to run for the door but she stumbled and slipped in the puddle of blood and grabbed hold of the table to stop herself from falling.

'Sit down,' Phil said. 'I'll check. You'll only frighten them. Look at you.'

She did and saw the whole of her upper torso was covered in blood. She sat and let Phil do the looking. Outside a blue light flashed round and round against the curtains. Sam looked at the door that opened out on to the balcony. The glass was shattered and a cold wind was blowing through the kitchen. Phil came back into the room.

'They're fine. He'd locked them in the cupboard under the stairs – a WPC's upstairs with them now.'

Sam nodded at the broken glass. 'It must have come from there.'

'We need to get you to a hospital.'

'There's nothing the matter with me, I'm just covered in blood.'

'All the same, we should get you checked out. You haven't seen what you look like, Sam . . .'

'I'll go to my mother's. She'll know if I need stitches or not. I'll take the children there. They mustn't see this,' she said, indicating Ballinger's body. 'Could you get me a coat from the hall? It'll cover the worst of this mess.' She pointed at her bloodstained clothes.

'I suppose so but your face still looks pretty shocking.'

Phil came back with a raincoat. Sam shrugged it on, wincing at her aching muscles. She called her mother.

'I need to come over and bring the O'Connor boys,' she said.

'Are those police cars to do with you?'

'Yes, Mum, they are.'

There was a pause. 'Well, come then.'

She looked at Phil. 'OK, she's had some warning. Let's go.' Sam waited for the children in the hallway. They came down the stairs with a WPC, looking pallid and scared. Sam held out her hands. 'Come on,' she said. 'We're going to spend the night at my mother's – she's a barrel of laughs,' she added under her breath. They took her hands and walked out of the house, past the police cars and the ambulance, under the blue and white police incident tape and up the steps of her mother's house.

Her mother opened the door and looked at her face. 'God, Sam . . .' Then she stopped. 'Come on, boys, let's get you something to drink.'

Peter was sitting at the kitchen table with the paper spread out in front of him. He took off his reading glasses and rubbed his eyes. He looked at Sam but said nothing, got up and pulled open a cupboard out of which he took a bottle of whisky. He poured a couple of inches into a tumbler and handed it to her. She muttered her thanks and felt the amber fluid burn down her throat and into her stomach.

'Peter, take the boys through to watch some TV,' her mother said. And Peter nodded.

Her mother sat Sam down in a chair. 'Right, let's take a look at you.'

Sam began to take off the coat. 'I'm covered in blood but it's not mine and it looks much worse than it is.'

'Give me some credit. I did work in an A&E ward for fifteen years.'

'Sorry,' Sam said. 'I just wanted to warn you.'

'Where are you hurt?'

'I just want you to tell me if I need stitches,' Sam pointed to her face. Her mother took out some cotton wool, swabbed it in antiseptic and began to clean Sam's face.

'This,' she said, swabbing the cut under Sam's eye, 'is the worst. She passed the cotton wool over the cut a couple more times. Sam winced. 'Keep still.' She peered at it. 'No, I think that should be fine. We just need to get the swelling down.' She walked over to the fridge and took out a large packet of frozen peas. She wrapped it in a clean tea towel and handed it to Sam. 'Keep it pressed over the whole of that side of your face.'

Sam was exhausted and for once did what her mother said. The whisky was starting to take effect and her face was throbbing and stinging in equal measure. She put her elbow on the table and held her face against the ice pack. Water dripped down through the tea towel, soaking her sleeve and forming a pool at her elbow. She shivered. She closed her eyes and dozed for a few minutes. She came to when her mother pulled the frozen peas away and looked at her face. 'Longer,' she said, replacing Sam's hand.

Sam straightened in her chair.

'Mark told me,' she said.

Her mother was over by the sink. She could only see her back. 'Told you what?'

'About Dad.'

She shook her hands into the sink.

'Everything,' Sam lied. 'He told me everything.'

'He didn't tell me he'd talked to you.'

'He hasn't had time. We've only just spoken.'

Jean Goodman turned round and leaned against the sink. 'I always tried to be fair. It wasn't your fault. None of it was your fault. You were an absolute innocent. I tried so hard not to blame you.'

'Blame me for what?'

'But it was so difficult. You looked so like him, it was uncanny. You were a constant reminder of something I was trying hard to forget. And temperamentally there were similarities.'

There was something here that Sam wasn't getting ... something ... but it was all beyond her at the moment, what with the whisky and everything.

'I'm sorry I looked like him,' she mumbled, even though she knew she was apologizing for something she couldn't help.

'Don't be silly. It's not your fault,' her mother repeated. 'But it is one of the reasons I couldn't bear you fighting. Even in judo. But you were so determined, so stubborn. That was very like him.'

'Yes,' Sam said.

'At least you didn't go into the army.'

'No.'

'I didn't know what to do, really. I could see it was good for you. But I so much didn't want you involved in anything violent.'

'I had to do it,' Sam said. 'God knows what would have become of me if I hadn't had it.'

Her mother nodded. 'Yes, I could see that as well.'

Sam's arm was soaked from the melting frozen peas. She shook it and sprayed water over the floor, and then squeezed her sleeve.

'I suppose I always wanted you to be as different to him as possible. I was always worried that somehow you'd be affected. It's silly but—'

Sam put the peas and cloth down on the table. 'These have melted now.'

Her mother took the soggy mess and placed it on the draining board.

'Has Mark told you what's been happening?'

'No, what?'

So Sam told her about the note, the fox and the gun and about Max. Her mother didn't say anything while Sam spoke. But her face registered no surprise, just strain.

Looking at her mother, it suddenly dawned on Sam. 'You knew. You knew he wasn't dead.'

'Yes,' she said, drying her hands. 'I knew he wasn't dead.'

Sam was confused. 'Are you still married to him? What about Peter?'

'I had his death certificate, Sam. That's all I needed to remarry.'

'But he's alive . . .'

'Officially he was dead. Officially that's all I needed. Officially he doesn't exist.'

'Did Mark know?'

'No, just me and his handlers.'

'Did Max?'

'I honestly don't know. He wasn't involved at the time.'

'And what was the deal?'

'He disappeared for good. He died. They could do what they wanted with him. It was useful. They had occasions where they wanted things done by someone who couldn't be traced. If he was dead they could use him.'

'For what?'

Her mother shrugged. 'But the deal was he never came near us again. That was the deal done. I wouldn't go to the police. I wouldn't prosecute him – they'd get to keep him. He was highly trained. They didn't want someone like that sitting in prison for years. For them it would have been a waste. And of course, they didn't want the negative publicity.'

'Why would you go to the police?'

'Mark didn't tell you everything, did he?'

'What don't I remember?'

Peter came into the kitchen. 'The children were falling asleep. I've put them to bed in the spare room.'

'Thanks,' Sam said.

The doorbell went and Peter left the room. He came back a few minutes later with Phil.

'Does she need to go to hospital, Mrs Goodman?'

'No, she'll be fine.'

'God,' Sam said. 'I haven't even phoned O'Connor.'

'We need to ask you some questions, Sam.'

'She needs to sleep,' her mother said.

'It's OK, Mum.'

'We'll leave you in peace,' Peter said, and he and Sam's mother left the room.

Phil sat down and took hold of Sam's hand. 'How are you?'

'Confused, knackered, covered in blood – take your pick.'

'Could you tell me what happened?'

Sam ran through the events of the evening.

'So he admitted murdering Meg?'

'Yes, he did, but not Alice. Although he said he knew who did it.'

'Did you believe him?'

'Why would he lie? He was going to kill me. It doesn't make sense. He was adamant he hadn't killed her. He wanted revenge on O'Connor. That's why he killed Meg. Old Testament. You take my wife, I take yours. That's what he said. I must phone O'Connor, he should be back here.'

'Yes,' Phil said, 'O'Connor.'

Sam rang O'Connor, gave him a somewhat toned-down version of events and assured him that the boys were OK and established when he would be back.

'The thing is,' Phil said. 'Ballinger was shot.'

Sam nodded. 'I heard an explosion, felt wet on my face and when I opened my eyes he was sitting there with blood pumping out of his mouth.'

'Did you see anyone?'

Sam shook her head. 'Whoever shot him must have been standing behind me. They must have been in the garden.'

'Who would be willing to kill for you, Sam?'

'Or who would want to kill Tony Ballinger? It might have had nothing to do with me.' But even as she spoke the words she knew that this was nonsense. Someone had killed Tony Ballinger to protect her.

CHAPTER TWENTY-TWO

It was like a dream you remember vividly at two o'clock but have forgotten by the time you wake up. Sam was sure that in the middle of the night she had been absolutely clear about everything. What had happened when her father was on leave, why her mother didn't like her, who had killed Alice Knight . . . But that was then and now it was eight-thirty in the morning and she was sitting bleary-eyed at her mum's table having breakfast with the children and trying to clear the fog from her head. Polite conversation was beyond her; at breakfast it usually was, even when she hadn't been beaten up the night before. She crunched her toast slowly, trying to avoid the lacerated parts of her mouth and waggled a loose tooth back and forth with her tongue. Her mother tilted Sam's face towards the light and peered at her.

'It shouldn't scar,' she said. 'It's not deep enough and the swelling is going down.'

The doorbell went and soon afterwards O'Connor came into the kitchen. He hugged the boys and grimaced when he saw Sam.

'Don't worry,' she said, 'apparently I'm not going to be scarred.'

'Good.'

O'Connor turned to Jean Goodman. 'The police won't let us back into the house and can't say when we'll be allowed back in. Is it OK if we base ourselves here until we get the go-ahead?'

Sam's mother nodded her assent.

Later that morning in the St Aldate's police station, Sam sat opposite DS Rowland, giving her version of what had happened. This time round he was gentler, presumably affected in some way by the sight of her battered face. He had been particularly interested in who might have shot Tony Ballinger.

'Did you see who did it?' he asked.

'I had closed my eyes,' Sam said wearily. 'Because I was expecting to have my throat cut.'

He nodded. 'Do you know any professional assassins, Miss Falconer?'

Sam laughed. 'What?'

'Tony Ballinger was shot twice through the mouth from quite a distance. That requires some accurate shooting. It requires someone who was confident enough of their shooting abilities to be sure that they would not kill you in the process. It has all the hallmarks of a professional hit.'

'Oh,' Sam said.

'So, do you know anyone who can shoot like that?'

'No, I don't.'

'Your father was in the SAS, wasn't he?'

'He died in nineteen seventy-four.'

'Kept in contact with any of his mates?'

'No,' Sam said. 'We came to Oxford in nineteen seventy-five and left all that stuff behind us.'

'So you've no idea who might have done it?'

Sam shook her head.

'No one who'd be prepared to kill for you?'

'I'd like to think that there was,' Sam said. 'But no, I can't think of anyone who would do that or even anyone I know who might have access to a gun.'

And that had been that, Sam thought. She knew that Rowland probably didn't believe her, but he wasn't going to go digging too much into this one. After all, the person who had been shot was a self-confessed murderer and had been about to commit several more, if you counted the boys. Why waste police time on that? But then Phil had joined them and another conversation took place, a conversation that lasted a lot longer and involved both men using their considerable persuasive powers to the full. It took them two hours to convince her.

That afternoon O'Connor and Sam took the boys to Christ Church meadow for a walk. Sam still felt weak and they walked slowly, the boys running ahead of them along the riverside path.

O'Connor wiped the end of his nose with his gloved hand. 'You know, when I bumped into her at Blackwell's I was so happy. Just to see her again. It's such a powerful thing, isn't it, the first time you fall in love? And it was still there after all those years; the desire I had for her was as strong as ever. And she always gave off this aura. You know, the promise that she would be the best fuck of your life.'

'Watch out for the sirens,' Sam said.

He shook his head. 'I'm afraid I didn't.'

'You should have put parsley in your ears.'

He smiled.

Sam prodded at the swollen flesh round her eye. 'I didn't like her. I thought she was highly manipulative.'

O'Connor laughed. 'Oh yes, she was that all right.'

They stood looking across the river at the university playing fields.

'But sex was never about intimacy for her; it was all about power. The amount of power she could have over someone. Sex with her was a game.'

On the other side of the river a gawky figure was wobbling along on a bicycle and shouting instructions at an eight. Sam laughed and waved. 'Mark's taken up coaching again.'

'Rowing saved that man's life. It was so good for his confidence. Getting a blue laid so many ghosts to rest.'

Sam nodded. They were walking towards Christ Church Cathedral.

'Did you phone him?'

For a second she thought he meant Mark, but then she remembered. She touched the piece of paper in her pocket tangled up with the dog tags. She shook her head. 'I got overtaken by events.'

'Don't leave it too long.'

'I'll see.'

'What I mean is don't leave it until you feel like it, just do it.'

Why was it, Sam thought, that people were always saying that to her?

'I talked to my mother about it.'

O'Connor looked startled.

'But it's still not clear. I thought I had it at two this morning. You know, the pieces made sense, and then when I woke up it was gone again.'

'You have a belief that if you remember it will destroy you. It's a powerful reason not to remember.' O'Connor stopped. 'Don't try to do that by yourself, Sam. Get professional help. Phone Reg. I think you'll like him.'

I doubt it, Sam thought, I bloody doubt it.

They walked on for a few moments in silence. Sam looked at O'Connor walking next to her in his brown corduroys and blue fleece. She thought of his two boys, Bill and Ian, and she thought of Meg drowned in the river, possibly raped, certainly murdered by Tony Ballinger. A string of events sparked off by something as commonplace as an affair and a ticking biological clock. And then she thought of Alice. She hadn't liked her but it didn't mean that she thought she deserved to be murdered. No one deserved that.

'You know Ballinger only confessed to Meg's murder?'

O'Connor didn't say anything.

'So Alice Knight's case remains unsolved.'

He nodded. 'He could have lied. He was there that evening. He had the opportunity.'

'But I don't think he did it,' Sam said. 'He was in love with her. That portrait was like an icon. I don't think he could have killed her. And why would he lie to me when he was about to kill me?'

'Isn't that what crimes of passion are all about? You kill the very thing you love?'

'Do you believe in confession?' Sam asked.

O'Connor looked at her and frowned. 'That's a strange question. I'm not a Catholic if that's what you mean.'

'Wasn't the priest the forerunner of the therapist? But more effective because at the end of confession you had God's forgiveness, or you thought you had it, which I suppose amounts to the same thing. Therapists can't deliver that, can they?'

'Therapist believe in self-forgiveness, in self-healing.'

'Rather an inadequate alternative, surely?'

'But you forget that for confession to work you have to believe in God.'

'Oh yes,' Sam laughed. 'I knew there was a catch somewhere.'

'Do you?'

'I've always found the devil a more plausible prospect.'

He laughed.

'Can you live with what you've done?' She said it casually, almost as if she'd asked him something as insignificant as the time.

O'Connor looked startled. 'I'm sorry?'

Sam didn't say anything.

'You mean the affair?'

Sam sighed. 'If you like. Did Alice tell you she was pregnant?'

'Yes.'

'When did she tell you?'

O'Connor didn't reply.

Sam tried again. 'What was she intending to do with it?'

'Oh, she was intending to keep it and raise it with Tony. I think it was the only reason for her having the affair with me. It was quite calculated. She wasn't interested in me at all. It was purely a matter of having the correct genetic material for her child. She said, "Well, you've had a more exciting sex life than you've had for a while and I've got what I wanted." She saw it as a trade-off. Sex was always a way of getting what she wanted. It's how she got Tony in the first place.'

'And how did that make you feel?'

O'Connor glanced sideways at Sam. 'Ever thought of being a therapist?'

Sam shuddered. 'I would rather go head to head with Bruce Lee.'

'Are you wearing a wire?'

Sam stopped on the path and held her arms out at right angles away from her body, inviting him to search her. 'You've been watching too many episodes of *The Sopranos*, but go ahead, you're welcome to check.'

He shook his head and they walked a few more paces. He took a deep breath. 'How it made me feel was used – very used, very stupid and very angry. She had absolutely no intention of discussing with me whether she kept the child or not. She just told me that was what she was going to do and that she did not want me to be involved in any way. She didn't want any money from me. In fact, all along she had wanted nothing from me other than my sperm. I couldn't bear the idea of a child of mine being raised by someone else, especially two people as narcissistic as Tony and Alice. She capped it by saying that if I made any fuss she would tell Meg about the affair. She said I'd lose Bill and Ian, and that I'd end up with nothing. I suppose you know what happened with my father?'

'He had an affair with his secretary. She got pregnant, insisted on having it and then he disowned them both. Then she spilled the beans and he had to resign.'

'Yes, roughly, that's right. But the thing I could never understand was that he never wanted to have any contact with his child. We were all forbidden to have contact with her. He just slammed the door on the whole thing and I swore I'd never do that to a child of mine – ever. And then there was Alice telling me, more or less, that that was exactly what I had to do. That she'd allow me no access and if I did try to get some it would put my relationship with Meg, Bill and Ian at risk. She was a very clever woman. She used me and then boxed me in to a corner. She was going to force me to do what my father had done and what I had despised him for. She was going to make me disown my own child.'

'The DNA tests will show it's yours. Ballinger said he couldn't have them.'

O'Connor didn't say anything and Sam continued. 'Of course, that in itself will mean nothing. They already know that you were having an affair with her.'

O'Connor stopped and leaned back against a tree, hands in pockets. He looked at his sons chasing each other around in the grass. 'To answer your earlier question,' he said, 'for them I can live with anything.'

For the first time Sam saw something steely in his face and realized that she had misjudged him. She had thought of him as weak, emotionally incontinent, an incapable person with blurred boundaries – a person too furry on the inside for her liking. But he had done something that she would not have been able to live with and he seemed barely to have batted an eyelid. He was much tougher than she had ever given him credit for. For the first time she felt a shiver of fear.

'You know, in some cases people hand themselves over to the police because they cannot live with what they've done. There is a compulsion to confess.'

'I know,' O'Connor said. 'I've heard that. But I assure you, I'm no Raskolnikov.'

'Perhaps it was an accident,' Sam suggested.

'What?'

'What happened?'

O'Connor looked into the middle distance. 'I lost my temper. She was taunting me, goading me about how easy it had been to seduce me, how pliable I was and how pathetic. She said if you offer men sex, they will do anything for you. She said if I ever sought any kind of contact with the child, she would tell Meg. I didn't want to risk that. She said I had meant nothing to her, it was just about getting the sperm she wanted. She was laughing at me. She was so pleased with what she'd done. I pushed her. She fell and hit her head against the mantelpiece and passed out.'

'So, it was an accident.'

'Up until then it was.'

'And then what happened?'

O'Connor looked at Sam. 'Oh, then I strangled her. You don't think I was just going to let her get away with it? It was the only way to bring the thing to an end. If she had lived she would have had the child. It was the only way I could have any say in what happened.'

'But you killed your own child.'

'Rather dead than brought up by those two. I'd rather it were dead. It was the only way to wipe the slate clean. To control the situation. To be free of her.'

'Did you write those notes yourself?' Sam asked.

O'Connor frowned. 'What?'

'The notes from *Jude the Obscure*.'

'No, I assume they were sent by Tony. He did come after the children. He was coming after me.'

'I found your copy of the book and three quotations had been underlined. I thought you'd only received two.'

'Oh, I see. I had. I'd underlined the third because I thought that's where it was leading. It seemed the natural follow-on to the others.'

'*Things are as they are and will be brought to their destined issue,*' Sam said.

'Yes,' O'Connor said. 'That's right.'

As Sam and O'Connor stepped out into St Aldate's, Phil and two uniformed officers met them. O'Connor looked quickly at Sam and then back at the three men.

'Would you come with us please, sir,' Phil said.

'I trusted you,' O'Connor said

'You shouldn't have,' Sam replied.

'However long it takes,' he whispered. 'I'll remember.'

'I've done nothing.'

'What happened to your so-called duty of confidentiality?'

'You murdered someone,' Sam said. 'That's not something you can just cry over and it'll go away. That's not something you can just forgive yourself for and continue your life as if nothing has happened. You murdered someone in cold blood.'

She watched the uniformed officers handcuff him and lead him off in the direction of the police station. Bill and Ian trailed behind, holding the hands of a WPC. Phil remained with her. Sam tore open her jacket and pulled a wire and tape recorder from under her jumper.

'Here,' she said, pushing it against Phil's chest. 'Next time you get to do your own dirty work.'

'You did really well, Sam.'

'Oh, shut up, Phil. Don't fucking patronize me.'

'We need to take your statement.'

'Not now you don't,' Sam said. 'I'm all talked out.'

Sam came back to London a couple of days later. An *Evening Standard* advert at Victoria coach station stating that a trial date had been set for the Jenny Hughes case did nothing to lift her depression. Sam went straight home. For three days she didn't crawl out from under the duvet. She pulled down the blinds, left the answerphone to pick up any messages and didn't answer the doorbell or the taps on the door that she knew came from Edie. She slept and she slept and when she awoke she tried to figure out what she needed to do next. On the morning of the fourth day a complete absence of any food for either her or Frank got her out of bed. She washed, pulled up the blinds, went and got some food from the corner shop and then listened to her messages from Alan, Mark, her mother, Max, Edie and Spence. She'd never known she was so popular. She phoned Alan first.

'Well, well, she's decided to rise from her deathbed.'

'Shut up, Alan.'

'You back in the land of the living?'

'I wouldn't go that far. More like the living dead,' Sam said. 'Fancy a trip to Dagenham?'

'Don't tell me,' Alan groaned. 'The Blue Posts.'

A couple of hours later Sam and Alan sat opposite Alfie Turner in the Blue Posts. His hooded, lizard eyes flickered back and forth between them but seemed to linger longest on Alan's well-developed upper body. A large Alsatian sat next to him, pink tongue lolling obscenely from its mouth. He hadn't offered them a drink.

'I want you to pass on a message to your brothers,' Sam said.

Alfie blinked and the dog closed its mouth and noisily swallowed its saliva.

'I'm not going to testify against you.'

Alfie smiled and blew smoke straight at them. 'That it?'

'That's it,' Sam said. 'So you can tell Bernie and any other pond life you've got out there that there's no need for any more psychopathic games.'

Alfie sniffed.

'So things are clear between us?' Sam said.

Alfie stubbed out his cigarette and stood up. 'Shouldn't get in over your head, girl.'

'That's exactly what I decided,' Sam replied.

Outside the pub Sam turned to Alan. 'I'm not going to spend the rest of my life looking over my shoulder. And I'm not going to move from my home.'

'Your choice,' Alan said.

'Yes,' Sam said. 'My life – my choice. And we both know, Alan, this isn't going to put a dent in the Turners. This is peanuts.'

'Didn't they end up putting away Al Capone for tax evasion? It was only for tax but they did put him away.'

'I'm not putting my life at risk over this – or Frank's.'

'Well, perish the thought the cat might get it—'

'Don't you dare judge me on this, Alan.'

'Come on, love, I wouldn't. Let's get out of here,' and he set off towards Sam's car.

Later that afternoon Sam sat in Max's office.

'I've spoken to Mark and my mother but there were some things I want to check out with you.'

Max looked decidedly uncomfortable.

'Mark told me what happened to him.'

Max nodded.

'But I don't know what happened to my mother.'

'Jean . . .' Max ran his hand over his head.

'You see, she said she had tried not to blame me. It's been going round and round in my head. She said she knew it wasn't my fault. What did she mean?'

'That night he smashed up the whole house. Ripped everything off the walls, smashed the furniture, plates, glasses, everything. Mark was unconscious when I got there and I thought he was dead and your mother . . .' He turned round, silhouetted against the light pouring through the window behind him. 'He beat her up pretty badly, broke her nose and raped her.' He paused. 'I don't think it was the first time either.'

Rape. As Max said the word, Sam recognized that she had

heard the truth. It all made sense. Why her mother had struggled to love her. Why she'd hated her fighting. Why she couldn't bear the fact that she looked like him. Also why Peter Goodman had seemed like such a good catch. He was intellectual, orderly, controlled. He never lost his temper and he was certainly never violent – a different world entirely. Oxford must have seemed like heaven to her. Sam saw herself clinging to her father.

She had been holding on to him to prevent him doing any more harm. That was why she couldn't let go of him.

'Are you all right?' Max's voice cut through her thoughts.

'Yes,' she said. 'What you've said. It's the only thing that makes sense of it all.'

'It wasn't your fault, Sam.'

'No,' Sam said. 'It wasn't.'

'And you know, that wasn't all there was to him. He was an incredible fighter, the sort of bloke you wanted on your side in a crisis. He got me through selection. I owed him for that, but his temper ... well, his temper was always a problem.'

'Tell me something else good about him, Max.'

'There was lots good about him. During the escape and evasion part of selection we had to cross a river. It had rained heavily overnight and I was never a particularly strong swimmer. By then I was exhausted but we knew we had to cross it. Your dad got across first but I ran into difficulties halfway through. He came back for me, dragged me out and gave me mouth-to-mouth. My heart had stopped. I'd have died without him. Without him I'd definitely have failed but he was like a terrier. He'd never let go. Once he'd decided on a thing that was that. He'd decided that I was going to pass and he dragged me through.'

Sam flexed her right hand.

'Some men are like that, Sam. They make good mates but they're wicked with their families. Geoff was like that. He should never have got married. It was a big mistake. SAS and family – it doesn't mix well at the best of times.'

'Why didn't you warn my mother?'

Max looked at her. 'I did.'

'And she went ahead anyway?'

'She was young, Sam. They both were.'

'Did you have someone following me in Oxford last weekend?' Sam said.

Max frowned. 'When was this?'

'Someone tried to kill me and was shot twice through the mouth. The police say that's a professional hit. Was it one of yours?'

Max slowly shook his head from side to side. 'But that's professional all right. It's how we're trained. Two shots to the head.'

'Has he been in contact with you?'

Max didn't say anything.

Sam stood up. 'Tell him I want to meet him, will you, Max?'

'Are you sure, Sam?'

She nodded.

The note came a month later. Just a postcard pushed through the letterbox with a time and the address of a café. It was the same writing as the first letter. So, Sam thought, face to face at last.

He sat at the greasy, grey table, a small man you wouldn't look twice at. His hands were dug deep inside the pockets of his black donkey jacket, as if they were too cold to take out, as if they'd always be too cold. Sitting opposite him, Sam looked at him in detail. No cursory look, this. She was absolutely clear what she was looking for in the planes of his face, the angle of eye socket to cheekbone to neck, even in the crevices of his ears. Finally, she looked into his eyes – red-rimmed, watery blue with sandy eyelashes. And she found exactly what she expected to find –

herself. She had imagined this so many times. How much love she would feel towards him and how open she would be. But she knew too much now. She sat with her arms folded. She was frightened, the adrenaline was pumping and her heart thumped in her ears. The last time this happened. No, she didn't want to think about that, she couldn't. She refocused on his eyes.

'Do you want anything?' He nodded towards the counter at the back of the café. She shook her head. Her mouth was dry; she couldn't swallow anything. She felt sick. Don't touch me, she thought, don't you dare touch me as you go by. He didn't. Just another nondescript man of medium height, joining the queue for a cup of tea. She sat with her back to him, looking at the open door. She could just get up and walk out. She could but of course she didn't. She watched the traffic rumbling past the window, and the people scurrying to work. What was she doing here? It couldn't possibly be happening, could it? She made patterns in the swirled, greasy surface of the table. It was what she had longed for all her life but it wasn't happening how it was supposed to.

He brought a cup of tea back, sat down and stirred two sugars into it, sipped it and looked at her. He reached across as if to touch her face but she swayed backwards, out of reach. He dropped his hand to the table.

'It was always you,' he said. 'It was you that kept me alive.'

She didn't understand him. What did it have to do with her? Nothing. What about her mother and Mark? She was only four.

'When you were born, I held you in my arms and it was like seeing myself newborn. It was different. It was always you.'

He was addressing her more as lover than daughter. She shuddered because she felt the way she had felt only one other time in her life: the last time she was in the presence of evil, in the presence of a man who had murdered his own child – Andrew Hughes. She sat opposite her father, knowing he was unsafe, a murderer. She held her arms tightly in front of her. A

315

clichéd image of a father throwing his child in the air came to her. The child squealed with laughter as she was tossed in the air. The sun was shining; it was like one of those cereal ads. Somewhere just out of shot you knew there was a large golden dog grinning and wagging its tail. And then other images came . . .

She's freezing cold, struggling to breathe; he's thrown her in the water. It's the only way, he says. You come to the surface, you swim – that's how you learn. She does eventually come to the surface but then down she goes again, gasping for breath, up and down she goes. Then he grabs her and pulls her out on to the edge. You have to swim, he says. You have to do something. That was when it happened. He pulls her on to his lap. She's struggling now but she can't move. She hears his heart beating faster and faster as if his heart will burst. She squirms, looks at her father's face but he is far away, his face rapt as if looking at a lost horizon. Now all she wants is to be thrown back in the water, to get away from him. She would prefer drowning to this. She struggles but can do nothing. She stares at the strawberries covering her swimming costume. She concentrates on the straw-berries, waiting for him to stop. Then there is a spasm and he throws her back in.

'You almost drowned me,' she said. She remembered now. 'You were a bully.'

She wouldn't allow him the fantasy any more. She wouldn't allow herself it any more – the benign but absent father, the dead hero. Fuck it, here was a man who threw her into the water and told her to swim and then . . .

He shrugged. 'You floated.'

All kinds of memories were piling up now, one after the other, yammering to be heard: the casual brutalities, the rows, Mark crying, standing in front of their mother holding a knife, her father taunting him, grabbing his wrist until he cried out and dropped the knife. Don't hurt him, her mother said. Don't touch her. There it was again. *Don't touch me.*

'You think I don't remember,' she said.

He said nothing, just sat there, sipping his tea.

'I remember,' she whispered. 'I remember all of it.'

He didn't look at her, but pushed his chair back and spread his legs, arrogantly. He looked over her shoulder, not outwardly concerned. No, he wasn't concerned one bit, this man who you wouldn't notice in a crowd, of medium height, this average, everyday sort of bloke.

'You fucking bastard,' she snapped, and slammed her hand down flat on the table, making his cup jump in its saucer. People at the table next to them turned to watch. Like a cobra from its basket, his hand flicked out of his pocket and grabbed her wrist, tight and hard. He pulled her towards him, closer and closer until she could feel his breath on her face.

'Don't ever talk to me like that,' he hissed. 'I'm your father.'

She grabbed his wrist straight back with her free hand, tightened her grip and was gratified by the surprise in his eyes, the flinch of pain. She squeezed as hard as she could, intending to bruise him right down to the bone, intending to really hurt him. He smiled but let go first.

'Don't ever touch me,' she snarled. 'Do you understand? Don't ever do that again.'

He put his hands back in his pockets. Didn't rub the bruised wrist. Wasn't going to show that kind of weakness. But Sam knew the bruises were forming, she could sense the red marks forming on his skin. She had the same marks on her skin. They had branded each other.

'I saved your life,' he said. 'I shot that man through the window. He'd have cut your throat without me. I told you, you were in danger. Why didn't you learn to use that gun, you little idiot?' He poured the tea, which had spilled into his saucer, back into the cup and sipped it.

But she wasn't having it. She wasn't having any of it. 'You fucking bastard. I almost got burned alive because of you. They only came for me because of you. I was bait.'

'I told you not to contact anyone. You didn't do what I told you. Why'd you go and contact Max? He's always played it by the book.'

'Why did you come back?'

'I thought I was safe. The Good Friday Agreement – I thought that had changed things. Turns out the government's all for the IRA pointing out where the bodies are buried but they don't like the idea of their own side doing it. Something to do with the moral high ground.'

'What were you doing in Northern Ireland?'

'The shittiest work of any army unit.'

Sam didn't say anything and waited for him to continue.

He lowered his voice to a murmur. 'At first we were assassinating members of the IRA who were handed over to us by the boys working on the borders. Then we were just shooting Catholics at random on the streets of Belfast. The idea was to escalate a full-scale sectarian war so that the army could stand back and watch the two sides tear each other apart. Then when they tired of it, step in and act as peace brokers.'

'You put my life at risk.'

'No, you put your own life at risk when you contacted Max.'

'Why did you come back?' she asked again.

'I'm tired. Tired of being on the run. I came back to see if something could be sorted out. I know where bodies are buried. I could let people know. We killed about forty during the course of a year. It seems they are not at all keen for me to do that. All the others in my team are dead. Johnny – car accident. Dave – fire. Jo – jumped out of a plane without a parachute. And why should he do something like that? All three accidents have been very convenient for the government. I'm not going to be the fourth. It was time to come home. You're the only home I've got, Sam.'

'Forget it,' Sam said. 'I'm nobody's home. So you can just forget it. I owe you absolutely nothing.'

'You owe me your life,' he said, and she wished it wasn't true.

And he just sat there, looking at her, as if having tea with his daughter was an everyday occurrence. Not as if this was the first time he had seen her in twenty-eight years. Not like that at all.

'I don't want you coming near me again,' Sam said. 'Do you understand? I will have absolutely nothing to do with you. As far as I'm concerned I have no father . . .' She felt tears prick her eyes. 'You were killed in nineteen seventy-four and that was the end of you.' She stood up. 'Don't come near me again.'

'I saw you become World Champion in nineteen ninety,' he said.

She looked down at him. So, he had been there.

'You fight like me, Sam – to the bitter end. You're a fighter to your fingertips. Where the hell do you think you get that from? Even if I don't come near you, you can't ever get away from me. I'm in every cell of you and I knew it from the day you were born.'

'You don't know anything about me,' Sam said. 'And you never did.'

Outside the café she leaned against a wall, her whole body shaking, then she began to run. She ran and she ran until her lungs were screaming and her legs were wobbling so much they could barely hold her upright. She bent over, gasping for air, drowning again, black spots dancing in front of her eyes. He was back and there was no place she could hide.

A month later. Sam sat in a bus shelter, looking at the house on the opposite side of the road, trying to imagine the man inside. Get professional help, O'Connor had said; but why should she pay any attention to a murderer? And the truth was she probably wouldn't have done it if it hadn't been for the nightmares and flashbacks and headaches. How many Nurofen could you take before your stomach lining turned into a sieve? She had hoped that remembering what had happened would bring an end to them but this hadn't been the case. She had been sitting in this shelter for the last half hour. She looked at her watch for the hundredth time and felt the lurch in her stomach as the minute hand hit the hour. She jumped up and walked slowly across the road. Better get to it; it was her money after all. At any time I can turn back, she said to herself, at any time I can change my mind. She rang the doorbell and waited. A broad-shouldered squat man with a shaved head opened the door. He was wearing a denim shirt and brown chinos and nothing on his feet. Much to Sam's relief he looked more like a bouncer than a therapist. He removed a pair of horn-rimmed glasses.

'Sam?'

She nodded.

'Come in, come in.'

She walked past him into the hall and he closed the front door.

'I've been warned not to shake hands but I rarely take advice.' He held out a broad, tanned hand with blunt, square fingers and Sam took it, concentrating on meeting pressure with equal pressure. She thought she'd managed quite well.

All Orion/Phoenix titles are available at your local bookshop or from the following address:

> Mail Order Department
> Littlehampton Book Services
> FREEPOST BR535
> Worthing, West Sussex, BN13 3BR
> *telephone* 01903 828503, *facsimile* 01903 828802
> *e-mail* MailOrders@lbsltd.co.uk
> (Please ensure that you include full postal address details)

Payment can be made either by credit/debit card (Visa, Mastercard, Access and Switch accepted) or by sending a £ Sterling cheque or postal order made payable to *Littlehampton Book Services*.
DO NOT SEND CASH OR CURRENCY

Please add the following to cover postage and packing

UK and BFPO:
£1.50 for the first book, and 50p for each additional book to a maximum of £3.50

Overseas and Eire:
£2.50 for the first book plus £1.00 for the second book and 50p for each additional book ordered

---

BLOCK CAPITALS PLEASE

name of cardholder ....

address of cardholder ....

delivery address
(if different from cardholder)
....
....
....
....

postcode ....   *postcode* ....

☐ I enclose my remittance for £ ....

☐ please debit my Mastercard/Visa/Access/Switch (delete as appropriate)

card number ☐☐☐☐☐☐☐☐☐☐☐☐☐☐☐☐☐☐

expiry date ☐☐☐☐   Switch issue no. ☐☐

signature ....

prices and availability are subject to change without notice